DARKLIGHT

BELLA FORREST

CHAPTER ONE

I focused on the five dark silhouettes perched atop the Ferris wheel of Navy Pier Park. The ride was closed for renovation, but crowds of tourists bustled on either side of its boarded-up enclosure: a steady stream of warm targets.

"Team A, be ready," I breathed into my comm, and glanced to my teammates behind me within the wheel's perimeter. Six helmeted heads nodded back, their hands tightening around silver barrels.

"Team B is going in," came the low, confident voice of my brother and second-in-command.

A large helicopter whirred overhead, drawing closer to the wheel and slowly circling it.

I glanced at my watch. "Greta, you should be in position."

"Yup, and waiting for your command, Lyra," the clipped voice of Team C's leader replied.

"Start the haze," I said.

The hiss of decompressing gas filled the cool spring night, and Greta boomed through a megaphone: "Please evacuate the pier. This is an emergency. Head for the children's museum. You will receive further information there. I repeat, please evacuate the pier."

Beyond the enclosure's walls, a semi-dense fog billowed from the ground, covering the crowd. Shouts and cries rang out, followed by a stampede of panicked footsteps. I refocused on the wheel's apex, ignoring the guilt that panged in my chest at the sounds of alarm and confusion. The smokescreen could be inconvenient and frightening, but ultimately it would prevent the tourists from being targeted.

The silhouettes started shifting, clearly noticing the helicopter and the commotion. I caught the rustle of an opening wing.

Placing some distance between myself and the base of the wheel, I raised my gun, and my colleagues did the same. "All right, Team A. On my count. Three, two, one…"

I aimed for the largest shadow and fired, my entire body vibrating from the force of the bullet's release. I heard the creature's rasping cry, as guttural and grating as a vulture's, followed by four others as my teammates hit their marks.

But the shadows barely jerked. Instead, their massive wings shot out, and they launched into the air so fast that I lost them in the darkness.

It was far from my first encounter with the strange avian species, but I still shivered when the light from the nearby Wave Swinger attraction touched their sleek, ink-black forms. In many ways, each resembled the common stork—long and graceful, with an extended beak, broad wings, and thin, dangling legs. But these weren't the kind you'd see carrying babies on greeting cards.

At least three times larger than the biggest earthly stork, they soared through the sky like dark omens, propelled by unnatural speed and a craving for blood. Their talons resembled an eagle's, while their beaks were sharp and strong enough to puncture metal—they could suckle a human dry in three minutes if they found a main artery.

There was a reason we called them "redbills."

"Zach, get to work!" I yelled.

Gunfire exploded from the helicopter, peppering the birds with artillery. It took more than a single shot to bring them down—even with bullets specifically designed to deliver their death.

"Spread out!" I ordered my team. "Don't let them dive!"

The redbills began to circle the aircraft. The chopper was their greatest source of aggravation, and, judging from the way their beaks angled toward it, they were preparing to strike back. I leapt onto the wheel's frame and pulled myself up the metal skeleton for a better angle. I fired a round at the largest predator.

"Focus on the biggest!" I shouted. "But don't let the others get close enough for a snatch-n-fly." *Rookie mistake of the year.*

My team fired, angry streaks of laser-blue cutting through the darkness. At least ten bullets struck the creature from my team's direction, in addition to a round fired by one of the chopper's gunmen. The redbill's wings beat violently but held its flight. I'd never seen one so large, and with its massive size came extra resilience.

After another onslaught, it finally floundered, an unearthly shriek ripping from its throat and spurts of dark blood raining from its body. It backed down, swerving shakily toward the water at the end of the pier. It would probably be underwater in moments.

My team's focus switched to the next target, a redbill spitting nasty hissing sounds which reminded me uncannily of curses. It darted right up to the aircraft, its powerful beak close to ramming the tail.

Swearing under my breath, I pulled myself higher up the wheel and leaned a little farther out of my comfort zone to get a better shot. I fired, my artillery joining my team's focused stream. Shots pummeled the bird's underbelly, but it didn't falter. It took two intense rounds before it fell away, hissing loudly as it plummeted with a crash into the roof of a snack joint.

"Good job!" I shouted. "Three more to go!"

I released three bullets in swift succession at our third target, then leaned out even farther to attempt a shot at its neck. My finger was on the trigger, pressing—

"Lyra, watch out!"

Something clamped around my waist. My feet slipped from the frame as an impossible force yanked me to the right like I was a rag doll. The gun flew from my hands and the breath left my lungs—then I was flying.

The pier bled rapidly away beneath me, and a mass of shimmering dark water replaced the ground. My eyes stung. I couldn't hear my breathing over the roar of the wind.

I winced as I felt the cold, painful press of armor against my flesh, as if it were closing in on me, and glanced down. Two blood-speckled claws engulfed my waist, the giant talons squeezing tight.

I didn't glance up, because I didn't need to. All but one bird had been in my peripheral vision before I was snatched. Clearly the first hadn't been as injured as it looked—or it had somehow recuperated and flown back with a burst of energy.

Either way, it didn't matter. If this redbill squeezed any tighter, it was going to crush me even before its deadly beak could gouge me.

Those realizations hit me within moments, flying disjointedly through my brain as my reflexes finally kicked in. I yanked my knees toward my chest and fumbled in my boots to reach the knives strapped there. I pulled both out and slashed them across the creature's claws, hoping it would drop me.

Its legs retracted, shifting me into a more vertical position, but the bird's grip barely loosened. Instead, it shrieked and thrust down with its beak, catching my right thigh. My suit dented into the muscle with a pain like being punched, and I gasped in both pain and anger. If it hit the same place twice, it'd cut right through.

Time for plan B. There was no time to replace the blades in their sheaths. I let them fall, then pulled out a small rectangular pulse patch from a sleeve in my suit's right shoulder while keeping my eyes on the creature holding me. As the bird thrust its beak down at me again, I jerked my head to the side, narrowly avoiding a second strike. I slapped the patch onto the bird's right ankle and pressed the center of it, hard. The patch glowed bright blue for a split second, then beeped.

The effect was instantaneous. The creature's talons loosened as the device sent a powerful surge of energy rushing through its body. My suit was specially insulated, but if it were damaged enough, the pulse would've killed me, too. Which was why the patch had been the backup plan.

My stomach dropped as the stunned bird and I hurtled down in freefall, the black, choppy waves rising to meet us at breathtaking speed.

The impact jolted every bone in my body, and though the ice-cold water didn't reach me through the suit, my skin prickled at the instant drop in temperature. I struggled against the instinct to gasp, preserving the precious air within my helmet.

I opened my eyes to a swirling confusion of bubbles, wingtips, and pale shafts of moonlight, and thrashed to put some distance between myself and the redbill. It was still alive, though it seemed to be struggling to get to the surface.

The surges created by its writhing body made it hard to fumble for another patch—especially with my suit dragging me down. I managed to pull one out and kicked back toward the bird. An insanely risky move, but I managed to catch the tip of its wing as it curved through the water. I held on for dear life, slapped the second patch on with my left hand, pressed hard, and let go.

The violent currents subsided a moment later. Lungs burning, I prayed that the redbill was finally dead while I struggled to remove my helmeted suit, the heart-stopping cold engulfing me as I kicked to the surface. The pulse was over, and I didn't have the energy to sustain the suit's weight.

Then again, hypothermia might kick in soon. But I trusted my brother to fish me out before that.

Breaking the surface, I heaved a gloriously deep gasp of air while I reached for my comm and wiped my eyes.

Two redbills hurtled toward me from the sky above, their razor-sharp beaks angled to strike.

My heart lodged in my throat, and in one motion I gasped again and dove hard and fast, bracing myself for beaks to slice through the water. I should've expected them. It was Bill Behavior 101. The birds saw their companion take down prey (or so it looked from a distance), and they wanted a piece of it. A snatch-n-fly had never happened to me before, so I wasn't as prepared as I should've been. Simulations only took you so far.

I wouldn't be able to survive this kind of attack even with a suit. The only idea I had was to get as deep as possible, rely on the water to hide me, and resurface far enough from them to get away, all before my lungs gave out. It sounded impossible.

It never came to that. The redbills didn't follow me. There was a commotion above the surface: two deep, echoing booms followed by a bright flash. Two enormous splashes disturbed the water around me.

I rose back to the surface to breathe, blinking furiously when I reached air. Our aircraft hovered in the sky. A tall, broad form dangled from its extended ladder, a wide-barreled grenade launcher gripped in one hand.

"Lyra!" Zach bellowed, his head swiveling wildly as he scanned the waves.

"I-I'm here," I managed, almost choking on an incoming wave. I raised a hand and flailed.

I could've sworn I heard his sharp exhalation even from this distance, and the helicopter moved closer. Slinging his gun over his shoulder, Zach climbed to the bottom of the ladder as it swung directly overhead. He reached his hand out to me, and I kicked hard to grasp it, allowing him to haul me up.

I swung around to the side of the ladder opposite him, both of us clinging to the same rungs, and met my older brother's brown eyes with a deep inhalation. His lips stretched slowly, the sheer panic I'd seen in him only moments before melting into his signature devil-may-care grin.

"Having fun?" he asked, reaching through the rungs to smooth back my sopping wet bangs.

"A friggin' ball." I batted his hand away and started climbing before I froze in the harsh wind.

Zach followed me up. "Are you hurt?"

"Mostly shaken. A few bruises. I'll survive." My teeth chattered.

"Not gonna lie, you had us all crapping our pants back there. I don't think any of us saw that sucker returning for more... At least all's well that ends well, eh? You gave me a chance to use this baby."

He was referring to the grenade launcher. We weren't supposed to use heavy explosives unless a location was cleared of citizens, which was why we'd started with weaker gunfire at the pier. Out here, though, we could blow things up to our hearts' content.

Something Zach enjoyed more than was probably healthy.

"You're welcome," I replied, my voice dryer than the Sahara.

As I reached the top of the ladder, a pair of strong hands grabbed me and hauled me up. The warmth of the aircraft's interior enveloped me like a sauna. Our captain—and our *real* first-in-command—stood before me, his sharp blue eyes narrowed in scrutiny. But before he or I could say a word, someone attacked my head with a towel.

"Better get you warm fast, Lyra." A familiar voice came from behind me, muffled by the towel scraping my ears as it swiftly transformed into a turban. Hands spun me around until I stood face-to-face with my brother's girlfriend. "Come and get changed," Gina said firmly. Her light amber eyes were concerned and relieved as she took my hand and led me to the back of the aircraft.

"Yes, get changed, Sloane." Captain Bryce's thick Scottish voice sounded from behind. "And then we all need to talk."

"That sounds ominous," I muttered.

"Pretty sure it's the usual drill." Gina sighed.

Passing Teams A and B, I saw that everyone was unsuited and wore relieved expressions, though some had a tinge of thinly veiled amusement, similar to my brother's expression on the ladder. I threw a playful scowl at those faces.

No, it hadn't escaped my crew that their first-in-command (albeit *in training*) had been the one to fall into what our trainers labeled Rookie Mistake of the Year.

But come on. This one had been different. After all those injuries, I couldn't have expected the bird to be that fast or stealthy. I needed more experience with bills of that size.

A set of warm, dry clothes had been laid out in a makeshift changing room. Gina waited outside while I peeled off my wet uniform.

"You got rid of all the birds, right?" I called through the curtain, realizing I'd only seen two come after me, which left one unaccounted for.

"Yeah. Once you got lifted, Captain gave permission to override grenade protocol so we could deal with them faster and get to you. Team C had mostly cleared the area by then, anyway. Pilot's taking us back to base now."

"Good." I caught the reflection of my face in a small mirror while reaching for the dry clothes. My hazel-brown eyes were bloodshot, my usually sun-kissed skin still pale from the cold. But after wringing out my ponytail and pulling on a cozy, fleece-lined getup, I felt much better.

I stepped back into the corridor.

"Now for some hot chocolate," Gina said. She turned and made for the front of the chopper, and I followed, watching the back of her short, blonde bob and ignoring my smirking colleagues on the way back. I sank into the seat next to my brother in the center of the common area while Gina fixed me a drink in the mini kitchen unit.

Captain Bryce's eyes lighted on me from the front of the room, and a moment later, he cleared his throat.

"We'll commence the Stripping, then," he announced, every syllable tart and sharp.

I recoiled involuntarily and felt the whole room do the same around me.

A verbal *stripping* for each of us was what it would be—there really was no other term to describe the *very* detailed performance break-downs Bryce gave his trainees after every mission. Nor was there any way to prepare for them.

I flinched when his eyes turned to me, but then, apparently changing his mind, he strode to the seats on the far left, the first of which was occupied by Colin Adams, a member of Team B. Bryce stopped less than a foot in front of him and crossed his arms over his chest.

"So, laddie. What made you think popping your first bullet before Zach's command was a good idea? Did you think you'd earn an extra point for enthusiasm? Were you wanting to get ahead of your colleagues? Naturally trigger-happy, are we? Or is there some great intellect in that hard helmet of yours that I'm missing?"

His blue eyes bore intensely into the Chinese-American, whose face flushed furiously.

"N-No, sir. I'm sorry. I was just… nervous," he mumbled.

"You might want to take something for that twitchy finger then, eh?"

Colin nodded, swallowing hard.

Bryce moved along to the next trainee: Sarah Lammers, also of Team B and the youngest of our crew.

"And you, Sarah. What made you think it was a good idea to skip to the loo in the middle of a firefight? Couldn't you have gone a few minutes beforehand? Were you paying no mind to my words before we took off?"

"I just realized that I… really needed to go." The eighteen-year-old's cheeks rapidly turned a blotchy pink.

"You should've done it in your knickers, then, and changed later. You put your colleagues' lives in danger."

"I-I'm sorry, sir."

"This isn't high school anymore, folks, in case you needed remind-ing. When you're out on a field mission, your first priority is each other's safety. Anything else is secondary. Your action this time might not have had significant consequences, Sarah, but in even a slightly different scenario, it could have had very serious ones."

Bryce moved on to the next Team B member.

"And you, Grayson. What made you think it was a good idea to keep glancing at Louise while you were supposed to be fighting? Do you have a crush on her or something? Didn't realize the best way to ensure you can *keep* looking at her is to focus on getting the both of you back to the ground?"

A mortified silence fell over the room. Louise's eyes were fixed stiffly on the floor, while Grayson's looked close to popping out. "I-I wasn't looking at her, sir," he stammered. "I'm not sure what you're talking about."

A wily smile cracked Bryce's leathery, suntanned face. He laughed, heartily. "You think I was born yesterday, son? You were ogling her like she were some sorta rice puddin'. Might as well just tell her you fancy her now, so you get it out of your system. Don't want your poor little heart getting us all killed next time we're in the air now, do we?"

Bryce moved on, leaving Grayson looking like he was choking.

The captain worked his way systematically through the rest of Team B's members, breaking down in brutal detail transgressions both small and large—he gave the same attention to both—and thoroughly dismantling all of the (few) objections he received. If he appeared to spare most of my Team A colleagues, it was only because his all-seeing eye hadn't quite extended to the ground where they'd been most of the time. But the closer the captain drew to Zach—and to me—the clammier my hands became around my cocoa. I doubted I'd be exempt.

Zach held his breath when Bryce finally stopped in front of him.

"And you, *Second-in-Command* Sloane." He paused, furrowing his brow, deftly drawing the tension out. "You were a bit too keen to get that grenade launcher out for my liking. Yes, we had an emergency, but if I weren't here, I suspect you would have been looking for any excuse to jump on it. That's not the way of a good soldier. You shouldn't be driven by personal preference in any way, only by what is objectively best for the situation, and of course your superior's orders. You're one of the older folks here, and I expect to see that maturity. I suggest you work on honing your objectivity."

He paused again, then spoke in a lower tone, as though it were meant only for Zach's ears. "And maybe play a bit less with your father's toys, eh?"

"Got it, sir," Zach breathed, visibly flustered, though obviously relieved his reprimand hadn't been worse.

Bryce started to move on, and then his head snapped back. "Also, get a damn haircut. I can hardly see your eyes anymore through that brown mane."

A titter of laughter broke out amongst the group. I couldn't help but smirk too, knowing how much Zach hated the super-close, cropped shaves the captain advocated. His aversion was likely due to the well-meant, yet categorically awful, home haircuts our parents used to give him when they didn't have time to take us on a trip to the salon. Which was most of the time.

"Oh, sir." Zach clutched his chest, feigning hurt. "That's a low blow. *Gina* likes it wavy."

Bryce gave him a stony, narrow-eyed look but said nothing. He continued on to Gina… skipping me entirely.

I frowned, unsure of whether I should believe my luck. *Maybe I'm getting off the hook after all?*

Bryce stared down at Gina intensely, his expression inscrutable. The hum of the aircraft was the only noise around us for several long moments, until he sighed softly.

"Ah, this one. What can I really say? She's an angel." A rugged smile tugged up the corners of his lips.

The room exploded in mock outrage.

"Come on, sir! I'm sure you could think of something!" Zach protested, leaning around me to poke his girlfriend playfully in the shoulder.

"Yeah, Captain. That's just straight-up favoritism!" Roxy complained.

Bryce whirled on the tall, burly girl from my team sitting behind us, his eyes flashing.

"What did you just accuse me of, lassie? *Favoritism*, you say? Aye. Well, I'd *favor* all of you if you showed the same damn work ethic, situational awareness, and efficiency as this young lady. When the rest of you have developed those qualities, I'll throw a bloody rave!"

Gina's freckled cheeks darkened as she tried to roll her eyes and shrug off the attention, while Bryce's gaze roved over the seats, daring anyone to protest. When nobody did, his eyes snapped back to... me.

Crap. I braced myself, tightening my grip around my cup as he returned to stand before me, fearing I *had* gotten my hopes up too soon.

But then I realized he didn't look like he was about to deal out a stripping. If anything, he looked... concerned.

His gaze held mine for several heartbeats, and then he shook his head slowly.

"Eh. Lyra gets a free pass, too. I'll be very honest with you all about something: I didn't see that bastard returning for more either, not after the battering we gave it. I've never encountered a bill as tough as that."

Vindicated! I felt like saying the word aloud and giving a little fist pump, but the seriousness of our captain's expression stopped me.

"Do you think it was just a one-off?" I asked, eyeing him. "Some genetic fluke?"

Bryce shrugged. "I sure hope so. Definitely wouldn't do us any good if they started breeding stronger."

He glanced around at us darkly, and I knew what he was implying. The Bureau was stretched to the max for personnel as it was.

There'd been an increased number of redbill sightings over the past year, around North America particularly, for reasons that were still unclear to the Bureau. It was as if the birds had spiraled into a breeding frenzy. Recruitment agents, my mom among them, were working overtime to keep up with the demand for new officers, and younger, less trained recruits were starting to be allowed into ground missions as a result. Which explained our motley crew.

Some state and city departments simply didn't have enough people. Our branch here in Chicago, for example, sometimes had to send out squads as far as Oklahoma to help deal with threats. It was lucky that tonight's sighting had been local... well, not so lucky for the revelers of Navy Pier Park.

A secondary, albeit unrelated, factor didn't help the Bureau's staff problems. The demand for soldiers, and law enforcement workers in general, had grown slowly but steadily over the past half-decade or so, thanks to a slight but continuous rise in the regular human crime rate. It meant there was a smaller pool of officers the Bureau could recruit to their specialized force, since more soldiers were out dealing with ordinary human problems.

I just hoped things would smooth out sooner or later, for all of our sakes.

"*Anyway,*" Bryce said, casting another strong look around the room. "Don't any of you take this as an excuse to start whining. Even a bird thrice the size of that one is nothing like the bloodsuckers *we* used to hunt."

"I find that hard to believe," Roxy mumbled from behind. *Too loud.*

Bryce spun on her again. "And what was that, my wee lass? Care to speak a bit louder, so we can *all* hear your precious thoughts?"

Roxy gave a soft sigh. "I find that hard to believe," she replied sullenly. "There's no way vampires were as strong or dangerous as these freaking monsters."

Bryce's lips formed a hard line. "Mm-hmm. And what, precisely, makes you say that?"

I turned over my shoulder to glance at Roxy's half-flustered, half-incredulous expression. She didn't know how wrong she was.

"I mean, how could they even compare?" she started. "Vampires didn't fly, for one thing, so it couldn't have been half as difficult to catch them. They had small fangs, compared to huge, snapping beaks. They kept way more to themselves, too, from what I've heard, and weren't a big threat to public places. Plus—"

"And what about their brains?" Bryce interrupted.

Roxy stuttered. "Their... brains?"

"Their brains," Bryce repeated, his eyes widening.

Roxy's brow furrowed. "Well, yeah. Vampires were smarter. But still—"

"Exactly." Bryce took a step back, shoving his hands into his pockets. "Vampires were cunning devils. They could outsmart a human in almost any situation, and usually the only way to match one was to put many human minds together. Bills are just dumb brutes, and any comparison is frankly offensive."

He gave an almost wistful sigh and sank back into his chair, facing us. His eyes grew distant.

"Honestly, if vampires hadn't been such a menace, I would've been sad to see them go. Watchin' them was like... pure poetry in motion... put any martial artist to shame. They could distract you by just the sheer skill and speed of their movement, and the way they used your own strength against you, you'd barely realize you were bleeding until it was too late."

He tugged at his collar and pulled it down to reveal the beginning of a massive scar on his upper chest.

"Aye." He grinned, watching our stunned faces. "This was done with my own weapon. But I'm not going to lie. As risky as the job was, it was more of a thrill hunting a vampire. You never knew what could happen. Would they lure you into a trap? Attack the moment they saw you, or wait a while and lull you into a false sense of security? Or maybe they'd do neither and instead slip away into the night, let you try to trail 'em some more until you tired out... But they were worth the chase. And when you finally caught one? Oof. The thrill was indescribable."

He finished with a crooked smile, and the whole room stared in rapt silence; even Roxy's brow had softened.

I'd heard plenty of tales of vampire chases before, but I'd never seen this side of Bryce. He spoke with such awe of the creatures that had snuffed out so many innocent lives, it was almost hard not to wish I'd seen one, too… even if they were the reason my uncle needed a permanent walking aid.

After all, Zach and I had grown up expecting to track the predators, just like our parents had done in their early careers. But by the time I turned sixteen, vampires had disappeared.

"It *is* weird how they died out so quickly," Zach mumbled, as if he'd followed the same line of thought.

Bryce leaned back in his seat, nodding slowly. "Aye. It was unexpected for a lot of us. Guess there couldn't have been as many as we thought there were to begin with, and once all countries started cooperating, we managed to drive them to extinction. Amazing how destructive we humans can be when we put our minds to it." He chuckled, though it sounded halfhearted.

"Where do you think they came from, Captain?" I asked. The origin of vampires was more of a mystery than their disappearance, and everyone and their mother had an opinion about it. I'd never heard Bryce's before, and I was genuinely curious.

The captain puffed out his cheeks. "I'm not sure what you're expecting to hear from me, when an entire research department couldn't come up with anything better than 'they just existed'. The honest answer is I don't know. But if you held me at gunpoint, I'd probably say the same—they just always existed. A so-called 'supernatural' creature living among us, perhaps since the dawn of time, for one reason or another. Who knew? Bram Stoker was onto somethin'."

I nodded, having basically come to the same conclusion. Some folks liked to swerve toward fictional vampire lore and present theories about vampires' ancestors having once been humans who went on to —*somehow*—develop unnatural abilities. But the science simply didn't back that up. Vampires had been caught, dissected, and studied in labs, and there was no proof that they were ever part of our gene pool, or that they could spread their condition to others. They actually showed no genetic commonalities with any earthly creature. Which led to *others* suggesting they could be a species from another planet. I wasn't even going to get into that.

"And what do you think about the redbills' origin?" Grayson muttered. "Given there's no record of their existence anywhere up until half a decade ago."

We all turned to glance at the blond man. It was the first time either he or Louise had spoken since Bryce's… exposé on Grayson's feelings— a fact that the captain's sardonic smile not-so-subtly acknowledged.

"Aye," Bryce replied. "We all thought vampires were an anomaly, the only species of their kind out there, until the redbills came along… right around the time vampires stopped showing up. I'm not going to *try* to speculate about that one. All I know is they're somehow made of the same stuff as vampires. Not natural."

"Do you believe in reincarnation, sir?" Zach asked.

My brother's smile clearly indicated that it was a joke, but Bryce's expression looked oddly strained.

"Not sure about that, lad. But karma, maybe? I mean, it is odd, isn't it, that we get rid of vampires, only to be saddled with this other huge, heaving problem." He cast Roxy a look. "Not that it's necessarily of the same caliber. But it's a problem nonetheless. And it appears to be getting worse."

He finished on a quiet note that seemed to infect the room. My brother and I exchanged glances, and the tension in Zach's jaw reflected what I felt in my gut. *Hopefully not too much worse*. Or at least, not too quickly. We struggled to keep pace as it was.

Unlike vampires, redbills could not be concealed from the public. Vampires had been discreet, and they had always attacked in seclusion —one on one. They rarely left witnesses. That had been the government's major advantage in preventing the mass fear and panic among citizens which would surely have followed a declaration that vampires walked among us.

With the redbills, the authorities had been able to get away with explaining them as an abnormal breed of stork, a strange fluke of nature—possibly even the result of past nuclear plant accidents—and saying that research was ongoing to determine their origin and the best way to subdue them. But if they bred too much and attracted too much attention, that explanation would become harder and harder to swallow. Our saving grace was that they hadn't spread to other countries yet —or at least, there'd been no reports.

We needed to keep it that way.

"Landing in five." The pilot's announcement broke through the quiet.

I shifted in my seat, wanting a distraction, and glanced out the nearest window as the aircraft tilted. I watched the thousands of lights of downtown Chicago rise to meet us. The evening felt so clear and calm, so comfortingly *normal*, that if it weren't for my still-damp hair and sore thigh, it would've been hard to believe we'd just been battling monsters.

This was what we were fighting for, I reminded myself. A world where we could all sleep peacefully at night, where families could vacation without fear, where couples could enjoy their late-night dates and children could play out on the streets. *The world as it* should *be.*

I was among the first to unbuckle when the aircraft touched down on the roof of our base. I stood up slowly, testing out my right leg, and winced slightly. It hurt more than when I'd sat down, probably due to swelling where the beak had caught my suit. I was going to have one ugly bruise. But it could have been a lot worse. Like, no-leg-at-all worse.

"You okay?" Gina asked from beside me, obviously noticing my grimace.

I nodded. "Yeah. I can still walk and run. I just need some rest."

I moved toward the door, wanting to get ahead of the crowd. I was definitely looking forward to resting. It wasn't that late, but my little swim had taken more out of me than I'd realized.

The door drew open, letting in a chilly waft of air, and I was on the verge of leaving when Bryce called, "Hold up, folks."

We all turned to see him staring down at his comm screen.

"We've just had another summons," he announced.

My breath caught. "Another one?" Our team had never had two calls in a single day.

"In Chicago?" Sarah asked incredulously.

"Nope. Washington, D.C. They're short-staffed because New York State borrowed from them. They're requesting any recruits available." Bryce glanced up at us. "Satellites flagged an unnatural frequency at a closed church, and the D.C. chief needs a team to investigate. Suspicion is there's a bird trying to nest there, because it hasn't posed a threat yet."

"And we have to leave *now*?" Roxy asked.

"First thing in the morning," Bryce replied. "They're keeping an eye on the building for the moment, but I need you all here by four a.m. sharp. Go to bed as soon as you get home, and you'll be bright and fine." His face twitched in a dry smile.

I glanced at my watch—*21:45*—before Zach grabbed my arm and pulled me down the stairs after him.

"No rest for the wicked, eh?" Gina murmured from behind us as she followed.

No... No, I guess not.

CHAPTER TWO

Captain Bryce gave us his usual cold "goodbye" grunt as my teammates and I hopped from the chopper to the air pad. He stayed behind to discuss the next morning's strategy with the pilots.

We entered the Bureau through sliding steel doors and were greeted by familiar obsidian-black walls. The tired shuffling of our boots echoed from the vaulted ceilings. After a night like this, the main hallway always seemed never-ending.

Everyone stayed silent until we reached the elevators. Roxy hit the down button.

"Have a good night," I called in her direction.

"Yeah, sweet friggin' dreams," she muttered. The rest of the crew shook their heads, trying to laugh through their sighs.

As they filed into the elevator, my brother, Gina, and I split from the group, heading toward the giant metal door that always reminded me that my bed was close.

Zach pulled his ID from his suit's breast pocket and pressed it against a dark gray pad on the wall. Three low beeps rang out, and a *clunk* sounded through the hall as the door unlocked. I reached to pull down the handle, but Zach slapped my hand.

"Take it easy, gimp." He grinned.

I rolled my eyes while he pulled the massive door open, and we started down a much smaller hallway into the residential staff apartments. *I wonder if Mom and Dad are still awake.*

The narrow white walls of the base's family housing were lined with sporadically placed numbered doorways. Zach and Gina pulled ahead of me. Whether I wanted to admit it or not, my pace was a little slower than usual.

Gina glanced back over her shoulder. "Want an arm?"

"I'm good," I assured her.

We finally reached 237. Zach once again pulled out his ID, pressed it to the pad, and opened the door to our family's apartment. I faintly smelled casserole. Zach made a beeline for the kitchen and started making himself a plate.

"I'll have a bite and then head to my apartment, if there's enough," Gina said, unlacing her boots beside me in the entryway.

"Mom always makes a full tray. Lyra, you want a plate?" Zach called.

"Not really hungry," I said, carefully bending over to untie my own boots.

Gina eyed me. "You need to lie down."

I nodded to acknowledge her concern but said nothing—I didn't want her going into mothering mode.

She half-smiled. "You and your brother. So damn stubborn. I'll see you at the ass-crack of dawn, Lyra," she said, accepting the plate of casserole Zach handed her.

I waved over my shoulder as I headed toward my bedroom, assuming my parents were asleep.

I was aware that most twenty-one-year-olds in America didn't live with their parents, but most people in America didn't grow up as second-generation OB soldiers. Bureau base housing was limited, so until Zach and I had families of our own, we shared quarters with our parents. Honestly, we were all so busy that we didn't see much of each other on a daily basis.

Halfway down the hall, I noticed a light shining under the closed living room door—and heard voices.

The sound of my mother's sharp tone halted my breath and footsteps. She rarely spoke above a gentle hum, albeit a hum that commanded respect. When I could hear her through a closed door, something was wrong.

I couldn't make out her words, so I inched closer. I heard my father's voice interject, lower and slower than my mother's but just as severe. I held my breath, now able to make out the words.

"I don't understand how the board hasn't taken action on this yet," my mom snapped. "It's unacceptable. This is not how the Bureau is supposed to conduct itself."

My heart jumped at another familiar voice, calm and thick as caramel. Uncle Alan. "Don't be so quick to judge, Miriam. We're dealing with something we don't understand yet."

It was hard to hear what they were saying over Zach and Gina chatting in the kitchen. *Quiet. Quiet!* I squeezed my eyes shut and focused on the living room door—after all, it wasn't like I could shush my brother and his girlfriend so I could snoop better.

Uncle Alan dropped his voice, and Zach's fork scraping his plate from the kitchen drowned out my uncle's words. Several moments passed, but I remained frozen.

My mother gasped. "Unbelievable." My heart pounded so loudly in my ears that her higher timbre was the only thing I could distinguish.

Uncle Alan raised his voice an octave in response to my mother's concern but then cleared his throat and returned to his hushed tone. "These are the facts we have. Like I've explained, even these vague details are strictly secret."

My mother didn't like her brother-in-law's response, apparently, because her voice peaked again, cracking this time. "People's lives are at stake! How could the Bureau keep something so dangerous a secret?! You and your damned red tape. Papers and signatures aren't more important than human lives!"

This time my father joined in. "How many more soldiers need to throw themselves at these monsters before we get this under control? These are our *children*. Your niece and nephew, Alan."

"Miriam, Russell," Uncle Alan replied calmly. "We all know why the Bureau has to do this. Something like this getting out could be catastrophic. I understand your concern. But letting this information reach anyone else's ears is out of the question. There's a reason it took me so long to tell *you*. And that only happened because of your promotion last month, Russell."

I bit my lip, and my eyes widened. My father was the new Head of Defense Technology.

"You are the only ones not on the board who know anything about this at all," my uncle offered.

A heavy silence fell in the room. I started to feel lightheaded from holding my breath.

Uncle Alan continued, his usual sweetness now turned slightly rigid. "Stability and calm are the most important things for the Bureau, this country—and the globe—right now."

Guilt knotted my stomach. I was beginning to get uncomfortable about eavesdropping for so long.

I cleared my throat and knocked softly on the living room door. My mother's voice became a hurried whisper, and my father called out, "Yes, we're in here."

I pushed the door open to reveal three weak attempts at smiles.

"Hi, everyone," I said cautiously.

My uncle sat in the armchair to my left, across the coffee table from my parents. His platinum hair was slicked back in its usual fashion, his trim gray suit predictably impeccable, even at this late hour. He whisked two papers from the coffee table into the depths of his shiny leather briefcase, but not before I recognized the emblem in the header: Bureau nondisclosure paperwork.

"Lyra! We weren't expecting you home so early," he said warmly, and I couldn't help but smile back at him. No matter how tired I was, I always had extra energy for Uncle Alan. "A successful operation tonight, I hope?" he asked, wavering slightly as he stood with the help of his cane.

The memory of crashing into frigid water jolted my mind. "Mostly."

My parents weren't as good as my uncle when it came to pretending nothing was wrong. I met their worried eyes, looking at each of them in turn. "Is everything okay?"

"Yes, Lyra, we're fine," my mother said, her usual tenderness returning. She smoothed over her pixie cut with a hand. "Come and sit with us."

I moved to join my parents, teetering lightly, but mostly from exhaustion at that point.

My father eyed me with concern. "Are you hurt?"

"Nah, she's just being a baby." Zach followed me into the living room. "Big Bird got the best of ya tonight, didn't he?"

I shot him a glare and eased onto the couch. My muscles sighed with relief as I sank into the cushions.

"Lyra enjoyed her first snatch-n-fly tonight, didn't you, sis?" Zach smiled.

"Are you okay?" my mother asked.

"Oh, she's totally great." Zach nonchalantly leaned a hand on the back of Uncle Alan's chair. "She and birdie even went swimming together!"

If my knives had still been attached to my leg, they would've gone flying. I kept my eyes locked on my smirking sibling, glaring the daggers I couldn't throw, while I explained to my horrified parents. "We'd hit the target multiple times, and I thought it was eradicated, but it bounced back and caught me off guard. It was the biggest redbill I've ever seen."

My parents tried to stay stoic, but they exchanged a glance. Zach's grin faded, and his eyes darkened. Uncle Alan wrung his hands.

"I need to get to bed," I said, breaking the sudden quiet I'd created.

"The Scottish ogre is calling us in at four a.m.," Zach said, stretching his arms toward the ceiling.

"Special summons in D.C., apparently," I added, rising from the couch.

My mother sighed. "It's always something these days."

"Get plenty of rest, you two," Uncle Alan said.

I smiled again, entirely for my parents' sake this time. They suddenly looked fragile... older than I'd ever seen them, and so much smaller than they did when addressing soldiers and coworkers at the Bureau.

I steadily lumbered down the hall to my bedroom. The mere sight of my bed was pure bliss. The weight of the day had finally taken over. I was thankful that the ache from my leg had started to quiet.

Too exhausted to change, I slid into bed in my uniform fleeces. I'd had to sleep in much less comfortable uniforms, that was for sure.

But I didn't sleep. All I could manage was staring at the ceiling, counting the circles of my ceiling fan and listening to the nighttime hums of our residence. Every time I closed my eyes, I felt the redbill's claws wrapped around my body, saw the dark feathers looming as I tilted my head back... and all I could hear was my mother's protest. *Papers and signatures aren't more important than human lives...*

I didn't know exactly what I'd overheard in the living room, but something didn't feel right.

CHAPTER THREE

Our seats vibrated as the chopper carried us over the still-sleeping territory below. The tiny window behind my head offered only dimly lit veins of highways and the deep violet and bronze of sunrise.

We'd transferred off the Bureau plane outside of D.C. and would only be in the chopper for a few more minutes. The team was in our usual circle, though somewhat cramped in the smaller aircraft, listening silently as Captain Bryce gave us the rundown. His tone was sharp even at six o'clock in the morning.

"We'll split into three teams once we reach our destination," Bryce barked. "All three teams will be on the ground; Teams A and B will enter the site, and Team C will be posted outside the church. Team C—Sarah, Grayson, that's you. If anything comes in or out of that church, it's your problem."

I glanced around, finding most eyes glued tensely to the chopper's floor. Grayson's knee was bouncing.

"Team B. Zach, Colin, Roxy, Louise, Greta. You will split into groups, enter the church from the west windows and main door, and cover the first floor." Bryce pulled on his gloves as he walked around the circle. "You will not leave that floor unless I *tell* you to. Only necessary use of comms inside the site. I shouldn't hear more than a mouse fart in my earpiece. I'll be on the floor with you, so any chitter-chatter will answer to me—and I promise you'd prefer the redbill."

We rarely had the captain on the ground with us. Sweat dampened my palms, and I hadn't even heard my station's details yet.

"Team A." Bryce paused to clear his throat, his icy eyes glancing down momentarily. "Gina, Lyra. You two will enter through the east wall's window. The site has multiple levels, and you will be the first to head up. Silence is golden, lassies."

I nodded, holding Bryce's gaze. Gina sat to my left, and I watched her hands clench.

"The main floor is somewhere around thirty thousand square feet," our captain continued. "We haven't placed the target yet, so step lightly. Redbills' sense of hearing isn't nearly as sharp as their eyesight, which is why I'm permitting an airdrop. But don't take anything for granted once we're in a closed space."

The head pilot's voice came through our earpieces. "Three minutes to site."

"Three minutes and fifteen seconds to drop," Bryce replied into his comm.

Zach cracked his knuckles from across the circle.

"Once we locate our target, you know what to do." Bryce tightened his artillery belt. "Safeties off when your little feet hit the ground. Understood?"

"Yes, Captain," the entire crew resounded loudly.

Bryce moved to the cockpit. Our comms were silent. He'd turned them off, but I could see his lips moving rapidly as he gesticulated to the pilots.

For the short time until the drop, our eyes remained locked on the tips of our boots. No one said a word. The droning of the chopper intensified, and my stomach lurched as the craft descended. I closed my eyes. *Breathe.* At least my thigh was feeling much better than last night. The rest had done it a lot of good.

I glanced up briefly in the silence and caught Zach looking at me. His mouth formed a small smile. He winked.

"Line up, children," Bryce snapped, returning from the cockpit. "Look alive, why don't ya?"

The group bolted from their seats, the sound of our steps blending with the chopper's hum. Gina and I locked eyes, then shoulders. We made our way to the open door. The tops of trees became clearer in the now-pale-violet morning light.

The church came into view from the doorway, just to the north. Its spire had shattered; what remained was a spike of pale gray wood pointing at the sky. The shingles were scattered about the roof, some stacked together like forgotten piles of papers. The air battered my cheeks. The thrumming of the blades above battered my eardrums.

"Thirty seconds to drop!" Bryce's voice bit through my earpiece.

I looked over my shoulder. The teams were paired and lined up behind us, facing the exits. I braced my weapon tightly against my side.

"Ten seconds!" the captain shouted behind me.

The main doors of the church were visible below, and the chopper now hovered in place just behind the trees encircling the building. Someone dropped the two lines on each side of the doorway, and they slithered down toward the ground.

Gina reached over and gripped my arm for a split second.

"Drop, teams!"

Sucking in a breath, I crouched alongside Gina, gripping my line, and the chopper floor disappeared from beneath my feet. Weightlessness overtook me. The speed blurred my vision, and the friction of the line whizzing through my gloves warmed their damp fabric.

Treetops surged closer, then branches, trunks—ground—

Gina and I hit the soil in tandem. We dropped our lines and stepped away silently, unlocking the safeties on our guns and moving into position. My peripheral vision showed the other teams landing behind us and filing toward the church. The building's walls may have been painted once, but all that remained were thin streaks of gray on the rotting wooden boards. It was taller than I'd expected, its roof reaching far above us amongst the treetops.

Gina led the way. The back window, our entrance, was at shoulder level. Pinecones crunched under my boots, so I lightened my steps.

We reached the window. Gina eyed the windowsill—no glass left, totally busted out—and swiftly lifted herself up and through the flaking wooden frame. I waited three beats and followed suit, heaving myself inside.

I landed quietly on the old floorboards. In front of me, Gina scanned the room, gun butt against her chest. The edges of the main sanctuary were entirely dark. The altar's giant cross loomed above us from the back wall. The window we'd entered was one of two lighting the room —crisscrossed boards covered the others, except for the one Zach and Roxy were crawling through on the west wall. Dust floated through the few beams of light we had.

Must and earthy mildew filled my nose. The now-distant and barely audible murmur of the chopper was the only thing I could hear besides my clipped breathing. Most of the pews were in scattered pieces, and old hymnals were strewn between them.

I followed Gina as she crept toward the altar. We knelt on either side of it, squinting through the haze. *One, two, three, four…* I counted my teammates as they shifted through the darkness, covering the perimeter of the sanctuary. Everyone was accounted for. Bryce's behemoth frame stood beside one of the massive, cracked pillars. I couldn't see his mouth moving, but I heard the gravel of his whisper in my comm: "Team B, say the word when all four corners are covered. Team A, stationary."

Zach and Roxy scouted the west wall, and I could see Colin and Greta securing the darkness framing the main door. I glanced above, mentally repeating my next orders. *You will be the first to head up.*

The vaulted ceiling was so tall I couldn't tell where the walls ended and it began.

"Team A, have you located the stairs?" Captain growled.

"Stairs near corner of altar and west wall, confirmed," Gina whispered. My eyes darted to the narrow staircase.

"Ground floor secure," Zach said softly in my ear.

"Right. Team A, visually secure the stairs. Then head up. If I've got your bearings right, there should be a balcony beyond that," Bryce instructed.

There wasn't much visibility up the staircase, but the next landing was clearly far up. Some of the slatted steps were cracked... some not there at all. Gina's gaze caught mine, and she nodded to reassure me.

"Stairs clear. Light steps, Lyra," Gina breathed over the comm, holding my eyes with hers.

"Team A, move up," our captain grunted.

Gina instantly responded, stepping delicately as she ascended. I left several steps between us as we climbed. My eyes bounced between her feet and the steps emerging from the dark above us.

A step groaned under Gina's left foot, and we instantly froze. She looked back at me, a warning to be careful. I nodded. Despite my care, the same step creaked under my weight, but it held.

Cobwebs latticed between the railing and the steps. I glanced at them for just a second, and I heard a step whine and then snap—*crack*—Gina's right foot was falling, and she was going down with it.

I snatched the back of her belt and threw my weight back as hers pulled me forward, my muscles straining. The broken wooden step clattered on the floor below, echoing off the east wall.

"*Freeze!*" Bryce hissed in my ear.

Gina's sharpened breaths were the only sounds that followed. I held on tightly to her belt; she gripped the railing, taking most of her weight off me. Her eyes closed in relief, but only briefly. She flashed a thanks to me with a glance. All remained still.

"Team A. Secure?" It was Zach.

"Secure," Gina replied.

"Continue," Bryce ordered.

Gina exhaled and turned back up the staircase. Shaking just slightly, I found my breath and followed her.

We covered over a dozen more steps, accompanied by one or two more creaks but thankfully no more collapses, until we finally found ourselves entering what looked like an attic—not a balcony. There were scattered wooden pillars, piles of old furniture, and a window in the wall far ahead. Another glowed behind us. The windows' light haloed above us from the opposite ends of the room, relieving the gloom just a little. We moved off the stairs and carefully tested the wooden floor with our feet.

"Next floor confirmed, Captain," Gina said quietly on her comm. "It's an attic. Moving forward."

Something pale moved in the corner of my eye, and I jumped. The tip of Gina's gun darted toward it. We halted. It didn't move again. I squinted, making out a sheet draped on an old table. Inches of dust covered every surface. It fluttered again in some unseen draft.

I nodded to Gina to move forward. *False alarm.*

We silently passed other tables and chairs, all enveloped in cobwebs. The attic was dead quiet. We peered around, our forms casting even more shadows in the extending darkness.

"Western stairwell visually confirmed," Zach whispered.

"Zach, Roxy, take the stairs. Hopefully you can confirm a balcony," Bryce said.

Gina and I planted our feet and held steady. The room was motionless, soundless. If there was a redbill here, it was the quietest I'd ever encountered, that was for sure.

Our eyes continued scanning the dark. I reached up and slowly picked a spiderweb off my chin.

"Balcony confirmed," Zach murmured over the comm. "No movement."

Gina stepped forward, and I looked behind us for any stirring. Still nothing.

She signaled me with her hand, and I followed her deeper into the thick beams and abandoned furniture.

Thwap, thwap.

The sound tore through the silence. Gina and I spun toward it. I planted my heels to secure my stance, the slick metal of the trigger under my finger.

A sudden, bright thrashing and whirling engulfed Gina's head. I jerked back and adjusted my aim, trying to get a bead on the cloud flailing above Gina's shoulders—until I heard a quick, flustered cooing.

"Pigeon," Gina gasped. She swatted at the bird, and it tumbled down to the wooden floor then bobbed off, its feathers mussed, vanishing into the gloom.

I pulled the tip of my weapon back up and away from my teammate, my hand instinctively pressing against my breastbone. My heartbeat throbbed in my ears. *Holy hell…*

The two of us stayed there for a moment, catching our breath. In the resumed quiet, we peered around for any other movement.

Zach spoke again. "Moving to western balcony."

After scouting the rest of the room, Gina gestured toward the staircase. "Attic clear," she whispered into her comm.

I watched my feet as I followed her, to avoid kicking a table leg or brushing any dust-choked sheets. I glanced around in search of the staircase we'd come up, when Gina stopped abruptly. I nearly walked into her and quickly side-stepped. Then I saw why she'd stopped.

A figure stood directly before the staircase, blocking our only way out.

As I stared, I realized I could barely call it a figure—it was more a blanket of obscurity. No clear shape to the body. An empty space of jet black, only finding form against the slightly subtler grays of the room it stood in.

My eyes strained to trace the outlines of the figure's shadowed face.

"Hello?" I called out, my voice reverberating through the attic, seeming to fill every jagged crack and crevice.

Silence. Stillness.

That was the only response from the living shadow in front of us.

The hair on the back of my neck rose as I felt a chill, thick and contagious. It spread down my spine, gliding through my extremities with a frigid wake. Still, I gave a small wave, beckoning Gina to follow me forward.

Thoughts tumbled through my mind. *It's not a redbill. That much is obvious. And we're highly trained. If it's a squatter, or some psycho, we can defend ourselves.*

Not to mention, this was our only way out.

Gina stayed two steps behind me as our boots crept closer to the figure and our exit point. A few feet away, I saw a face begin to take shape amidst the darkness of its boundaries. *His* boundaries, I realized. And his eyes… My heart froze in my chest. Something about his eyes was so familiar, yet so foreign, that I felt my brow furrow, my mind scrambling to understand. I couldn't make out their color from here, but there was… something about them.

I felt my body tense suddenly—some primordial instinct that somehow pieced the puzzle together and hardened before my brain had a chance to do the same.

Then his hands were on me.

And despite his impossible speed, I felt it happen in slow motion. Like an almost-lucid dream, one where I was a full participant but couldn't respond fast enough. My gun flew from my hands and clattered to the ground, the sound echoing off the thick, wood-slatted floor. My comm was ripped from my ear, and my body was heaved over his shoulder.

In the time it took me to gasp, he crossed the room. So light and fast it felt like we were floating, then, without warning, angling upward. I saw it in a blur—the window. He was *scaling the wall to the window.* I regained my voice, shrieking frantically into the attic space, and heard

Gina's voice yelling back. A gunshot rang out, but the man didn't falter. My screams grew stronger as Gina's grew farther away, and I was plunged into empty space with only the body beneath me to cling to.

We were freefalling. As we plunged toward the ground, he made a sound—a sharp, guttural growl—and a huge shape appeared out of nowhere.

Broad wings and thin, dangling legs. An extended beak that had featured in my nightmares a few hours before. A redbill.

It swooped under us, catching us with a heavy shudder as the man straddled it and hauled me in front of him.

What is happening?

I didn't have time to ask myself anything beyond that. To think. To wonder. I barely even had time to breathe. Because a moment later, the redbill accelerated to cut through the air like a torpedo. I knew redbills could fly fast. But this—*this* was beyond comprehension.

The world screamed by in a blur, too fast and jumbled to be anything but a mix of faint colors and the meshing of space and time. My helmet detached from my suit, and I gasped, choking on the wind. I felt the skin on my face being pulled backward. My eyes burned. And I clutched his cloak with everything I had.

Until, at some point, I realized we'd slowed. We weren't clipping through space anymore. I blinked, willing my dry eyes to moisten enough to function. To figure out where we were and what was happening. The surrounding shapes took form just as the redbill landed with a brain-rattling jolt.

Cliff, I grasped. *We're on a cliff.* My senses darted in every direction, trying to take everything in. Gray skies splayed out in front of me. Clouds rolled and tumbled in the sky, churning—matching how my stomach felt, tossing and twisting inside me. I heard the roaring of waves as they crashed into the cliff, salt spray cutting up into the air.

The man slid gracefully off the bird. The wind billowed through his dark cloak, causing it to flare behind him. He turned to me, and I remembered what I'd pieced together before he'd grabbed me. Before the power and momentum and speed swept all thoughts from my brain. My eyes flew to his face. To his *eyes*. Wondering if what my instincts had jumped to in the milliseconds before he snatched me could possibly be correct.

The wind swept through his dark hair, and strands of it skated across the pale, yet strangely shadowed flesh of his forehead. I gasped as my gaze caught his once more. I could see his eyes better now that we were free from the dimness of the church attic. Yes, they were blue. But not *just* blue. They were an icy, crystalline blue that seemed to shift and melt in his very irises, tinges of silver and gray surfacing with them. Like glacial waters, haunting and bottomless.

I knew what those eyes meant. What they were. The depth—the darkness. The shadows. I knew what they were from every story Bryce had ever shared about his past. I was reminded of them every time I saw the cane Uncle Alan still had to use—an ever-present connection to his days as a ground soldier, the dangers he'd faced. I knew them from every whisper between my parents. I knew them from so many of the people who had done everything possible to prevent those eyes from ever seeing a human again.

And yet, here I was. Staring at them.

I felt it then: fear. Thick and dark, its talons sinking deep into my core. He reached out, his hands latching onto me. And for a split second, I wondered what it would feel like when he sank his teeth into me. Would it feel like his hands, the strong pressure I felt in them as they clutched me? As though his skin had melded into mine and I could no longer tell where I started and he ended... Or would it be fierce and fast, an anchoring of fangs in my flesh without warning?

Improvise. Adapt. Overcome.

The dizzy thoughts flashed through my head one after another until he jerked forward, and I felt my training kick in.

As he swept me downward off the redbill, I prepared to roll, assuming he meant to throw me to the ground; I wouldn't go down without a fight. Instead, my feet landed on solid rock. My fists clenched. I saw his lips part. Barely. And just when I gathered the energy of fear and anger coursing through my body, feeling it surge into the fist I was going to throw his way, he spoke.

His words rolled around us, deep and resonant, as though they'd ridden in on the waves crashing against the cliff behind us.

"Ah," he sighed. "I always prefer to have a conversation one on one."

CHAPTER FOUR

"What?" I croaked, staring.

Changing strategy, I shifted backward, my wobbling legs getting as much distance from the redbill and the man—the *vampire*—as possible. The cliff's edge appeared in my vision as I backtracked, the sheer drop sending alarm jolting through my core, and I reversed one step toward the two creatures. But just one.

They gazed at me, indifferent and silent. The redbill turned its monstrous beak under its wing, fixing a few feathers. The vampire cleared his throat and crossed his arms, his cream linen-like shirt frayed under his thick black cloak.

The wind howled past us again. Sucking in a breath, I braced my feet firmly on the rock. I raised my fists to my midsection.

"Who the hell are you?" My voice cracked.

"So we're past the stage of '*What* are you?' Good. I don't have a lot of time." He pulled his cloak from his shoulder.

I blinked hard. It was really true? A vampire?

"How are you even…?" I breathed.

"I may get to that." He flipped a hand nonchalantly in the air. "Or I may not. That depends on how you answer my questions."

My heart punched the back of my ribs. "*Questions?*"

This can't be real. There's no way this is real.

"Yes. Questions." He nodded, his arctic eyes piercing me. He tapped a finger to his lips and held it there for just a moment. "How old are you?"

I looked around, turning just my head, assessing the terrain. A thin beam of light broke through the clouds briefly, flashing across his opalescent face. I'd heard that sunlight didn't bother them, and apparently that was true.

He snapped his fingers this time and raised his voice, the effect of it pulling the little air left from my lungs. "How old are you?"

"I'm twenty-one," I managed, regaining as much of my composure as possible.

He didn't miss a single beat. "What are you called?"

"Lyra—"

"Not your name, your *rank*," he replied impatiently.

I instinctively flinched. "I'm..." I started, but cut myself off, clenching my fists tighter.

He was definitely going to kill me after he questioned me. Of course he would—he was a vampire. My suit covered most of my neck, but he could easily get past that. My knives hadn't been restocked since I lost them last night. And pulse patches were too dangerous to use in tight quarters, so I didn't have any of them on me either.

"Tell me your rank." He crossed his arms again.

I swallowed, finding the strength to hold his stare with my own. "First lieutenant." *Why in the hell is he asking me this?*

"For how long have you worked with the Bureau?" he pressed.

"Three years," I said. I continued scanning the area, searching for a sharp rock or stick within reach. *Nothing.*

His eyes bounced about my frame for a moment, then fixated on my chest—on my badge, I realized. He furrowed his brow, frowning.

"Sloane," he said.

My heart leapt again. The wind gusted against my legs, but my footing held solidly.

"As in… *Alan* Sloane, the director of Chicago?" he asked.

How does he know that? I licked my lips quickly and clenched my jaw.

I opened my mouth, but nothing came out. *Don't answer him. Do. Not. Answer. Him.*

Then the thought of my throat being torn open sent a rattle through my body. Swallowing, I decided to answer, because if there were a way to survive this, I would.

"No relation," I told him.

His eyes narrowed. "I don't believe you." The threat went unspoken.

Is there a mole at the Bureau? I paused, reconsidering my approach. I had no way of knowing what he knew, and it was clearly far more than he should've.

"He's my uncle," I admitted.

His eyes grabbed mine again, and they looked darker suddenly, with shades of indigo tingeing the wintry swirls. He cocked his head. Another knot tied itself in my stomach; my armor suddenly felt much thinner.

The vampire sighed. Strange, gray ripples curled under his skin, then vanished, reappearing under his eyes. His shoulders shifted, like a massive weight bore down on them.

He looked dimmer, drained. Almost… worn.

His voice carried across the wind. "In that case, I definitely need your help."

CHAPTER FIVE

"*Help?*"

My mind frantically weighed which option was worse: being held hostage for God knows how long by a *vampire*—or having my blood drained all over the cliff and my body thrown into the raging ocean below.

The vampire nodded at the redbill, and a low rumble came from the monster's closed beak.

"We need to move first," the vampire announced.

I immediately retightened my fists, preparing to lash out. "I'm not going anywhere."

"You'd rather starve to death in the wilderness?" He swung me through the air before I could strike him, and then I was staring at the redbill's wings again. My stomach hadn't forgotten the last ride on this monster, and it churned in protest. The vampire leapt onto the redbill and sat behind me.

The giant bird shifted its weight, and I grabbed fistfuls of long, rough feathers, my ears already ringing. This wasn't good: I wouldn't be able to attempt to fight him and stay balanced on the bird at the same time.

"A pitstop is in order, if you don't mind," the vampire murmured, in a tone that made it clear that he didn't care whether I minded or not.

The redbill stretched the tips of its wings straight out and stepped forward toward the edge of the cliff. I held my breath, bracing myself for the drop.

My back collided with the vampire's chest when the redbill dove over the cliff, dropping, plunging almost straight down.

Then the bird extended its wings and caught a gust of wind, the drop stopping so suddenly that my stomach lurched in a different direction. We flew forward, the roaring speed blinding me. I leaned into the redbill's back, bracing myself. Snippets of whitecaps darted by below. Clouds dampened my cheeks.

The vampire's arm around my waist felt like a tree trunk. Strands of my hair blew loose and whipped the sides of my face. Even if I'd been able to think, I wouldn't have been able to hear myself.

I squeezed my eyes closed, my muscles rigid. I tried to breathe.

And then it was over.

The air swirled around us when we landed. The beast's wings stretched, then calmly returned to its ribcage, covering my legs. I released a clump of feathers, wiping the tears streaming across my face from the whipping wind with one hand.

My head still spun, but I searched the location. Now we were in a thickly wooded area. Heavy storm clouds hung above us still, like the ones I'd seen over the cliff. A gravel road cut through the trees ahead. No cars, no people, but I thought I heard a very faint hum of a highway in the distance.

The vampire appeared on the ground to my right. I hadn't felt or heard him dismount. He pulled his hood over his head and adjusted the sleeves of his tattered shirt. He looked around as if he saw or heard things that I didn't, and I wondered how much better his senses were than mine. The shadows under his pale skin rippled up his neck and toward his cheekbones, now almost as dark as the clouds.

"Do not move," he said. His eyes cut through me. "I'll be back momentarily."

He strode down the gravel path, which led to a sagging old motel partially obscured by trees. Orange paint peeled from the few room doors I could make out through the branches. There was a logo on the glass of a window: "Woodland Lodge." A flickering neon sign hung below the words. *Vacancy.*

I glanced back to where he'd been, but the vampire had vanished. Silence sank in around me... and the redbill.

The bird seemed entirely unaware of my presence. It preened its chest, grumbling slightly. I looked down. My left hand was still buried in its feathers. I slowly released them, holding my breath. The last thing I needed was to piss off a bloodsucking demon stork.

A cricket chirped. I glanced around. *Um... okay. Just... hanging out with a redbill.*

I spotted the vampire again. He'd already reached the motel, which seemed too far away for that to be possible. He walked through one of the orange doors and immediately closed it behind him.

Run. This is your chance. He couldn't possibly hear and see me from where I was. *I can get to the highway.*

I slowly pulled my right leg up, my eyes glued to the back of the redbill's head. *Easy. Easy.*

Just as I'd almost gotten my right foot over the bird's spine, its head jolted up toward my leg, its broadsword of a beak releasing a rasping groan. Its eye caught mine for the first time: a massive black pupil encircled by a deep crimson iris. It did not blink.

I froze. Our staring contest held as my heartbeat hammered in my ears. The monster clacked its beak. I could see that the inner edge was serrated, like the world's biggest carving knife.

It was almost like I could... feel... the vampire's voice echoing inside me. *Do not move.*

I released a breath but held my right leg still, refusing to fully remount the beast.

Then the bird growled, tossed its wings, and snapped its beak twice, just inches from my left leg. My heart pounded, but I still refused to lower my right leg.

Wait for it to get distracted again and slide off its back... just a few moments. Then roll into the bushes and—

A faint scream sounded from the motel. My head snapped in that direction, searching for movement, and I caught sight of the vampire's cloaked shape slipping through a tall, open window. He stalked toward us, wiping his chin with the back of his pale hand. He carried a large sack over his shoulder. His eyes never strayed from where the redbill stood.

At first, I noticed that the sack over his shoulder was denim, and then I saw a leather belt wrapped around it. There were shoes dangling from the ends. It wasn't a sack. It was a person.

The rippling shadows under the vampire's flesh were now the color of dark smoke. When he reached me, he tossed the body off his shoulder, its weight hitting the soil with a sickening thump. He nudged it with his foot, turning it over, and I saw a man's face.

Blood covered the man's shirt from a gaping crevice in his throat. I saw muscle. Then the man twitched violently, and a spurt of blood shot out from the hole, then another—his heart was still beating.

My breath caught in my throat. *My God.* The smell of iron filled the air.

The redbill leaned down and jabbed the tip of its beak into the mess of the man's neck. Blood speckled the grass. I heard the bird sucking the blood up through its beak, its throat gurgling as it swallowed.

Vomit threatened the back of my throat, but I forced it back down. My nausea turned to white-hot anger inside my chest. I glared at the vampire. Adrenaline pulsed through my arms. *Murderer.*

His arm crossed his stomach, his other hand pressed against his temple, his eyebrows furrowed. I squinted, confused.

The redbill's sucking sounds began to slow.

"It's okay. It'll pass," he muttered. I wasn't sure if it was to himself or me. He turned to the side, facing a tree trunk. He rubbed the nape of his neck as if he'd pulled a muscle. He flinched.

What's wrong with him? The vampire's eyes were clenched shut in a wince. He gave a strained exhalation.

After a long moment, his glacial eyes turned to me again. The body on the ground was stone still. Congealing blood caked the man's neck and pooled in the surrounding grass.

"You shouldn't fret over him," the vampire said finally. His voice was coarse. "Raped three women. Including his sister. Was planning to murder two others."

I stared. My lip curled from his accusation. I shook my head slowly, eyes burning. "I don't believe you."

He sucked in a breath, eyeing me.

Another yell sounded from the motel, this one followed by the shuffling of loud footsteps. More shouting. A door slammed.

The vampire pulled his hood over his forehead. "Time to go."

I flinched as he wrapped his arm around me, but before I could struggle, the redbill tossed its beak to the side, a squawk caught in its throat. With one immense lunge, we rose over the treetops, the redbill's wings thundering rhythmically.

The clouds had grown even darker. Lightning broke through the air in the distance. The trees dwindled in size, hundreds of feet below us. The altitude stifled my breathing.

With only the slightest of pauses, the redbill pointed into the storm —and then the roaring wind and speed blinded me again.

CHAPTER SIX

We swooped over a red rockface. Beneath us, the landscape was covered in sand, rocks, and brush. Sharp mountaintops lined the horizon. I had lost my sense of time during the flight; it felt like it could've been seconds or hours. The clouds were gone, and the sun glared down on the desert below us.

The redbill tossed its wings back to land. I covered my eyes as a burst of sand blew over us from the backdraft, biting my face.

Thud.

The bird screeched, and the piercing sound echoed back from towering rock formations. As I tried to wipe the sand from my eyes and lips, the vampire appeared beside the redbill, patting its neck feathers. Harsh sunlight reflected on the rocks, hurting my eyes as I squinted around. I unclenched my fists and pulled two feathers from between my fingers.

This nightmare just wouldn't end.

I blinked, and all I could see on the back of my eyelids was that dead man, his gaping throat. The gurgling, suckling sounds filled my head again... and the vampire's indifference.

"Where are we?" My rasping voice escaped my lips.

"Canyonlands. Utah," the vampire replied. He held out his palm—an offer to help me down.

My nose filled with the smell of iron again, remembering that man's blood glistening on the grass.

Don't let him touch you.

I looked at the vampire's outstretched hand, then met his leaden, icy gaze. The last thing I wanted was to be any closer to this murderous animal. I stared, unmoving. I wasn't going to let him tear *my* throat out.

The vampire didn't move, either.

Would you rather... sit on a redbill that obeys a vampire, or stand on open terrain next to a redbill and a vampire?

There was no way I could outrun either of them.

"Back up," I demanded.

He blinked back at me, unmoving.

"Back *up*," I snapped.

He pursed his lips and took three short strides backward.

I pulled a leg over and slid down, angling so that my back never turned to him. Our eyes remained locked as my feet hit the sand. My muscles protested, stiff and sore from clinging to the redbill's back, but I held steady. I didn't want him to see me stumble.

I stepped to the side to put more space between us, and exhaled.

The vampire continued to stare, stone-faced. My lips parted as I reached for the list of questions that had built up in my head over the journey, but he spoke first.

"I'll explain everything, I promise."

I wiped my forehead with the back of my hand.

He went on, his voice clipped. "We need a place where we won't be disturbed for a while. Follow me." He broke our gaze to scan the rocks around us, reminding me of a lion surveying his grassland. He turned toward the tall, thin rocks ahead.

"Keep your head down," he grunted over his shoulder.

From the corner of my eye I saw something floating through the sky, black against the bright blue. It had a huge wingspan—and a massive beak. *Another redbill?*

My eyes glanced back to the vampire. He was already making his way up a small incline, his cloak brushing the rocks as he passed. His redbill groaned in its throat, one of its beady eyes locked on me. I flinched, then followed the vampire. The redbill remained where it had landed, scratching its claws under some brush.

I wonder if this is how Stockholm syndrome starts.

We approached a tall line of standing rocks, and I spotted a vertical crevice in the stone. The opening was narrow, a sharp, toothy slice through the rock barely wide enough for the vampire's shoulders. He slid inside with ease, but I paused when I caught sight of the jagged rock lining the walls of the gap. I released a shaky breath, tucked my arms, and followed him, pivoting around the jutting stone. *Just keep going. He would've killed you already if he'd wanted to. Just keep an eye on him until you find out what he wants.*

I carefully stepped over an exposed root, only taking my eyes off the back of the vampire's head for a moment. We continued through the passage in silence. Then he turned to his right, and his arms and back tensed. I heard rock crunching against rock, and then he vanished into the stone wall.

I reached the spot and found a small entryway carved into the rock, opening into a totally unlit space. Cool air seeped through the doorway. Bracing myself, I stepped into the dark.

Stone ground on stone behind me—the vampire pushing a rock against the opening. One sliver of light shone on my boots from behind, then disappeared. I froze in the sudden darkness.

And... I've just locked myself in a cave with a vampire. I spun around, straining to locate his figure in the blackness, my fists balled and guarding my neck.

"Take my arm." His voice came from directly in front of me, muffled somewhat by the stone.

"No." I stepped back.

He sighed. "Fine." After a pause, I felt cloth brush against my right hand. "Just hold that, then."

It was the corner of his cloak. I gripped the fabric. It tugged, and I stepped forward through the pitch black. My toe caught on a rock, and I felt the vampire pause as I regained my footing. I still couldn't see him, but somehow, my mind *felt* where he was.

I must be delirious.

As we continued—how far, I had no idea—the cooling air calmed me somewhat. Our steps became consistent, rhythmic. My muscles were still rigid from the flight, but the quiet of the cave slowed my racing thoughts. I assumed exhaustion was taking its toll.

My eyes bounced around, but I couldn't orient myself. With nothing to focus on, I started seeing spots. *Don't faint.*

It slowly dawned on me that the spots were actually patches of flickering light—real light. The light slowly intensified, until I could make out stone walls illuminated by an orange glow.

When my feet became visible, I dropped the vampire's cloak. I walked a few paces behind him, the ceilings of the passageway growing taller as the light grew brighter.

The ceiling and narrow walls of the passage opened. An expanding cavern spread before our feet, more torches lining the sprawling space. Shadows lurked around the perimeter, but there was enough light for me to make out a group of figures.

Vampires.

My breath caught in my throat. I immediately started counting them, wondering how far I could make it back through the black passageway on foot.

Several were small. Children? *Child* vampires? Their heads drooped. A female—a mother?—held a small girl with matted hair. A little boy stood beside them. His arm was bound in white cloth, like a cast.

As the creatures saw me, they began murmuring to each other. The mother clutched the little girl to her chest and backed away, urging the boy closer. Two other young vampires gaped at me in the dim light. One covered her little mouth with her hands. The other's face was heavily bruised. They scuttled away toward a group of mothers and children. There were at least thirty vampires.

The vaulted stone ceiling heightened their voices and resounded with echoes. A baby started crying. My palms dampened.

"What the hell are you doing?!" A male voice rang out, and several adult vampires separated from the group, advancing on us. The only thing standing between me and their teeth was the vampire who'd just murdered a man in cold blood.

My "guide" held up a hand, but it did nothing to quiet the group.

"Why did you bring that here?" one of the male vampires snapped. His eyes were an icy blue, much like my guide's.

Behind them, one of the vampire mothers called out. "How could you think this was a good idea, Dorian?"

I finally had a name for him.

I slowly retreated a few paces, my eyes darting over the group. If Dorian couldn't protect me from this horde he'd dragged me into, I had no chance against so many vampires.

Another pair of vampires appeared, a man and a woman in their early twenties, their eyes dark with worry.

Dorian raised both of his hands now. "She's not dangerous."

Excuse you?

Another male vampire, exceptionally tall and sinewy, tried to brush past Dorian. "Like hell she isn't," he growled.

"I need you to trust me, Kane," Dorian said.

"You *would* pull something like this."

Dorian blocked the vampire's shoulder with his own, his hand gripping the other's large bicep. Their eyes locked, muscles straining as Kane tried to push through—and failed. Instead, he shoved Dorian's hand away, backing up a step.

"You're being reckless and selfish. Step aside and I'll fix your mistake." Kane's fangs grew sharper and longer as he spoke, shining in the torchlight, his eyes now fixed on my throat. Ice coursed through my veins. My muscles tensed. I wouldn't go down without a fight... but I knew how it would end.

"Kane. Enough." Dorian moved, using his body to block me from Kane's sight.

He'd found the one circumstance that made me feel almost grateful to have him near me. Almost.

I clenched my fists. Including Dorian, six vampires stood before me —some clearly more dangerous than others. I caught sight of another adult female standing against the wall, but she didn't move. She watched us all, seemingly unphased.

Kane, still clenching his teeth, knocked his shoulder into Dorian's. "How could you risk the only safety we have left?"

"This one won't hurt us." Dorian's voice rang out over the group. "I would not play with your wellbeing."

"How can we know for sure?" the female barked. She looked to be in her twenties, short, but built like a tree trunk.

"Judge for yourself, Bravi," Dorian replied. "Anyone want to take a bite?"

Excuse me?

I tensed at the sudden, but not unexpected, betrayal. The vampires surrounded me. Their pointed canines were much more noticeable now as they sneered. Children peered at me from behind the adults' legs.

I shifted my weight, but my legs were like cement. *I'm going to be torn apart.*

Their eyes glowed with anger, boring into me. My armored suit felt like paper. I could see the ripples under their skin now. Dorian had looked at me like that, but this was far more unsettling.

As the pack studied me, Kane stepped closer than I liked. I readied myself for something desperate, anything to take one of them down with me.

"Humans are unpredictable," Kane spat at Dorian, curling his lip up over a fang. "Anything could make her change her mind!"

"Maybe so," Dorian said evenly. He intercepted Kane once more, placing his hand on the other vampire's chest. "But if we want to gain humans' trust, we'll have to trust them, too."

A quiet settled over the cavern. The only sound was my labored breathing.

"The last thing I want is to put what's left of us in harm's way." Dorian's voice remained steady. "But we have to remember that we're all in this together."

Kane grunted, shaking his head, his eyes still locked on me.

The group looked at each other, questioning. Someone grumbled. I stayed wary, scanning the circle in case one of them lunged for me.

Dorian's hand gripped mine then, his hold cool yet firm, and he pulled me from the group, toward another passageway that I hadn't seen in the shadows. I looked over my shoulder at the furrowed brows and tense gazes that followed me, feeling just as puzzled as some of the vampires looked. Kane moved back to stand beside an older female vampire that I hadn't seen before. She leaned over a bent leg wrapped in dirty fabric. Her expression was just as foul as his.

Dorian led me down the hallway, and we wound around a curve. He ducked down through a small doorway in the stone. I bent down and followed him.

When I stood and looked up, we were in some kind of grotto. It was much smaller than the large cavern I'd nearly been murdered in. Natural ledges were carved into the rock walls. A single torch cast light around the room. A thin wooden frame held a bed. A ripped old book sat on a ledge to my right, alongside a little figurine carved out of wood —a bird slightly resembling a redbill.

Dorian eased himself onto the stone floor and exhaled heavily. He gazed down at his feet, then looked up at me over his knees, his hands resting on his worn gray pants. From this angle, I could clearly see the strain of fatigue on his face, darkening the skin under his eyes. He gestured toward the bed.

Sit down? I glanced at the spot, then back at the vampire. A moment passed; then, I eased myself onto the fraying cloth covering the bed. *Yep, Stockholm syndrome. Great.*

He leaned forward. The torchlight caught the pale blue of his eyes. "Now I can give you some answers."

CHAPTER SEVEN

I studied Dorian's face, his cheekbones high and jaw sharp in the flickering torchlight. Dozens of questions raced through my head. He'd kidnapped me and fed a man to a redbill before my eyes. Why should I trust any explanations he offered at all?

He rested his elbows on his knees and laced his fingers together.

"Let's clear something up first," he said. "I imagine the Bureau has taught you that vampires are evil and depraved. But there's been a catastrophic misunderstanding." He paused, as if waiting for my response.

"Enlighten me," I murmured dryly. I was trapped underground with thirty vampires. It wasn't like I was going anywhere.

He held my gaze. "We're not the heartless, savage killers you probably think we are."

I hadn't seen anything to the contrary today, but I didn't imagine telling him that would go over too well, so I figured I might as well let this play out.

"Vampires have a purpose, a role in the universe. I'm sure you understand that things require balance. We don't just recklessly murder whenever our hearts desire. We are drawn to feed on specific kinds of people. Remember I told you that man at the motel was a rapist? That he was preparing to murder other people?"

I shuddered, not wanting to relive it. The way he'd served that man to the redbill like some bag lunch...

"We—vampires—can sense someone's goodness, and, more specifically, their lack of goodness. I was naturally drawn to hunt him because I could sense the darkness in him." He paused, searching my face.

I did my best to reveal nothing. This was an awfully convenient narrative for vampires. It didn't escape me that I had no way of verifying that man's crimes.

"Think of it like fish that bottom-feed to keep the entire lake clean for the other lifeforms."

Keep him talking. If being perceived as a hero was important to him, maybe I could use that to convince him to release me.

I glanced over the room's carved-out ledges again, searching for a potential weapon.

He clenched his jaw for a moment but then shifted his shoulders, regaining his air of detachment.

"We do this not just on Earth, but in other places, as well."

"Other places than Earth?" *That took a left turn.*

"Specifically, one other place. Think of this planet as a plane where the population is mortal," he said evenly. "The other world is a plane where the population is immortal." The vampire set his hands out palm up, using them to illustrate the two planes.

"Have you seen this other 'plane'?" I asked.

"I was born there." He nodded his head, as if he were acknowledging his homeland face-to-face.

"Vampires aren't immortal." The Bureau had killed plenty of them, and our scientists reported signs of aging. They estimated vampires had a lifespan of 150 years.

"We're not entirely *mortal*, either," he retorted, creasing his brow.

"We're supernatural, the only beings that are meant to travel between the mortal and immortal planes. And we're hated by both."

I watched his unfaltering expression. His eyes held steady with conviction. A dangerous thought surfaced at the back of my mind. *What if he's telling the truth?*

But Uncle Alan and Bryce always said the most dangerous thing about vampires was their conniving mental acumen. He could be playing an elaborate mind-game, whether it was to get my guard down, get information out of me, or just to amuse himself by convincing me that vampires were good before he tore me apart. Even the crowd's reaction earlier could have been staged. I'd have to be out of my mind to trust him.

"Our purpose is even more important in the Immortal Plane," he continued, the evenness returning to his tone. "The creatures that live there have far more strength than humans, and if they're ill-intentioned, they can do a lot more damage to the balance. My kind has lived almost entirely in the immortal world, since humans have made the Mortal Plane incredibly difficult to inhabit." He pursed his lips.

"Yeah—because vampires made living on Earth so pleasant for us." I narrowed my eyes, then exhaled. What in the hell was he talking about? *Planes?* I got a grip on myself to keep him talking.

"I'm sorry," I bit out, going for polite but just coming out strained. "Continue."

"Whether you want to admit it or not, when vampires were around, there were fewer crimes, weren't there?" he asked, and raised his eyebrows at me.

I didn't respond. Even if that was true—which, to be fair, I had been hearing a lot recently—that just meant that before, there was an unaccounted-for vampire-on-human crime rate. *Is that supposed to be better?*

"The balance has shifted since humans drove out the vampires. And not just in the Mortal Plane." Dorian rubbed his temple. He paused for a moment and cleared his throat. "As you're with the Bureau, I'm sure you've heard about the death of Senator Canley."

"The *murder* of Senator Canley," I corrected sharply.

Of course I knew the story of why the Bureau had been founded, a few years before my brother was born. The vampires had finally murdered the wrong man.

He ignored my remark, his voice cool, yet focused. "Something happened after that, and it wiped out my kind on Earth."

"We hunted you to extinction," I said bluntly. Although, apparently, we hadn't been as thorough as we'd thought.

"No. That had an effect, but something else humans did was far more devastating." His jaw clenched, and fury briefly touched his gaze.

Unease prickled my spine. The only potential weapon in the room was the torch on the wall. Directly behind him. I tried to scope it out in my peripheral vision without looking directly at it, in case my glance betrayed me again.

"The vampire that killed Canley was captured by the Bureau. They tortured him until he eventually broke. It took twenty years, but he finally told them about the Immortal Plane. And then they forced him to take them there."

The firelight tinted his dark hair, giving him a demonic halo.

"The space between the planes is not meant to be treated like a highway. Not for humans. The boundary… the fabric… tore. Right over our city. Vampires are intrinsically tied to the boundary, because we traveled it for eons, before this tear. It's part of us." He paused. When he went on, his voice sounded like gravel. "There were no survivors for miles. Our home was basically destroyed when the fabric tore."

I'd never heard of anything like that. *If the Bureau had discovered where vampires came from, they would have told us.* But my mind flashed to the nondisclosure paperwork on the coffee table the night before.

"The opening between the worlds is still there. Permanently open, since the humans' breach." Dorian laced his fingers together again and paused in thought before continuing. "And if more humans found out about it, they could try and cross—and that's the most dangerous thing they can do."

"Why is that?" I figured he was trying to reason with me. He was trying to make it sound convincing, like he cared about what happened to humans. But what did he want?

"Since so many vampires in the Immortal Plane died when the tear happened, we could no longer keep the Immortal Plane balanced. That world grew corrupt. Immortals are greedy, and that greed is even more dangerous than humans harming humans." He shook his head, his face forlorn.

I pinched the bridge of my nose. "Are you seriously painting vampires as superheroes?"

Dorian sighed. "No. Vampires have flaws just like any sentient creature. But without us, evil will continue to grow. In the end, it will consume everything. Everyone."

I stared at him. His voice echoed through my head again, exhausted and direct: *Then I definitely need your help.* Was this what he wanted me to help him with? He wanted me, a lieutenant in the Occult Bureau, to help him keep vampires alive... in order to save the universe?

"If your kind are needed so badly in the Immortal Plane, why are you here?" I questioned, unwilling to ignore any inconsistency in his story.

"I told you, the Immortals and humans both hate us. After the tear devastated our population, the Immortals took advantage of our weakness to try and destroy us entirely. We're hunted and killed in both planes." He paused and rubbed the back of his neck. "We're here because the Immortals are more dangerous than humans now. They want to do away with the balance for their own benefit, turning a blind eye to the consequences."

I held my head in my hands. If this was a mind-game, the vampire might as well have just eaten me then, because he had me far outclassed. Between his apparent sincerity and the fact that he hadn't killed me yet, I caught myself wondering if he was telling me the truth. Why go to this trouble for a lie? But I still hadn't seen any proof, and the existence of another plane was tough to swallow without it. I couldn't afford to trust him.

"This is bigger than both of us." He leaned back against the stone wall. "Without vampires, humans could be wiped out. And without the help of humans, vampires *will* be wiped out."

I set my hands back on my knees. My head reeled. "You want me to believe that everything I've seen and know is just a façade, and vampires, bloodsucking murderers, are actually out to save everyone."

"Did you see those children back there?" he asked. "Carwin, with the broken arm?" He winced at his own words, and the pain in his eyes looked real. At least, to my human gaze. "The Immortals ambushed us. We had to cross over to the Mortal Plane to escape. We're hiding."

My voice softened. "Why here? Utah?"

"The tear. We're right beneath it. Redbills can travel it, as well—that's why redbills are so common around here. We think so many redbills have come through that it's become more of a gaping, open hole, like a highway instead of a gate—and travelable for humans now, too. Also, the constant energy leaking from the tear covers our auras on human surveillance here in the desert. At least for now. They know the tear is here, so it's only a matter of time before they find us during their searches."

The Bureau is searching here? That makes no sense. How could they keep this secret? And why?

"Can't the Immortals just cross over and find you here?" I asked, trying again to catch him in a lie.

"The Immortals don't know about the tear. It's imperceptible to them; only vampires are able to see it, and redbills can also somehow sense it," he replied. "In any case, the Immortals tend to avoid our mountains, except to hunt. And vampires don't enter the city. There's nothing left for us."

On that note, quiet filled the room. The conflicting voices in my head deafened me. I watched the dark ripples fading in and out across his face like storm clouds.

"I still don't understand why I'm here," I said.

"My kind have to come together and grow strong again," he said firmly. "We must bring back balance. For everyone's sake. And we can't do that while we're scattered and dying." His irises gleamed white on the word "balance," and I jerked back a little, unnerved by the change. In the moment it took me to recover, his eyes returned to normal. "We need refuge to recover our strength. We need safety on Earth, away from the Immortal Plane."

I tilted my head. I thought I saw where he was going with this.

"That's why we need you." A muscle tensed in his angular jaw. "You can be the link between us and the Bureau. I *must* speak with them in order for us to work together and make this right. They have to know how far the consequences of the tear will reach."

My face froze. *He wants to talk to Uncle Alan. How can I trust a vampire near anyone on the board? It'd be a perfect opportunity for revenge.*

"They have to know the truth. We—all of us—have to come to an understanding. Everything relies on it." Dorian smiled humorlessly. "These negotiations will benefit humans, too," he went on. "Humans need the redbill attacks to stop; vampires can make that happen."

Words caught in my throat. If he was serious about stopping the redbill attacks, the Bureau would be very interested.

Why would a ravenous killer ask his own enemy for help if he weren't serious? I couldn't dismiss the earnestness in his face. Then Uncle Alan's words found me again. *Conniving.* Why would the Occult Bureau hide something so important from its own members?

If it wasn't the vampire in front of me, then *someone* wasn't being completely honest. Which made this even more difficult.

"What's stopping you from using me to get into the Bureau and kill everyone?" I asked. "Try to see this from my perspective. This 'save the universe' thing could be your opening gambit for taking out the human race. Last I knew, vampires were extinct. How do I know there aren't thousands of you in hiding, waiting to annihilate everyone?"

He leaned back and released a weary breath.

"How do I know this Immortal Plane is even *real?*" I pressed.

This time, Dorian's eyes darkened, shadows flickering through those swirling crystalline irises. "I'll show you," he said grimly.

CHAPTER EIGHT

Dorian didn't wait for me to answer. He strode through the stone doorframe, assuming I would follow. I hated to reward arrogance, but I couldn't just sit here and wait for a hungry vampire to wander by—especially one of those who'd made it so clear they wanted me out of their hideout.

We hadn't made it two steps into the main cavern when four vampires broke from the shadowed crowd and blocked our path. Some of them had been in the tear-Lyra-apart circle earlier. I recognized the short young woman called Bravi and the mother vampire who'd kept her children close. A gangly young male vampire lingered behind them.

The man who resembled Dorian stepped directly in front of him and crossed his arms. I looked around the cavern for other vampires and found Kane scowling at me from a corner. His eyes reflected only the torchlight; they seemed almost black otherwise.

"Where are you going?" the man asked in a low tone, glancing at me over Dorian's shoulder.

"There's something that she needs to see," Dorian replied coolly, seemingly unperturbed.

"What does that mean? What is your plan?" the man growled.

"I can't expect her to believe something she's never seen, Rhome," Dorian said. "For any good to come of all this, she needs to see it before she decides what to do."

"What do you mean, *she* will decide what to do?" Bravi hissed. "What if she decides to take off?"

Rhome grabbed Dorian's shoulder and pulled him a few paces away. The other three vampires surrounded them in a huddle, their interrogation muddled but fierce. I couldn't make out their rushed words. The mother vampire threw her hands in the air. Rhome never released Dorian's shoulder. Bravi shot a sharp look at me and then launched a whispered assault on Dorian.

Their voices rose as they continued arguing. I stood alone, prickles of alertness crossing my skin, watching Kane stare at my throat. I couldn't make a run for it with his eyes glued to me.

"...keep her hostage." It was the mother. "We can't let her go."

"If she tells them where we are, we'll have to flee into wide open territory and pray for another safe spot," Rhome said.

"What makes you think humans will talk peacefully with us without some incentive?" the mother vampire snapped. "You know how humans are. They only care about themselves. Stop being so blind."

"What, Kreya, you think they'd be more willing to work with us if we threaten her?" Dorian returned.

"We need to think offensively. They'll try to slaughter us no matter what, whether we're just sitting here or keeping her hostage." Kreya's eyes leapt to me and then back to Dorian. "Why not get one step ahead?"

"I'm sick of waiting for the Bureau to find us," Bravi snarled. "We need to act. Now."

"Enough," Rhome said, with an air of authority that silenced the group. "Dorian." He gripped Dorian's shoulder again, leaning to look him directly in the eye. "I can't handle the thought of losing someone else." His sentence trailed off at the end as he swallowed hard and lowered his head. I could barely make out his next words. "Your brother was enough. Too much. We have to stay as safe as possible until we figure out what happened to your parents. And my parents. We can't put ourselves in the crosshairs again. The less risk, the better." Rhome's hand fell to his side.

Dorian looked toward me for a moment, long enough that his eyes clouded over.

Kreya crossed her arms and shook her head, her eyes downcast. A veil of silence fell over the group. The cavern stayed quiet, until Dorian cleared his throat.

"I understand your concerns," he said. "I don't trust the humans either." My heart skipped a beat. "That's exactly why we need to *convince* them to help us of their own volition. Threats and hostages will not do that. If we start with those, we give them reason to harm us. If we coerce them, they will inevitably betray us."

"They'll certainly betray us if we let them know where we're hiding," Bravi said tightly.

"We don't have time for this." Dorian shook his head. The others gazed down at the stone floor. Bravi shook her head. Rhome's eyes remained closed. He exhaled.

"We can't waste our resources and our lives trying to subdue the humans when there is a larger threat snapping at our heels," Dorian continued. "At least my way we have a chance, even a slight one, of avoiding violence."

Kreya set her hand on Rhome's shoulder, and he leaned into the touch ever so slightly. It dawned on me that vampires had partners like humans did. Even faced with vampire children, it had never occurred to me that these creatures might love each other, might have families like mine.

An indiscernible mumble escaped Bravi's lips. Dorian looked around the circle at each of them individually, holding their eyes.

The gangly young male vampire, who'd kept quiet so far, opened his mouth. "He's got a point, you know."

"Please don't encourage him, Sike." Rhome sighed.

"If we show humans that Dorian and this girl—lady—person—have come to an understanding, and she thinks we deserve help... that's more convincing than us threatening to kill her, isn't it?" Sike shrugged, then cringed. One of his arms lay in a sling.

"We cannot assume anything about humans," Bravi said.

"Well, sure, but we'll be in more trouble if they get angry and come after us, right? Starting peacefully and hoping for the best would be 'less risk.' Like Rhome said." Sike's voice grew in confidence, and his thin frame straightened.

"That's my thought." Dorian nodded. "I agree with you, Bravi: we do need to take action before they find us. And this is the most low-risk action we can take. They'll only have access to me. The imminent threat would be more controlled. And if it comes down to a fight in the end, then you'll be ready for it... but let me try this first."

Rhome gazed at Dorian again. Bravi's face softened from angry to something more forlorn. Kreya turned from the group, her auburn hair falling down her back.

"You'd better be right," she said. "It's not like you gave us much of a choice."

Rhome squeezed Dorian's shoulder once more before he followed Kreya to a dark corner of the cavern.

"I still don't like this," Bravi said, her green eyes sharp. She glanced up at Sike, then stalked after Rhome and Kreya.

Sike stood beside Dorian for a moment, but they said nothing to each other.

Even though the immediate danger seemed to have passed, adrenaline still coursed through me. My body was ready to fight my way out of there. Dorian had said I wasn't a hostage, but I felt like one.

Now that the others weren't scrutinizing his plan, his face creased with pain, despite the confidence of his words from moments ago. I couldn't fully trust him, but those feelings weren't put on for my benefit. I could see that they were real.

He nodded at Sike and then turned to me. "Let's go."

He led me toward the cavern's doorway. That's when Kane finally spoke up.

"First you drag us to the middle of a desert to waste away. Now you're handing us over to the humans?" he growled. As he spoke, the older female vampire with the injured leg limped toward us.

"We'll die faster if we do nothing," Dorian said curtly.

The older woman spoke for the first time. "Whose side are you on?"

"This isn't about sides anymore," Dorian said. Once again, he stood between them and me, but that offered little comfort. I'd seen how fast vampires moved.

"It's the humans' fault any of this happened in the first place," the woman spat. Her lips seemed permanently curled downward. "Our kind shouldn't have to placate such vicious fools." When she reached that final word, her eyes fixated on me. I didn't react, not wanting to provoke them further.

"Kane, Halla, have you two heard nothing that I've said?" Dorian asked.

Kane snorted contemptuously. "Yes, we all know what a loving, caring pacifist you are. Even when it comes to those who have no problem destroying every other living thing on their own planet and beyond."

"They have to pay for what they've done." Halla now spoke directly to me. "We can't grovel at their feet. They've sown—it's time to reap."

My fight-or-flight response told me to book it out the passageway.

"You haven't been listening to me, either," Kane said. "I've said a hundred times that we should return to the Immortal Plane and rally our clans there. There is safety in numbers."

"You think that we're in danger *here*?" At that, for the first time, Dorian seemed to lose his temper. His shoulders rose like a hissing jaguar. "You want us to return to the place where we were attacked and torn apart?"

"The Immortals will have our necks faster than the humans, Kane," Rhome said tersely, his deep voice echoing as it drifted over to us. He must have been listening from where he sat with Kreya and their two children.

"You know that," Dorian said to Kane, then looked at Halla. "Your mother knows it, too."

So, hatred of humans runs in the family. Great. As much as I wanted to believe their animosity was unfounded, I felt a pang of guilt in my chest. If the tear were real, and humans *had* caused it...

We were defending ourselves, I reminded myself. *From brutal murders.*

"It's shameful, what you're doing." Halla curled her lips into an even deeper scowl. "Vampires groveling at the feet of humans, begging for asylum. It's a disgrace that our kind should even consider stooping so low."

Dorian matched her tone. "Your pride blinds you."

"You're one to talk!" Kane snapped.

Dorian dropped his gaze and exhaled sharply. "This is why I didn't ask. We have to do *something*, but all of this bickering amongst ourselves is cementing our fate."

Kane and Halla fell silent, but their glares did not break.

Dorian raised his palms. "This is the best we've got right now. It's better than throwing our lives away by returning to the Immortal Plane. At least this way, we have a chance."

"Just let him go, Kane," Kreya said. "The damage is already done."

Kane snorted again, shook his head, and turned to his mother. "They've all lost their minds," he said, loudly enough that the entire cavern echoed with it.

Rhome and Kreya stared at the ground in the corner. Sike aimlessly drew lines in the sand with a rock.

After one more smoldering stare, Kane and Halla removed themselves to an unoccupied corner, Kane with a parting shot: "We're putting a lot of trust in you."

Dorian stood still for a moment, breathed out hard, and then stalked off again. I followed closely, looking back every so often to check that nobody planned to attack us from behind as we made our way back into the pitch-black passage.

I felt surprisingly grateful to be walking blindly through the dark again. It was preferable to the intense stares in that cavern. Dorian must've heard me sigh with relief in the cool air, but he said nothing about it.

We walked for a long time, but I didn't mind, as each step put more space between me and Kane and Halla. Despite the growing distance, their words rang sharply in my head.

One thing was clear to me: unless this was elaborate playacting, the rest of the vampires believed the same crazy stuff that Dorian did. They were just as upset and worried for the survival of their kind as he appeared to be. Staging this kind of tension just to pull the wool over my eyes seemed less and less likely.

I listened to the rock door scraping open, then winced as a crack of light stabbed my pupils. After one more grind, Dorian led me out of the dark. He closed the door in the rockface, and we slid between the narrow stone walls.

Outside, the desert air shimmered across the horizon. I plodded behind him as he scanned the brush and rocks. *Could he be watching for Bureau soldiers?*

I followed him down the incline and spotted the redbill standing amongst the brush. It caught sight of Dorian and grumbled, as if waking up.

He stood beside the redbill for a moment, looking around, his eyes calculating, then back at me with a stony gaze. "I'm not sure how to help you mount without touching you," he said.

I watched him for a moment, gauging his sincerity before deciding. "I'll take your hand."

He nodded, then leapt onto the bird's back and gazed down at me, offering an open palm. I took it, his firm grip easily helping me climb up behind him. His skin was cool and smooth as he slipped it from mine.

"Hold on tight," he murmured.

I placed my hands on his waist, every nerve in my body tightening as I considered what we were about to do.

The bird shook its head. I gripped Dorian as the bill jogged across the sand, extending its wings.

We shot into the air, and my stomach dipped, my heart pounding. I squinted my eyes and hid my face behind Dorian's shoulder as the wind roared around us.

What have I just agreed to?

CHAPTER NINE

Everything around us vanished in a burst of blinding white light that forced my eyes closed. The hair on the back of my neck stood up. A snapping sound filled my ears, like the fountain fireworks Zach and I used to set off when we were kids. The crackling intensified, and it felt as though the air was pressing into my body. Electricity tingled down my spine, a static blanket of heat that made me gasp.

Then it was over.

I opened my eyes to darkness. The air was gentle as a breeze coming off a warm ocean, but thick in my nostrils like humidity. It held a hint of something akin to cedar. My lungs felt heavier.

We were still flying, but the bird's wings made no sound. *Did I go deaf?*

I looked above and saw only a shroud of black. It had the texture of water, but it didn't ripple. I could not find a sun, moon, or even a single star in that watery ink, but somehow, I could still see my surroundings. A faint amber glow filled the air, staving off the pitch blackness. Below, I took in an endless stretch of mountains. Their distant peaks looked as if they'd been carved from charcoal. Ribbons of gray mist drifted around their bases.

A gust of wind flowed over us, and my eye caught something gliding through the air. It was a wave of glinting golden lights, drifting across the sky like twinkling pollen. They ebbed and flowed with the shifting breeze, growing bright and then softening. The wave washed over us, and suddenly thousands of them surrounded us. The lights darted, caught in whorls and eddies of the air under the redbill's wings.

Something moved in the gray below us—a flock of redbills circling over a misted peak. One of them screeched, and the sound drifted through the heavy air up to us.

Our bird drifted lower, and more redbills came into view below us. As we neared the ground, other specks of light shone on the rocks. These were duller, darker than the ones flowing through the sky. They reminded me of dwindling campfire embers.

"What are those lights?" I breathed into Dorian's ear.

He didn't respond, instead leaning over to pat the redbill's neck, and we dipped lower to catch another breeze, soaring downward toward the mountains.

The peaks and valleys came into focus, and some of the mist moved off with the wind. I thought I saw an expanse of gray water, but once the clouds cleared, I knew I was mistaken.

Miles and miles of rubble stretched over the mountainsides. Hollowed-out stone buildings jutted from the scorched ground. A fallen bridge lay crumbled in the basin of a dried-up riverbed. The broken skeleton of a massive open-air colosseum protruded from the black dirt. Little square rock foundations clustered together. None had a roof. Shattered stone walls trailed through countless burnt-out homes.

The air soured in my nose. My eyes burned more the lower we soared.

I scanned the horizon but saw no end to the dilapidated city. It reminded me of photos of atomic bombings. I tried to swallow, but my throat felt closed shut.

We flew over a valley with a massive hole carved into the ground, like a manmade lake. There were piles of… were those bones? This time I clenched my eyes shut of my own volition.

Were we really responsible for this?

I opened my eyes again, and in front of me, Dorian's shoulders sank. He looked out to the side instead of down. In profile I could just about make out his eyes, darkened and rimmed red. "I think you've seen all you need to."

I nodded, speechless.

He exhaled and placed his hand on the redbill's neck. The bird ascended, turning back the way we came. I set my forehead on the back of Dorian's shoulder for a moment, too dizzy to keep my eyes open. Thankfully, the bird increased its speed, and the putrid air drifted away behind us.

As we flew away from the city, a sound cut through the breeze from somewhere in the very far distance—it was like a lilting, wavering trumpet call. It echoed away but then grew louder, like an approaching train's horn. My muscles went rigid as the call filled my head and reverberated inside my chest. It enveloped us, sharpening every second. The air vibrated around us.

"It sounds closer than it is," Dorian said. "They must have found someone. We should go. I don't want to draw them here."

He clicked to the redbill, and our speed suddenly increased. Barely five seconds later, the white light exploded over us again, replacing the sound with zaps of electricity. The buzzing wrapped around me, jolting through my head. Sweat instantaneously covered my entire body. The last crack dissipated.

The familiar heat of the desert sun on the back of my neck returned. The redbill cut through the clouds. We soared over the red stone and sand again, the rock formations blurred into a pale red finger painting.

"What was that noise?" I gasped in Dorian's ear, between the beating of the bird's wings.

He turned his head, one of his glacial eyes meeting mine. "There are a lot of strange noises in the Immortal Plane, and you don't want to know what any of them are. Forget it. It was never meant for human ears."

The redbill circled lower. I loosened my cramping grip on Dorian's waist. The shrubs and rocks drew closer, and we landed on the sand.

Dorian dismounted, and I slid off behind him. He walked a few paces away before turning back to me.

I felt his question in his eyes before he said a word.

The crumbled houses and burnt soil flashed in front of my eyes. The broken fences. The heaps of crisscrossed bones.

I exhaled. I couldn't confirm exactly what I'd seen, but if it were what Dorian had described, his plea for help was understandable. I knew this could still be some elaborate ploy, but I couldn't dismiss the possibility that it was true. I needed to present this to the board, either way.

"Yes." My voice rang the clearest it had all day. "I'll help you."

CHAPTER TEN

As our redbill thundered through the sky, my thoughts roared louder than the bird's wings.

They're going to think I've gone insane. An Occult Bureau lieutenant trying to convince the board to help vampires. Can they commit me for that?

The redbill descended through a wet patch of clouds. I recognized D.C. once we cleared the vapor; the bird pointed toward a forested stretch northwest of the city.

The air blasted over its wings, pushing Dorian's back into my chest. I braced my face against him, waiting for my intestines to return to their proper place.

Our downdraft waved through the long grass as we landed on the edge of a field, flanked closely by trees. The sun hadn't reached its peak. Birds called from the forest. The calm was unsettling and foreign after the morning I'd had.

Dorian dismounted and turned to offer me a hand, but my boots had already hit the ground beside him. I was so done with flying. I saw him smirk slightly out of the corner of my eye.

I scanned the edge of the field for signs of civilization and spotted a hiking trail marker through the trees. *There's my way home.*

I turned back around, and we held a stare. The bird grumbled.

I sighed, then scrunched my nose, gathering my thoughts. "I'm going to talk to my uncle first," I began. "Today. I'll see what his response is. This won't be easy."

Dorian nodded slightly.

"I don't know whether I can convince him that I'm telling the truth, or if he'll believe you brainwashed me." I set a hand on my hip. "I'm going to sound like a lunatic. And a traitor, too."

Gina saw Dorian, so at least I had a witness to prove his existence. *But how can I prove he's not a threat?* I stared at the grass, searching my mind for a strategy.

"I need proof," I told him, testing my thoughts aloud. "But I can't just waltz home with a vampire in tow."

Dorian reached inside his cloak and thrust a closed fist toward me. His fingers opened, revealing my ear comm and cell phone, which I'd switched off before the mission that morning.

You're freaking kidding me. This whole time?

I shook my head. Relief and a grin replaced any sense of anger. "Are vampires also expert pickpockets?"

He suppressed a smile. I snatched them from his hand, immediately checking to see if the phone responded, noting the lukewarmth of his skin as my fingers brushed it. The phone turned on. As I stared at the device, an idea occurred to me. A kind of ridiculous idea, but...

"I have to take a picture of you. No, both of us. To show them you're not a threat, that you let me go," I said matter-of-factly.

"Seriously?" He shied away.

"Got any other ideas?" I gazed up at him over the phone screen, the camera app already open. "What, you've never had your picture taken before? Vampires don't have family photo albums?"

He frowned at me and rolled his shoulders. "If it'll help."

"It will." I held the phone up.

I could see him frowning through the phone's screen. I snapped a photo, then looked at it, shaking my head. "You just look like a pale guy in a field. A bad senior photo. I need some teeth."

He squinted at me, then pulled his lip open with his finger, exposing one of his unnaturally elongated canines.

"Got it," I said. "Okay, now one of us."

I stepped toward him, realizing as I did that I wasn't afraid. It felt strange. Given the crazy things I planned to go do right after this, I probably wouldn't know what "normal" felt like ever again.

I positioned myself at his elbow and leaned toward him, leaving plenty of space between us, then held my arm out in front of us to take the picture. Neither of us breathed until I stepped away.

"Well, that'll work," I said. In this photo Dorian's eyes were a brighter blue. I angled the screen toward him. "We caught the redbill's head, too. Talk about proof."

Yeah, this is still going to be an impossible conversation.

I put my phone in my vest and tucked my comm into my pants pocket. A wave of exhaustion flooded my body. My head buzzed. "I'm gonna go, then." It felt surreal, being released by a vampire. This wasn't supposed to happen.

But if even part of what Dorian said was true, then I hadn't been told the whole truth, had I?

"Wait," Dorian said, just as I turned to leave. He reached inside his cloak again, then offered me an onyx-colored stone wrapped in a piece of cloth. The edges of the stone were tinged with gray, making it look a bit like a carved piece of charcoal, but not enough that it looked like any stone I'd ever seen.

"This should help you convince them that there's a world they don't know about," Dorian said. "This doesn't exist on Earth. It's from my old home. The mountains you saw." His voice softened and trailed off on the breeze.

I cautiously took the stone from him, making sure to touch only the fabric wrapped around it, then searched his face. "Why do you carry this with you?"

He contemplated the stone in my hand but didn't respond, his eyes faraway. In that moment, he didn't look like an otherworldly creature who'd kidnapped me with unnerving speed and rode about on bloodthirsty beasts. He looked like he was reliving something that I could only imagine.

I looked away as if the sight burned, focused on carefully tightening the cloth around the stone and slipping it into my pocket.

I cleared my throat. "Thank you." It seemed a bit of an underwhelming response, but what else could I say?

Dorian nodded. "Please don't lose it. I'd like it back."

"I understand."

A silence fell between us.

I cleared my throat. "How will I contact you? After I've spoken to my uncle and the Bureau?"

Dorian mounted the redbill in one fluid, sweeping motion. He held my eyes for a moment, his blue gaze sharp.

"I'll find you in a few weeks," he said, and the bird leapt into the air, hammering its wings. The resulting gust of wind pushed me back, and the animal hurtled away into the sky.

I stared until they disappeared into the clouds hanging over the horizon.

Show-off.

CHAPTER ELEVEN

I made my way down the hiking trail, following signs leading to a ranger's station. I needed to call my family—they would be scared to death—but I had to collect my thoughts first. I'd never been so grateful to have my feet on the ground.

After only a couple miles, the ranger's station appeared through the trees, and I broke into a sprint for the water fountain on the side of the building. I shoved my face into the water stream, the coolness welcome on my skin. Then I pulled back, took a breath, and sucked down water until my sides ached.

The station was empty, so I sat beside the closed building and pulled out my phone.

"*Lyra?*" my mother gasped on the other end after only half a ring.

"Mom, it's me. I'm okay."

"My God, Lyra, where are you?"

"I'm in a national park. Near D.C., I think." I looked at the sign in front of the station. "Rock Creek Park. Station D3."

My mother repeated my location to someone who was with her. I heard my father's and brother's voices, fuzzy yet distinct, in the background.

"She's okay?" Zach hollered.

"Lyra, we're in D.C. We have a helicopter. We're coming," Mom said, struggling to keep her voice even.

"Okay." I breathed out.

"You're all right? You mean it?" Her voice lowered, becoming wavery.

"I'm fine. I really am." *I think.*

"We're coming."

I scooted against the wooden building, leaned all my weight onto the wood, and closed my eyes. Images flashed across the back of my eyelids like lightning strikes. The man's throat spurting blood. The way Kane's eyes cut me. The countless bones. I shuddered. My mind shifted to Dorian—the storm clouds swirling under his skin.

I'd drifted off slightly when the beating of the chopper's blades snapped me back. The scouting helicopter lowered to the pavement in front of the station. My parents waved frantically. I bolted.

I hurled myself into the chopper, the closest to safety I'd been since sunrise. My family's voices blended together in a warm thrumming alongside the chopper's vibrations. There were so many arms around me, familiar smells, relieved tears. My mother held my face like she'd thought she would never see it again. My father kissed my forehead, his beard tickling my skin. He hadn't done that since I was eight. Zach hugged me so tightly I choked. Uncle Alan clutched my hand in his shaking ones, tears welling in his eyes. Seeing him like that shook me.

My brother pulled me into the seat next to him, wrapping an arm snugly around my shoulder. Gina gripped my hand, her face furrowed with guilt. I smiled at her. *It's not your fault.*

The chopper rose, and I leaned my head against Zach's shoulder. Muscles I didn't even know I had ached. *Turns out there is something that daily training exercises don't stretch. Who'd have thought.*

I glanced around the circle again, savoring the sight of every face. It made it even more surreal to remember the circle of vampires around me, their eyes mistrustful and predatory, trying coldly to decide whether they should let me go, keep me hostage, or worse. It was hard to imagine those otherworldly creatures showing this kind of warmth, having this kind of family bond.

"I don't know where to start," I said, squeezing Gina's hand.

"You don't need to yet," Uncle Alan interjected. "They've called an emergency national board meeting at the D.C. headquarters due to Gina's vampire sighting. We need you to recount what you've seen today."

My father pulled a few bottles of water and granola bars from a bag of supplies beside him, and only once the bars rested in my hands did I realize how hungry I was. They vanished in moments, and the water shortly after.

I set my head on Zach's shoulder and closed my eyes.

The D.C. headquarters' meeting chamber had a long mahogany table and matching chairs. An entire wall of windows overlooked the city. Twenty board members gathered around the table when we walked in. My nerves were so shot that the presence of this many higher-ups didn't even phase me. What strained my mind was the inconceivable task at hand.

Uncle Alan had entered the chamber before me and Gina. He sat at one head of the table, and he smiled and gestured for me to sit next to him. Another four seats remained empty, intended for my family and Gina. It was unheard of for this many family members to be at a debriefing, but Uncle Alan had clearly pulled some strings for me.

I lowered myself to the smooth, polished mahogany and looked around. Crisp suits and golden name plaques stared back at me. My mother sat to my right and Zach sat on her other side. Mom patted my leg under the table.

"Thank you all for coming so quickly." Uncle Alan addressed the room. "Board, we call this meeting to order to hear testimony regarding a vampire sighting by Lyra Sloane, Occult Bureau First Lieutenant under Head of Command, Captain Bryce. Event occurred today at approximately 06:20 during the operation you were all briefed on immediately after it occurred." My uncle's professionalism never failed, regardless of the circumstances, or the fact that half the people sitting around him happened to be immediate family.

Several members shuffled papers and clicked their pens.

"A second witness is present. Gina Blackwell, also First Lieutenant under Bryce's command." My uncle gestured toward Gina, and she nodded in affirmation.

"Lieutenant Sloane," Uncle Alan continued. "Start your testimony from five minutes before the sighting and describe in detail everything that followed until your rescue."

I inhaled and cleared my throat, unnerved by hearing my uncle call me "Lieutenant Sloane." *Tell them the facts. Deciding what to do about them isn't my job.* Relief flickered through me at the thought—until I remembered Dorian's haunted eyes. I leaned forward, determined to do this to the best of my ability.

"Lieutenant Blackwell and I were scouting an abandoned church for threats registered by Bureau surveillance," I began. "We believed we were alone on that floor. We surveyed the perimeter and returned to the staircase."

"Had any threats been visually confirmed at the site?" Uncle Alan asked.

"No," I breathed. "Nothing had been spotted yet. When we neared the staircase, we saw a figure. I called out to him, with no response. He rushed me, removed my weapon, comm, and phone, and carried me out the church window."

"He?" a female member asked over her glasses.

"Yes, the vampire was male. He called himself Dorian."

I grew more confident as I continued speaking. Pens scratched rapidly. I explained how we flew on a redbill's back to reach the cliff.

"I have no idea where the cliff was located," I said. "That's where we spoke for the first time." I paused.

"What did the vampire say?" Uncle Alan asked.

"He asked my name, age, and rank. He didn't seem overtly threatening," I replied.

Several eyebrows rose. My mother wrung her fingers in her lap. I summarized our conversation. I saw more eyebrows rise and subtle sideways glances when I pointed out that Dorian had known some of the Bureau's inner workings—including my uncle's name.

"We rode the redbill to a motel in a heavily forested area. It was called the Woodland Lodge. I heard a highway somewhere nearby." I inhaled. "The vampire and the redbill fed on a human man."

Zach rubbed his temple.

"Do you know who the man was?" a member questioned.

"I had no way to identify him, sir." I shook my head. "He's dead. The vampire said that he had committed multiple rapes and planned to kill, soon."

The room stood still.

"How did the vampire know that?" Uncle Alan inquired, setting his hands on the table.

All eyes fixed on me.

"I... I'm not certain." I furrowed my brow, forcing my mind back to the surreal moment. "He... appeared to have a negative physical reaction to the feeding. It looked painful. Almost like he was experiencing the bad things the man had done, from... drinking his blood." *If that makes sense.* It hadn't fully occurred to me until now. If vampires literally consumed darkness, I supposed it did make sense.

Uncle Alan wrote on his pad of paper.

"We flew again," I continued—but then swallowed, unsure of how to follow up. I saw Carwin in my head, his tiny broken arm. Rhome and Kreya. Kane's face twisted with resentment. A stab of guilt slid between my ribs. What if the board decided, despite my plea, to exterminate all the vampires I'd seen? If I'd heard of a hidden vampire enclave even twenty-four hours ago, that would have been my first reaction, too.

Withholding information from the board was treason. But what if the board had lied? Indecision twisted my insides. I felt like I was freefalling—but not on a redbill this time. The room's silence rang in my ears.

If there's even a chance that Dorian is telling the truth... if there's even a chance that those vampire children are innocent... Besides, if Dorian's plan went through and he got a meeting with the board, they would have plenty of time to find out about the other vampires from him. I closed my eyes briefly, ignoring my knotted stomach.

I looked around the circle again. "We went to another world. Another realm. It may be the source of the occult occurrences in our world. I know it sounds completely unbelievable, but it's what I saw."

Every face was stone.

"The vampire called it the 'Immortal Plane.' We flew through a blinding white light to reach it." I continued describing what I saw, including the mountains and the redbills.

I studied the members' faces. Nothing.

"We flew over a huge city that had been completely destroyed," I said. I steadied my voice, remembering. "I saw rubble, burnt buildings. And a grave—a mass grave filled with hundreds of bones. They may have been deceased vampires," I stated. Describing it made it feel more real to me.

Papers rustled. Still no visible reactions.

"The vampire told me that only his kind are meant to cross between Earth—he called it the Mortal Plane—and the Immortal. But the barrier tore, and that was devastating to his species. He said that humans caused the tear by trying to reach the Immortal Plane. And the tear is still there, making his species vulnerable."

Uncle Alan tapped his pen on his chin. Some members shifted in their seats or exchanged glances.

I took a deep breath. "He told me that he needed our help. He said that this tear is dangerous for both humans and vampires, because if vampires are entirely wiped out, the imbalance in the universe will harm humans. After the tear weakened the vampires, immortal beings in the other plane tried to wipe them out. Now, he and other vampires seek asylum on Earth, and they want to cooperate with us. They want peaceful relations. In return, he said that they would help us with the redbill problem. He will contact me for your answer in a few weeks."

No one was writing anymore. The female member had taken off her glasses. Their stares bore into me.

"The vampire brought me back to D.C. You can see he did not harm me; he let me go. I have proof."

I pulled my cell from my pocket and opened the photos of Dorian, feeling only a little silly about showing off my vampire selfies. I handed my phone to Uncle Alan, keeping a perfectly straight face.

He studied the photos for a long time. "Did the vampire force you to take these pictures?" he asked, after giving my phone to the next board member. It passed slowly around the circle, each member swiping back and forth between the two images.

"It was my idea to take the pictures," I replied.

Uncle Alan raised his eyebrows and nodded.

The phone returned to me, and I put it in my pocket. I felt Dorian's stone in my pocket when I slid my phone in. Dorian's face flashed through my mind, the sound of longing in his voice when he'd said the stone was from his home. My gut told me to hold steady—maybe the pictures were enough proof. It felt likely that if the Bureau took the stone, it would never be returned. I didn't pull it out.

No one spoke for a few moments.

"Thank you, Lieutenant Sloane. You've given us all a lot to think about and discuss. You've had a very tiring day, so let's get you home to rest." Uncle Alan placed his palms on his papers and smiled at me. "And in the meantime, do not discuss what you've shared with people outside this room." He nodded at Zach and Gina to follow the same orders.

And… that was it. I had no idea what the board would decide to do. I wasn't sure whether I was disappointed I hadn't seen more reactions, or glad. My mother stood and placed a hand on my shoulder. We left the chamber. I felt eyes on my back until the door shut behind us.

As we made our way to the building's exit, Uncle Alan's voice from the other night looped through my head. *Letting this information reach anyone else's ears is out of the question... Stability and calm are the most important things for the Bureau, this country.*

I turned to my parents. "Did you two know about the Immortal Plane? About the breach?"

My father sighed and stared at his shoes. My mother pressed her lips together and looked at me, her eyes troubled. I took that to mean they weren't allowed to answer the question—which sometimes happened in our working relationship—so I didn't ask again.

My feet dragged over the marble floor. Exhaustion squeezed every muscle, but my brain still ran at full speed. Some of the guilt had dissipated after I spoke Dorian's request aloud. I'd done my best to help him without endangering my own species. The board would handle this. It was out of my hands now.

Guards escorted us to the tarmac of the D.C. headquarters airstrip, where a small Bureau charter plane waited to take us to Chicago. My mother ushered me onboard first, and I plopped into a seat beside a window. Zach sat beside me and ruffled my hair.

The sun was finally setting. We took off, and I watched the city disappear below us. With my forehead pressed against the window, I drifted from consciousness.

This is a lot slower than a redbill.

CHAPTER TWELVE

"Lyra, you awake?"

I cracked an eye. I had no idea how long I'd been out. Zach came to my bedside with a tray and a glass. Oatmeal, toast, and orange juice.

"Thanks," I mumbled, angling myself up on an elbow. "What time is it?"

He set everything down on my nightstand. "It's evening."

I pulled my phone out from under my pillow. Five o'clock. *Yikes. And I'm still tired.*

I accepted a spoon from him and sat up to shovel oatmeal into my mouth. "Is Uncle Alan here?" I asked after swallowing.

"Not yet. He called and said they're still finishing up meetings in D.C. They had a lot to sort out."

I nodded, chewing on my toast.

"Are you feeling all right?" Zach asked, his face lined with concern. He sat on the bed beside me.

"Pretty beat. But I'm okay."

Zach nodded and paused for a moment. He was fidgeting and picking at his thumbnails like he always did right before expressing something he'd been thinking about for a long while. I swallowed another spoonful of oatmeal.

"Do you remember that time when you were about six, and I was nine—we walked off Bureau property to that corner market to get candy? You said you wanted gum." Zach rested his chin on his hands, his eyes intent on me.

I thought for a moment, but nothing rang a bell. By the time Zach was that age, our parents let him take me for walks regularly. It was usually his idea. That was Zach—man about town.

"And I ran into my friends and left without you?" he added, a small, guilty smile pulling at his lips. Zach had always been the more outgoing, charismatic one. He saw friends every time we were out in public. It wasn't that I was unpopular—just kept to myself a bit more, especially when I was younger. My training with the Bureau had cracked a lot of my shell, and I'd found that I was a natural leader, too.

"Oh, yeah," I said, after swallowing some more toast. "I got lost on the way home even though it was only seven blocks." I closed my eyes, shook my head, and laughed at myself. I'd gotten distracted by a dog walking by, and once I'd stopped petting it, I'd accidentally started walking again in the wrong direction. I mean, I was six years old, after all. My sense of direction had definitely improved with age and Bureau training, too.

"It was my fault. I left you there. I was supposed to take care of you and watch you." Zach's eyes trailed over the carpet and fixed on a random sock I'd tossed and forgotten about. I watched the side of his face; the rims of his eyes were reddening, and he was chewing on the inside of his mouth. On the rare occasion that my brother got emotional, there was always a trigger reaction for me, like we were internally synced to feel what the other did. My lip quivered.

"Please don't cry. You know that always makes me cry," I said softly. I set my plate down on the nightstand beside my bed and reached over to squeeze his arm.

"I abandoned you that day. And when I heard Gina over the comm, saying you'd been taken, that a vampire had attacked you, that same exact feeling punched me right in the gut," Zach whispered. He used the butts of his palms to rub hastily at his eyes. "I just thought, *Damn, Zach, you lost her again. You're a terrible brother.*"

My lip kept quivering no matter how hard I pursed or rubbed my lips with my fingers. It wasn't that I didn't like emotions or people showing them. I just hated that rising discomfort in my chest immediately before my eyes welled with tears, that pressure that pushed the air out of my lungs. I hated seeing my brother experience it, too. For me, sometimes watching someone I loved feel emotional pain hurt more than experiencing it myself.

"Well, you didn't lose me. And you didn't do anything wrong. You were a kid and you got excited to see your friends. You are not a terrible brother. I couldn't ask for a better brother," I assured him. I squeezed his arm again, sniffed, and wiped at the corners of my eyes. "I'm right here. I'm okay. I promise."

"My friends, job, possessions, whatever—they'll never be more important than you." Zach turned, and his bloodshot eyes stared directly into mine. "Ever. I just wanted you to know that. To hear that." He cleared his throat of phlegm and emotion. He pushed some wavy hair out of his face.

"I hear you. And same. Ditto. You're my number one." I rested my head on his shoulder, and he put his arm around me after rubbing at his eyes one more time.

I was an incredibly lucky woman.

"Here comes hell, it's Z and L," Zach said quietly through a faint smile. That was the catchphrase our father said regularly when my brother and I entered a room together.

We sat in silence for several long heartbeats, until he finally exhaled and extended a hand to take my plate. "Gotta head down for work," he murmured. "I'll catch you later. Enjoy your free days off. Don't do anything I wouldn't in the meantime." He cast me one last grin before padding out the door.

I leaned back in bed and let a slow sigh roll out of my chest, then downed the glass of juice and stood on aching legs. Due to the kidnapping, I had at least a week off for "physical and mental recovery." Bryce had informed me via text the night before. I was worried about how bored I was going to get, waiting for an answer from the Bureau and wondering if or when the vampire would randomly show up again.

My uniform pants caught my eye, lying folded at the end of my mattress. I reached out to squeeze the pocket and felt the stone, still inside. I was grateful the board hadn't argued for more proof or outright denied my claim about the existence of the Immortal Plane, as my gut still told me that I definitely needed to give it back to Dorian. He'd handed it to me to be used as proof—but I was sure his eyes had said differently.

I made my way to the bathroom and turned on the shower, then stared at my swollen eyes in the mirror until it fogged over. The running water sounded like heaven. And it felt even better.

Steam filled my lungs, thick and warm, like the air of the Immortal Plane. Those dancing golden orbs passed through my mind. There had been something so soothing and beautiful about them. *Dorian never told me what those were.* He also hadn't explained the specks burning out on the mountainsides.

Shampoo dripped down the side of my face. Given how easily Dorian had swayed me to consider his cause, I understood why he'd chosen me. *Opportunist.* He had been convincing at the time, but time would tell regarding his honesty. I still wasn't sold. Parts of the whole situation seemed too convenient.

I sat on a low stool and scrubbed my feet with a loofa. The whole "I'll find you" thing worried me a little bit. Even if he had told me the truth about his species' devastation, that didn't mean he wouldn't stick his teeth in me given the chance. I didn't like the idea of Dorian thinking he could find me wherever and whenever he pleased.

I examined the redbill bruise on my thigh, which slowly but surely was going down, then massaged a twinging muscle in my foot. I needed to get with Bryce and tighten up on my hand-to-hand combat. Or would that be hand-to-fang combat?

I turned off the water and dried myself. Sweatpants and a T-shirt were my plan for the evening. I dressed and wrapped my damp hair into a bun, then grabbed my phone and sat on the edge of my bed. I started scanning back and forth through the pictures of Dorian, looking for clues to weaknesses I could exploit. His face on the screen looked so different—lighter—than it had on the cliff. Or when he'd had blood on his face. *He looks about mid-twenties; how many people has he killed?*

If I feigned compliance with Dorian, I could probably get him to drop his guard a bit more, just in case I needed to use that to my advantage. I reminded myself that his earnestness served as a great disguise. The opportunity he'd nabbed by persuading the family of a Bureau board member to listen to his proposal proved that.

I closed my eyes and imagined what Dorian had seen when he drank that man's blood. *Rapist. His own sister. Planning murder.* My muscles shuddered, and I rolled my shoulders, trying to shake it off. If Dorian only killed evil people, what else had he seen? That was one hell of a burden to carry for sustenance.

If Dorian had been honest about the duty of his kind, then I had to admit that they'd gotten a tough deal. To be naturally driven to cleanse the world's evil by poisoning yourself with it? How strange, to consider the words "vampire" and "martyr" in the same sentence.

It also created an excellent excuse for their behavior, making vampires look like saviors, when historically they were known as the exact opposite.

I sighed. Just two days prior, I'd hated vampires and was grateful I'd never run into one. I found it hard to swallow that everyone I'd ever known, everything I'd ever been told, could be entirely wrong.

Is Dorian's brother somewhere in that mass grave?

I shook my head and glanced again at the lump in the pocket of my uniform pants.

CHAPTER THIRTEEN

I went stir-crazy waiting for word from Uncle Alan after just two days, which was longer than I thought I'd make it. I spent more time at the gym than my apartment. Sure, I loved to work out. It helped my nerves and kept me in shape while I was on a short break from missions. But I was also paranoid about being alone. I had no idea when Dorian planned to show up. He could decide to come early, for all I knew.

I called Alan every day for updates. His voice was always heavy, exhausted. He rarely had uplifting or exciting feedback. Through his drowsy words, he described the board's constant bickering, endless debates, and emotional arguments. He wasn't the only one on the board who'd been personally affected by vampire violence. Many of them were ex-ground soldiers, or had friends and family who were. This was a big deal for all of them. It was a big deal, period.

My uncle promised he'd visit me in person as soon as the board came to some kind of agreement. I wasn't going to hold my breath, but the uncertainty was burning a hole in my stomach.

Gina made a point to take me out for breakfast a few times over the following days to take my mind off things. We never talked about my kidnapping. Any time I mentioned the word "vampire," her eyes glazed over, like she couldn't connect the word to the object. That girl was tough as nails, but her inability to save me back at the church visibly weighed on her. So, we'd eat croissants, drink coffee, and I'd retell jokes from when we lived together during training. Zach kept an eye on her —I made sure of it.

It was so hard to sleep. Most nights, I'd jolt from a dead, dreamless sleep, terrified. Like I was falling, being watched, and soaring through the air at insane speeds, all at the same time. Naps between workouts filled in for the sleeplessness, but not knowing when the vampire was going to show up again haunted me.

My mom was filling a flask of water in the kitchen when I walked in to make another piece of toast one morning, nine days after my testimony. She told me that Dad had gone downstairs to the headquarters meeting rooms. She would join him shortly. Zach and Gina had just left.

I seized the chance to ask a question. "Do you know of any civilian weapons that have an effect on vampires?"

She eyed me, and her perfectly arched, dark eyebrows rose slightly over her eyes, as they did when she was fighting off concern. My mother had a beautifully intense, angular face and striking elflike features. I'd gotten more of my dad's babyface. "From what I've seen, mace momentarily disoriented them," she replied. "But that's about it."

"Hmm." I recalled a conversation I'd had with Zach a while back. He'd stashed an extra can in his room a year or so ago. It probably hadn't expired yet.

My mother didn't ask any questions immediately. But I could see the worry pulling down the corners of her lips, the strongest wrinkle in her forehead creasing. My mother had always been the worrier of the family, a trait I had inherited a bit of, too. In this case, though, she defi-

CHAPTER 13 | 95

nitely had a valid reason to be concerned. The day Dorian kidnapped me had probably given her an ulcer.

"You're going to look out for yourself, right?" she finally asked, her anxiety pushing words from her throat.

"Absolutely," I replied, giving her an assuring smile and a shake of my head.

A knock sounded from the door. I rushed to swing it open.

Uncle Alan greeted me, leaning a little heavier on his cane than usual. Lack of sleep hung below his hazel eyes. Anticipation coursed through me.

"Alan! You've finally made it." My mother hurried up behind me to greet him. "Oh, I wish I could stay. Lyra will have to fill me in when I get back, unless you stay late. I have to rush down for my meeting now. Things have been picking up—as you know."

"No problem, Miriam." He sighed. "She or I will fill you in."

As my mother headed out, I offered him a drink, and after I poured him a glass of water, we made our way to the living room. He leaned his cane and briefcase against an armchair and sank into it.

"How are you feeling?" he asked, clearly fatigued.

"I'm fine. Been exercising a lot these past days," I said, and offered a smile from the couch. He returned it.

He took a sip of water and leaned back. "Where do you want to start?"

I paused to prioritize my questions. "Did the Bureau actually breach the Immortal Plane?" I asked. That one had been bugging me for too long.

"Yes."

My stomach twisted. That explained the lack of surprise I'd seen in the room, when I had described a whole different world.

"We attempted to, at least. Five years ago. Unfortunately, none of the soldiers survived. This was at the peak of vampire attacks, and we hoped to learn everything we could about them to stop the murders.

We wanted to get to the source and stop them there to protect our people."

I leaned forward slightly in my chair. "How did they do it?"

"The Bureau's director of strategy at the time put a captured vampire through interrogation for many, many years. That's when we learned about a gateway to another realm, where the vampires originated."

My voice flattened. "They tortured the vampire?" *I doubt he started chatting about the Immortal Plane over brunch.* It confirmed what Dorian had told me.

"Yes," my uncle replied. "In fact, most vampires caught by the Bureau over the years were interrogated—but unsuccessfully. Vampires are remarkably stubborn. All refused to say a word about their origin, even after torture, so they were killed soon after their capture. But the director kept one vampire alive, for an experiment of prolonged inter-rogation, to see if that would finally crack him. It culminated in the director making an executive decision to authorize a mission, in which soldiers forced the vampire to 'straddle realms' while in an aircraft. The vampire opposed the idea; he went on about the damage it could cause, but the soldiers assumed he was bluffing. They had to be very persuasive."

I swallowed.

"There were soldiers on the ground at the time of the event. They said that the aircraft disappeared in a huge burst of light, and then the sky spit them out. Pieces of aircraft and bodies falling everywhere. Terrible scene. They reported a sound like thunder, and apparently the sky seemed to wave, then went still. The team on the ground was incredibly shaken. Several left the service." My uncle bent forward and took two gulps of water.

Thunder—cracking. That's exactly what it sounded like when we went through the tear.

"We never got proof of the other realm. It was as if the craft got struck by lightning and shattered. The vampire could very well have lied to lure them into a murder-suicide trap. Soon after that, massive amounts of supernatural energy and redbills began to swarm the area, but that didn't explicitly prove the existence of the 'other side.'"

"What did the Bureau do with the director who authorized that? He acted above his command." If I knew anything about the Bureau, an action like that would be harshly punished. I bit my lip. *They aren't exactly forgiving of liars, either.*

"Obviously, he was fired. The loss of human life alone was beyond reconcilable, setting aside his arrogant disregard for protocol and equipment. The Bureau barred any members from going near the area again." Uncle Alan eased deeper into the chair and exhaled heavily, his voice sorrowful. "But the loss of life didn't end there. A group of young rogue soldiers attempted to reach the other realm shortly afterward. They were never seen or heard from again."

I took this in, turning the facts over in my head. "What did the Bureau do after losing so many soldiers?"

"After that the existence of the breach, or whatever it was, became a larger issue, one of public health and safety. If civilians found out about it, the repercussions could've been catastrophic. People can be very stupid when curious. You know that—and those rogue soldiers further proved it to us. I suppose that the vampire wasn't wrong in claiming that damage had been incurred. But the Bureau had no way to re-approach or even understand the situation, so it sealed the area, and personnel who knew about the tear were forbidden to speak of it."

Uncle Alan looked me in the eyes, his own warm, sorrowful, and firm all at once.

"Lyra, you must realize that the Bureau isn't deliberately keeping secrets. We understood nothing about what this event meant, or if the other plane was even real. We only knew that it was dangerous. It didn't prove anything regarding the origin of vampires, in the end, and we didn't want to waste more lives in the search."

I sank between two couch cushions and gazed at my uncle for a moment, relieved. Considering the circumstances, it was what I would expect the Bureau to do. Civilian protection was the most important thing—that was the whole purpose of the Bureau to begin with. It would've been irresponsible to take further action without understanding the nature of the situation.

Maybe Dorian had been right about this all being a huge misunderstanding.

Uncle Alan sighed heavily and rested his intertwined fingers on his abdomen. "Forgive me, it's been a very long nine days."

"Were any decisions made?" I asked carefully, tempering the eagerness in my voice.

"Yes. We did come to a consensus. Finally," he replied. "And, Lyra, this is not to discredit anything you experienced or said. This is simply the Bureau acting in the best interest of our people."

I nodded as I would to Captain Bryce, settling my demeanor into its most professional stance.

"We can't trust the vampire. Yes, you had pictures proving that he and the redbill didn't hurt you. But that doesn't eliminate the possibility that he was manipulating you and plotting to use you to infiltrate the Bureau."

My thoughts exactly.

"One verbal account of this other plane isn't enough evidence. We can't agree to help a species that has historically hunted and murdered us based on this. I know you understand that we can't risk something like that."

I kept my face steady, trying to will away a kind of tightness in my chest.

My uncle narrowed his eyes on me, as though gauging my reaction before continuing.

"This was the first vampire you've ever encountered. I know that you remember the stories your parents and I have told you, but engaging with one in person is very different from hearing tales or visualizing one in training. Now you know how overwhelming and terrifying they are. You were kidnapped, taken hostage. To survive, you obviously had to do whatever he said. I'm asking you to consider that he lied, using you due to your rank and family placement in the Bureau, because he probably knew it. He did ask about your surname."

"That occurred to me," I agreed, ignoring another twist in my stomach.

I considered showing him Dorian's stone. Would that make any difference? I mean, Dorian could've given me a rock he found anywhere.

If I did, I would probably never see it again.

Dorian had wanted me to use it as proof—but he hadn't known that would risk not getting it back. The Bureau wouldn't want to give up an artifact that was literally from another plane of existence, and I'd look kooky trying to argue for it.

"They are the most calculating creatures on the planet," my uncle went on. "Wicked smart, predatory senses. There's no way for us to know whether this was an elaborate act. I don't doubt that you saw a ruined city, a mass grave, but we have no way of knowing whether those bones were even vampires or another species they've preyed on more successfully than humans. I'm sure it was all very convincing, even his request for asylum. I would want to help if I saw something like that, too. But we can't just believe, after everything we've seen vampires do, that they're actually victims."

I nodded, even though I wasn't entirely pleased. Something itched in the back of my mind.

"The vampire said something else. Remember when I mentioned he had a negative physical reaction to feeding on the man at the motel?"

"Yes," Uncle Alan said.

"The vampire stated that his kind only hunt people that are evil. He said he could feel their darkness, sense it."

Uncle Alan set his chin in his hand and thought for a moment. "Interesting. The captive vampire said something like that. Again, it can't be trusted. How can we be sure? Without being able to prove that every vampire victim in history had committed acts against other humans—in a court of law, mind you—there's no way we can believe that. And it's a very convenient justification for his kind's past behavior. It only seems natural that they'd have to fabricate something like that in order to gain our assistance."

Every gnawing doubt I'd had since meeting Dorian grew stronger. I rubbed the back of my neck.

"Beyond that, Lyra, it's not justifiable to *kill* a rapist without a trial. Isn't murder evil, as well? There is a good reason our justice system does not work that way. If we sanctioned the murder of a 'bad' person, based on a vampire's 'feeling' alone, that would be chaos."

I sighed. "I understand." I couldn't prove anything I'd been told.

And then he continued. "But don't be discouraged quite yet."

My back straightened.

"We will not discount your testimony. There could be some truth to this situation that we must accurately uncover, as we are dealing with something potentially outside our realm of understanding. The Bureau wouldn't be doing its job if it labeled this as lies without proof. It's our duty to learn about the unexplainable." He paused and sipped more water. "As we do have some reasonable grounds to think that a breach happened that incurred damage, some of what this vampire said could be true. What the board proposes is that the vampires prove their good-will before we offer them asylum."

I leaned forward, intent on his words.

"This will involve a trial period. There are three requirements that the vampires must abide by, no matter what. First, they will not harm a single human being. For any reason. Even if they sense 'evil' in them, as your vampire claims. They will have to find another form of suste-nance. No exceptions."

"Yes," I said.

"Second, they will have to agree to reside in a controlled environ-ment. We will make space in one of the Bureau facilities. They will be tracked and monitored at all times."

That's going to be an interesting situation.

"Lastly, they will work closely alongside a team of our soldiers to begin resolving the redbill problem. That way they can prove their trustworthiness under our observation. We'll also be able to monitor how safely they can coexist with humans."

"How long will this trial period last?" I asked.

"Six weeks. No less. Any issues and it's over. Should they fully cooperate, the board will consider their request for a long-term asylum agreement and invite more of them to stay, but we make no promises at this point. That will require another round of meetings." He paused to wipe his brow. "I must emphasize this, Lyra: should anything go wrong, the vampires will not receive amnesty, and the board will return to its standard protocol for protecting our people from vampires."

"I understand..." This was really happening. It took several moments for it to sink in. I blinked, hard, and swallowed my apprehension.

"Confidentiality is paramount. Any information regarding this 'Immortal Plane' and the tear will be strictly monitored. People could get seriously harmed or killed if it's made public. The soldiers assigned to work with the vampires will receive information only on a need-to-know basis, for things to run smoothly."

"Okay," I said, rubbing my hands together, my heart beating a little faster as I considered this outcome.

If Dorian had told me the truth, and the safety of his species was of the utmost importance, he would understand the terms. The vampires would probably dislike it, but if it kept them safe and developed trust, it could be a win for everyone. I just had to send them the message.

My uncle cleared his throat and laced his fingers. "So, now you're all caught up. I believe the next move is theirs. Or Dorian's. How exactly will you contact him?"

I pursed my lips. "Um, yeah... I'm still figuring that one out."

CHAPTER FOURTEEN

Two nights later, I was in bed, my mind still whirring after speaking with my uncle. I had barely been able to sleep since his visit. I wanted to get in touch with Dorian immediately, to let him know what was happening, all the ideas spilling around inside my brain. But there was nothing I could do. He'd said he'd find me. *What does that even mean?*

As I lay there, trying to slow down my thoughts enough to sleep, something creaked on the balcony outside. Silhouetted against the orange sky was the curved neck and pointed beak of a redbill.

Oh, my God.

I leapt from my bed and grabbed the can of mace I'd swiped from Zach's room earlier, tucking it into the waistband of my sweatpants and inching toward the sliding balcony door.

The massive bird perched on the reinforced steel railing, and Dorian stood on the balcony with his arms crossed, staring at me in the dim light. The faint glow cast from my bedroom shadowed and elongated his already angular face and sharp nose and jaw. His black eyebrows remained stationary in an arch over his glimmering pale eyes. His dark cloak covered his broad, sharp shoulders, and his ragged, cream-colored shirt looked dirtier. There was a new tear in his worn gray pants.

Holy crap. This guy has balls, showing up at headquarters like this.

I slid the glass door open a crack.

"Don't worry, I won't keep you long," Dorian said. His slender lips were straight, emotionless.

I tightened my throat to a whisper. "How in the hell did you even find me?"

"I must be a good guesser," he replied flatly.

I shook my head. *Wily, that's for sure.* I stuck my head out the door, glancing at the other balconies, but all remained empty and dark. "I'm not inviting you in."

He ignored that. "Did you speak with your uncle? What did the Bureau say?"

I pulled the door open a bit more but remained behind the glass. "I testified at the Bureau and spoke with my uncle," I replied. "They're going to help you, but there are terms."

Dorian raised his eyebrows expectantly.

"A trial period of six weeks is required," I started.

I studied his face as I covered the rules my uncle had set down. Dorian stayed stoic, giving nothing away until I mentioned the "no preying on *any* humans" and "monitored living situation on Bureau property" parts. At that, he rubbed his forehead and leaned back against the railing. I had figured those stipulations would be a tough sell. Just past him, the redbill nibbled at its breast feathers.

"This will be difficult," he said, his face dour. "Not impossible, but difficult. Vampires are fueled by the dark energy we receive from our prey. Regular blood is useless—because blood is merely the carrier for the dark energy. We can only be sustained by beings with ill will. We can feed heavily and be nourished for a while, sometimes for extended periods of time. But eventually we weaken and die." He looked away, as though calculating, drumming his fingers on the balcony rail. "We can prepare for a fast by going to the Immortal Plane for a short while, and we should be able to survive under these requirements for about six weeks. It's going to get rough toward the end, though."

"The children can survive for six weeks, too?" I asked, Carwin's little face jumping back into my mind.

"They can feed on the adults," he said grimly. "Which will make it harder for us. Even so, this is as much as I could have hoped for." He tilted his head back and sighed with what sounded like relief.

"Good," I replied. I spotted my uniform pants still on my bed. "Hold on."

I retrieved the stone and reached through the crack in the door to return it. "I, uh, didn't show it to them... I didn't want them to take it and possibly not give it back."

"Keep it," he said, his eyes locking with mine. "Consider it my way of saying thanks."

I bent my brow. "So, you're using this to track me somehow. Got it."

He chuckled, his head tilting back slightly and exposing a sharp canine.

"How do you think the others will react?" I whispered. Remembering Kane and Halla's vicious stares gave me a chill. I leaned against the wall, just inside the door, and rubbed my arms.

"We will discuss it, and I hope that they will come to see this as an opportunity. All of them." He obviously knew whom I was thinking of.

I looked down at the wrapped stone in my palm. Keeping it seemed wrong—not to mention dangerous, if he really *could* somehow use it to track me.

"Are you still afraid of me?" Dorian asked, his tone quieter and his face less playful. I found myself surprised that he genuinely cared that I might feel fear. Or at least, seemed to. A bit of warmth filled my chest, but I wasn't going to let my guard down with this guy anytime soon.

I straightened up, put the stone in my sweatpants pocket, and scoffed. "Since when was I afraid of you?"

"My mistake." He grinned down at the mace canister poking from my pants.

"Well." I narrowed my eyes on him. "You're probably still planning to eat me."

"No, thanks," he said. "What an unappealing thought. In the 'food' sense, I mean. You'd taste like cardboard."

In the food sense? As opposed to what?

I set a hand on my hip. "I'll take that as a compliment."

He smirked. We stared at each other. I felt like I was missing something. Then I remembered.

"Oh, there's something I want to give you, too." I jogged to my nightstand, ignoring his slight eyebrow raise, and returned to the cracked door with an old smartphone and charger.

"You can contact me with this," I said, eyeing the bird from behind the glass. "So this whole… thing… isn't required every time we have to talk."

He took the phone from my extended hand but squinted at it as though it were an alien artifact. "How do I use this?"

I reached out, took it back, and held down the power button. "Get with the times."

He smirked knowingly, as the device's power-up screen lit up his face. "Now who's tracking who?"

Warmth traveled up my neck. I should have known he would guess my intention. *Vampires.*

"Well, you made it easy by showing up at headquarters." I reached out to point my finger at an icon on the screen. "Press that, and then you can see my name and call me." When I'd gotten the idea before bed, I'd done a factory reset and programmed myself as the only contact, so it wouldn't be too hard for him to figure out. I didn't plan to tell him about the "Find My Phone" feature which I could use to see exactly where he was whenever I wanted to. It was extremely possible that would come in handy in the future.

"Don't forget to charge it sometimes," I added. "If you can find an outlet every now and then."

"Thank you," he replied quietly, and the change in his tone stilled my breath for a moment, bringing my eyes from the phone screen back up to his face. His brow softened, and his mouth relaxed. "What you've done means more than I can put into words."

We stared at each other. The foul vampire I'd met on the cliff no longer stood in front of me.

"You're welcome," I managed.

He considered me for another moment. The heat rose from my neck to my cheeks.

A little smile crept onto Dorian's face, like he had a joke he wasn't going to tell, and then he turned and leapt onto the railing. He mounted the redbill with a click of his teeth, and he didn't look back as the bird soared up and away, through clouds tainted amber by the city lights.

CHAPTER FIFTEEN

I woke up the next morning feeling rested, despite the guests I'd entertained before bed.

Mom had left some pancakes on the counter, and I made a plate after getting home from a run at the gym. By that time, Zach and Gina were sitting in the living room.

"How are you feeling?" Gina asked.

"Good," I said through a mouthful. My phone vibrated in my pocket. I pulled it out and recognized my old number flashing on the screen.

"Gotta go." I swallowed and abandoned my half-finished plate, racing to my room and closing the door behind me. "Hello?"

"We accept the Bureau's terms," Dorian said simply on the other end.

"Oh," I replied, sitting on the corner of my bed. *They don't have conditions of their own?*

Dorian didn't try to negotiate. It sank in, my stomach dropping at the idea that the vampires truly wanted safety and reconciliation. They must, to be desperate enough to accept whatever they could.

"We need to know what they would like us to do next," he said, his voice cool and businesslike. "I assume you will figure that out with your uncle and call me back this evening?"

"I can do that," I said.

"In that case, we've got a bit of feeding to do, so I'll speak with you later," he said flatly, and hung up.

I shuddered, then dialed Uncle Alan. He picked up quickly.

"The vampires have accepted the Bureau's offer," I told him. "The trial period and all of the rules."

"I'll alert the board," he replied, and his voice matched Dorian's. I'd never thought I'd compare my uncle to a vampire. It felt surreal for this to be happening, just like that. "We still need to set a location and prepare the necessary provisions for their housing. That will take several more days."

"Okay. Is there anything I can do to help?"

"I'll let you know. Thank you for calling. I'll get in touch again soon," he said, and ended the call.

I took a deep breath. *Well, here goes.*

The Bureau chose a remote location in Arizona to house the vampires for the trial period. My uncle said the facility had been used to detain vampires and conduct behavioral research in the past.

"It's well-equipped for this purpose, and it's far enough from civilization that it should minimize any immediate threats if things don't go according to plan," he'd added.

They had a list of senior and experienced staff that they wanted on the project. But seeing as Zach, Gina, and I were already aware of the situation, we'd been asked to join the team of soldiers that would live at the facility for the extent of the trial phase. My uncle referred to me as the "liaison." Captain Bryce would be one of those in command. Some other younger soldiers, including Greta, Colin, Sarah, Grayson, Louise, and Roxy were also asked to join. The information we received about the tear and Immortal Plane was strictly confidential, as made clear by the piles of paperwork we had to sign.

The Bureau started shipping out equipment by aircraft during the night. The soldiers would fly out within forty-eight hours of signing papers.

Dorian agreed to meet us at the facility on the requested day and time. We'd have a short stint of prep with Bryce before the vampires arrived. Captain seemed markedly excited about this operation—more than I'd ever seen him before.

My parents held a going-away dinner for us and invited Gina's family. They remained positive, although I noticed Mom excused herself to the restroom when my father made a toast to our safety.

Like everything the Bureau did when the board made up its mind, things moved methodically. And soon enough, the day was upon us, whether we were ready or not.

I walked beside Zach across the facility's tarmac. It was early morning, but the Arizona sun glared full force. I gazed at the long metal building in front of us. The last of the supplies sat organized on the asphalt, near a series of open utility doors.

"Home, sweet home," Zach said.

We strode up to Captain Bryce, who held a clipboard and surveyed the supplies with a critical but enthusiastic eye.

"Thanks for joining us, children," he said with a nod as we filed past him into the building. "We're having a briefing in thirty minutes. Main meeting room. Do not make me wait for you."

The building was split into two wings, with several labs and meeting rooms in the center. The entrance to the vampires' quarters was made obvious by three sets of massive deadbolts and a security keypad.

Guards escorted us to our quarters, passing surveillance rooms on the way. Dozens of screens already monitored the vampire housing. I lost count of how many armed guards milled about.

The guards directed the women to our room, and the men followed them down the other hall.

Gina and I dropped our giant bags on our bunks and grabbed our notebooks and pens. We'd packed heavily for this trip, knowing that the Bureau tended to skimp on such luxuries as warm blankets and extra bedding.

Gina exhaled. "Ready?"

"Yep," I replied.

The main meeting room held new faces. My team sat together after introducing ourselves to the new soldiers. Two or three looked young, but most were middle-aged, and their faces showed experience. I counted fourteen of us in total.

Captain Bryce called our meeting to order by slamming the door behind him.

"Quiet," he snapped, though the room was hardly full of chatter. He made his way to the head of the room, set down his stack of folders, and cleared his throat. "Right, now that you've got your formalities out of the way, let's talk about how to not get killed for the next six weeks."

He set his hands down heavily on the table in front of him.

"Everyone here answers to me and the other captains, Finley and Clemmins. Understood?"

"Yes, Captain," the whole room responded.

"Once Finley and Clemmins join us, we'll be running drills. But first, the one thing you must not forget is this: never underestimate these creatures. You are not dealing with humans, so don't expect them to behave, speak, or move like humans."

The room filled with the scratching of pens.

"We are up against abnormal speed, precision, instincts, and predatory drives. They're going to be twenty paces ahead of you mentally and physically. Learn to think and move faster, and maybe we'll be able to share a drink when we're done here." Bryce chuckled to himself at the thought.

The door opened, and a man and woman sporting captain patches entered.

"Captains." Bryce nodded to them, and they returned the gesture. "I just informed these folks what they've signed up for. Are we ready for drills?"

"All set," the woman responded. Her uniform read "Finley," a detail I filed away for future reference. Her skin was ivory and taut—but that could've been because her red hair was tied back in an extremely tight bun.

"On your feet," Bryce barked. "Follow your captains to the warehouse."

The warehouse, we soon discovered, mostly contained wooden crates stacked to the metal ceiling. Gym mats covered an open section of cement floor.

"Form two lines facing each other," Finley ordered.

And, just like that, training began. Gina and I instinctively placed ourselves across from each other in the bustle.

Captain Bryce sauntered between the lines. "I'm sure you're all aware that a vampire will strike the neck. But if that's not the easiest target, they will find other ways to terminate you. We're going to focus on defensive and disarming moves. If you are attacked, it's much more likely that a two-step disarm will buy time for others to come to your aid."

Captain Clemmins spoke to the group for the first time, his tone even as he smoothly picked up at the end of Bryce's sentence. His dark brown eyes were thoughtful but focused. "In the event of such an attack, guarding your neck is your first move. Arms up. The metal on your forearms should be directly in front of your neck, between you and the vampire's mouth."

We all set our defensive poses.

"Good." Clemmins nodded, running a hand over his tan, bald scalp. "Fists ready to strike."

"I could knock you over with a sneeze, Grayson," Bryce yelled. "Find your feet."

Grayson quickly corrected his stance.

Captain Finley demonstrated with Clemmins how to restrain a vampire, using Aikido techniques to use their momentum against them, then put them into a rear armlock. Pretty basic stuff modified for vampires.

"It's extremely important that you capture both hands in this process," she said. "Vampires aren't just teeth."

"Bring it into the center and run drills as pairs," Bryce ordered.

Gina and I flowed through the moves they'd showed us together and increased our speed to the extent possible, knowing that even our fastest speed would be much slower than a vampire's. We'd seen that firsthand when we'd met Dorian in the attic.

Bryce and Clemmins demonstrated two other moves, and the soldiers recreated them.

"One thing that we have on our side is that vampires anatomically resemble humans. If one is shot or wounded in a vital place, they will die," Bryce stated. "This is where your core training will be essential. You know the spots to hit. Make them bleed. If you're being attacked, use the time you have before contact. If I see any of you without your issued firearm on you at any point in time in the next six weeks, consider that moment your resignation from the Bureau."

"Yes, Captain."

"Keep running drills." Captain Bryce tossed a hand at us and turned to confer with the other captains.

By the time we broke for lunch, sweat poured down my face. But that was just the beginning; we were only given a short time to eat at the long lunchroom-style tables before we returned to the main meeting room for more briefing.

"Our honored guests will be here before you know it. Pick up your feet," Bryce had shouted as we chewed, and nobody had even rolled their eyes.

The next day was similar, filled with more drills and meetings in the low-ceilinged building. The team seemed more confident by the time we sat down for dinner that evening in the hum of the air conditioning. The place sometimes felt more like an old factory than a Bureau facility, to be honest, and the brown-and-beige color scheme reminded me of my high school.

One of the new soldiers walked up as I ate. "I'm Lily. We met yesterday."

I nodded, covering my chewing with a hand. "Have a seat."

We made small talk, though I primarily focused on my food. She came from California and had trained at the L.A. headquarters. She'd gathered her black hair into a clean bun, and her brown eyes were happy above her freckled, bronze cheeks.

"You're a lieutenant, right?" she asked.

"Yes," I replied through my chewing.

"Planning on being there, too. Sooner rather than later." Her voice had an edge to it, a seriousness. I immediately believed she'd achieve it.

"You remind me of myself," I said with a smile. "Let me know if you ever need anything or have any questions."

She reached out to shake my hand, and we exchanged a nod before she got up from the table.

Later that night, I walked off some anxious energy around the facility. The rest of the soldiers had already returned to their bunks. I made my way down the main pass and noticed the bolted door to the vampire quarters hung open. I looked around and saw no guards.

I slipped through the doorway and cringed. In this wing of the facility, the aisle was lined by rows and rows of bars. Inside the cells were flat beds with one thin blanket each. Bare, stainless steel toilets sat in plain sight, and no windows broke the grim gray walls. I'd seen nicer prisons.

Multiple padlocks and chains hung from every cell door. I chewed my bottom lip. This wasn't exactly welcoming.

I walked the hall, gazing into each cage. Some had enough beds for families, while others were intended for a single occupant. Everything smelled of bleach.

I gripped a bar and stared at the concrete floor. An idea jolted me. I rushed back to the women's quarters. Some of the soldiers complained to each other about the facility gruel, while others read.

"Ladies," I said loudly. "Did anyone bring an extra blanket or two?"

Gina and Roxy squinted at me.

"I have two," Gina said.

"I think I brought a spare," Louise called from the corner.

"Okay, everyone." I put my palms together. "Let's gather up whatever extra blankets and pillows we have. And then follow me."

"Slumber party in the warehouse?" Roxy joked.

I dug through the sack of possessions I'd brought to the facility with me and pulled out the small pillow my grandmother had embroidered for me, as well as an extra knitted blanket. I watched a stack of assorted bedding grow in the aisle between our bunks.

Gina held up a stuffed bear. "Does this fit the bill?"

"Perfect," I said, snatching it and putting it under my arm. "I think we need a bit more… Grab all of this and come on. You guys are okay with temporarily donating these to a good cause, right?" They shrugged and nodded, but Roxy didn't respond at all.

The ladies and I crossed the hall, several of us lugging big, colorful lumps of bedding in our arms. I knocked on the door to the men's quarters.

One of the new soldiers pulled the metal door open. I'd learned his name was Hank, which was extremely ironic, because it rhymed with "tank." He towered over me, a wall of early-twenties muscle.

"Hi, Hank. We were wondering if you or any of the other guys had extra pillows or blankets they'd be willing to donate to our incoming friends," I said.

Hank blinked at me, then turned around and hollered my request to his bunkmates. After the expected confusion, Grayson and a few other newbies came through for me. They appeared behind Hank's hulking frame carrying sports teams throws and other plushy additions.

In the meantime, Hank had procured a stuffed crocodile from his luggage. "This is Dilly," he said.

Roxy snorted into her fist behind me, and I elbowed her in the side.

"He's perfect," I said.

We shuffled down the main hall, and I pushed the vampire quarters door open wider. The rest of the group followed me, but I caught concerned glances out of the corner of my eye.

"Are we supposed to be in here?" Lily asked.

"The door's open," I said innocently, which wasn't exactly a yes. Some of the soldiers laughed. "Divvy out the blankets. Let's make the beds look nice," I encouraged.

I walked into one of the family-sized cells and put my embroidered pillow and Gina's teddy bear on the beds, then stepped back and assessed the décor. Did vampires even care about this kind of stuff?

"Miss Lieutenant's got her bossy pants on tonight," Roxy said, under her breath but loudly enough for me to hear. "Impressing her vampire friends is pretty important, huh, Louise?"

Louise ignored her, but I didn't. I didn't want her to get bitter and undermine me at every opportunity.

"Roxy, I know you and the others may not really want to donate your personal belongings, but I think it'll really make a difference," I said, smiling at her in an attempt to melt her iciness. "Do you have any ideas we could work on?"

Roxy shrugged but offered me a small, sheepish smile.

In the end, we were able to get a colorful blanket on every bed.

"Talk about hospitality," Louise said, her hands on her waist. Everyone laughed.

"Hank," Grayson called out, "where did Dilly end up?"

"In here," Hank said, pointing into one of the two-bed cells at the end of the aisle. "They'll probably get along. Sharp teeth."

Gina and I bit our lips to fight laughter.

The quarters still reeked of bleach and echoed emptily, but it was something. I tried to picture Dorian's response.

"Perhaps this will make them less inclined to kill us." Sarah grinned.

Roxy scoffed. "That would be nice."

"They're uprooting themselves and moving into a jail for six weeks to show us that they want better relations. I think this is the least we can do," I said gently. "We're not putting our safety at risk by lending some blankets."

"Fair enough," Gina replied. Several of the boys raised their eyebrows in consideration.

The group scuttled back through the main hall to our quarters. We passed Zach and Colin chatting outside the entrance to their own. They had missed our little party.

"Well, that can't be good," Zach muttered, eyeing our furtive group, with particular apprehension directed at me and Gina. I grinned at him.

Back in our bunks, everyone settled in for the night. The murmurs of conversation drifted off. I listened to Roxy snoring. I couldn't tell if my heart raced because I was excited or terrified for the next day. The rhythm of Gina's breath eventually lulled me into unconsciousness.

The next morning, the frantic vibration of my phone jerked me awake. I fumbled with the device, squinting around the barracks. Everyone else was still asleep.

I blinked and focused on the phone in my hand. My old number glowed on the screen. Suddenly, I was wide awake.

"We're almost there," Dorian said.

CHAPTER SIXTEEN

The sun rose as our team lined up on the tarmac. Security flanked the soldiers on both sides, and in the center of our team stood Captains Bryce, Finley, and Clemmins. Gina, Zach, and I, all first lieutenants, stood directly next to the captains.

Bryce mumbled something into a walkie, then whispered to the other captains. I readjusted my artillery belt and gun strap.

A board member I recognized from my testimony strode across the tarmac from a small Bureau charter plane that sat off to the side. He looked young, mid-thirties, probably a recent addition to the board, but otherwise looked the part in his gray suit. His black hair was parted and slicked back.

"Soldiers," Captain Bryce barked over our heads. "We have the pleasure of having a board member and former captain with us here today. Salute Captain Fenton."

We saluted him in tandem, and he nodded in return.

"Good morning, everyone. I'll only be staying to help our guests get situated, but thank you for having me. Honored to be here." His smile was genuine.

"Captain Fenton, may I ask you to step behind our guards until we secure the vampires?" Captain Finley said softly to him.

"Thank you, Captain," Fenton said, leaving my line of sight.

I squinted into the brightening sun from behind my sunglasses and glanced down my team's line. All lenses were glued to the end of the tarmac where the vampires had been instructed to arrive. As absurd as it seemed, we'd set cone markers for their descent. Everyone had their issued handguns on their waists in addition to their rifles. The Bureau guards kept AR-15s poised under their arms. The night's coolness lingered, but already most of us had sweat on our foreheads.

Surveillance came on over our comms. "Arriving party located. Beginning descent."

Everyone stared into the sun. I spotted a speck of black flitting out from some low-hanging clouds, followed by multiple others. A flock of redbills.

"Soldiers. At the ready," Captain Bryce hollered. A wave of hands unlocked rifle safeties, and weapon tips angled up to the sky.

I squeezed my eyes closed and opened them again, adjusting to the light. The birds drifted closer, weaving over and under each other in the air. They descended quickly. Soon I could make out Dorian in the lead.

"Hold steady unless you hear otherwise. Got it?" Bryce growled.

"Yes, Captain."

The bills' wings fluttered as their talons neared the asphalt. There were about twelve birds, some carrying more than one vampire. Dorian's cape billowed over his shoulder. I couldn't see his eyes, but I felt them.

His redbill landed first. It let out a deafening shriek that made two soldiers readjust their footing. Dorian glanced back at his group, landing behind him, then back to our line. I could see his furrowed brow.

Several breaths passed where no one moved. The vampires stared. Even though Dorian's clan had about thirty members, I counted only fifteen here. Dorian hadn't mentioned that the others would remain in

Canyonlands, but maybe it had been a last-minute decision. For their kind, this was probably scary and dangerous. Not to mention unpleasant. Who'd want to spend six weeks in a military facility, starving and working for a species they historically fostered dislike for? It was probably unnecessary for them all to come to Arizona, as this test group could feel out the situation and report back to them, should the trial period go well.

The clothes of the vampires present were worn with frayed edges, the fabric looking like some sort of rugged, thick linen, all shades of dark greens, browns, and creams. Most of the women had their hair tied back with torn strips of cloth, and the men sported unruly locks tucked behind their ears. I spotted Kreya with Carwin and her daughter sitting in front of her on her redbill. I assumed it was her daughter, as they hadn't been apart since I'd met the group.

I looked to Bryce as he surveyed the small crowd. He caught my eye and nodded to me. I stepped forward and slung my rifle over my shoulder.

Dorian stayed on his bird until I was twenty steps away. Then he dismounted, gesturing to his group to remain seated. He met me in the middle.

My heart hit my ribs when he got close enough for me to see the dark, defined shadows rippling under his cheeks. We stared at each other for a moment. He glanced behind me and clenched his jaw.

"Shake my hand," I murmured, barely moving my lips. I extended my gloved palm.

Dorian peered into my face as though looking for something, then gripped my hand, watching closely and letting me guide the gesture. Vampires probably didn't do this very often. Or ever.

He narrowed his eyes as we released hands. "That's a lot of guns." Still, he turned and gestured for the others to dismount their bills.

The group of vampires slowly moved toward me, all cautiously reaching out to emulate the hand motion they'd seen. Kreya and Rhome stepped forward, nodding to acknowledge me, but Kreya gestured for her children to stay back. Kane and Halla lingered on the outskirts of the group. Their glares were just as I remembered them, but for now they remained silent.

"Welcome, everyone," I said. "Please, come meet our team."

The vampires followed me at a distance; I could feel their presence keenly as I returned to the line. The captains stepped forward, but Fenton remained behind the guards.

"Captains, this is Dorian." I introduced them, indicating each in turn. "Dorian, Captains Bryce, Finley, and Clemmins."

They nodded to each other, and Dorian awkwardly held out his hand like before.

"At ease," Bryce called to the line of soldiers, before shaking Dorian's hand. "Nice to meet you."

"Thank you for inviting us," Dorian said evenly. He looked back, jerking his head toward his team, and I did the same to mine, encouraging introductions.

Soldiers and vampires stared at each other, then lightly grasped each other's hands. There were murmurs of greeting. Kane and Halla continued lingering behind everyone else, refusing to greet anyone— until Dorian cleared his throat in their direction. Carwin, his little sister, and many of the other children hid behind Bravi's legs at the back of the group. Bravi whispered something to them and then approached me, hand outstretched. I shook it, smiling. She avoided my eyes, though I saw the children watching her curiously.

Once Dorian had shaken hands with all the captains, Bryce spoke into his comm. "Please escort Fenton to join the captains."

Bryce visibly relaxed, and his eyes took on an odd light, like he'd suddenly turned twenty years younger—or maybe like he'd just walked into an ammunition factory.

The soldiers cleared a path for two guards and Fenton. Dorian and the board member looked at each other.

"I'm Captain Fenton of the Bureau's national board. Welcome to our facility," Fenton said through a tight smile.

"Thank you. I'm Dorian Clave." Dorian offered his hand, and they shook. Apparently, vampires had last names, too.

Fenton greeted the other vampires while maintaining several feet between himself and whomever he smiled at. The guards remained attached to his shoulders.

The groups cautiously parted from each other, and quiet reigned over the tarmac. Kreya and Bravi slipped through the vampires to rejoin the children.

Dorian looked back at the redbills and clicked his teeth. They tossed their heads and leapt back into the air, winging into the desert.

Almost simultaneously, most of the gathered soldiers reached for their guns, but Bryce held up a hand. He cleared his throat. "Mr. Clave, where are those bills headed?"

"They're finding a place to roost for our visit. They'll be close by but will not harm anyone unless provoked," Dorian said, his voice clear and confident, loud enough for all the soldiers to hear. "These creatures are docile and answer to us."

Several of my team exchanged skeptical glances.

"Aye," Bryce replied. He bent his brow and cleared his throat. "I suppose we will trust you on that, then. If the soldiers can step inside the main hall, we'd like to show you to your accommodations."

The vampires knit into a cluster and waited. My team filed into the facility, but I remained beside Dorian and Bryce in front of the line of vampires. On Finley's word over our comms, we led our guests inside.

I studied Dorian closely as he and his people entered their quarters' hallway. He was stone-faced, but his jaw looked locked, and I could see his heartbeat pulsing in his neck. Kane grimaced and wrinkled his nose upon entering, probably at the chemical smell. As the vampires drifted down through the aisle, Kreya's daughter pulled her mother's hand and whimpered.

"Quiet, Detra." Kreya immediately shushed her.

"Please, make yourselves at home and choose your quarters however you please," Captain Bryce said, attempting a smile but rubbing his hands together as though nervous.

"Thank you." Dorian nodded in the captain's direction.

At the two words, Bryce's smile stretched, genuine and giddy, and he placed his hands on his hips, looking dazed as the group explored. I knew the feeling. I couldn't believe this was actually happening.

The vampires, however, were silent. They split off into the cells, shuffling like nervous zombies. I looked to Dorian, and although I couldn't read his expression, I could somehow tell that, to him, the bars on the cells said more than Bryce's geniality.

I tapped Kreya's shoulder and pointed to one of the family-sized cells. She bent her head in acknowledgement, showing her children cautiously through the door. The little girl leaned down and poked the teddy bear.

Zach and Gina had remained at their posts by the doorway. I flapped my fingers for them to come over and introduced them to Dorian.

"We've already met," Gina said under her breath, her face tight, but she tried again after I eyed her. "Welcome."

Zach said nothing but gave Dorian a curt little nod. Neither he nor Gina removed their hands from the handguns on their hips.

I gazed around. Most of the vampires had chosen their beds, but Kane and Halla remained in the aisle. Captain Bryce side-stepped toward them.

"Do hope you can get comfortable," he said through his awkward smile. "Isn't five stars, but eh, military housing."

Kane's glare could have lit kindling.

"Aye, then we'll leave you to it," Bryce said, taking the hint. "First Lieutenants Zach Sloane and Blackwell, please remain posted at the door until First Lieutenant Lyra Sloane has made sure everything is set." He raised his eyebrows at Zach and Gina, and they complied. Four guards stationed themselves beside the entrance, too. I knew they weren't going anywhere.

Kane and Halla chose a two-bed cell at the very end of the aisle. As I walked around, I peeked in to see how they reacted; Kane knocked Dilly to the floor, seeming alarmed and confused by the stuffed animal's presence. I could almost see him wondering if it was an intimidation tactic.

I continued walking the aisle. The vampires murmured amongst themselves, seated on their beds or standing nearby.

Dorian stood in front of the last single-person cell, his shoulders heavy.

I approached him. "This one gonna be yours?"

He exhaled and stepped inside.

I lingered at the cell door, glancing down at the knit blanket on his bed. It was the one I'd donated. "How are you?" I ventured.

Dorian shot a look down the aisle, momentarily eyeing a bearded security guard near the door, reminding me again of a lion on the prowl, this time one looking out for danger. He licked his lips and set a small cloth bag on the bed.

"Maintaining," was his only response.

"Okay," I said softly. "Well, I'm going to head back and let you rest. I'll visit when I can."

He nodded twice but avoided my gaze.

When I stepped back into the main hall, Gina, Zach, and the guards followed me. I stopped to watch the guards heave the massive metal door closed and enter the code that locked the bolts, the *chunk* rattling through the corridor. Two guards leaned against the wall beside the door, the barrels of their weapons poised against their shoulders. I couldn't see their eyes behind their dark glasses.

"Come on, Lyra," Zach urged. "We have another briefing."

I glanced once more at the massive bolts on the locks to the vampires' wing, and then followed my brother and Gina to the meeting room.

CHAPTER SEVENTEEN

Late into that night, our quarters still buzzed with chatter. None of us could even think about sleep.

"Their skin is so strange," Louise whispered across the aisle. "It almost... moves."

"That little boy had a cast on his arm," Lily added. "Lyra, do you know anything about that?"

Roxy snorted. "She's not going to tell you anything. She signed more NDAs than you did."

I stared at the bottom of the bunk above me. My stomach gnawed over the way Dorian had looked earlier.

"When did Captain Bryce become so chatty?" Roxy continued, trying to hold back laughter. "With vampires, of all people. Maybe they have more in common than we realized."

That was fair. This time, a grin cracked my lips.

"Maybe they'll adopt him once this is over," Louise muttered, flipping a page in her book.

I rolled my eyes and turned onto my side. The weight of the day pulled at my eyelids, but every time I tried to doze off, the thought of Dorian's unease made me fidget.

Gina hadn't spoken to me since I'd introduced her to Dorian. She sat on the side of her bunk playing with her hair tie. She had memories the other girls couldn't understand, just like I did.

The whispers subsided, the conversations slowly dying down around me as the women on the team tried to get some sleep, when a muffled yell resounded through the barracks. A moment later, it was joined by the sound of an alarm screaming into the night.

We all bolted from our beds, staring at each other. The screeching alarm didn't stop.

On the first *night?*

"Guns, now!" I yelled, and we snatched our weapons and rushed through the door.

Zach and Colin tumbled out the door to their quarters, joining us in the hallway, handguns clutched in white knuckles. We darted through the main hallway and found the door to the vampires' wing slightly ajar. I sucked in a breath and flung the door open.

A security guard slumped against the wall, clutching a bleeding wound in his neck. The other night guards had bent over, restraining someone against the wall. I recognized the tiny form as Detra.

Blood dribbled down the child's chin, and she cried in terror, trying to squirm away from the guards. Her screams sounded shrill, like a baby animal cornered by wolves. They were echoed by the threats and wordless howls of vampires down the cell block—all of them still trapped behind bars.

Captain Bryce tore through the doorway behind my group with his gun angled at the floor. "What the hell is going on?" he yelled.

"It got through the bars—I don't know how—it slipped through the bars and attacked him," a security guard stammered, his automatic weapon pointed at the girl's face.

Bryce swore.

"There were two other guards closer to her cell, but she went straight for him, Captain," the guard carried on.

I spun around to face the cells. Every vampire pressed against the bars of their cells, screaming and reaching helplessly toward the girl.

"Detra, come back! Come back now!" Kreya cried, her face twisted in agony. She turned around in her cell, thrashing an arm. "Carwin, stay at the back. Don't come toward the bars!" she yelled to her son, who was hidden from my view.

"Listen to us! She didn't know what she was doing. We tried to stop her. Please let her go." This came from Dorian, his voice low and as desperate as I'd ever heard it.

Rhome strained his fingers in an attempt to reach his daughter, but even when he jammed his shoulder as far through the bars as it could go, he couldn't reach her. "It's okay, Detra, just be still. It's okay."

Detra's bloodstained fangs glinted as she writhed and shrieked, the dark ripples under her cheeks circling rapidly. One of the guards holding her arm twisted it and bent her face toward the floor. She whimpered and it turned into a cry, tears welling in her eyes.

"Easy, easy!" I yelled. "Don't hurt her."

"Don't hurt her?" another guard snapped, throwing a glance at the man gasping on the floor. "What about him?"

That was when I recognized the guard on the floor. He was the bearded guard that Dorian had stared at before I left him earlier that day. They all must have sensed something dark in him... but the children didn't understand that they couldn't hunt now.

I spun on my heels and looked to Dorian. His eyes confirmed my fear. What if this ruined everything? It hadn't even been twenty-four hours.

"Return her to her cell. Now!" Captain Bryce bellowed. "You, keys! You three hold her! Move it!"

"Please don't hurt her," Kreya called out.

Detra wriggled and wailed as the guard fumbled with the three separate padlock keys. Tears streamed down her cheeks. The door finally swung open, and the girl tore from the guards and flew into her mother's arms. Sobs echoed down the aisle. Dorian banged his forehead against the bars of his cell.

A medic leaned over the bleeding guard and pressed gauze against his neck.

"Get him to the medical wing," Bryce said.

I heard Clemmins and Finley shouting orders from the main hallway, having also arrived.

The guards relocked Kreya and Rhome's cell before helping to carry their colleague. As they lifted him, giving him words of encouragement, I couldn't take my eyes off the man's face. If Dorian and his kind sensed bad deeds like rape and murder in their victims, what had Detra and Dorian sensed about him? It must've been a powerful lure, for Detra to contort herself enough to get through the bars.

"Captain," I said. "I will muster a fresh set of guards."

"Thank you, Lieutenant," Bryce said, moving to check in with Finley and Clemmins.

I rushed through the main hall to the surveillance rooms. More guards had already arrived, strapping on their belts.

I selected the four who looked the calmest and assigned them to the vampire quarters. The rest I told to disperse. I had to tell them twice, with a bite in my voice the second time.

With the new guards at my heels, I returned to the vampire quarters. Before I opened the door, I leaned against it, snapping my fingers to grab their focus.

"Don't do anything stupid," I said, looking each of them in the eye in turn. "We don't have all the information yet. If this experiment works, it will be a huge win for the Bureau. If you get nervous and shoot somebody for twitching, it won't work."

They nodded and gave quiet "yes, ma'ams" of acknowledgment.

Inside, the vampires had retreated from the bars to huddle in the backs of the cells. Detra still wailed.

Dorian lurked in the corner of his cell. His face was dark. The quarters felt even more miserable and cold than before we'd put out blankets and pillows.

The fresh watch was stationed, so the other soldiers and I headed back to the main hall. Everyone looked dazed. We passed the captains, and I slowed my pace, an idea bouncing in the back of my mind.

"Gina, Roxy, go ahead. Need some words," I told them quietly.

They nodded and continued. Zach grabbed Gina's shoulder when she walked past, raising his eyebrows at me.

I stood a respectful distance from Bryce, waiting my turn as he discussed the situation with the other captains. I couldn't pretend, however, not to hear something about contacting the board, then something about relocation.

My cheeks burned. "Excuse me, Captains," I interjected, eyes on the floor. "Might I have a word?"

"Sloane," Bryce hissed in warning, then rolled his eyes. "She should probably be involved in this conversation. *Briefly*."

"Captain, I do not believe that the other vampires should be held responsible or punished for a minor's actions. The girl didn't understand the circumstances."

"We understand that, Lieutenant." Captain Finley closed in on me. "But what if this happens again—and the attacker is not a child?"

"I propose a quarters reassignment," Clemmins said evenly. "No bars. Solid walls only to house children and their parents. We clearly were not prepared for this situation." He turned to a security guard nearby and demanded a floorplan of the facility immediately. She bolted.

"Aye, we'll discuss moving the families." Bryce exhaled heavily. He grabbed the arm of another passing guard and demanded that two extra guards be placed directly beside the cells holding children.

"Captain," I said again.

"Sloane. I understand that you don't want there to be retribution due to a child's misconduct. Now, move on to your barracks."

"There's something else I need to speak with you about." I held my shoulders tall.

He closed his eyes and exhaled sharply. "Okay. Let's move to my office. Finley, would you please join us?"

The three of us made our way into Bryce's tiny office. He waved an impatient hand for us to sit.

"Captain, I know the board discussed the 'specified feeding' theory with you," I began. "That vampires only prey on threats to society."

Bryce sat at his already-cluttered desk and rubbed his face. "Make this quick."

"Assuming that theory is valid, wouldn't Detra's attack tonight call that guard's character into question?" I asked. "Especially since she targeted him preferentially over the other three guards. Two of them were closer."

"Lieutenant, are you implying that the Bureau doesn't perform thorough background checks on its staff?" Finley snapped.

"That guard has been with us for years," Bryce said. "All of them have. They were each *handpicked* for this assignment."

"A seven-year background scan doesn't necessarily mean that he's squeaky clean," I said quietly, trying not to add tension to the room.

Bryce eyed me over his hands. Finley looked like she'd sipped sour milk.

I spread my palms. "What would it hurt to investigate?"

"He's one of us, Lieutenant," Finley warned. "Drop it."

"If he's innocent, he's got nothing to worry about." I turned to Finley. "And if there is something unsavory in his past, this would illustrate another extremely useful vampiric skill that we can use for the greater good, alongside resolving the redbill issue. The Bureau doesn't want to hire ethically questionable staff, does it?"

The room went quiet. My eyes bounced from Captain Bryce to Finley and then back.

Finley swiveled to Bryce. "This is not proper conduct from a young lieutenant, Captain." She raised her voice. "Do you typically allow this? I'd say this is bordering on insubordination."

Bryce held up a hand. I gritted my teeth.

"Captain Finley, if you'll excuse us, I will take care of this," my captain said. "Lieutenant Lyra Sloane forgets her manners when she's vexed. Don't you, Lieutenant?" Bryce glowered at me.

"I simply meant the best for our team and operation," I said after unclenching my jaw. "Captain Finley, no disrespect intended, ma'am."

"Just handle it, Bryce. As if we don't have enough to worry about," Finley muttered. She stormed from the office.

Bryce tapped his finger on the side of his face.

"That will not happen again, Lieutenant," he said. His voice sounded like gravel scraping under metal. "I understand your concern, but that is not the way to conduct yourself with your superiors."

"Yes, Captain. It will not happen again, sir," I said with straightened posture.

He eyed me, then sighed. "I'll look into the guard. Now get out of my office."

"Yes, Captain."

Just jogging down the main hall took the wind out of me after the stress I'd had. I retreated to the women's latrine before returning to my bunk. I placed my hands on the sink and stared at my taut face in the mirror. I assured myself things could've been worse. It wasn't like the vampires had staged a coup. Despite everything, no one had died. And the event might have inadvertently shown more of the vampires' value.

I sighed.

But it hadn't exactly been the smoothest first day.

CHAPTER EIGHTEEN

We stumbled out of our bunks like drunkards the next morning. "Jeez," Roxy croaked. "I feel like I just blinked, and then that damn horn was blowing."

The barracks were woken every morning with the standard bugle call, and it never got any easier. I rested my forehead on the frame of the bunk above mine for a moment before I could muster the energy to reply.

"You just have to persevere," I muttered, shooting her a grin. Roxy and I had a tradition of ribbing each other first thing in the morning.

"Yes, oh, thank you, thank you, wise one, oh, second-in-command," she sneered. Roxy was always one to throw my crap back at me.

Louise snorted. Some of the women smiled through their hazes.

Breakfast in the commons was exceptionally quiet. Captain Bryce started the meal with an announcement that the injured security guard was making a steady recovery and would be back on duty in about two weeks. He'd concluded the report by tossing me his side eye, to which I responded with a quick eyebrow arch.

While we ate, Captains Finley and Clemmins briefed us on the day's schedule. Most of the adult vampires would join us in one of the larger common spaces, and we would go through interactive exercises. A few parents would be left to supervise the children, who would remain in the cells due to the previous night's events. Finley addressed everyone but me while she spoke. Clemmins looked like he'd gotten even less sleep than the rest of us.

An hour later, the soldiers filed into a meeting room. The table had been removed, and chairs circled the perimeter of the space. I scanned the ceiling and found six cameras mounted on the walls. Bryce had mentioned that the activities were to be "monitored" (which Captain Finley had hastily corrected to "studied") from the surveillance room.

I glanced over and caught my brother assessing the camera as well.

"Like fish in a bowl," he said softly, as if he didn't want to be heard.

"Comforting," I mumbled, trying to dismiss my uneasiness with the setup as crankiness from fatigue. I knew they needed to gather evidence, but I felt like an animal at the zoo.

Once our team had taken seats together in a row, filling half of the chairs, the vampires were escorted in, surrounded by Captain Clemmins and a handful of Bureau guards.

"Welcome, everyone." Clemmins mustered up an enthusiastic face. "You're going to do a series of engagement practices. Getting to know and understand each other better, if you will." He turned around and noticed that some of the vampires had clustered near the doorway, unsure of where to go. "Please, come and sit." He showed them to the other half of the chair circle.

I smiled at Dorian. He didn't seem to notice. Bravi and Sike sat beside each other, and Kane, naturally, entered the room last. Halla was absent, I guessed due to the pretty bad leg injury she'd acquired when their clan was attacked in the Immortal Plane; or perhaps she was helping to supervise the children. Discomfort lined the vampires' faces.

"I need human-vampire pairs." Captain Clemmins cleared his throat. "Link up with the person directly across from you."

I looked across at my partner—Rhome. His hands rested on his thighs and he gazed at his feet, as if meditating. He'd tied his black hair back, and with it put up like this, I noticed streaks of gray at his temples for the first time. As if he could tell that I was looking at him, he caught my gaze. I smiled. He nodded in acknowledgement.

"Ask your partner a question, then answer one of theirs, until the exercise ends. I have the list of questions here"—Clemmins rustled a sheaf of papers in his hand—"so no need to worry about thinking of questions. Just follow my lead. Pull your seats closer to your partners, now."

Chair legs screeched. I noticed my brother sliding his chair toward Kane, who refused to move his. That was going to be a fun time.

Rhome and I met in the middle and took our seats. He tried to maintain a smile, but his eyes were strained.

"Is Detra okay?" I whispered. My stomach still churned over thoughts of the little girl.

"She was very scared and confused, but she's calmer now," he replied softly.

"This first question should be asked by the human partner to their vampire partner. Question one: What is your favorite thing to do?" Clemmins read from his paper, his voice completely flat. "Begin."

I took a deep breath. "Well, Rhome, what is your favorite thing to do?" I grinned, knowing he must find this as odd as I did. I'd never been to one, but I imagined this was just like an awkward college orientation.

Rhome blinked, his gaze dropping to his knees again. "Before we were forced from our home, I loved taking my children up into the mountains. I taught them how to speak with creatures that way."

"Speak with creatures?" I squinted, unsure whether he was pulling my leg.

"Redbills, in this case," he clarified gently.

"You can actually speak with them?"

"It's not always speech you hear," he said. "Often it's like forming a thought, and right before you open your mouth, you 'send' it to the one you want to hear it. Like you visualize the words already in the creature's head." His forehead creased. "That probably doesn't make sense."

"It's strange to imagine, but I think I understand," I assured him, filing away the information that the vampires' relationship with redbills was more intimate than I'd realized. When Dorian had pulled me out of the church window, he'd growled right before the redbill appeared—it seemed they had two modes of communication.

At that, Rhome cracked a genuine smile through his obvious weariness. "Detra was exceptionally quick to learn," he continued, as if encouraged. "She made friends with the redbill hatchlings very quickly. Always wanted to visit them."

I set my chin on my palm, imagining the little girl playing with a gaggle of man-eating storks.

Rhome cleared his throat and looked directly in my eyes for the first time. "I wanted to apologize," he whispered. "For not keeping closer watch on Detra last night."

"It wasn't your fault. She was doing what she's biologically designed to do," I said. "I'm just glad everyone's okay."

"There's something else," he said, his voice low, so I had to lean closer to hear him. "When I first met you, I was terrified for my family's safety. Keeping you hostage to ensure that we weren't attacked seemed like a plausible idea. I'm sorry I considered it without looking for other options first."

That was something I'd never imagined hearing. I breathed out, just a little shakily. "Apology accepted. I think it was understandable in your circumstances. But... you didn't harm me in the end. So, thank you, too." I nodded to him, trying to show him my sincerity.

"The vampire should now ask their human partner the same question," Clemmins called from the other side of the room.

"What do you enjoy?" Rhome asked quietly, his eyes still focused on me. He folded his hands in his lap.

I hadn't thought of my own answer yet, still caught off guard by the seriousness of our previous conversation. "You know," I said, glancing at the ceiling, "this may be boring, but I love going to the gym."

"Going to the 'gym'?" Rhome asked.

I considered my next words. "Going to a building with equipment that helps you exercise. I enjoy working out my thoughts while running as hard as I can on the treadmill. A good sweat is like therapy for me."

He still looked confused. "You physically exert yourself for fun?"

That probably sounded insane to someone who was constantly running for his life.

"I guess that is a little weird from a different perspective." I stifled a laugh. "Uh, I also like playing board games. Like chess."

"Board games," he echoed, rolling the words around on his tongue, as though trying to figure them out.

I felt a flash of surprise. Vampires spent a decent amount of time on Earth before humans drove them out, and I realized I'd assumed a lot about their knowledge of my kind. "Have you ever played chess?"

"No, I haven't," he said earnestly. That was one thing I was learning to appreciate about Rhome: he seemed sincere, regardless of the situation he was in.

"It's a strategy game," I told him. "It's very old, and we—I mean, humans—have been studying it for centuries, but it's still one of the best games there is. If you want, I'm sure I can find a board around here and teach you."

Rhome let out a quiet breath, thought for a moment, and then nodded in agreement.

I looked around. Rhome and I sat closer to each other than most of the others. Many of the pairs were silent, including Zach and Kane. Dorian and Roxy didn't exactly look chummy, either. I imagined for a second what it would've been like to starve in a cell under constant supervision, especially so far from anything familiar. With all that in mind, Rhome was handling himself more than gracefully.

I was thankful that Louise and Kreya were speaking more than the others. Louise's soft matter-of-factness mirrored Kreya's. Grayson and the quiet, dark-haired female vampire named Laini struggled to maintain eye contact during their short exchanges, and Grayson's focus on shooting glances at Louise didn't help, either.

"Next question," Clemmins announced. I wondered if he cared that not everybody seemed to be handling the exercise very well. I also wondered if he found this whole thing as strange as we did. "Humans, ask your partner whom they admire most."

I posed the question to Rhome.

"My mother," he replied without hesitation. "She is the fiercest of protectors. I try to be the same for my children."

My insides warmed a little. Apparently even grown male vampires could be momma's boys.

When it was my turn to answer, my response came easily, too. "Uncle Alan. He keeps his cool in every situation and is dedicated to the Bureau."

Rhome's eyes clouded for a moment. "I see," he said, his smile faltering.

"I admire the hell out of Teddy Roosevelt," I overheard Zach say. "You know, 'Speak softly and carry a big stick.'" Out of the corner of my eye, I saw Kane stare at him blankly. I had to cover my grin with a hand.

Perhaps thankfully, at that point, Clemmins rallied everyone's attention and told us to switch partners.

I ended up with Sike. "You're Sike," I said, as I pulled my chair next to him.

"And you're Lyra. And now we have a chance to meet properly without arguments or security guards staring at us." A blinding smile warmed his voice and face.

"Humans, ask your vampire partners one place they'd like to visit someday," Clemmins ordered. I did.

Sike crossed one of his ankles over a wiry thigh, his dark brown eyes thoughtful as he leaned back. "My grandpa told me about a place where humans give money to walk around and eat food, and ride on machines that go up and down. And people dress in animal costumes, like mice and ducks."

I blinked a few times. "Are you talking about Disneyland?"

"Yeah! That was it. I just found it fascinating—dressing up like another animal for fun—and paying currency to see it. It makes no sense." He smiled, scratching his sandy brown curls.

I laughed. "Well, it's a real thing. And I guess it is kind of weird."

"And, yeah, at some point I'd like to go home. But everybody gets homesick, right?" he said lightheartedly, though his eyes lost their amusement.

My chest tightened and I nodded. "I can understand that."

Louise suddenly leaned into our conversation. "By home you mean the Immortal Plane, right?" she asked Sike under her breath. "What other things live in the Immortal Plane?" Louise was usually not this assertive unless provoked—and something sparkled in her eyes as she spoke to him.

Sike gazed at Louise with a small smile but returned his eyes to me without responding, lacing his fingers in his lap. A very polite—if not slightly cocky—wordless "no."

At the head of the room, Clemmins advised the pairs to reverse the question.

"This is like interspecies speed dating," Roxy muttered from a few seats to my side. That caused a laugh to explode out of Grayson, and he clapped a hand to his mouth to muffle it.

"Where do you want to visit?" Sike asked, with genuine interest.

"I've always wanted to visit the Amazon rainforest," I said, trying to smooth things over. "There's sadly not much of it left, but there are so many different kinds of animals in one place. It's an amazing ecosystem." I caught Dorian looking at me from the corner of his eye a few feet away, and I smiled, thinking back to our conversation in his cave room about vampires' place in the universe.

"Wow. That's a part of Earth I've never been to, either. Sounds fascinating," Sike said thoughtfully.

Beside us, Sarah asked Dorian about the Immortal Plane, too. "Why did you have to leave the Immortal Plane?" she murmured, her hushed voice thrumming with curious excitement. I couldn't hear Dorian's response, but I saw his face turn to stone. Sarah didn't seem to notice his discomfort, because she continued asking for more details, whether she received them or not. She'd been painfully inquisitive during briefs when she first joined the Bureau, but Bryce had quickly put a stop to that.

Apparently, I was doing a better job of hiding my biting curiosity than my teammates that morning. The others didn't know as well as I did that the vampires were discreet about their homeland. Honestly, if I hadn't seen the Immortal Plane with my own eyes, my curiosity would consume me, too. It's not every day you hear about another plane of existence.

Clemmins rustled his papers again, as if that would somehow relieve the room's awkward mood. "New activity. Humans, find the vampire closest to you whom you haven't spoken with yet."

"It was a pleasure getting to know you a bit more, Lyra," Sike said, that beaming smile unfading. "Do humans do this when saying good-bye, too?" he asked, extending his hand toward me for a shake.

"Yeah," I replied, giving his hand a firm grip and a few hearty shakes. "Thanks for chatting."

My new partner would be Bravi. When I looked at her, she rolled her eyes and crossed her arms. I made my way over to her.

"Hey." I offered a little wave.

She raised her eyebrows under her short black hair. *All right, then.*

"Everyone paired? Good." Clemmins heaved himself into a chair and adjusted the handgun on his waist. "This next activity is simple. Humans, you will make basic hand gestures and body movements. Vampires, you will copy everything your partner does. Got it?"

"Yes, Captain," a few soldiers replied, their voices weaker than normal. Even without looking too hard, I could see a rustle of murmurs and looks passing around the room.

"This is a little weird," I said sheepishly.

Bravi raised her eyebrows again and nodded. "You gonna start?"

I looked down at my hands and decided on a series of movements. I placed my palms together like a prayer. She followed. I raised my right hand to the ceiling and splayed my fingers. She didn't miss a beat.

As I continued moving, extending my arms and even raising my feet here and there, she never paused or delayed. It was like she already knew what I was going to do—like looking in a mirror. What shook me a little was that, unlike Rhome and Sike, Bravi never once broke eye contact. At all. I wasn't sure she even blinked.

"You're really good at this," I said, masking my nervousness.

"It isn't exactly hard." She scoffed. "You move so damn slowly."

"Ah." I pursed my lips, hoping the remaining time would pass quickly. So far, this exercise confused me, but I assumed the purpose would become clear. I glanced at a camera directly behind Bravi's head, still uncomfortable with being watched.

"Switch it up." Clemmins waved a hand. "Vampires make gestures and humans emulate." Then I got it, and the rest of the exercise supported my suspicion.

Bravi began immediately. Her movements were fluid, effortless. I'd seen a few tai chi tutorials in my combat training, and she could've put the demonstrators to shame. I held her eyes just as she had mine, but I couldn't keep up. I couldn't close the constant delay between us, no matter how hard I focused. She kept her face still, but her vibrant green eyes laughed at me.

The scientists were testing the difference between our reflexes, but how did they plan to use that information?

"Good, moving on." Captain Clemmins opened a new manila folder.

This time, Clemmins had the entire room count off in threes. The vampires seemed confused by the practice but caught on quickly. I got paired with my brother and Dorian.

"Howdy," Zach said as Dorian joined us.

"Hello." Dorian's voice sounded like sandpaper. Apparently, he'd worked out the last exercise, too. Between that and the intrusive questions, I guessed he was finding his plan more painful in practice than in theory.

I eyed him. "Nice to see you, too."

Dorian made a clear effort to shake off his mood, rolling his shoulders back and offering us a thin smile.

"Listen to the questions I pose and discuss how you feel about them amongst yourselves," Captain Clemmins ordered.

Dutifully, the three of us found empty chairs and pulled them together.

"First question. What is the most important thing about being alive?" Clemmins asked.

"Oh, that's easy," Zach said. "Always being right."

Dorian stared at him, unamused.

"I'm kidding." Zach returned his expression. I winced internally. Humorless was Zach's least favorite kind of person. "My real answer is doing what one feels is right. Sticking to one's convictions, and so on. Yada yada. What about you, Lyra?" He turned a questioning gaze on me.

"I'd say, uh... helping others," I replied with a shrug. That answer came to me pretty easily, given it was what I'd basically dedicated my life to doing.

I glanced at Dorian. He remained quiet, eyes watchful. If I were in his position, I would probably act the same, gathering as much information as I could before deciding how to act. But that wasn't the point of an icebreaker.

I cracked a grin, hoping to thaw him out. "You're so talkative today."

"The most important thing about being alive is seeking the truth and acting on it," he replied after a pause. He gave me a searching look. Vampires probably didn't do icebreakers.

Zach and I sat in thought for a moment, and I decided to play a little further into this game. Dorian clearly needed loosening up.

Sure, what he said was important, but was it the *most* important?

"I would think you'd agree with that idea, Lyra," Dorian continued before I could voice my thoughts. He met my eyes. He was trying.

"I mean... as long as it helps people." I smiled at him, but I was not budging on my answer. I thought Zach's answer was important, too.

"Eh, some are lost causes, though," Zach said. "Like that Kane guy. Who shoved a stick up his butt?"

Dorian narrowed his eyes on my brother. "Kane has reasons for being the way he is. I may not agree with him all the time, but he is justified in disliking this situation."

I glanced at Zach. He had raised an eyebrow.

Dorian set his hands on his knees and let out a slow breath. "Imagine if vampires slaughtered your father in front of your eyes and then forced you to open up to them on a video recording in between locking you in a cell. Oh, and they wouldn't let you eat for six weeks."

Zach nodded and sighed softly. "Yeah, I get that. It's not ideal."

Dorian wet his lips. "Yes, his behavior isn't always helpful. I agree with you there. But his attitude is understandable."

Zach nodded, taking that in for a moment. Just when I thought we were going to move on to something else, he looked Dorian in the eye again.

"On the other side of things... imagine if humans considered you so mentally and physically inferior that they used your species as a food source and didn't feel any qualms about it. Imagine that they crippled your uncle and nearly killed him." Zach leaned forward, his tone level.

In my mind, I saw my uncle's beaming smile falter because of his pained limping. The image punched me in the gut.

"What I'm saying is, we've all got beef, you know?" Zach said, his face serious. "I'm not thrilled that I have to hang out with the guy who kidnapped my sister. We just need to work it out and set our crap aside."

Zach leaned back in his chair and crossed his arms, mirroring Dorian's body language. Dorian studied him, expressionless. Then he raised his eyebrows and offered a nod in acknowledgement. Each had valid points—and their eyes met in unspoken understanding.

I opened my mouth to move the conversation on, but Clemmins interrupted.

"Next question." His voice broke my focus. "Everyone in the group tell a joke."

"What do you call a guy with a rubber toe?" My brother started us off with his worst, and I was already rolling my eyes before the punch-line. "Roberto!"

Zach chortled, and Dorian looked confused.

"Okay." I jumped in. "So, an amnesiac walks into a bar. He goes up to a pretty lady and asks, 'Do I come here often?'"

Zach snorted even though he'd taught me that one. I took a quick glance around, and my ears told me that this rather dubious approach wasn't totally off. Laughter filtered across from the other sides of the room. Roxy and Bravi, to my surprise, were making silly hand gestures at each other. Louise was trying to explain knock-knock jokes to Sike. Clemmins watched the groups, smiling even while his sharp eyes analyzed the scene. Dorian scanned the room as well, and I could see his body slowly relax, his broad shoulders leaning farther back into his chair, causing it to creak. I felt my body emulate his growing ease, a little wave of relief flowing through me.

"Dorian, you got one?" Zach asked him, his voice fully returned to its natural lighthearted timbre.

"I picked up a human joke a while back," Dorian responded carefully, the shadow of a smile playing on his lips. "What is a vampire's favorite fruit?"

We waited.

"A blood orange." He grinned at his feet.

"Wow," Zach said, through a wide-eyed laugh. Apparently, Dorian had redeemed his earlier lack of humor with his bravery.

"Interesting setting for that one," I replied.

This time, Dorian smirked at me, holding my eyes so long I felt a flush rise from my chest. I broke his gaze and cleared my throat in the quiet.

I noticed Zach's gaze bounce between me and Dorian. He cleared his throat, and it looked like he was about to say something, when Clemmins cut in.

"Okay, time to break," Clemmins called, rising slowly from his chair. "Vampires, please line up and file out to the hall. Guards will escort you back to your quarters. Soldiers, you have an hour to yourselves, then we have another activity session scheduled."

Dorian rose to his feet. "See you soon," he said to us both. Then he turned directly to me, his tone softening. "I really look forward to it."

My blushing reached my ears. "Me, too," I replied gently. As he walked away, I almost wished Clemmins had a few more sheets of those ridiculous questions.

Zach leaned back in his chair, squinting inquisitively at me. I didn't offer a response, instead focusing on calming my blush.

I wasn't sure if I imagined it, but I could have sworn the other vampires left looking less dejected than when they entered, too. They seemed to carry themselves with more ease, like Dorian. My teammates definitely did. I was relieved that the discomfort of the activity hadn't totally ruined everyone's interactions.

Zach stayed by my side as we headed back to our side of the facility.

"That was... interesting," he remarked as we stepped out into the echoing, cement-walled main hallway.

"Yeah, a week ago I'd never have imagined answering psychological analysis questions with mutually embarrassed vampires," I replied, shaking my head. This stuff made workplace sensitivity training look so much less awkward in comparison.

"That's not what I meant," Zach said pointedly, and I turned to quirk a brow at him. "You and Dorian. You guys seem to get along... pretty well." His voice undulated with not-so-subtle insinuation.

I stopped, not wanting to be overheard by someone who didn't understand Zach's creative sense of humor. *Like Roxy.*

"Well," I replied flatly, turning to face him fully, "we've had more time to get to know each other, due to the circumstances."

If he was smart about this, my brother would read between the lines. *Drop it, dumbass.*

"Oh. I suppose so."

Nope. Zach was wearing his condescending older brother look. His I-know-what's-*really*-going-on-here look.

"I guess it doesn't mean anything that he didn't crack a smile once during the 'activities,'" he went on. "Except when he was looking at you."

My stomach did a little flip. Dorian had to have smiled other times during the exercise, right? Zach was obviously exaggerating. I rolled my eyes. Was he seriously suggesting I was flirting with a vampire?

"Believe it or not, Dorian is a lot like you and me," I replied tartly. "He wants what's best for everyone. And we're *friendly* because we both want this alliance to work. That cooperation has got to start somewhere." *Honestly.* Zach could push my buttons like no one else on Earth. *As if.* He knew better than anyone that I'd never had the time, or real interest, for dating—and I didn't intend for that to change, especially over a *vampire.* He must've wet his Cheerios with booze that morning.

"Okay, that's a totally fair point," my brother replied, nodding, his tone evening out.

I eyed him. "I think that if you got to know each other more, you and Dorian would get along," I said, firmly changing the subject.

"You're probably right. Guy has good jokes." Zach gave one last smile and then walked to his quarters.

I shook my head and headed back to my bunk to try and take a power nap, pushing Zach firmly out of my head. I hoped I would be able to sleep. My mind was already busy, dissecting everything the vampires had said to me, analyzing and categorizing and wondering whether all this hokey teambuilding could really make a significant difference.

After the day's activities ended and evening fell, I found myself sitting cross-legged on the floor of the communal area, staring at Rhome across the chess board I'd scrounged up. He watched seriously as I demonstrated the different ways his rook could take my pawn. Dorian sat nearby with Bravi, Sike, and Roxy—Bravi explaining to Roxy in intimidating detail what it was like to ride a redbill. As I knocked over a piece and Rhome nodded intently, Louise found a way to join their conversation, pulling her chair next to Sike.

"Sike, what's your favorite part about flying?" Louise asked him. I wondered if she'd had too much coffee that day; she was so assertive. I mean, she was always matter-of-fact, but she wasn't usually the type to approach someone who was basically a stranger and start an unannounced game of Twenty Questions with them.

"Well, I'll just have to show you sometime," Sike replied, turning in his seat to face her. "My bird and I have this fantastic spinning trick we're working on."

Everything felt... well, almost comfortable amongst the sixteen or so evenly split humans and vampires.

The two groups had been scheduled for "free activity time" together in the meeting room, and I'd taken advantage of it to make good on my promise to Rhome. On the other hand, not everybody took the opportunity at face value. Some soldiers clustered together in a corner, chatting in low voices. Some of the more aloof vampires did the same, like the young brunette named Rayne, talking only to their peers. The older gentleman vampire named Thoth sat by himself, reading a *National Geographic* magazine. Kane and Halla just sat silently near the door, obviously waiting to go back to their quarters.

I watched Thoth for a moment, and then quietly asked Rhome how vampires learned to read in English.

"Vampires have a universal understanding of languages, kind of like the way we have a natural understanding of how to communicate with redbills," Rhome answered quietly, his eyes fixed on the chessboard. "To be honest, from being able to inherently speak languages, putting alphabets together and understanding them comes easily to us. We read lots of things... well, mostly whatever we can get our hands on these days." He cleared his throat after he finished his soft-spoken thought, then took my pawn with his rook in a way that I hadn't realized he could. I raised my eyebrows and gave him two thumbs up. He smiled, his canines glinting.

These creatures are intimidatingly intelligent.

"Well, isn't this a lovely picture," Captain Bryce chirped, walking in just as I finished my rook tutorial. He took in the room and nodded contentedly. "Clemmins says things went decently well today. I have to agree, from what I saw." He'd been in the surveillance room most of the day—I'd only spotted him after lunch when he invited a Bureau staffing manager into his office.

He looked around the room and set his hands on his belt. "And that's a good thing," he announced. "Because tomorrow is our first fieldtrip."

CHAPTER NINETEEN

The night passed peacefully, and, despite our extra-early bugle call, lively voices filled the halls the next morning. We'd been given twenty minutes to get ready and eat breakfast. I didn't usually need a ton of time to get myself ready for the day, but that was even difficult for me to work with. And then, at five thirty a.m., we convened with the vampires in the main meeting room.

By the time my team found their chairs in the room, the vampires were already seated, the same group we'd done exercises with the day before. I waved good morning to everyone, and I was happy to see the white-blonde female vampire, Harlowe, wave back. A few of them looked groggy, like Bravi, who was probably still adjusting to waking up to a screaming bugle. I noticed several vampires missing, including Halla... again. Of course, she was injured, so it made sense that she wouldn't be going out on "field trips" just yet—she was probably with the children. But I couldn't imagine she was disappointed to stay behind, either. Kane, on the other hand, had decided to suffer us again. He sat crouched in a chair at the back.

The captains filed in after my group and talked amongst themselves at the front of the room for half a minute. Then Finley took a seat, surveying the room with an expressionless face, while Bryce and Clemmins remained standing. Bryce called us to order.

"Good morning, teams," he said, his tone unusually chipper. "Right to it. We have an op today. We've received intelligence that a cluster of bills has gathered in the Franklin Mountains in Texas. This is an imminent threat to the city of El Paso."

My eyes roamed in search of Dorian, and I spotted him listening expressionlessly on the other side of the room.

"Our teams will be working together to eliminate that threat," Bryce continued. "All of you have been cleared by the medic for this op, although some will need to take it easy." He eyed Sike, who feigned awkwardness and tried to hide his very obviously wrapped arm, which pulled some giggles from the room. "We will travel via aircraft to the location. The vampires will take the lead in persuading the flock to leave the area. Vampires, we trust that you can discuss and organize amongst yourselves how best to achieve this."

I heard whispering and glanced back. Bravi and Rhome had leaned toward Dorian and appeared to be questioning him about something.

"We had special tags made for this operation and the ones that follow. These bands"—Bryce raised what looked like a bright yellow plastic bracelet—"will need to be placed around the ankles of each redbill that is… safely contained, for tracking purposes. We need to know which ones we've interacted with so that we can monitor their behavior post-op."

The three vampires were still whispering, and now Kreya leaned into their conversation as well. I strained unsuccessfully to hear their words. *What are they talking about?* Captain Finley eyed them.

"Captain Bryce, please forgive our interruption." Dorian finally spoke up, clearly and calmly. "We request to ride our redbills to the location."

Bryce's face grew stern, and he frowned at him, then exchanged a look with the other captains. "Mr. Clave." He cleared his throat. "It is clearly stated in the regulations of this trial period that vampires must be monitored at all times. If you are riding man-eating storks, we obviously can't supervise properly."

By now the rest of the soldiers on my team had also pivoted in their seats, their eyes glued to Dorian in a mix of curiosity and confusion. I was perplexed by Dorian's request. *Maybe I'll see Dorian get his head bitten off by Bryce for the first time today.*

"We understand and honor the requirements of the trial period," Dorian responded, his voice clear and unintimidated. "But we believe the other flock of redbills will be easier to persuade if we arrive with some of their own kind, demonstrating our trustworthiness."

Captain Clemmins raised an eyebrow and looked at Bryce. "Interesting thought," he muttered.

Dorian's point was valid. And to be fair, the vampires knew a lot more about the inner workings of redbills than we did, regardless of how many missions we'd been on in the past. To me, treading lightly and carefully in the beginning was logical.

Finley stood up and placed her hands on her hips, a few red curls falling out of their tight bun. "Out of the question. Captain Bryce has already told you that it's unacceptable by the terms of our agreement. Not to mention dangerous to everyone else."

I met Bryce's eyes, raised a hand, and waited. He gestured for me to speak. My throat tensed a little with nerves, but I cleared my throat, found my confidence, and briefly caught Dorian's crystalline blue eyes before speaking.

"With respect, Captains," I started, "the vampires understand these creatures better than we do. Their thoughts should be taken into account when strategizing. Why don't we compromise? Each vampire can ride a redbill accompanied by a soldier. It might even be safer this way. A Bureau aircraft on its own might antagonize the wild bills. Besides, the vampires will need to have soldiers with comms close by to ensure we all know what's going on."

Finley's jaw clenched visibly. "Lieutenant Sloane, you have a very interesting definition of 'safer.'"

Bryce held up a hand, still frowning. "Just hold it. Finley, Clemmins... outside, please."

The captains walked into the hallway and shut the door behind them. The security guards at the door held their eyes steady on the vampires.

"Ballsy. I like it," I heard Roxy mutter under her breath.

I smiled at my feet. When I looked up, into Dorian's eyes, he gave a deliberate nod of thanks. Laini smiled softly, and even Rayne gave me a long, considering look.

Captains Bryce and Clemmins re-entered first, and Finley followed, wearing a frown and tightly crossed arms.

"Mr. Clave," Clemmins began. "Is Lieutenant Sloane's proposal acceptable to you?"

I raised my eyebrows and turned back to Dorian. I watched the vampires with anticipation, hoping that they'd found my suggestion helpful. He murmured something to the others, then, after a few moments, faced the captains again.

"We accept," he said. "We will communicate with each soldier on safe practices and what to expect during flight."

"Right." Bryce clapped a hand on his chest and energetically drummed his fingers against his uniform. "Vampires, you will also be tagged during this operation. In case you get... lost, we'll be happy to track you down. Remember that your cooperation is necessary for your cause to be considered."

"That will not be an issue, Captain," Dorian replied, without expression.

"Good. We stipulate that your redbills will not fly faster than the Bureau aircraft that will escort us with more soldiers, guards, and artillery."

"That's fine. However, we hope to resolve this peacefully, Captain," Dorian said.

"Don't we all," Bryce replied sternly, but his eyes gleamed with excitement. Thinking back to the enthusiasm he'd shown when describing vampires the other night, before Dorian burst onto the scene, I figured he must be beyond thrilled at the thought of getting to see the vampires and redbills *both* in action right off the bat. It'd probably been a secret dream of his for years. "But if you're about to ask us to go unarmed, you can save your breath."

Dorian paused, and I noticed his slender hands tighten over the back of Bravi's seat in front of him. "I ask that you please allow us to handle the creatures as we deem fit, and only use weaponry as a last resort," he replied. His words may have been deferential, but his tone was anything but.

All around me, soldiers' eyes widened. If Dorian had been a soldier, Bryce would have had his head mounted to a wall by now for sure. Dorian's vampirism was certainly saving him here.

"We will do what we need to do in order to keep our soldiers safe," Bryce growled. "Is that understood?"

"Yes, Captain." Dorian nodded curtly. "I simply ask that weapons be avoided if possible. As part of our compromise."

Clemmins cleared his throat. "We hear you, Mr. Clave. Thank you. Bryce, why don't we continue the brief?"

Dorian leaned back in his chair, pushing his dark hair back from his forehead, but I couldn't tell from his face whether he was satisfied with the interaction or not. The vampires remained silent for the remainder of the meeting. Part of me worried that Bryce had pushed some unnecessary buttons, but I reminded myself that the vampires knew the stipulations before agreeing to the trial. This could hardly be unexpected.

We went directly to the tarmac at the end of the meeting, and I felt tension build up in my chest that we were actually *doing* this. I was equal parts excited and anxious. While the soldiers hung back near the aircraft to prepare with Bryce, the vampires walked across the pavement with security guards to where they planned to "summon" their birds. Some soldiers looked uneasy with the plan—especially Gina, who had started biting her nails. Sure, I was nervous, but my previous flying experience probably took some of the edge off.

A group of redbills soon flew toward us, drifting low over the sand and the few blooming desert bushes. The sun was already beating. The vampires moved to greet the birds, some calling out to them, names and growls.

"Soldiers assigned to redbills, double-check your weapons and munitions if you haven't already, then please join your vampire," Clemmins directed.

Bryce's face was hard, as usual, but the spark hadn't left his eyes. Every time I spotted it, more of my anxiety turned to thrill. Sike slouched beside him, his expression somewhat miffed. Due to his injury, he would have to ride in the plane for the operation.

As we approached the vampires, some of the redbills tossed their heads and screeched. Louise's pace faltered, but she quickly recovered. That was the tough, quiet girl I knew. I made sure to keep my footsteps steady, as I didn't want the redbills to think they had the upper hand. Some of the other soldiers' hands hovered over their handguns, which made a lot of the vampires fidget.

With barely a conscious decision, I found myself gravitating toward Dorian and his bird. Roxy went to Bravi, Gina to Rhome, and Zach to Kreya. Sarah had the guts to cautiously approach Kane, who spoke to her without looking at her. Her face turned from eager to apprehensive as Kane instructed her, but she maintained intense focus. Each of the vampires, in turn, accepted yellow tags that the Bureau guards affixed around their ankles. Thoth even bent over to help the guard adjust his. Harlowe said "Thank you" once she'd received her tag. For as cold and bitter as some of the vampires were, it seemed to be evenly balanced by the others' manners.

"We meet again," I said to Dorian and his bird. Dorian's shoulders were held squared and confident under his cloak, and he rolled up the thick cream fabric of his sleeves. The bird tossed its head and snapped, looking less than pleased at my arrival, insofar as I could guess any emotions in that round, red eye.

"Lieutenant Sloane, I ask that you refrain from pulling feathers, making sudden noises, or making forceful movements around our friend here," he said formally.

"Yes, Captain," I replied, holding back the beginnings of a smile.

"Please maintain a safe hold on me until we've landed," he continued. "Happy to be here on Redbill Airlines."

A soft chuckle caught in Dorian's throat. I tightened my gloves and adjusted my handgun holster.

All around us on the tarmac, other vampires taught soldiers to mount the birds. Dorian simply leapt onto his and stretched out his hand. I took it and slid up behind him, with a weird wave of déjà-vu.

Some of the storks eyed the Bureau aircraft as its propeller blades thrummed. The boarding doors rolled closed as soon as captains, security soldiers, and backup soldiers finished boarding. I adjusted my comm, trying to focus on the mission ahead and not fidget. I hadn't forgotten what flying on this bird was like, so I braced myself as best I could.

"Let's hope this works." Dorian turned his head toward me, his eyes indicating the small plane. "There are a few unpredictable elements."

"Well, we won't know unless we try," I murmured, my mouth becoming drier the closer we got to takeoff. I mentally checked myself and didn't let Dorian's comment get under my skin. It was time to focus.

"Redbill soldiers, sound off when prepared for flight," Captain Bryce's voice barked in my ear.

"First Lieutenant Lyra Sloane ready for flight," I replied, my heartbeat quickening.

"First Lieutenant Zach Sloane ready to fly," Zach added.

As everyone else indicated their readiness, the aircraft pulled off to the right and accelerated down the strip. Our bill watched it warily.

"Redbill soldiers follow post-takeoff," Bryce ordered.

"Follow the plane," I said in Dorian's ear.

He nodded. He cracked his knuckles above his head, just like I did sometimes, and brushed his hair from his face. He moved his legs closer up under the bill's wings and tightened his grip. I followed his lead without being told.

The airplane's wheels left the pavement and it curved into the sky, ascending sharply until it banked toward our destination. I cautiously put my arms around Dorian's firm waist, my fingers now positively tingling from the nerves. I thought I felt him lean back into my chest. My heart was already racing, but it quickened again. Was he doing that on purpose? The thought seemed ridiculous to me—or at least I immediately convinced myself it was ridiculous, so I tossed it from my mind.

Our redbill ran first, and in the sudden bouncing I almost bit my tongue. We were followed closely by the rest of the flock. I glanced back and spotted Zach grinning over Kreya's shoulder.

All around me, wings extended, flapping loudly. When our bird leapt into the air, I tightened my arms around Dorian's waist. We ascended rapidly, closing in on the plane.

As the facility drifted away below us, the redbill's ascent straightened, the desert expanding around us as far as I could see. My stomach clenched, but this was nowhere near as bad as the first time. Maybe it was possible to get used to this.

The redbills eased into a V-shaped formation a safe distance from the aircraft, pulling back their initial speed. Our bird led the flock. I caught myself smiling—Dorian led the vampires, and his redbill led the birds.

I wore my sunglasses under my helmet this time, so the bright sunlight didn't blind me. The slower traveling speed made this… almost pleasant, compared to the rides I'd taken with Dorian previously. *Not too much déjà vu after all.* I watched the sand beneath us turn to hills, then back to sand. Mountains loomed on the horizon.

"Traveling by plane must take ages." Dorian spoke for the first time over the wind.

"Some people enjoy transportation that doesn't make you sick or deaf," I retorted, and felt his diaphragm move just slightly under my hands as he chuckled.

I watched the side of his face as he looked over the approaching mountain range. His ivory jaw was flawless, and it occurred to me that he didn't have a single sign of stubble. Ripples under his skin danced under his jaw and up toward his ears, constantly in motion. I didn't know if that feature of vampires would ever cease to fascinate me.

The cobalt sky was endless and cloudless. The sun continued to rise in the northeast, slowly turning cobalt to turquoise. Sepia peaks dotted the horizon. And after a while, I found myself wondering what it would feel like to hold onto Dorian without the metal breastplate of my suit between us. Would I feel his heartbeat? Did he even have a heartbeat?

I blinked the thought away. There was *much* about him that I still didn't know, but I needed to focus on the approaching mission, run scenarios in my head.

As trees and soil blurred together at the base of the mountains, my mind continued to wander. And soon I was thinking back to my previous conversation with Rhome about the redbills. *Maybe I should allow myself to just enjoy the ride.*

"Rhome told me a bit about communicating with redbills yesterday," I called, attempting to make myself heard without literally shouting into his ear. "Can you hear the redbills speaking to you?"

"It's not exactly hearing," Dorian replied, his voice strained. He tilted his head so the wind wouldn't snatch his words away. A few strands of his black hair whipped around the side of his face, the sunlight illuminating a shine of sepia undertone. "It's a feeling. We think in words, sometimes, but a lot of what we sense from them is feeling. We've been linked to these creatures for ages, which has created a lot of closeness in our communication."

I scrunched my nose, trying to understand. I guessed what Dorian was describing was a kind of sixth sense, another mode of perception? When I thought of it that way, it did make more sense.

I lost track of time as the sun rose higher, and I decided not to distract Dorian with more questions. Even with his enhanced hearing, the guy struggled to hear me over the wind, and I didn't fancy drying my mouth out with more yelling.

The mountains soon pulled away behind us, and the desert sprawled out ahead, seemingly endless. A few buildings speckled the landscape here and there as we passed.

Finally, my comm buzzed in my ear.

"ETA ten minutes," Bryce's voice announced. "Surveillance has indicated that the target redbills are in flight. Soldiers, inform vampires."

I checked the watch under the lip of my glove. We'd been in the air just under an hour.

"We'll be there soon," I said loudly in Dorian's ear. "The other flock is in the air, too."

"Got it," he replied as he turned his ear toward my mouth. My lips nearly brushed his earlobe. I didn't lean back immediately. The sky had fully brightened, and the mountains diminished to mounds. As the minutes ticked past, Dorian's back grew more rigid, and I wondered what he was thinking. My folded hands on his stomach rose and fell with his quickening breaths. *Definitely nervous... at least a little.*

My own tension heightened in response.

"Target flock spotted at three o'clock," Bryce shot over the comm.

I narrowed my eyes and found a tiny cluster of black dots weaving through the sky in the distance. "Do you see them?" I asked Dorian tightly.

"I've got them," he replied.

We drew closer as the birds calmly circled in the air. I wondered what Dorian and the other vampires would "say" to them. Although the other redbills didn't seem bothered by our approach, Dorian remained tense.

One of the larger wild birds' wings banked, its beak angled toward our group. Even through the wind, I could hear the piercing screams as it signaled to its companions. The rest of the flock dipped and wove faster. They all saw us now.

Their screeching intensified, a raucous chorus that grated on my ears even at a distance. I managed not to flinch, though the sound made my insides quiver.

"What's going on?" I shouted.

Dorian didn't respond right away. He jerked his head to each side, locking eyes with Rhome and Bravi on our flanks.

Before us, the wild flock gathered into a tight cluster. They rapidly beat their wings to hover, snapping their beaks in all directions. I glanced behind us at the other birds in our formation, noting worried glances from other soldiers. Nevertheless, our redbills continued to approach at a steady pace.

And that's when the biggest bill zeroed in and launched itself at us.

"They think we're dangerous," Dorian yelled, his arms stiffening against his body and around my own arms. "They're confused by the humans and the plane. Hold on and keep your face covered!"

The other vampires shouted to their passengers, and I saw Gina brace her head against Rhome's back. Our redbills trilled to each other, a sound which quickly escalated into cries.

The other flock attacked.

Dorian had just enough time to fire a sharp glare back at me. "Lyra! Head down!"

As I tucked my chin, our bird went into freefall. From the corner of my eye, I saw the rest of our team follow, their birds tightening their wings against their bodies. I caught snippets of the enemy bills closing in, diving to pursue us. Kane and Kreya's birds spiraled and bolted out to the sides while we held our course, the approaching earth getting larger and larger.

I swallowed. Dorian and his bill wouldn't let us smash into the ground, would they? I peered back at our flanks. Some of the attacking birds split off and chased our team, but I still heard wings hammering behind us. *I hope he knows what the hell he's doing.*

At the last minute, as the ground took up my vision, our bird went into a spin so violent it detached my helmet. The sky and ground bled into one jolting picture. I clung to Dorian, the only sense I had of the rest of the battle coming from my comm hissing in my ear.

"We're under attack!" Roxy hollered, as if anyone could have failed to notice.

With a stomach-rolling jolt, our bird straightened, then swooped upward again. I no longer heard wingbeats behind us, but as I opened my eyes, five other wild bills zipped past us.

The confronting flocks screamed at each other. Above us, an attacker snapped at Rhome's bird's wing. I didn't see if the attack landed, but the bird dropped, quickly passing us on their way to the ground. I prayed it was on purpose. I feared it wasn't.

I pressed my finger to my comm. "Captain, we're taking hits!" I yelled.

"Cover each other if you can! We're dropping the ladder so soldiers can get off the birds!" Clemmins cut through.

I watched Dorian's head turn as his eyes caught sight of a ladder dropping from the plane, and, as if in sync with his gaze, our bird suddenly swung toward the aircraft.

Then I heard an explosion. A grenade tumbled toward the earth, and its target redbill dove toward us, serrated beak open. Dorian let out a deep growl, just like the first I'd ever heard from him at the church. Our bill dropped so fast I lifted from my seat for a second.

By now every bird was screeching, including Dorian's, the sound deafening at this range. I heard machine gun fire from the direction of the craft—and the blast of the second grenade.

"The weapons are scaring our redbills. They're not listening!" Dorian bellowed over his shoulder, and I glanced back up at the plane. The enemy birds chased our bills away from the ladder.

"Can you keep the bird steady? I'll get a ceasefire," I cried. I watched the back of Dorian's head nod. "Soldiers, hold fire! We're scaring our own bills," I snapped into my comm.

I glanced around again as our bird tried to ascend. A wild redbill swooped toward us from the right, gaining on us quickly with huge wingbeats.

"Dorian! Try to divert the flock's attention! If they chase us, the others can get away."

Dorian said nothing, but his body stiffened in what seemed like fierce concentration, and he placed his hand on the back of his redbill's neck. A noise came from the bird that I'd never heard before, like train wheels screaming to an unexpected stop. It gurgled like a dragon preparing to blast fire. I could only imagine it was a redbill war call.

The enemy bird on our right closed in, but all of the others had pivoted toward us, too.

"Dive again! Dive!" I screamed.

Our bird dove as I spoke, and the wild flock fell in behind us. I held tight to Dorian and looked back. Behind the wings of the pursuit I spotted our team rising toward the plane, no longer in enemy crosshairs.

"We've got them! They're following us!" I yelled. A wave of excitement coursed through me alongside the adrenaline. Dorian responded to me so quickly it practically felt like we were connected beyond our voices.

"I'll keep this up as long as I can," he returned. Another incredibly warlike shriek escaped our bird. The enemy screamed at us from behind.

We were in total freefall again. The largest bill gained on us, staring me down from the right flank. Once again, the ground grew uncomfortably close.

"Dorian, we've got one on the right—pull left!" I shouted.

"We have to push it to throw them off our trail!" he growled back.

The lead bill snapped at our wings. I could see the saw-toothed edge of its beak as it narrowly missed our bird's outstretched feathers.

"No, Dorian, he's on us!" I screamed.

I saw brush and trees, closer than they had been before—this time, surely, we were going to crash. I opened my mouth to tell Dorian, when something slammed into my back, adding an instant pressure. I cried out, all the air escaping my lungs and my eyes clenching shut.

Through the pain, I felt our bird bank left, sailing on its side. I wrenched my eyes open, blinking back tears to stare into the sky. Above us now, the enemy birds, including the one just pursuing us, pulled back. Then they were whisked out of my frame of vision as we straightened out and whizzed over low-growing brush—so close I could have touched it, scraggly trees whizzing by to our right and left.

The pressure on my back remained. I realized whatever had hit me —likely a beak—had damaged or dented my armor. I tried to inhale, but my throat and chest felt constricted. I yanked on my side-strap, and the back panel of my suit went careening away, followed by my now-unsecured breastplate, which clipped my chin as it bounced up off the bill's back and tumbled away. My head snapped back, and I tasted blood.

I heard Dorian curse. "Don't let go of me!"

I jerked my head forward just in time to see a thick copse of tall brush. We were heading straight into it.

The bird tried to rise at the last minute, but its feet didn't quite clear the branches—and then its solid body jerked out from under us, and we went somersaulting through the air. I lost my grip on Dorian's waist in a tangle of limbs, and we slammed into the ground and rolled together through the spiny shrubs.

Dorian took the initial impact, but our momentum kept us rolling for what felt like forever. My eyes clenched shut as branches clawed my limbs and sand pummeled my face. We slid to a stop, Dorian below me, both of us coughing in the billowing dust.

I groaned and opened my eyes.

All I saw was icy blue.

Our noses were touching. Air heaved out of me. My ears buzzed. Dorian looked paler than usual, his expression grave. His eyes felt as though they were pinning me to the desert sky.

Veins of gray threaded his irises. I felt every motion of his chest as both of us heaved out relieved breaths, still not moving. My heart thundered.

From this close, it was impossible not to notice as his gaze traced my face. His exhales tickled my neck and collarbone, the skin feeling too sensitive where my armor normally covered it. My arms began to shake.

"Your mouth is bleeding," Dorian murmured.

I blinked the dust away and rolled off him, onto my back.

Trying to recover, I quickly glanced up at the sky. Our redbill was nowhere to be seen—but another cloud of sand swirled. From a crouch, I spotted what looked like Bravi's bird swooping toward us. Roxy's absence made me hopeful that she and the other human riders had escaped into the plane.

"Are you planning on helping us or not?" she yelled. "Come on!"

Without a second's pause, Dorian and I leapt to our feet and mounted Bravi's redbill. I sat behind Bravi, and Dorian sat behind me. Her bird launched back into the sky. Dorian breathed on the back of my neck.

"The humans are in the plane. They got the gunfire to stop," Bravi shouted. "Dorian, we're dropping her off and then getting this other flock on the ground."

Her bird sped through the air to reach the plane. The vampires and their birds, now free of human passengers, encircled the enemy flock. I noticed with the slightest touch of relief that Dorian's bird flew along-side them, rider-less, seemingly uninjured from the crash. As much as I disliked that particular bird, I had to admit he had gone above and beyond on this mission. The redbills no longer screamed challenges at each other. As we passed, I heard them gurgling and chirping instead.

Our bill hoisted us higher. It lurched farther in a powerful burst, and the ladder dangled in front of us.

The bird steadied its beating wings into a rhythm, keeping us flying in place. I stretched out an open hand. The rungs were only inches away.

I leapt forward, clutching a rung with both hands, and then the bird, Bravi, and Dorian fell away below me.

For a dangerous moment I dangled, and then I growled and dragged myself up. The ladder swung in the turbulent air. I found the rungs below with my feet and started to climb.

Go. Go. Go.

A hand appeared in front of my nose. Captain Bryce gazed down at me from the airplane's side door. I clutched his offered wrist. A moment later, I landed on my knees in the plane.

"Thank you, Captain," I shouted.

He didn't respond, his steely blue eyes fixed on the vampires, whose birds still circled with the wild flock, the whole knot of them slowly descending.

"Take her down," Clemmins yelled through the comm. "Carefully."

Our plane performed a gentle, angled tilt through the sky. I peered out the open door at the vampires and the bills, all now on the ground. I couldn't see any sign of a struggle, but before I got a good look, we touched down a safe distance from the two flocks, and my view was briefly eclipsed by the angle of the plane.

The craft's wheels slipped slightly through the sand. I braced my shoulders against the wall as the plane shuddered to a stop.

Once we were stable, I placed a hand on my lower back where I'd been hit before we crashed. There was no blood, but the skin felt tender. The big bill must've rammed me; its beak had definitely dented the back plate I abandoned.

Everyone stared blankly at the floor or each other. Zach's mouth hung open a little bit. I wondered if that's what I'd looked like after my first redbill flight. No; if I was being honest, I had probably looked worse.

Pain pounded dully through my whole body from the crash. I felt around in my sore mouth with my tongue. I'd bitten my cheek when my breastplate clipped me, but it was nothing major, and the bleeding had already stopped. Dorian hadn't needed to sound so concerned.

I stepped toward the door at about the same time Captain Bryce ordered, "Soldiers, remain on the aircraft. We will monitor the situation from here." His bulky frame blocked my view.

With an exhale, I hurried to the nearest window instead, craning my neck to watch the vampires. Our bills clustered safely together off to the side, and the vampires walked steadily toward the other flock. The wild bills continued their grumbling, but eventually quieted as Dorian neared the biggest bill.

They all stood staring at each other for a time. Then, with shocking synchronicity, the vampires stepped forward and bent to secure yellow tags around each redbill's ankle. The enemy birds held still, gazing straight ahead.

"How are they doing that?" Gina mumbled from where she stood beside me, her fingers slipping strands of her blonde bob behind her ear.

One by one, the vampires straightened and stepped directly in front of the captured redbills. Dorian extended his hand and placed an open palm on the large bill's forehead, holding it there. Around him, other vampires did the same.

"They're letting the vampires touch them," Louise reported to the soldiers who didn't have a good view of the scene. Her voice and pale brown eyes displayed awe.

The wild—*formerly* wild—birds tossed their heads and leapt into the sky. They ascended, heading northwest...

"What the hell just happened?" Zach snapped.

Sike, his narrow frame sandwiched between sweaty soldiers on the airplane's bench seat, cleared his throat loudly to call attention. "They wanted to speak more clearly to the creatures. So the flock would know what we're asking them to do."

"What do you mean?" Louise asked, the wind throwing her long hair around her shoulders.

"When vampires touch a redbill, it helps them hear each other better. Like leaning in, when someone's whispering. It enhances the connection, I guess." Sike shrugged, blinking his dark brown eyes a few times. "You won't see those bills again. They're headed home."

The surrounding soldiers exchanged looks. Sike's words excited me, and I couldn't help but shoot Zach a thumbs up, which he enthusiastically returned. The entire wild flock was only a collection of dots in the distance. The vampires walked toward the plane, their redbills plodding along behind them. Captain Bryce jumped out the door to speak with them.

"Travel back with us… monitor…" I heard over the idling engine.

The vampires boarded the plane, Rhome and Kreya first. Rhome lifted his partner through the doorway, though I was pretty sure she didn't need help. Bryce sidled in around them, returning to his station before the cockpit entrance.

"Soldiers, make room for our friends," my captain ordered.

Everyone, vampires and humans alike, looked around at each other, winded but excited—or relieved. Some of the vampire-human pairs gave high fives. An intense gratitude filled my chest, and I made a point to shake hands with every single one of my new vampiric teammates.

We shuffled about until everyone found a seat. Soldiers leaned their heads back and closed their eyes. Vampires sat stoically, gazing at their knees. I felt a buzz flicker through me. This had been a much more effective teambuilding exercise than the previous day.

The aircraft's propellers whirred, and we eased into the sky.

For some reason, I didn't dare look at Dorian until we were well into our flight. I watched him for a moment, and then his eyes found mine. I snapped my gaze away.

What had happened back there? Why were my fingers still tingling, my chest pounding? Even when I avoided looking at him or forced myself to think about something else, the feeling didn't go away. At all.

I kept my eyes closed the rest of the way back to the facility.

Maybe Zach had seen something I hadn't.

CHAPTER TWENTY

I t was only early afternoon when we returned to the facility, but the desert heat rippled on the tarmac. As we deboarded, Bryce announced a meeting to recap the mission.

All of us, humans and vampires, quietly seated ourselves in the main meeting room. The intensity of the morning hadn't worn off. I sat in the front row to avoid eye contact with anyone. My stomach knotted with nerves, remembering Dorian's breath flowing over me.

After a brief word in the main hallway, the captains entered, pulling at the dark green sleeves of their still-starched uniforms. Their eyes were exhilarated—even Finley's seemed brighter, the first time I'd seen her look anything other than stern, though her military bun was as tight as always.

"Well, we hit a few snags. Some of us literally," Bryce said as he surveyed the room. He threw a sarcastic glance in my general direction, and I tried my hardest not to fidget.

"But I'd like to congratulate everyone on a successful first inter-species mission," Bryce continued from the front of the room. "Overall, the redbill response to the vampire interaction was positive. I've spoken with the other captains and sent word to the board. El Paso doesn't know what you've done for them, but if they did, I'm sure they'd thank you."

It seemed we would avoid a Stripping. The soldiers' shoulders sank with relief, and a few vampires nodded to each other.

Zach raised his hand. Bryce allowed him to speak.

"How often should we expect these types of missions, Captain?" my brother asked, barely masking the hesitancy in his voice.

Finley was the one who answered. "It would be wise to expect this to be a regular occurrence," she said, her green eyes serious. "Some of these missions will be planned in advance, but you will be on call at all times."

"I know the board will be impressed with everyone's work today, so expect to maintain standards," Clemmins added.

"And should we plan for more… um, 'structured social activities' this afternoon if we don't get called out to the field again?" Gina added, her tension mirroring my brother's.

Bryce's eyes sparkled. All the captains seemed pleased, but he looked almost gleeful. He simply couldn't hide his enchantment with the vampires anymore. *Just let it out, you fanboy.*

"Seeing how everyone's getting along so well, we will continue social activities," he said. "But this time, I think we should go outside and stretch our legs. We'll meet on the tarmac in forty-five minutes."

I studied Bryce, searching for any clues about what he had in store for us, but his usual stoicism returned. Kane rubbed his eyes irritably, but Dorian and Rhome exchanged nods. Gina raised her eyebrows in my direction, and I returned the look: *What did our captain mean by stretching our legs?*

And with that, Bryce dismissed both groups to rest with a curt nod. The humans went to revive with food and beverages, and the vampires headed off to… well, I guessed to sit around their bare cells.

Lost in thoughts that refused to move on from the feeling of sitting atop Dorian's muscular frame in the desert, I returned to my bunk without interacting with anyone, making my way quickly through the overly air-conditioned hallways.

In my room, I put an icepack on my lower back to prevent swelling. It looked like it would only bruise, which was amazing, considering I'd taken a direct hit from a massive redbill. That was twice I'd been lucky now. With all these new missions, I just hoped I'd continue my streak.

Our break passed far too fast. It felt like I'd barely put my feet up before Gina alerted me it was time to head out. Once the group from the morning's mission gathered on the tarmac, both Thoth and Roxy looking slightly drowsy, Captain Bryce signaled us to follow him off the pavement into the desert. The other captains had remained at the facility to communicate with the board. The sand glared in the sunlight, and I hoped a breeze would spring up to move the heat in the air. I didn't join the little conversations that surrounded me as we walked, but I was happy that the human and vampire voices were intermingling more than usual. Through the looping, jittery thoughts of Dorian's nose touching mine, I noticed him walking beside me. We didn't speak, but I felt his eyes on me.

Part of me wished he'd leave me alone. I hadn't been trained on what to do in situations involving… "non-professional" feelings. If that's even what it was. It irritated me not knowing what to do around him. I felt hyper-aware of the motions of his body, the swing of his steps next to mine.

Another part of me wanted to give myself a mental slap—and make a firm note to keep a rein on my imagination. I was here to do dangerous work, and I wouldn't be a capable team member, let alone a leader, if my thoughts kept spiraling like this.

Bryce led us to a sandy area lined with spiny desert trees and shrubs. Everyone, human and vampire alike, was already visibly sweating.

"Circle," Bryce ordered.

We gathered around him.

"Soldiers, today is an excellent and rare opportunity for you," he began, barely able to hide the curve of his lips. "Our guests are experts in combat, and to the extent that they're willing, I would like to ask them to teach you."

Some of the vampires shifted their feet. Worry filled my head with images of a playful spar gone awry, especially with tempers like Kane's and Roxy's thrown in the mix. Hopefully the teamwork from that morning would carry us through.

"I figured we had so much chitchat the other day that some action might benefit everyone," the captain added, setting his hands on his hips. He wore the familiar smile that meant he would enjoy watching his team get put through the wringer. "Soldiers, you will remove your weapons and set them near me while we do this exercise." Roxy scrunched her nose and opened her mouth to protest, but Bryce ignored her.

"Pair up. Guns here. Move it." The captain clapped his hands together, and that was it—we were doing this.

I loosened my belt, wrapped it around my handgun, and set it in the sand. Its absence was a relief, and not just due to its physical weight. The vampire's faces reflected my reprieve.

When I turned to find a partner, Dorian stood directly in my path, his crystalline eyes on me, making it quite clear whom he'd chosen to spar with.

"You planning on tackling me again?" he asked, his lips quirking up.

Heat traveled up my neck. All I could think about was how his breath had tickled my collarbone.

"It was an accident," I managed, fighting the smile that threatened to tug up the corner of my mouth. "But no promises for next time."

"I'll prepare myself."

We headed to a clear space away from the other pairs. I tried to walk casually, to hide the fact that my heart was beating too fast for a normal training exercise. Whatever made me feel this way was not helping, and I struggled to even pinpoint what I was feeling at all. I tried to push down the resulting frustration.

Louise made her way to Sike, an excited bounce in her step. Zach and Colin both sought out Bravi, most likely impressed with her performance that morning. She looked them over smugly, probably looking forward to the chance to teach some humans what was what. Grayson and Laini paired off to our right, and I wondered if such quiet people would be able to interact at all, especially since they'd been so quiet together during the previous day's exercise.

Kane sat alone under a bent, leafless tree. Bryce walked around, observing the pairs, and had noticed Kane's silent protest. Bryce angled a smile toward Kane which was met with a stone-cold stare—effectively freezing it. Bryce kept moving.

Roxy and Rhome claimed a spot to our left. I noticed Roxy's hand kept returning to her waist, where her missing weapon would have been.

"I don't know where to start," Dorian remarked, drawing my attention back to him. His fingers scratched absently at his neck.

"Hands up," I replied, grinning at his terribly feigned naivety. My fists were in position at eye- and chin-level.

"I don't need to do that." He lowered his hand, self-assured to the point of amusing me.

"Suit yourself." I gave him a wink and, before I could think too much about it all, stepped toward him.

Dorian's hand snapped to my wrist, twisting my arm and then my body into a hold, pressing my back against his chest. I caught myself noting his pecs and immediately shook it off.

"I—" he started.

I didn't give him a chance to finish. Instead I dipped, swung my right leg around, and threw him over my hip.

Dorian hit the sand, his shirt slipping up over his lower abdomen. I looked down at him, fists back in position, avoiding looking down more than once at his exposed, taut skin.

"All right," he said, eyes narrowed in what I thought might be approval. He rose and brushed off his arms.

"Hands up," I repeated, my lips twitching in a half-smirk.

"That was good," Dorian admitted.

In my peripheral vision, I caught a glimpse of Zach grinning in our direction. Bravi took advantage of the distraction and kicked him in the ribs.

"Come on!" he protested. Colin bit back a laugh.

Roxy and Rhome in tandem had achieved surprising gracefulness. Unfortunately, some of the other soldiers and vampires still hesitated to touch each other. Rayne reached to touch Sarah's wrist to show her a move, and Sarah instinctively recoiled—then caught herself and cautiously offered her hand back to Rayne. Laini and Grayson had decided that simply discussing moves was better than attempting such awkward closeness.

I refocused on my own fight, waiting for Dorian's next move. He remained motionless, one eyebrow cocked, waiting for *me*.

I moved to strike his neck, one fist protecting my face as I threw the other out on the offense. He deflected the blow easily and swept me behind him in one elegant wave.

I turned to face him again, hands ready.

"It's not always about offense," he said, his gaze locked on me.

"I know that."

"Our main advantage is speed, but it's not everything." He paused for a moment, his expression turning thoughtful. "Think about it like chess."

I nodded, and this time, the impending smile managed to crack my calm façade.

"In chess, you're always thinking several moves ahead, right?" Dorian continued. "If you do the same in fighting, you'll save your own energy and consistently find ways to expend your opponent's."

I nodded. This was pretty basic martial arts philosophy.

"Let your opponent act first and observe what they do consistently. Even a little observation can prepare you a lot."

"Do humans always do the same things?" I asked, stepping toward him again.

"Some humans are very predictable, yes," Dorian replied, putting his fists up for the first time. "Others, less so." I leaned a shoulder in, and he mirrored me. By this point, our smirks matched, too.

I ducked under his arms and brushed my foot toward his ankles. My boot never made contact—he landed a hand on the back of my neck, muscling me down into a crouch. His grip was both startlingly firm and gentle.

"That's what you mean by predictable," I said to the sand.

"I would never call you predictable," Dorian replied. I wasn't sure from his tone if he was humoring me.

I reached over my neck and grabbed his wrist, wrenching it around in a circle and bending his arm backward. His foot slipped, and he landed on a knee in front of me. Our foreheads bumped.

"Good," I said.

Our gazes locked again for the first time since our crash. The tingling sensation from when I'd landed on top of him flowed through me as the frosty blue of his irises consumed my vision. His gaze didn't falter.

I released him and bounced back to my feet, glancing away, my cheeks reddening. From one side of the sparring area, Bryce had been watching us. At least I had the excuse of being in the sun. I took stock of the ongoing situation while Dorian and I took a breather.

Around us, the pairs continued grappling. The previously hesitant soldiers and vampires were grabbing each other and starting to share ideas about moves—Sarah and Rayne exchanged a smile as I watched, and Laini and Grayson now risked a few arm twists and ankle kicks. Louise chattered at Sike about how good he was at fighting, even with an injury, and he simply gave her a "no duh" nod and shrug in response. At which point, she did something I couldn't see that brought him crashing to the ground, laughing in surprise. Bravi had Zach in a head-lock. He appeared to be trying to bend her fingers back and escape, but she tripped him and sent him spinning down to the ground.

"Okay! Uncle! Seriously!" Zach said, sprawling on the sand. Several onlooking vampires tried to hide their grins; Bravi didn't even bother.

"Sloane, you're embarrassing the Bureau," Captain Bryce barked. He crossed his arms.

Zach bounced back up and brushed himself off, fighting off a scowl. "Okay, best six out of ten."

A few feet away, Sike demonstrated to Louise how to restrain someone's hands and bite their neck, when he accidentally got her strawberry blonde ponytail caught in his mouth.

"I'm not sure I'm going to use that one," Louise said evenly, wiping spit off her hair. "Thank you, though."

Rhome and Roxy were running an organized drill with three deflective moves that I logged in my memory.

My gaze returned to Dorian. My cheeks were still a bit warm, but I rolled up my sleeves. "I wouldn't call you predictable, either," I announced.

"One of the many things we seem to have in common," Dorian replied.

I studied his face with a hint of suspicion but didn't spot any flicker of teasing in his eyes. Rather, they looked... earnest. Like he meant what he said earlier.

A sudden, piercing screech shattered the lull in our fight. The air above us filled with the sounds of heavy, rushing wingbeats. I snapped my gaze to the sky, adrenaline coursing through me.

Redbills.

Bryce shouted in surprise. Roxy raced to retrieve her weapon from the pile at his feet, and I instinctively did the same. Zach and Colin were right behind us, picking a flapping target and aiming. Other soldiers scrambled around us, ducking and trying to get to their weapons. Bryce's handgun aimed at the sky, unfaltering.

The redbills circled above us, screeching and diving.

"Hold your fire!" Dorian's voice boomed over the commotion, surprisingly loud and guttural. "These are our redbills! They're tame, they won't hurt you, put your guns down!"

Captain Bryce found his words. "Soldiers, hold!"

"They thought we were under attack." Dorian held his hands up, swiftly approaching the soldiers with weapons. But the soldiers didn't back down.

The bills continued circling and throwing their heads.

Dorian looked to me anxiously, his eyes imploring. What I feared more than getting scolded by a redbill was ending this day in an unnecessary bloodbath, so I lowered my weapon and motioned for the others to do the same. Another redbill snapped its beak in the air, and several soldiers flinched, the tips of their guns angling for the bird.

"Please, lower your weapons," Dorian repeated in a commanding tone. His gaze snapped to Bryce when no other soldiers followed my lead. "Captain, the animals won't leave until your soldiers set aside their weapons."

Bryce's leathery face creased with conflict, and he waited a few beats, but ultimately nodded. "Soldiers, lower your weapons," he said slowly.

Roxy stared at Bryce incredulously, her stocky shoulders and thin lips rigid in protest.

Torn between who was scarier—the birds or Bryce—the soldiers lowered their weapons. But they took a few moments to do so.

Rhome began speaking softly up to his bird, the one with a few broken-off serrated teeth. It slowly lowered to the ground, clacking its crimson beak. Rhome placed his hand on its broad forehead, just as he'd done with the wild redbills earlier that day.

Some of the redbills still circled overhead, as if uncertain whether to land. Bravi whistled, and two more birds descended to the sand, hopping toward her while keeping suspicious eyes on the nearby humans.

The other vampires held their palms to the redbills' foreheads as they continued hesitantly landing on the sand, which swirled around our feet.

"Thank you for pulling back the artillery," Dorian called to the soldiers, a palpable edge in his voice. His redbill came to rest beside him, nuzzling the tip of its beak slightly against Dorian's torn gray pants. Its beak was larger than the others', and it growled like it knew it. Dorian gently placed a hand on the bird's neck. The animal gurgled and made a trilling noise in its throat, aimed at the flustered birds still hovering above.

We soldiers backed away as more birds landed and the vampires soothed them. Watching the vampires soothe their man-eating monsters like terrified kittens, I had a moment of surreal disorientation. I wondered, just for a moment, if we were doing the right thing. Then I gave myself a mental slap. *Of course we are.*

The birds eventually stopped jerking their heads and began chirping to each other instead.

"I think we should talk about how to keep everyone safe around the redbills," Dorian said pointedly to Captain Bryce, though his sharp gaze encompassed all of us. "Weapons will not resolve everything."

Roxy clenched her weaponless hands into fists and glowered. Some of the vampires returned her frustrated look. Finally, Kane was on his feet, arms crossed in annoyance. He'd sat through most of the event like he was watching reruns on TV.

"Soldiers, can you please approach me and my redbill?" Dorian asked. *"Slowly."* He exhaled, clearly tempering irritation, which only pricked mine. Between that and the remnants of my earlier fear, the last thing I wanted to do was approach that bird.

Zach and Louise looked to Bryce and then me. At Bryce's nod, I began walking toward Dorian. My teammates followed with hesitant steps.

"The best way to show you mean no harm is to keep your voice soft and palms upward. Like this," Dorian explained, demonstrating. His bird clawed at the sand as we neared but thankfully kept its serrated beak closed. "See. It's not difficult."

His tone was a little too condescending for my liking.

"I think it's understandable that we want to protect ourselves," I muttered in Dorian's direction, keeping an eye on the giant beak.

"Especially since we can't assume that all redbills are controlled by friendly vampires."

Dorian gave a curt nod. "Yes, I'm fully aware that they're predators and can be extremely dangerous. But if you approach them peacefully, they're likely to respond the same way. Once you've gotten close, something else that helps is clicking your tongue. The sound comforts them." Dorian trilled his tongue against the back of his teeth, and his bird chirred back softly.

"Let's have everyone return to their previous pairs and follow Mr. Clave's instructions," Captain Bryce said from behind us. The enthusiastic note had returned to his voice.

I couldn't help rolling my eyes.

The soldiers returned to their partners with a marked lack of enthusiasm, emulating Dorian's open palms. The birds remained calm, except Rhome's. It hissed at Roxy, its shoulders hunching defensively. The soldiers froze, watching. I held my breath.

"He's picking up on your tension," Rhome said evenly.

Roxy's cheek twitched. Then, with a deep sigh that heaved her chest, she visibly relaxed her muscles. The bird eyed her for a long moment, then blinked and began to preen its feathers. From the crowd, somebody whistled.

I stepped closer to Dorian's redbill—the same one that had carried me during the last mission, the same one that Dorian had flown when he kidnapped me. *Had that really been only a couple weeks ago?*

It seemed the redbill sensed my trepidation. It jerked its head toward me as I approached, its eyes hard and suspicious. My insides flipped, but even if it felt a little ridiculous, I clucked my tongue. I wasn't going to fail at this. *Not in front of Mr. Know-It-All.*

The redbill listened silently but gave me no other response.

"I know you two already know each other, but let's get friendlier," Dorian said, his voice irksomely chipper. He no longer addressed the group but came closer to speak to me personally. "He's a little flustered, but let's see if you can get him to let you touch his neck."

Touch his neck? The thought didn't thrill me. I'd been on the redbill's back, sure, but the last time I'd been alone with it, it had tried to bite my leg off before drinking a man like a juice box. Did I even want to get friendlier with it?

I kept my palms up and carefully approached the bird. Every few steps I clicked my tongue. The bird remained unamused, grumbling to itself. *Yeah, you're not the only one, pal.*

"That's good." Dorian continued his encouragement. He crossed his arms over his sinewy chest, watching me closely. "Just take it slow." The other soldiers crept closer to their redbills, too. It was mostly quiet, save for some clicks and chirps here and there.

Trying not to grimace, I stepped forward again, only a few feet now remaining between me and the bill. I clucked a little louder, hoping to encourage it.

Its throat gurgled. I stopped.

"It's okay," Dorian said calmly, but I could've sworn he suppressed a chuckle. "He knows you don't have a gun, so he'll warm up in a little bit."

I cast Dorian a pointed side-eye. "You know, it's not like a few of these things haven't attacked me before. And not just that—they've killed countless people." Afraid to startle the redbill, I tried to keep my tone gentle, despite my prickle of frustration. It was easy for Dorian to chuckle. "I've got a few scars to prove it."

"I understand," Dorian replied. His lips straightened, though a shadow of a smile lingered as he watched me. "I don't want that to happen again. I don't want anyone to get hurt. We're a team now, right? If we learn to communicate, we'll all be safer."

I had to accept that he had a point, albeit grudgingly. I swallowed my nerves and clicked once more. The bird gave me a curt chirp. Just one.

"See? There you go," Dorian said, his smile returning full force.

"Yeah, thanks." I scoffed.

I took another small step and delicately extended a palm toward the bird's neck. Three feet of air were the only thing between that beak and my hand. I closed my eyes and inhaled, then reached. My fingers lightly brushed some of its neck feathers. I froze, gauging its reaction.

Dorian's redbill kept as still as I did. I offered another cluck, and it gave me another in return.

"You'll be riding him without me in no time." Dorian grinned.

"That doesn't sound like much fun," I whispered. I closed the last of the space between me and the bill, my hand now firmly pressed against its neck. *It's kinda like the horses I used to ride at summer camp... kinda.* The bird closed its eyes in response to my neck pets, finally pleased. Once I heard a chittering in the redbill's throat, I knew we'd reached an understanding. My shoulder was just inches from Dorian's chest, which, annoyingly, I was almost as aware of as the giant, human-eating bird.

"Glad you think so," he replied, a smile in his voice.

CHAPTER TWENTY-ONE

I smiled before I opened my eyes the next morning. Somehow, I wasn't even irked by the bugle call, which was definitely a first.

I brushed my teeth at the latrine sink, remembering the feeling of my forehead bumping Dorian's. I touched my fingers to the spot, humming to myself. *You planning on tackling me again?*

I absently rubbed my forehead as I walked to the mess hall. Of course, just at that moment, Captain Bryce stepped in front of me, jolting me from my thoughts.

"Captain, good morning," I said, immediately dropping my hand to my side.

"Lieutenant. Please join me in my office," he said, and promptly stomped down the hall without waiting for my response. I blinked, before hurrying after him.

Reaching his office, I closed the door behind me, wracking my brain for anything that might've happened over the past twenty-four hours that I could possibly get scolded for. I eased into a chair as he shuffled papers on his desk.

"Thought you'd be interested in what we found on your security guard friend," Bryce announced.

I paused as my brain processed this unexpected shift in the conversation. "You... You have intel back already?" I asked. A mix of curiosity and nerves spiked in me.

"I have friends in high places, Lieutenant," Bryce said with a smirk, still rustling papers. "Got a mate who's ex-Bureau. Currently a top dog with the federal police. He was able to immediately assign a wee task force on the case. That, and it turns out your friend is crummy at being a criminal."

Bryce finally got the papers into some kind of order and shoved them toward me, his eyes lowered in stern disapproval. This time, it wasn't directed at me. "Crummy and guilty," he clarified, jerking his hand impatiently.

I took the papers and scanned them. My eyes widened once I got to the words "child pornography."

"That was my reaction, too," Captain Bryce said, watching my face harden. He pursed his lips. "He got a home visit from investigators yesterday. They clearly found quite a bit. I'd hate to be the one to tell his mother."

I continued reading, my hands tensing around the papers. The report noted that investigators suspected intent to distribute. I curled my lip.

"Needless to say, you won't be seeing your friend at his post again," Bryce said, tapping his pen on his desk in a furious staccato rhythm.

I lowered the papers to my lap, my thoughts rushing.

"This could open quite a door, Lieutenant," Bryce remarked, before I could get my first thought out. "If it's not just a coincidence."

Excitement bubbled in my chest. Bryce was seeing what I'd intended in that heated moment with Finley.

"Imagine the crimes that could be prevented," I said, holding up the papers. "This is a huge reason to support a human and vampire alliance."

"Easy, lassie." Bryce raised a finger. "Don't get ahead of yourself. This is just one piece of evidence in an ocean of anti-vampire history.

This isn't enough to take to the board and make a case on. We need more."

I knew he was right; supplemental data would only benefit the vampires more, and his tone told me we were on the same team with that. But I felt a flurry of impatience between my ribs.

"I don't see how most people wouldn't at least *consider* allowing vampires back into society, if they saw this," I said.

"Agreed. It's only one piece of data, but it's definitely a start to supporting the 'specified feeding' concept they've been throwing around," Bryce replied. "However, there's still the issue of murder. I don't see the government agreeing that it's acceptable to drain someone because they've robbed a convenience store or two."

I chewed on my lip, thinking. "That's true. But... on the other side of the coin, they'll have to take into account that crime rates have increased since the vampire extinction."

"That'll be another selling point, yes." Bryce steepled his fingers, a calculating look crossing his face. "And if we could dig a little deeper—say, figure out if it's possible for vampires to identify these people and detain them..." He leaned back in his chair, trailing off for a moment in obvious thought. "But, like I said, one incident isn't enough to build a case on. We must find clear, explicit correlations between all of these pieces. I'm not risking my rank on your overzealousness."

He paused, and I held my breath.

"So. When would you like to start?" A smile cracked his sun-tanned face.

A pulse of excitement raced through me. "Are you serious?"

"Well, yes. How could we ignore this? You and I will work on it in our downtime and build a case to present to the board. Mr. Clave might be willing to answer some questions." Bryce raised his eyebrows at me, a conspiratorial spark in his light blue eyes. "And my mate with the feds shouldn't have a problem pitching in here and there. This would be a lovely cherry on top of a successful-six-week-trial-period, no-more-redbills sundae, wouldn't you agree, Sloane?"

My head bounced up and down. "Yes, sir," I replied, my mind rushing with possibilities. *This could be our winning ticket.* If this worked, our mission—aiding the vampires and therefore the entire universe— could be a slam dunk. This could blindingly demonstrate the value of vampires on Earth and beyond, and that's what we needed to show the board.

"Maybe we could start by asking the vampires about their past attacks," I went on. "Instances where they knew the person's name or unique descriptors. And we can check records to validate."

Bryce nodded. "Live experiments would probably gather some convincing data, too. A controlled setting where we expose the vampires to people they've never met, some innocent, some with nasty records. See if they can sniff out the bad eggs. Obviously, they'd have to be under heavy supervision. We won't risk anyone involved. No more bloodbaths."

My mind jumped back to the bleeding man in the grass at the motel. "I may have one specific lead, actually, Captain," I said, my enthusiasm sobering a little as I remembered how serious this project could be. "When I was captured, I witnessed Dorian kill someone he claimed was a criminal. I didn't get the man's name, but I know the date and some location details. Do you think your friend could run a search?"

"Don't see why not," Bryce answered, his eyes serious. "But post-humous searches would be needlessly time-consuming at this juncture, I'd say. Let's focus on live criminals. We catch dirtbags, and the vampires score points with the board. Win-win. There's always time for the police to investigate those who are already deceased once we've built a convincing foundation for the case."

I nodded sharply. His argument made sense. "Yes, sir."

"And, obviously, Lieutenant, keep this under wraps for now. This is strictly need-to-know. Last thing we need is everyone rubbing our noses in the dirt if the whole thing flops."

I nodded once more. *That* made sense too. Especially for Bryce.

He rubbed his palms together. "Right, then. You get the ball rolling with Mr. Clave, and I'll chat with my mate and pull strings. Now, Sloane, get the hell out of my office."

"Yes, Captain," I said, rushing toward the door; halfway there, I had to turn back around, like an overexcited high schooler, to drop the report papers back on Bryce's desk.

As I exited and walked down the main hall, there was an energy in my step. This could be huge for Dorian, his people—his entire species. All species. A deeper feeling of communion with the vampires flooded me as I visualized my uncle and the rest of the board commending us and welcoming the vampires back into cities with open arms.

I hurried toward the vampire quarters, forgetting about breakfast entirely.

CHAPTER TWENTY-TWO

A rriving at the vampires' residence, I nodded to the Bureau
security guards posted on each side of the entrance, panting
slightly. They didn't respond.

"Need you to open the door, gentlemen," I said with a smile.

This time, they visibly hesitated.

"Do you really want me to get Captain Bryce and have him explain
to you how rank works?" I asked, squaring my shoulders and dropping
my previous manners. My usual friendliness wasn't necessary when
lower ranks were unnecessarily stubborn. Just the snap in my voice was
enough to get their hands fumbling for the keys.

In the vampire block, I walked down the aisle between the unlocked
cells, waving to Sike when he looked up, which got me a thumbs up.
The vampires' good behavior had earned them free time every so often
with their padlocks open so they could visit each other. I paused and
imagined how awful it would feel to have to be uncaged to visit my own
family and friends.

Reaching Dorian's cell, I drew a breath before stepping in front of
the bars. I realized I was looking forward to seeing him again—a lot.
And not just to share the news.

I wasn't sure how to feel about that.

Attraction to Dorian sure as hell wasn't appropriate. Leaving aside the little fact that we weren't even the same freaking species, we were at a military facility. I was on a job. So was he, in a way.

What am I even thinking?

Shaking my head, I shoved the bizarre thoughts aside and mustered up my best joke about how Dorian's redbill and I would soon be best friends and forget all about him. Zach had one thing right: jokes were the best diversion.

Dorian wasn't there. Of course I'd psyched myself up for nothing. I walked down the aisle to see if he had joined someone in their room, ignoring that I felt a little foolish.

I had reached the end of the adult vampires' cell block without finding Dorian when Rhome appeared silently beside me. I almost jumped when I noticed him.

"I think he went to the children's quarters," he said with a smile. He pointed toward a door around a corner at the end of the aisle, toward the separate block that had been designated for the young vampires and their caretakers after the incident with Detra the first night.

"Thank you," I replied. *Jeez. Am I really that obvious?*

I opened the door quietly, slipping gently into the beige hallway. I hadn't been to the children's quarters yet and imagined I should treat it like a nursery. So far, it was less stark and prison-y than the main vampire quarters—the chambers had walls instead of bars—but the glaring fluorescent lights didn't do it any favors. The air was softer without the constant clattering and scraping of metal.

I stepped silently past closed doors before I noticed one cracked open. I thought I heard the low, deep lilt of Dorian's voice, so I made my way over. Then I heard crying.

My heart jumped in my chest, and before I could stop myself, I stole a glance into the room. Dorian and Laini sat together on a bed. I'd never heard her speak before; she'd always been on the outskirts of everything, even from that day in the vampires' cavern. She crumpled under his arm, leaning into his side. Sobs shook her shoulders as her long, dark hair tumbled over them. Her delicate hands hid her face.

I stepped back to avoid being seen, deciding I should just come back another time. The way he held her seemed almost brotherly, and it dawned on me that they might be related. Then my mind was arrested by their words.

Laini's voice cracked as she wept. "I just want him back." She sucked in a breath. "I miss him so much."

"I do, too," Dorian whispered.

I'd never heard Dorian sound like this. His voice was so low, and it… trembled. "Whenever it becomes unbearable," he told Laini, "I always think back to when we used to spend afternoons at the river. Remember?"

"Yes," she replied, her voice so soft I could barely hear it.

"There was that one spot he found. With the little waterfall."

"That's where he stole your clothes," Laini said, sniffing. She laughed gently for a moment, but it faded into another sob.

Dorian let out an uneven chuckle, too. "I never did find that shirt. It was my favorite."

"Your brother kept it. He was going to hide it for you to find," Laini said with a sigh, and then her voice went painfully blank. "It was probably lost in the fire, with everything else."

They went quiet for a moment.

"I'm sorry, Laini," Dorian said hoarsely. "I couldn't… It's my fault he's gone."

"Stop," she croaked. "You have to stop saying that. There was nothing you could've done."

"I think about that moment every day," Dorian said. I thought I heard a raspy sigh. "I… I could've fought harder. I should've reacted faster."

"You were wounded. You couldn't save him and yourself."

Dorian exhaled, and I heard him swallow sharply. Yes… he was crying too. "I would give anything just to hear him whistling again."

Laini moaned. "Me, too. Just once. One more time."

My throat tightened, and I backed away. It didn't feel right to hear this. Laini sounded like my mother had after my grandfather passed away. It made my head spin. I breathed in carefully, trying to be soundless, and made for the exit of the children's wing. I'd just have to come back to speak with Dorian later.

I crept out the door into the adult vampires' cell block and silently closed it behind me.

I turned to leave and nearly collided with Kane. A wave of nerves shot down my legs, and I leapt back, automatically tensing into a fighting stance.

Kane's hair was wet, and a few strands dripped water down his cheek. He held a towel over his arm. He didn't speak, just shot me a glare before swerving around me in an exaggerated manner. He must've just come from the shower.

I realized this was the first time that Kane and I had been alone together. And I was definitely overreacting. I swallowed, deciding to make the best of it, and willed my body to shift into a relaxed, conversational pose. "Sorry, you startled me. How is Halla's leg?"

He glared at me. "Fine."

"Good. That's great." I searched my brain for a way to continue the conversation, my face hot in a way that was totally different from the way it heated around Dorian. "I know the cells aren't exactly comfortable. Sorry about that. Do you or your mom need anything to feel more at home?"

At this his eyes turned, if possible, even colder. "This will never be home," he scoffed, not-so-subtly putting even more distance between us.

I didn't give up. "I suppose not. For any of us. Please don't hesitate to let me know if there's anything you need. Really."

Kane paused and analyzed my face for a moment, and I attempted an I'm-not-scared-and-this-is-totally-normal smile. I didn't need to see my face to know that it wasn't convincing.

"I... I heard that you recently lost your father," I said, trying to mind my tone as I broached the subject.

Kane shifted his weight. I couldn't read his face, so I forged ahead on hope.

"I'm sorry for your loss." I swallowed. Talking about things like this never got any easier. "That must've been awful. For both you and your mother. I wish you hadn't experienced that."

There was a second when his face softened, but, even as I watched, it quickly turned to confusion and then back to bitterness.

"Just another example of humans showing their lack of humanity," he muttered. I knew he'd wanted to sound meaner, but his surprise dampened the heat.

"I'll be the first to admit that my species has wronged others," I said, nodding solemnly. "So I can't say that's not true."

He curled his lip as though preparing to retort, but nothing came.

A second later, the door behind me opened and Dorian slipped out, coming up in my peripheral vision. Kane seized the opportunity to escape our conversation and stalked past me into his cell.

Dorian watched him, then turned to me, his brow bent in concern. "Everything okay?"

"Yeah, everything's fine," I said, swallowing my nerves.

His eyes were red, but his face retained its stoicism. I was shocked by how well he could curb his emotions, after what I'd just heard.

"I actually came here to find you," I said. Saying that felt strangely intimate, even though it was just the truth. "Do you have a moment to talk?"

Dorian tilted his head, and his eyes sharpened with interest. "Yes. What is it?"

"It's a confidential matter," I replied. "Do you mind if we speak privately?" I was impressed with how professional my word choice was. At least I had that going for me... if I could keep it up.

"Not at all."

"Let's step outside." I led him out of the vampire quarters. The guards shifted when they saw Dorian exit beside me, but I shot them a *look*, and they let us pass without a word.

We left through one of the facility's side exits to a backyard area, this one slightly less boring and sandy than most of the outdoor spaces the facility had to offer. Scruffy clumps of grass bumped the bottoms of my boots. The sun beat down on us, directly overhead. I wondered if I'd ever adjust to this heat.

Dorian surveyed the yard and then pointed to a pair of small boulders in the sand. We sat down facing each other, a few inches between our knees.

Once we were at eye level again, all of my prepared professional words and highly organized sentences evaporated from my mind. I cleared my throat and cracked my knuckles in an attempt to snap myself back on task, but for a moment, the only thing I could think was that this was the first time Dorian and I had been alone since he'd come to my balcony. That rushing in my chest returned, pleasantly infuriating.

I exhaled. "I just had a talk with Captain Bryce, and we have a proposition for you," I began. "It was discovered that the wounded security guard from the other night—the one Detra attacked—had a criminal record. An investigation was done, and he has been released from Bureau employment. Facing some unpleasant charges."

I expected Dorian to say something to that, an agreement or even just an acknowledgement, but he simply gazed at me, an expression on his face that I couldn't read.

"Based on that... Bryce and I want to run our own investigation between redbill missions." I looked into his eyes, offering the proposal with as much confidence as I could muster. "We want to build a case to show the Bureau that vampires can help us weed out evil people before they harm anyone."

Still, Dorian said nothing. I replayed my words in my mind. Was I not making sense? He hadn't blinked in a long time. His eyes were as piercing as ever, but they held a new softness that made me feel calm and anxious in equal measures. In the silence, I kept going, fumbling through my speech.

"I hoped you and maybe a few others would be willing to run tests with groups of humans—some known criminals, and some innocent," I continued. "That way we can document and prove to the Bureau that vampires really do have an internal sense for bad intentions. Darkness, as you've called it. Would…" I hesitated at his continued silence. "Would you be willing to do that?"

Dorian leaned forward, setting his elbows on his knees. The hair on the back of my neck stood as his face neared mine. His eyes suddenly had a spark of white in them again—I'd almost forgotten they did that. I'd never noticed how perfectly symmetrical his face was, either, sharply halved by his chiseled nose.

Finally, he broke his gaze from mine and cleared his throat. "I can do that," he said, his voice changing from raspy to lilting as he spoke. "This is… better than I'd hoped for. This way, our role can be clearly illustrated, and it's best that humans learn of it as soon as possible."

"It'll be huge for the alliance," I added, thrilled that he was on board. "Not only would the redbill issue get worked out, the Bureau would have a way to deal with crime and protect our people. And the balance could recover, right? Vampires could do what they're naturally inclined to do." *Well, maybe without the actual killing.*

"It'd be a start," he said, a smile darting across his face. I liked the way his eyebrows naturally arched when he was happy, no matter the size of his smile.

"For now, though, we have to keep the project quiet," I told him. "I'm not sure which other vampires you might want to ask, but only those participating should know."

"Of course," he replied. "I'll have to think about who to involve."

"Thank you," I said.

He laughed—a deep, lush laugh, like he'd just heard his new favorite joke for the first time. "I have no idea why you're thanking me. I should be the one thanking you."

His laughter sent a ripple through me, and a grin cracked my lips. Another speck of white flashed in Dorian's irises, as if in response to my smile, and the rushing in my chest made my fingers shake slightly. I felt myself leaning in his direction without knowing why, almost like my forehead wanted to bump his again.

I swore I saw him lean, too.

I tried to find words, but the search was useless. All my brain registered was his face. We exhaled in tandem.

"Dorian." A small voice echoed across the yard, and we both jumped.

I spun to search for the source of the high-pitched sound and spotted Detra standing beside the side door, coyly chewing one of her fingernails.

"Detra!" Dorian choked. "What are you doing?"

"Found you," she said, and giggled.

"We're not playing a game," Dorian growled. He rushed over to her, but she scurried out of his grasp and across the sand. As she giggled and scuttled away, a reluctant smile twisted his mouth.

"Detra, come here." He gave chase, but not as quickly as I knew he could, his bumbling lurches comically staged. "Your parents are going to be irate." I couldn't help laughing.

I rose from the boulder to help him, but as I took the first step, I nearly tripped as an invisible vise tightened around my ribcage. For just a moment, breathing hurt—a dull ache, like a pulled muscle.

I held still and waited for it to pass, whatever it was.

When the pain dissipated, like a receding wave, I blinked and looked back up. It seemed Dorian hadn't noticed my embarrassing misstep. He was still zigzagging around the yard behind the little girl. When he caught her, he swept her up into his arms. Detra's laughter bounced off the metal facility walls like birdsong.

CHAPTER TWENTY-THREE

Dorian quietly carried Detra through the doorway into the vampire quarters. The guards looked confused but held their tongues, probably because they realized they'd messed up. I made a point of standing there with my arms crossed for an uncomfortable amount of time. Detra shouldn't have been able to slip by them. Vampires were cunning and quick, but they weren't invincible, and these guys needed to do a better job of keeping their eyes on the doors. The look of worry in Dorian's eye when Detra had appeared in the doorway bothered me more than I liked to admit. For him, the little girl escaping wasn't really a joke.

Maybe that was why my stomach still churned. After the moment of chest pain in the courtyard, something still wasn't settling right. I'd never had nauseous anxiety before, though maybe skipping breakfast had caught up with me. I was considering the fastest way to grab a snack when Gina appeared. She caught my arm and told me that Captain Bryce was looking for me.

"He wants you *and* the vampire," she added with a grin, playfully emphasizing that she was *not* surprised, before continuing on. Yeah, I bet Bryce was looking forward to another close encounter of the vampiric kind. Apparently, I wasn't the only one who'd noticed his interest.

I raised my eyebrows to the guards, and they jumped to reopen the door for me, clearly not wanting to give me further reason to resent them after slacking on their duties.

Dorian sat on his bed in his cell, holding and studying his carved wooden redbill statue. He must've brought it with him from Canyonlands. I quickly stepped back before he saw me and watched him rub his fingers over its soft, worn wood. I wondered if he had carved it or if someone close to him had—it was one of the very few possessions he seemed to own, and his affection for it showed. It reminded me of a doll my uncle Alan gave me when I was five, which I still kept on a shelf in my closet. Every time I saw it, I would hold and study it, just as Dorian did with his little bird.

I cleared my throat to attempt subtly getting his attention, and his eyes snapped up. His lips quirked into a questioning smile. "Back so soon?"

"Bryce called for us," I replied.

He arched a brow. "Then we'd better not keep him waiting."

We walked to Bryce's office in silence. But I noticed that Dorian's left foot fell exactly when mine did, even when I slowed or increased my pace. The sound of our footsteps echoed softly through the hallway. I peeked at his face, wondering whether he was doing it on purpose, and met his cool gaze looking back at me. When he caught my eyes, I looked away, but not quick enough to miss the warm look in his eyes. As though he'd been looking at me the whole time, waiting for my response.

My heart thumped in my chest. Fortunately, we reached Bryce's office before I decided what to do.

I knocked on the door and received an indiscernible grunt in response. That seemed… not entirely discouraging, considering it was Bryce. I opened the door and motioned for Dorian to enter first.

At the sight of the vampire, Bryce's eyes—predictably—lit up.

"Mr. Clave, hello! And you, too, Sloane. I assume you've updated Mr. Clave about our proposition?"

"Yes," I told him with a nod, just a little bit proud. I hadn't only updated him; I'd convinced him to help.

"And?" Bryce prompted.

I tilted my head to Dorian, inviting him to offer his own answer. He seemed to know what I was thinking.

"I accept your proposal," he said confidently, sitting in one of the chairs before Bryce's desk. I took the other.

"Excellent," Bryce said, pleased that our plan was falling into place. "Because I just spoke with my mate, Jim, the ex-Bureau-now-federal gentleman. In case Sloane didn't explain that part, Dorian." Bryce laced his fingers atop a stack of new, yet already disorganized, papers.

"She did not," Dorian replied.

I wondered whether I should've, then shook it off. Dorian's voice sounded cool and professional. I could recognize the difference between that and the real gratitude and cautious excitement he'd shown when I'd first told him about my and Bryce's idea. A part of me felt a little special that I'd gotten to witness it.

I pushed the thought aside as Bryce went on; I wanted to hear the details of the project. "Jim is generally on board with our plan," he said. "In fact, he has a lead on it. He's keeping details under wraps, though. He needs to meet Mr. Clave first."

That… could prove difficult. The Bureau wouldn't allow an outsider on-site.

"Would a video conference work?" I asked dubiously.

"In person, Lieutenant," Bryce replied. "At his office. In Vegas. This evening."

"Oh," I said. I hadn't even considered that he might allow Dorian off-site for a non-redbill mission, especially to a populated area. Bryce was taking this more seriously than I'd expected him to. My heart beat a little faster at the realization of how quickly my idea was taking shape. That hint of pride I felt before returned, and I swallowed a smile.

"Think of it as a test run. He wants to see what you can do." Bryce spoke directly to Dorian, his eyes intent.

Dorian paused. "Will this breach the trial period regulations?" he asked after a beat. I watched his face—his professional coolness remained intact, but he carried a hint of tension underneath. Maybe he was trying to figure out whether this was a trap or test of some kind. I wished I could reassure him. Bryce might be tough, but he wasn't the type to purposefully trick someone.

"Ordinarily, yes... but I'm making an exception. This could be a gamechanger for our mission." Bryce sat up in his chair, playfully narrowing his eyes on the vampire. "And don't get all cheeky and think you two will be sauntering off into the sunset to gamble and drink bubbly when you're done with your meeting. I'm going with you. I doubt you'll do anything stupid, but I encourage you not to try anything cute, either. All three of us need to travel via redbill tonight."

Dorian smiled, only a bit stiffly. "We can take my redbill. And don't worry. With the reputation of my entire species on the line, I don't think I'll find wasting money in a crowd of drunken fools as tempting as most humans seem to."

I bit back a smirk at his tart reminder that none of us could take this lightly. Dorian, more than any of us, knew that this could be a really big deal for both species—if we pulled it off.

"Fair enough," the captain said, though his eyebrows had risen. "Ah, one more little detail, Mr. Clave. You'll be incognito during this visit."

"Sorry?" Dorian asked, seeming genuinely confused at the term.

"You're going to be disguised as a human on the excursion. You'll be around folks who have no knowledge that your kind even exist." Bryce didn't even attempt to hide his smirk. "Lieutenant Sloane, you will be in charge of this costume change. Can't wait to see the beautiful transformation. Oh, and you don't have much time to figure it out. We just got called out for another redbill mission this afternoon, so you'll be playing dress-up directly afterward." Bryce winked at me.

An exhale whistled out of me, and Dorian and I exchanged wide-eyed looks.

The redbill mission took us to an abandoned quarry, and the soldiers had a more hands-off approach this time. We stayed in the plane, ready to provide backup. Sike hung back with us to answer our questions and run interference. He caught me watching Dorian and gave me a knowing look that made me reevaluate him. So far only Zach had noticed the signs of my attraction to Dorian, and I knew how smart Zach was. If Sike had put it together as well, that made him someone to watch, despite his class-clown act.

Soon, the small flock of redbills took off toward Canyonlands with a distinct lack of drama, which impressed all of the humans present. If they could replicate this, the vampires' request for asylum would be difficult to deny.

When we returned to the facility with news of the success, the captains allowed everyone a few hours of personal time. I immediately seized the opportunity to get things in order for the evening; a few hours would go by fast, and I hoped the more I prepared I was, the lower my nerves would be.

Hoped—but wasn't convinced. A lot hung on the success of this evening.

I swiped a plastic plate and spoon from the cafeteria, then went to the women's bathroom. Maybe Bryce was making fun of me, but more likely he was totally clueless about the fact that I was the worst person to do a vampire makeover. I could barely even put makeup on myself for special occasions. I didn't dislike the stuff, I just rarely found the time, and with my lifestyle, it was impractical. Eyeliner didn't help you kill man-eating storks.

I rifled through my cosmetics case, though there wasn't much to look through—a tiny amount of blush, a bit of almost-dried-up mascara, and lip balm. The old bottle of concealer I owned definitely didn't match Dorian's complexion. I chewed my lip, considering the other options. Assorted makeup bags sat scattered about the sinks, each one's colors and patterns giving away the owner. Roxy's was black with hot pink flames on it, while Louise's had a vintage floral pattern. Mine was blue camo—an old Christmas gift from my mom. The other bags looked better stocked than my own. Maybe one of them would have what I needed.

Keeping a wary eye on the door, I picked through them carefully and quietly, trying to use my best judgment as to which products looked like the best quality, and therefore the most long-lasting. I wished I could just ask, but if I did, they would want to know why. In my ethical discomfort, I began to rush, simply grabbing the palest foundations I could find. I really didn't have any other choice, given the predicament Bryce had put me in, and most of the girls probably would have donated them to the cause if they'd known.

With only the haziest idea of what I was doing, I squirted the tubes over the plastic plate and stirred the products together like paint with the spoon. I tried not to think too hard about what I was going to be doing with this mixture in just a few short minutes. Never mind that I was staring at a paper plate trying to envision Dorian's skin... the image that kept popping up in my head was his face, only an inch from mine, his pale cheekbones swarming with shadows as I lay on top of him in the desert sand. Maybe Bryce *had* given me this part of the mission to torment me.

After my hurried stirring, I was mostly satisfied with my work and nabbed a bit more from Roxy's stash, as she was the palest in the group. My concoction wasn't perfect, but it would do—Dorian could use a tan, anyway.

As I replaced Roxy's foundation, I imagined what Roxy would say if she caught me "borrowing" her makeup for a vampire. It didn't bear thinking about. I pocketed a blending sponge and blush from my own makeup bag, just in case.

I turned to leave and found Gina leaning against the wall, blocking the doorway.

Her arms crossed over her petite but muscular frame, and her eyebrows lifted questioningly high on her forehead.

"Lyra?" she asked, peering down at the plate and assorted makeup bits in my hands.

"What?" I asked a little too loudly. My heart pounded. *Crap*.

I tried to look calm. There was no easy way to explain this without simply telling her what I was doing. And, honestly, I *did* want to tell her. Gina knew almost everything about me and vice versa. We'd been friends for years, even before she started dating my brother.

But this was for a mission, and Bryce had specifically asked me to keep it confidential. I didn't want to let him down. I wracked my brain for the best way out.

"Are you doing what I think you're doing?" Gina asked with a frown.

I didn't bother to hide the paper plate. She'd already seen it. "Well, it depends on what you *think* I'm doing," I replied, stalling for time.

She sighed, and a wry smile curved her lips. "Oh, Lyra. After *all* the times I tried to get you to wear a little eyeshadow when we played pool at Book's—or get one of those full-face makeovers with me at the mall. Or dress up a little snazzier for Zach's twenty-third birthday… Are you finally starting to wear makeup… for a *vampire*?"

I gaped at her. Had she caught onto my feelings about Dorian, too? Had Zach talked to her? Or was she just joking?

My cheeks heated to tomato-red temperatures regardless, and my lips parted to correct her, before I stopped myself. As embarrassing as I found it, this was my way out.

"What can I say?" I pushed out a grin, shrugging. "You caught me."

Gina stared for a minute, then shook her head fondly. "Well, if you want to look good for him, all power to you. I could help, you know, instead of you being all cloak and dagger about it. That color's clearly too pale for you."

Wait, she's not joking? She actually thinks I'm putting makeup on for Dorian? Another protest bubbled up my throat, but I forced it down. I'd have to file that little fact away for... future me to deal with. When I wasn't in the middle of an incredibly important mission.

My job was so strange.

"Don't worry about it," I managed, struggling to maintain my grin. "I just felt like trying it out for a change. A bit of practice in my downtime, ya know? I'm fine for now."

Gina tilted her head at me. "You know I'm always here to talk, okay? Don't make me worry about you."

"Ah, we both know you'll never stop worrying about me." I gave her a toothy smile, this one genuine. She worried about me almost as much as my mom, sometimes.

She smiled back at me. "And we both know you'll do your own thing no matter what. I get it."

And, just like that, she walked out.

I held my breath for a few moments, to make sure she was truly gone. Then I exited the bathroom, my face more flushed than I would've liked as I headed directly for Dorian.

I was lucky my embarrassing fake admission hadn't gone worse. At least I knew Gina wouldn't say anything to the other women. She wasn't the type to gossip. *But she really believes I've got the hots for Dorian?*

It was one thing for Zach to find out I was attracted to the vampire; he'd known me since birth. If anyone would know, it would be Zach. And Sike knowing didn't bother me for the exact opposite reason: he was only a stranger. But for Gina to pick up on it meant I was being obvious. What if Roxy, Louise, and Sarah found out? What if they thought it compromised my work and went to Bryce? My mind went blank from horror, and I stopped in my tracks until I recovered.

Doing my best to shove all thoughts of the bizarre conversation aside, I hurried to the vampire quarters, walking as swiftly as I could. Now it was time for the *real* test.

The guards let me through with only a brief skeptical look. They were probably getting used to this.

I found Dorian lounging on his bed, his lean frame propped lazily against the wall, dark hair hanging low over his forehead.

"Come in," he said, his voice neutral, though I could've sworn I heard a bit of smirk somewhere in there. I couldn't really blame him for that.

I stepped into the cell and held up the splattered plate. "Ready to change species?" I asked, trying to keep it light, then regretting the joke. My breathing already felt disjointed.

He sighed with a hint of drama, but his eyes glinted at me—almost as if he was looking forward to this. "If I must," he said.

I grinned at him, then sat beside him on his bed, careful to keep a couple inches of space between us. I surveyed the vampire's face.

He watched me as I watched him. "I don't see what's so exciting about looking human," he remarked.

"Didn't you know? It's all the rage these days." My answering smile felt too big for such a basic joke. I gathered my courage. "All right," I told him firmly, "I need you to tilt your face toward the light so I can see what I'm working with." Maybe he didn't hear me pulling in deep, measured breaths to calm myself, but with our bodies this close together, I didn't hold much hope.

Dorian leaned forward and tipped his face obediently, his eyes amused.

The tips of my fingers tingled, and my mouth went dry. A new feeling came over me as I looked down at his still, stoic face waiting for its paint. When his eyes closed, he looked like an ancient statue of a warrior king, his strong features calm and resolved. My anxiety returned, thumping against my chest.

Come on. You can do this. It's only touching a vampire. We'd even touched before. Somehow, that thought didn't help. I needed to get a grip. This wasn't life or death. Actually, life-or-death circumstances didn't stress me this much.

"I wonder which of your hidden talents I'll discover next," Dorian muttered as I started dabbing the foundation onto his cheeks with the sponge. His skin was taut and porcelain, and when the tips of my fingers brushed it a few times, I immediately noticed how soft it was. He was putting off a surprising amount of heat, and I found myself questioning my vampire knowledge—sometimes old vampire myths still popped into my head, even though I hadn't read Stoker's *Dracula* since high school. They were closer to mammals with their temperature fluctuations and normal, live births and family systems. They didn't sneak around turning humans into vampires. In fact, that seemed preposterous to me now. They definitely weren't cold, dead, ugly, coffin-dwelling dudes who feared the sun. Especially not the one right in front of me.

He grimaced as the makeup touched his skin. "That's unpleasant."

I smirked. "You get used to it," I told him, trying to keep up a casual conversation. "Though, I'm not used to it, either. This isn't my area of expertise."

Dorian chuckled. "I never would've guessed."

The sound of his laugh, with a bit of vampiric growl to it, made me feel oddly proud to have caused it. "Do you really think it's wise to sass a person painting your face? I could turn you into an old granny. Or cake your eyes shut with this."

Dorian's lips quirked again, which messed up my sponging, but I found I didn't want him to stop. "Terrifying," he said dryly. "Why would you wear makeup when you're not in disguise? Is that normal for humans?"

The question caught me off guard. I guessed I'd never thought about it quite that way. "Uh… it's normal for lots of human women. You wear it for fun, or to make yourself look more professional, or feel better, or look more attractive to get a date." I was glad Dorian's eyes were closed; at least he couldn't see my cheeks redden.

"I see. So, you never wore makeup because you wanted to 'get a date'?"

I heard the teasing in his tone and took a deep breath to calm myself, watching the foundation slowly covering up the shadows that danced under his skin. Of all the reasons I'd mentioned, he had to fixate on *that* one? "I guess not. The Bureau's my life. And, uh…"

The words hung between us, no doubt reminding him that I'd trained for a life of exterminating redbills and hating his species.

"Go on," Dorian said, after a pause.

I swallowed, looking down to daub more foundation off the plate. "I mean, I admire the women who are good at it, but I figured going without it shouldn't be a dealbreaker either, if the person was attracted to me for what I did with my life, what I believed in and accomplished."

Dorian's eyes opened, the vivid blue stunning me for a moment. "That seems likely to me," he said.

The pounding of my heart had to be audible across the whole room. "Thanks," I managed. We fell into a charged silence.

I leaned back to assess my work and get a bit of space from the unexpected turn of the conversation. Below the foundation, still-visible dark ripples swirled below his eyes and on his forehead.

"I'm not sure this is working. You look like a clown who got into a bar fight," I muttered.

Dorian laughed in response. "I guess that's more like a human than a vampire."

I narrowed my eyes on him. "I definitely wouldn't sass me right now. I can still do serious damage with this sponge."

The conversation had gotten off the topic of our mission rather quickly. I focused as I applied another coat to his cheeks and then slathered his forehead. It looked like a can of eggshell paint had exploded on him.

Think. Think. I wracked my memory, trying to remember how Gina had taught me to blend. If I just distracted myself with half-remembered makeup tutorials, and not how much my hands wanted to shake… *He shouldn't have such an effect on me.*

"I guess I need to, uh, fix it a bit," I said, trying to keep from looking like I had no idea what I was doing. "Just bear with me, here."

Being so close to him made me awkward. My dabbing with the sponge was just messing it up more. I swallowed again. Attraction was pretty damn irritating.

"What's taking so long?" Dorian asked. "My neck hurts." He opened his eyes a sliver to see my reaction.

I gave him my best stone face in response. "Don't be a baby. And stop moving your lips. It's messing me up."

Despite the complaining, he seemed to be in an exceptionally good mood. Part of me hoped it was because he was excited for this mission. I certainly was.

"I should get a special accolade for allowing you to convert me into a human," he muttered, making a visible effort not to move his lips as he spoke.

"I'm just following orders," I replied, reminding myself as much as him. It was hard to remember that I was just doing my job, when I had to sit next to Dorian on his bed.

After blending more thoroughly, I finally thought I was getting the hang of this. I decided to do one last layer, then added a touch of blush to mimic human blood flow. I leaned back once more to evaluate my handiwork.

His ice-blue eyes seemed too alive for the rest of his human-toned face, and his jawline and sharp cheekbones looked weird without the flickers of shadows. Still, even if my disguise wasn't professional, in dim lighting it would be convincing. I had always been a perfectionist, and I had to say, given my limited experience, this actually wasn't too bad.

That ache in my chest had returned, though, in spite of my having eaten earlier. Maybe the lunch had been too acidic—too many tomatoes on my salad? I rolled my shoulders, ignoring it. I'd take something when we got back if it was still an issue.

"How does it look?" he asked, his eyes narrowed with a hint of suspicion, searching my face for clues.

"It'll do," I replied. "Now, what options do you have for clothes?" My professionalism returned to my voice.

I glanced at the small stack of folded clothes on the end of Dorian's bed. He reached over and pulled out a simple black button-up shirt and khaki pants.

"I found these a few weeks before we met. I was exploring a city, and someone tossed them in a dumpster," he explained, touching the fabric. "I was lucky. I think they'll work for this." He looked up at me, the hint of blush on his cheeks warming his face.

I imagined Dorian dumpster-diving and realized I shouldn't be surprised that he was so resourceful. I was dealing with someone determined to survive. I wondered how I would fare with my skillset, if I had to struggle to make it day-to-day like Dorian and his kind.

"We should get going. Bryce will be waiting for us," I said curtly, practicing my professional tone for when we were around Bryce again. It needed to be perfect before we joined him.

"Right," he replied grimly. "Let's hope nobody is paying attention."

I frowned at that, confused, but backed out of his cell so he could change. I stood beside his door, back turned, trying to ignore the sounds of brushing fabrics and a *zip*.

Do not think about him putting on pants. And definitely don't think about what he looks like before *he puts on his pants.*

I was usually focused and professional. This wasn't me.

He stepped out of his cell, looking like he was ready for a business casual day as a bank teller. I studied him for a moment and nodded with satisfaction. He looked perfectly ordinary, though that face could never be *entirely* ordinary.

The two of us headed toward the door while I wondered what he'd meant earlier. It became quite clear as soon as we stepped out of his secluded cell.

"Ooh, look at that!" Sike craned his neck around the bars of Bravi's cell. "Hey, pretty lady, what's the occasion?" he shot at Dorian.

Of course the other vampires would find this just as weird as Gina had found me stealing foundation. In fact, it was probably weirder.

Dorian jerked his head, signaling me to keep walking. But the others weren't going to let him get away that easily. All around us, shocked stares bombarded us, and a few more hoots and hollers came from some of the other vampires. Kreya sat on her bed, covering her laughter with her hands. Rhome stared, his head tilted in confusion, amusement glittering in his eyes. Apparently, the entire facility's worth of vampires just happened to be out in the hallway to stare. Even Laini watched with a small smile, her usually sad eyes brightening slightly, and Harlowe called for Rayne to come look. Even old Thoth set down his book to watch the "Dorian the Human" show; he stood in the doorway of his cell, arms crossed over his stomach, emitting slow, booming laughs.

"I know we're getting along with the humans really well, but you don't have to turn *into* one, Dorian," Sike called.

Bravi snorted. "Leave them alone so they can go enjoy their"—she grimaced—"date."

Gina had thought so, too, but the vampires' jibes, some good-natured, others less so, were fifty times more embarrassing than my friend's had been. I snatched a glimpse at Dorian and found his face exasperated but amused. He rolled his eyes, but a reluctant smile tugged at his mouth.

Kane watched from down the hall, his face displaying his usual lack of amusement, but this time there appeared to be genuine worry in his eyes. That disconcerted me. Because of their intense bickering, I hadn't realized he might also care about Dorian.

Laughter rippled through the cells. Before we had gone more than six more feet, Dorian raised a hand.

"Now, now, everyone, I know that I'm irresistible. But please control yourselves." Laughter broke out around him, and he grinned back at his friends and family. I caught myself laughing too, startled. Dorian could roll with the punches.

"I'll explain everything later," he said, holding down a laugh.

Sike howled and leaned against a bar. "Oh, don't kiss and tell, Dorian!"

Kane scrunched his nose in disgust and retreated into his cell.

I sealed my lips together, containing my own laughter. Dorian grinned at me, then shook his head with raised eyebrows. We made our way out of the vampire wing, dodging echoing laughter and weird looks from soldiers in the halls—one of whom I handed the used makeup plate off to.

"Nothing like friends and family to knock you down a peg, huh?" I joked to Dorian as we walked.

"Any chance they get," he muttered absently, looking ahead to where Captains Bryce and Clemmins spoke quietly at the main entrance.

"The transformation is complete!" Bryce said, with an enthusiastic grin. He was getting to see vampires do all kinds of things lately, and his enjoyment was palpable, as always.

"Indeed," Dorian said. I caught a glimmer of humor in his eyes. Had he realized that Bryce behaved differently around vampires? "Much to the amusement of the entire wing."

"We're ready, Captain," I said, my voice tight with excitement. My nerves shifted to anticipation of flying and our mission for the night. Professional Lyra was back in the building, although weird-and-anxious-around-Dorian Lyra lingered in the back of my mind.

"Best of luck, everyone." Clemmins winked to us. "Knock 'em dead." Bryce had informed the other captains of our side project in order to ensure things would be handled properly back at the facility while he was gone. I was excited to see Clemmins as pumped about this as I was. I nodded to him, relieved that I wouldn't have to hide this secret project from my higher-ups.

The three of us made our way across the tarmac. The desert expanded out around us, and the crickets thrummed loudly.

Dorian surveyed the sky expectantly, and it seemed our excitement had rubbed off on him, because he shifted unnecessarily on his feet. After no more than a moment, his redbill whizzed overhead.

The bird circled above us and made a point of slapping its long black wingtip feathers over the back of my head. I glared at it, pushing my hair back out of my face, but I had to admit it was a little funny. For a bird. The redbill chirped and gurgled sweetly at Dorian, ignoring me and Bryce. At least it wasn't trying to eat us—that was definitely a step in the right direction.

Captain Bryce typed into a handheld GPS device. It beeped, and he handed it to Dorian.

"That'll keep you on course," Bryce said. "Keep your bird in the loop, so to speak."

"Yes, Captain," Dorian said. "Thank you for choosing Redbill Airlines." His tone was so curt and his face so stoic, it took me a moment to register the joke. I bit back a startled laugh.

As the redbill landed and bobbed over to us, I caught myself staring at Dorian. In the fading evening light, the makeup wasn't quite so noticeable, and it was a shock to see him looking so different. So *human.* I realized that I preferred him the way he was naturally. The makeup covered that otherworldly, opalescent glow of his skin, turning him into a mannequin of himself. That could've just been my mediocre makeup job, though.

"Captain, may I ask you to sit in the rear to evenly distribute weight?" Dorian asked politely.

"All right," Bryce said, rubbing his hands together. He *would* be eager to get on a murderous flying monster. He rolled his shoulders like he was warming up for a workout. "Any advice for a first-time flier? Tips and tricks of the trade?"

"Don't fall off," Dorian said, deadpan. Bryce raised his eyebrows in amused appreciation. It didn't surprise me that these two were starting to get along so well.

Dorian mounted first, soothing his bird with a hand on its neck.

Then he helped Bryce up, giving him instructions in a calm, even tone. Bryce listened intently, nodding when Dorian paused. I was last, hauled up by both men and sandwiched in the middle. The bird was big enough for all of us to sit relatively comfortably, but it was definitely cozier—and weirder—than it had been with just me and Dorian flying. I wasn't exactly comfortable with Bryce straddling me from behind, but duty called.

The bird clacked its beak and loped down the tarmac. It leapt into the air, and Bryce remained calm and quiet but noticeably tightened his arms around us.

We rose toward the clouds, and the redbill circled once before pointing northwest. The wind rose to a howl, peeling at my eyelids as our speed increased.

I put my face behind Dorian's shoulder and closed my eyes. *The flight won't be too long. Just don't think about Bryce's thighs touching you.* I felt the warmth emanating from Dorian's flexing back muscles against my chest. This was going to be a practice in thought compartmentalization; I had to not think about either of the bodies around me.

I knew this was just business, but I couldn't help but wish Dorian and I were alone.

CHAPTER TWENTY-FOUR

Our bird soared over the blazing lights of Las Vegas. After the long stretch of complete desert blackness, the size and brightness of it was awe-inspiring. A million headlights traversed serpentine highways, and downtown, towering structures flashed and glittered, showing off the whole spectrum of visible color. Even from above it looked loud and gaudy. It would've been an incredible view if I hadn't been wondering about the next step in our plan—and been a little squished between Dorian and Bryce.

The redbill twitched its head nervously as we descended, but every time it seemed too unsettled, Dorian brought it back to ease with the touch of his hand.

The federal police building stuck out amongst lines of strip malls and towering apartments. It was taller than the others and completely black, serious and forbidding compared to the bright palaces of escapism in downtown. Our bill circled twice before landing in a flurry of wings, tossing back its head.

A tall, lanky figure emerged from the roof access door as we dismounted. Bryce must have alerted his friend to our arrival.

The captain wavered on his feet after hopping off the bird, shaking his head a little. Even after all his years of experience, I guessed he found it hard to adjust to flying so fast. But, just as I would expect, he quickly regained his composure as he greeted his friend. He rolled with the punches, just like Dorian.

"Jim, you've gotten taller," he said as they clapped each other heartily on the back. Up close, Jim had thin-rimmed glasses and an angular face.

"And your accent has gotten uglier," Jim replied coolly. They grinned at each other. Jim's eyes bounced between all three of us and the redbill, though he seemed remarkably calm for being in close proximity to two supernatural creatures, regardless of the fact that he'd been briefed.

Captain introduced me. "This here is First Lieutenant Sloane."

I leaned in and shook Jim's hand. "Thank you for inviting us, sir," I said. The man's handshake was firm, almost testing. He seemed competent, even though he had a sense of humor.

"My pleasure," Jim said to me, though he looked past me to Dorian with intent, fixated eyes. He showed no fear; it seemed more like he was analyzing the situation, trying to suss it out. "And this must be our newly humanized friend." Jim's voice lilted with just a touch of humor again, but it didn't mask his seriousness. I imagined working under Jim would be rewarding. His manner had a good balance of businesslike and easy-going.

Dorian offered a smile and nod, extending his pale hand to Jim for a shake. "Dorian Clave," he said evenly. His posture was straight, his shoulders set in perfect confidence.

"Let's head to my office, shall we?" Jim turned and led us into the police building.

We entered his office, a dark room with wood-paneled walls. Jim had a desk somewhere beneath the mounds of papers—clutter was apparently another thing he and Bryce had in common—but Jim sat on the same side we did, his knees pointed toward Dorian's.

"I'm going to get right to it," he said, and folded his hands in his lap, maintaining his businesslike air. "As harrowing as it was to have vampires among us back in the day—no offense—I honestly believe that right now, overall, things are worse. That's why I left the Bureau. I think I'm more needed here."

Bryce nodded, his eyes serious. Though the two had greeted each other like friends, it was clear that this was no casual meeting. Dorian and I leaned forward in tandem, listening intently.

"You two know how out of control our crime rates are," Jim continued, turning his gaze on Captain Bryce and me. His face turned to stone as he spoke. His humorous edge completely dissolved. "This past half-decade has seen unprecedented growth of all types of crime. It's so bad that we've had to control how much the media is allowed to cover, in order to keep some semblance of calm among the population. Not only are we fighting skyrocketing crime rates, we're having serious personnel issues inside the police force itself. Corruption just keeps rearing its ugly head, I'm afraid."

He sighed and leaned back, the gravity of his words weighing heavily on the room for a moment as we all took them in. I'd known things were bad, but hearing it put like that was sobering.

"You never were much good at interviewing people," Bryce said, in an attempt to lighten the solemn mood. "Hell, you hired me."

"Biggest mistake of my life," Jim said, breaking his stoicism with a smile, which faded as quickly as it arrived. "Another interesting fact is that we've seen a decrease in missing persons. Most murder victims are found." Jim glanced at Dorian this time, evaluating his reaction.

Dorian remained calm, listening intently.

"That said, my deepest concern is for the future. If this trend continues, how bad will it be in five, ten, fifteen years? We can't keep up. We need to find another way to get a handle on the situation." Jim's eyes were somber. Dread filled me at the thought of the violence growing exponentially year after year—we couldn't let that happen.

He cleared his throat and lightened his tone. "So, I'm currently looking at… nontraditional resources. Hell, I must be desperate if I'm willing to work alongside this nut-bag again." Jim tilted his head to indicate Bryce.

"Missed you, too," Bryce said under his breath. These two would've been a handful to work with together.

Jim turned his attention to Dorian, adjusting his glasses on his nose to inspect the vampire. "I'm invested in your cause, Mr. Clave. Not only for professional reasons, but for everyone's wellbeing. Depending on how this evening goes, I'd like to help you build a case to present to the Bureau. Hopefully they'll listen, for once."

I squinted at him, rolling his last sentence back through my head. His intentions sounded good, maybe even promising. At least he seemed to be taking the situation seriously.

"I appreciate that, sir," Dorian said.

"I'm sure you're aware that even if this works out, the government won't let you and your pals run around killing whomever you please like you did in your heyday," Jim said. "But your alleged skillsets could bring some stability to this dumpster fire we've been trying to put out for years. Everyone, even vampires, could benefit. If you *do* have this 'specified predation' thing, whatever you call it, we could pinpoint certain cases for rehabilitation before they even harm anyone."

Dorian frowned, shaking his head with a somberness that mirrored Jim's earlier tone. "That won't work. There is no way to cure a human of their darkness." An uncomfortable silence settled after that matter-of-fact pronouncement.

"Leave that to the therapists, sonny," muttered Bryce. Dorian shot him a skeptical glance but shrugged it off.

Quiet filled the room as the humans pondered what Dorian had just said. Jim tapped a finger on his bottom lip, his eyes still calmly studying the vampire. Bryce squinted in concern, though he'd initially been his usual brash self. He couldn't hide the fact that he deeply cared for people, just like I did; it was why we worked at the Bureau to begin with.

Even if vampires couldn't cure someone of their ill intentions, they could help us locate those who needed help in order to change. I'd always firmly believed that anyone who wanted to change could do so.

It was in everyone's power to control their actions, and even more so, it was their responsibility. People could struggle with their darkness, but no one was beyond help. Dorian might believe that, but he didn't know everything. I knew that if this project succeeded, he could be proven wrong.

"So," Jim said, leveling his voice to pull us back on track and away from our thoughts. "I assume you were briefed on the little exam I have arranged for you this evening. I need to see for myself what we're dealing with."

"I was informed that you were curious about my skillset," said Dorian. His composure remained steadfast and earnest. Bryce and I exchanged a look of anticipation, our excitement rising again to see what was in store for the evening.

"We have a lineup downstairs with a variety of individuals. Some may be innocent, and some may not be. I'd like you to tell me who's who." Jim rose from his seat, and the rest of us did the same.

Just as Jim twisted the knob of his office door, his cell rang in his pocket. "One moment, pardon me," he murmured, swiping his finger across the phone's screen to accept the call.

We stood in silence as Jim listened to the voice on the other end. He blinked at the floor a few times, and then his jaw went rigid and his brow furrowed in the dim light from the desk lamp.

"Okay, I've got somebody on it," Jim said into the receiver. He hung up and looked at Dorian appraisingly, sizing him up again. "Change of plan."

"Pardon?" Bryce asked, his voice heightened with wariness.

My eyes were glued to Jim, and adrenaline mixed with anxiety in my blood. The air weighed heavier on me.

"A pair of newlyweds were just murdered in their hotel room at the Hyzanthia. The guests in the next room heard the gunshots and immediately called the police. The culprit fled the scene recently, so he won't be too far yet. The hotel is close by." Jim's words flew from his mouth rapidly, his tone flat.

His intention was clear. I shot a glance at Dorian, the words sticking in my throat. I knew there was no need to worry; Dorian knew what he was doing. And even if this project already felt personal to me, it shouldn't feel so difficult to imagine Dorian putting himself in harm's way. I swallowed. My chest felt tighter than normal. I really needed to get these feelings under control.

Jim evaluated Dorian, a calculating look in his eye. He set a hand on his hip. "What do you say, Dorian? Looks like we've been handed a golden opportunity. You want to take a field trip and track down our guy?"

Bryce interjected before Dorian could answer. "Jim, we can't just set him loose in the streets," he said gruffly.

"Why not?" Jim asked with a crooked smile. "This seems to be a very practical application of what he claims to be able to do, with an immediate real-world benefit. Why waste time?" Jim crossed his arms over his chest and gave Bryce a "so what are you gonna do about it?" look. He knew how to get his way with Bryce—and probably most people.

"For one, it breaks Bureau restrictions for our trial period. He's required to be under supervision at all times." Captain Bryce said what he was required to, but his voice wavered a bit between displeasure with breaking rules and knowing Jim was probably right. We all knew that if Dorian pulled this off, Jim would be sold.

I inhaled. I knew what the right call would be. I knew that Dorian was willing to take a personal risk to prove vampires were useful. But it didn't make me any less tense.

"Don't you trust him?" Jim asked, his voice prodding. I'd never seen anyone push Bryce's buttons so fearlessly, and though my nerves clenched my throat, Jim was relentless. "You're a captain. Can't you make the call, in serious circumstances?"

Bryce blew air out of his nose. He rubbed his temple, then slowly cracked a wry smile. I watched with wide eyes, not convinced that Bryce wasn't about to blow a gasket. "All right, I'm making an executive decision. Due to the imminent threat to human life, I'll allow this. Just once." Jim grinned at that, and Bryce rolled his eyes at him.

I wondered how many oddball plans Jim and Bryce had talked each other into over the years. At least Bryce wasn't going to throttle anyone. Now all I had to fear was what the heck Dorian was walking into. I clenched my fists in an attempt to relieve some muscle tension.

"Mr. Clave, if you would," Jim said, signaling Dorian over to his desk. "It's not the most high-tech, but I think it'll suit our purpose." Jim pulled out a camera and a comm earpiece. He fixed the camera to Dorian's chest and wrapped Velcro straps around him to secure it, then tested Dorian's comm with his own. Dorian remained still as Jim worked around him. He pressed his lips into a tight line, and his eyes stared intently at a spot on the floor. He looked uncomfortable to be in such close proximity to Jim, in a way that he hadn't with me, earlier.

"We'll see everything you see, and I'll be speaking with you the whole time. And no one dies during this operation—injure and restrain only. Understood?" Jim asked tersely.

"Yes, sir," Dorian responded. I watched him, wondering if he was at all worried. His cool, professional demeanor hadn't broken since we sat down. If he hoped to impress Jim, I imagined that would do it.

Jim reached into another desk drawer and removed a taser. He handed it to Dorian. Dorian held his hands up in refusal.

"That won't be necessary, sir," he said, and this time I saw his quick half-smile. It was a smile that told all of us humans that we were about to get a very good show. I wasn't sure whether it made me feel more or less worried—I knew plenty of self-assured soldiers who'd overestimated themselves.

"Cocky, isn't he?" Jim said incredulously to me and Bryce with raised eyebrows. Then, to Dorian, "All right, let's cut you loose."

Jim opened the door, and Dorian disappeared down the stairwell. We rushed after him, but he was quick—quicker than even I remembered. My mind flew through memories of his inhuman speed when he'd captured me, disarming me instantly. Had I ever seen him at full strength?

"We're going to monitor your progress from the surveillance room on the first floor," Jim shouted at Dorian's retreating figure, sounding slightly winded, but with more than a tinge of excitement in his voice.

We humans burst out of the stairwell door behind Dorian, and Jim clicked on his comm to continue his instructions. "Out the main door and to the right. The hotel is six blocks down. Do your thing." By the time we got to the lobby, I could see the rotating glass door spinning too fast, but Dorian was already gone.

"In here, folks," Jim barked quickly, directing us with a waving hand into the building's surveillance room, which was mostly filled by a two-tier desk crowded with screens. "I'll have this hooked up in just a second. Then we'll see what this guy's really made of."

The biggest screen in the middle of the array flickered as Jim toyed with some controls, then a screen to the right turned on with a display of satellite and CCTV footage for the twenty-block radius around us. The middle screen blinked a moment later, and there was Dorian's chest cam, vibrating wildly as he sprinted.

"Dorian." Jim spoke into the comm with precision and energy. "Tell me what's happening." Bryce leaned over Jim's shoulder to listen to Dorian's reply, and Jim tilted the earpiece toward him. These two were a sight to behold in action. Their interplay looked seamless, like they'd never stopped working together.

I heard Dorian's tinny voice reply in Jim's earpiece. The CCTV screen flashed to a different camera, and we watched a grainy Dorian race down the sidewalk.

"Good. I see you're nearing Cleveland Street. You're going to take a right there. The Hyzanthia is a block up on the right. The culprit won't be in the building anymore, but they may still be around it," Jim instructed into the comm. "This kid is fast," he mouthed to Bryce, his eyes alight, and Bryce nodded back at him, his eyebrows raised in an I-told-you-so. Bryce drummed the tips of his fingers on the desk eagerly.

Dorian was in front of the hotel by the time the CCTV screen flashed the image of the lobby doors. My eyes jumped erratically between all of the screens, trying to piece together this jumble of images into a smooth picture.

"I'm walking around the building," I heard Dorian say through Jim's earpiece. "I've got a sense of the target. Vile."

Jim leaned back in his chair. Everyone fixated on Dorian's chest camera in tense silence. Bryce still drummed his fingers, his face stone. All three of us were gripped, frozen. We watched Dorian slide past darkened windows and parked cars.

Maybe I should've worried that the vampire would use this opportunity to pull a fast one on us, grab a quick snack of innocents, and take off into the night. But instead, the blood and carnage I imagined resembled a headstrong guy biting off more than he could chew and regretting it. I didn't like the idea of standing by while he got beaten to a pulp on CCTV, but knowing Dorian, my worry was probably wasted. I was so curious I couldn't hold my leg still, my thigh bouncing nervously. I watched, willing myself to wait and see.

Was that confidence I'd seen in Dorian earned, or was it all hot air? That wouldn't bode well for our side project. But inside I knew it was more than that, too.

Bryce seemed too enraptured to blink, while Jim watched with his arms folded, his gaze anticipatory.

We watched Dorian creep around a corner, following his sense of the culprit's darkness. He swiftly walked a few more blocks. Then he slid into a surprisingly well-lit, random alleyway, the glow of the street reaching far into its depths.

I sucked in an anxious breath. A group of four men jogged ahead of Dorian in the alley. Were they the ones he was looking for?

"Got 'em," Dorian said, his voice low and confident, coming through the comm distinctly this time.

"Four of them?" Bryce asked the room, with a frown that gave away a hint of worry.

"This is an interesting turn. We have had increased gang activity in this neighborhood. Probably connected," Jim said, tapping his cheek with his finger as though this was all some sort of practice scenario. Neither of them instructed Dorian to pull back.

"Captain, this isn't what we expected," I murmured. "Should we send backup? Have him follow from a distance?"

I squeezed my hands together to release some of my muscle tension, calmly reminding myself to stay levelheaded.

If he has to go into danger, I'd rather be fighting at his side. I hated watching from a screen.

"If there's a problem, Sloane, we'll send you after him," Bryce said. "But he'll back out or ask for help if he needs to. Let's see how this plays out."

I knew Bryce was right, but my chest tightened. I couldn't help but worry that if something went wrong, I wouldn't get there in time.

It looked like the men had dressed in staff uniforms in order to pull off their stunt and make a clean getaway. I thought I could make out the shape of gun butts under a couple of their shirts, but the TV image wasn't clear enough.

Well, Dorian, all that attitude better not be for nothing. I'd never seen this guy take on a human before, besides ambushing me, and I hadn't been able to fully analyze and appreciate what he was doing at the time, since I was under attack. I highly anticipated watching Dorian cut loose—not fully, but enough to land some hits. I couldn't wait to see how hard he could go without snapping necks. And then there was that flutter of attraction inside my chest, which kept springing up from under my metaphorical boot heel.

The CCTV snapped to a bird's-eye view of the alley from a camera mounted on a light post. In flickering black and white, it clearly showed Dorian stalking up behind the four men. Only about fifteen feet separated them now.

Dorian closed the distance swiftly, assuredly. Dorian's approach must've been dead silent, because he got close enough to swipe the two guns from under the men's shirts at the back of their pants, one in each hand, then dart backward. I was impressed with Dorian's speed, but also with my ability to initially catch the detail of the guns hidden beneath the perpetrators' shirts.

One freshly unarmed man turned and spotted Dorian, his mouth stretching in surprise, alerting his friends with a shout I couldn't hear. The man beside him stumbled, reaching for where his gun used to be. His face contorted in anger at its disappearance. Their stances immediately went defensive, and one's mouth moved quickly, planning their attack. Dorian stood and studied them motionlessly. Then, his movement almost casual, he tossed the guns out of sight over his shoulders.

Not one of us breathed.

The yelling man pointed, indicating to his friends to surround Dorian.

Before they could, Dorian made his move.

He went for the man farthest to the left first, leaping over him— actually over him—and snapping his arm behind his back, breaking it at the elbow, using it to restrain him in place. The man's face wrenched in a scream, and Dorian dropped him to the ground, where he writhed, clutching his arm. The next closest man lurched toward Dorian, enraged, but the vampire aimed a high kick at his jaw, sending him tumbling backward to the concrete.

The light from the lamppost glinted on two more guns, the other two men having fumbled them from their pants.

"Watch out," I whispered on a strained outbreath.

A flash erupted from one of the guns pointed directly at Dorian, and his chest cam went dark. But the CCTV showed that he hadn't fallen; instead, he'd dived to the ground and shielded himself with the broken-armed man's body on the ground. The man jolted, dark blood streaming from a bullet wound in his shoulder, another wave of pain warping his face. Dorian pushed the now-bleeding man away toward his unconscious colleague and dodged another bullet, moving toward the remaining men almost too fast to see.

When he was nearly upon them, Dorian leapt into the air again, landing on the shoulders of the first shooter. The man staggered backward under his weight and smashed into the concrete. Dorian landed on top of him and pounded a fist into his temples, knocking him unconscious. The vampire snatched the gun and pitched it deep into the shadows.

The remaining gunman had fumbled to aim, unable to get a good shot so close to his friend's head, but Dorian was too fast. He lunged into the man's midsection with such force that the two flew backward, landing on the concrete about seven feet away, by my estimate.

I quickly scanned the surveillance room. Bryce and Jim were dead silent, their jaws hanging open. No one said a word. I didn't even hear breathing, which prompted me to inhale for the first time in who knows how long. I'd never seen Bryce so... awestruck. Jim's glasses had slipped down his nose, but he didn't move to fix them.

With that last man sprawled beneath him, Dorian crouched over him and threw his gun into a nearby dumpster. Dorian's face turned to the sky for a moment, almost directly into the CCTV cam we were gaping at. He twisted his neck, his fangs suddenly lengthening and shining in the light, visible even in the security camera. The criminals' darkness was getting to him.

"Oh, sh—" Bryce choked.

I felt my hand press against my mouth in an entirely new kind of worry. Was this it? Would he break down and prove to us that his bloodthirsty nature couldn't be controlled? Were these criminals too "dark" for Dorian to control himself? Until this moment, I hadn't even realized how much control I'd expected of him. Dorian's face twisted in a silent howl. On the black-and-white visuals, for a moment he truly looked like a monster from some old film, about to commit unspeakable evil. His pain was palpable through the screen.

Then he clenched a fist against his throat, his face constricting in a wince while his fangs retracted. A wave of relief washed the grimace from his face.

My own echo of relief didn't last long. While he was distracted, I saw motion on the security camera.

"He's getting up!" I warned. One of the shooters stumbled to his feet, directly behind Dorian.

At almost the same moment, Jim curled his lip in irritation. "What the hell? Who are they?" he snapped. "Dorian, you've got more company," he said into the comm.

Two people rushed down the alley, breaking into the security camera's line of vision—civilians, probably trying to help break up a drunken street brawl.

Dorian extended his hand for them to stop. The man coming up behind him pulled a switchblade from his front pocket and angled it at the spot between Dorian's shoulder blades. A gasp escaped my throat. Dorian could die.

Just as I was about to wrench the comm out of Jim's hands and shout a warning, he breathed into the comm again. "Dorian, behind—"

Before he finished his sentence, Dorian spun on the balls of his feet, one hand still signaling the civilians to back up, the other clearly preparing to defend himself from the knife. He'd known the whole time.

An exhale rushed out of my relieved chest, the tightness transforming into rising bubbles of something other than worry.

Dorian yelled something to the civilians, and then dodged as the criminal slashed the blade clumsily toward his face, his apparent concussion fouling his aim and stance. The vampire arched gracefully backward to dodge the knife, then dipped down and swept his leg in a wide circle, knocking the man's legs out from under him.

I raised my eyebrows. He'd stolen that move from me.

The criminal's head cracked on the pavement, and Dorian leapt onto him, grinding his skull down once more. The man flailed the knife wildly until Dorian broke his wrist, the impossible angle of the bone looking painful even from our vantage point. The guy's face broke into a scream. The knife dropped to the ground, and his struggle turned to pained twitching.

The civilians on the cam hadn't come any nearer—they stopped and stared, their mouths hanging open, just like ours.

Dorian gave the man a swift fist to the temple to knock him unconscious and then yelled something else to the civilians. They held their hands up and backed out of the alley, leaving the camera's view.

When I looked back to where Dorian stood, he had disappeared. The four men lay completely debilitated on the concrete. Not even twitching.

Flashing lights danced across the wall, and a swarm of police filled the screen.

We sat in silence for a while. Dazed excitement filled the room like fog. My head spun, not from worry, but from a dizzying sense of pride. He'd done it. He'd proven all that I'd hoped for and more. If I'd had any doubts left, I knew now that this project of ours could turn the tide of history between humans and vampires. Those flutters between my ribs turned into pounding wings.

And we started it. Dorian and me. Just by trying to understand each other instead of killing on sight.

"He did everything except put a bow on 'em," Bryce mumbled in disbelief.

"Couldn't find any." Dorian's bored voice came from behind us.

I jumped in shock and spun to face him.

His chest heaved, emphasizing his defined muscles, but his breathing was silent. "They smelled terrible," he said, crinkling his nose in disgust. Then he shot me a cocky grin, fanning the flames of my attraction. He'd just taken on *four* armed career criminals, singlehanded. I could barely think straight. I wanted to throw my arms around him, and if we'd been alone, I might have. Instead I maintained professionalism, staying silent in my chair, waiting for Bryce's cue. Did vampires even hug?

Dorian's eyes never left mine, and his grin turned knowing. Jim then drew his attention. Jim had finally closed his hanging jaw, regaining his calculating demeanor as he pulled his cell from his pocket and dialed. While he waited for a response on the other end, his eyes locked on Dorian, who leaned against the doorframe, composed and professional. He must have remembered that he needed to impress this man.

Bryce sank into a folding chair in the corner to wait for Jim to finish his call, still looking a little dumbfoundedly in Dorian's direction. The screens continued to buzz, the cops silently milling about in the background.

"Yeah," Jim said into his phone. Clearly whoever was on the line had no need for introduction. "I need a confirmation on the type of bullets. Now."

Bryce blew air loudly out between his lips and stared at me, his eyes like saucers. It might have been the first time I ever saw that much shock on the Scotsman's face. My gaze drifted over to Dorian, who leaned casually in the doorway, watching Jim expectantly. Specks of blood spattered his cheek, smearing his makeup into a gory mess. My eyes traced the lines of his shoulders, the evidence of toned muscles hidden beneath his black, long-sleeved shirt, accentuated by the way he leaned on his extended arm. The worry and pride I'd felt before swirled into a different kind of tingling. I couldn't remember a time I'd felt so many overwhelming emotions at once. It didn't hurt, but my chest was so full it felt like I would burst.

A voice on the other end of Jim's call rattled something into his ear, and he hung up without responding. He lowered back into his seat and rubbed his lower lip with his thumb as though calculating something, his eyes far away. He sat still for a moment, his brows furrowing thoughtfully. Then he turned to Dorian and cleared his throat.

"The bullets in the alley matched the type in the hotel room," Jim said softly, his eyebrows rising in consideration.

Every eye drifted back to Dorian.

Jim nodded once, decisively, that little smile spreading into a grin, his eyes flickering. "Yes… I think we can arrange something."

CHAPTER TWENTY-FIVE

We stood by a river. Water gurgled over green, mossy stones. Flowers bloomed nearby. The air smelled sweet. Dorian waded through the water, tossing a splash at me. "Lyra," he called. "Did you see where my brother went?"

A field replaced the river. The grass swayed. He walked toward me, the sleeves of his white linen shirt rolled up past his elbows. He called out, smiling. I waved. Something weighed down his right arm.

The wind cut through the grass, exposing a man whom Dorian held by the shirt collar. The man thrust a switchblade at him. Dorian wrapped his fingers around the man's throat and hoisted him up. He held the man to the sky, rapid heartbeats pulsing in both their necks. Darkness billowed beneath Dorian's skin like storm clouds. His lips curled back, revealing fangs dripping with thick, black blood. They slanted down, curved to points at the ends, a second away from piercing the man's flesh.

My scream never left my throat.

I bolted upright in my bunk, gasping for air. My eyes focused, and I hurriedly shivered off the tremor traveling my spine, chilling my insides. *Dreaming. You were dreaming.* I blinked, trying to shake the last vivid image of the knife, Dorian's teeth...

I took a moment to steady my breathing. The barracks were mostly dark, but shades of purple seeped through the windows. It must have been just before dawn.

Lily's heart-shaped face watched me sleepily as she lay sideways on her bunk across the aisle.

I waved a hand through my labored breathing. "Sorry," I whispered. "Weird dreams."

She offered a little smile and rolled back over, disappearing underneath her blankets.

I tried to go through my dream, digest what about it had left me so shaken, but the images faded and blurred together even as I thought back through them. Dorian... something bad was happening with Dorian. But was he in danger, or was *he* the danger that had terrified me in my dream?

I thumped a fist softly into the bedding. I'd been arranging so much in the rest of my life around the vampire that he was sneaking into my dreams now. *Great.*

Giving up the effort to remember, I wrapped my arms around my pillow and reattempted sleep through my disrupted, jarring thoughts, trying to find comfort in Roxy's snores.

I awoke to the bugle and that creeping ache in my chest again. My dad had fought heartburn for the past few years, so it was likely my turn now. I grabbed the water bottle sitting beside my bunk and chugged. The aches felt worse this time. There was no point in my daily performance suffering due to stomach issues, so I promised myself I'd grab something from the medic if it felt the same tomorrow.

The other women left their bunks, chatting about their expectations for our next redbill mission. As we entered the bathroom, Roxy called dibs on her favorite shower stall.

"But you promised I could have the big shower today," Lily contested groggily.

"I'll write you an IOU," Roxy replied flatly. It was clearly not up for debate. Lily rubbed her eyes, yawned, and muttered incoherently to herself. Gina and Louise placed bets on how many redbills we would send off next.

I blocked them out, instead focusing on recapping the previous night in my head while stretching my toes against the bathroom's cold concrete. Jim had finished the evening by telling Dorian that he'd have another task as soon as he checked his files—a task that would continue to bulk up our case. I couldn't wait to hear back from him.

I took such a long shower that morning that the women in line yelled at me for being a hog. I leaned into the stream of water, treading through my thoughts. Despite the stomachache and strange dreams, I was sure the captains had a full day for us, and I wanted to be as clear-headed as I could. And I wanted to check in and see how the vampires felt after the last successful redbill op. And, of course, to see Dorian.

I eased myself against the tile wall, breathing in the steam, thinking maybe just a few more minutes would clear my head or dissolve the lingering pain in my chest.

Captain Bryce still had sleep in his eyes when he greeted us at our morning meeting, which was highly unusual for him, but I probably looked about the same. Dorian, on the other hand, looked unusually cheerful. Perhaps it was because of our mission, which had certainly put a spring in my step.

"New mission this morning," Bryce said energetically, cracking his knuckles. "My mid-level team—for the most part—knows how to be light on their feet, but today, some of our newer soldiers may get the chance to show me their dance moves."

Roxy rolled her eyes. Hank, on the other hand, swiveled his bulky shoulders excitedly, as though pumping himself up for the challenge. I remembered him putting his stuffed crocodile in one of the vampire cells and smiled to myself. He'd been getting along with the vampires pretty well, and I was glad to see him adjusting. I appreciated that no matter how tired he was, he was always in a good mood.

"When I say 'light on your feet,' I mean aware. We're entering a heavily populated area today," Bryce said, directing the end of his sentence toward the vampires. "The number of redbills reported isn't terribly high, but we will be surrounded by humans. Circumstances are delicate—people don't know the bills are there yet, but it's only a matter of time. We're trying to remove this issue before it becomes a reality to anyone besides the Bureau. Quick and clean."

"What Captain Bryce is telling you in a roundabout way," Captain Finley said dryly as she walked in the door, "is that your mission today is in a suburb. Specifically, a golf course. The Bureau asked the establishment to close to the public, which they did, but some of the managerial staff are still on site."

I immediately thought back to our recent encounters with civilians, especially at Navy Pier, the night before everything changed. With the vampires' help, I hoped this afternoon would go more smoothly. But this also meant that the vampires would be around people who weren't carrying handguns, and they'd potentially have to fight their urge to feed. I shuddered, remembering Dorian's face on the CCTV feed the night before.

Beside me, Grayson rubbed the back of his neck after Finley spoke. I couldn't read the side of his face, but he scribbled some notes in his memo pad. He always took notes, mentally preparing himself on paper before a mission.

I shot a glance at the vampires to see if their faces gave away any feeling regarding civilians. Harlowe looked pensive and picked at a nail as she sat beside Rayne—per usual—who looked even more bored than normal.

"I'd like the vampires to brainstorm the most efficient way to approach this mission under these circumstances," Captain Bryce said.

I loved to see Bryce progressively put more and more trust in the vampires. To me, that was the biggest sign of victory for the trial period yet, alongside our growing friendships and the increasing number of relocated bills. Maybe watching Dorian last night had left Bryce convinced that the vampires would create a good plan for our approach. Or maybe it had been the near-disaster with the first joint redbill mission, where we'd tried it the Bureau way and messed things up immediately.

Either way, I was glad to see him treating the vampires less like criminals and more like partners. Around me, though, some soldiers muttered to each other, suggesting that not everyone felt the same. Not yet, anyway.

When Dorian heard Bryce's request, he immediately swiveled around and whispered to Rhome and Bravi. Bravi's eyes watched him intently, and she nodded a few times. It irritated me that I was too far to hear what they said.

The meeting adjourned. We had an hour before we departed for the outskirts of Salt Lake City, Utah. The vampires returned to their quarters to formulate a plan. Dorian lingered at the back of his group as they exited. When he caught my eye, my heart rate picked up. Another reminder about reining in "unprofessional" feelings sounded loudly through my mind.

As I walked back to my quarters, I saw Dorian, Rhome, and Bravi in conversation with the captains. The vampires appeared to be asking questions, the captains nodding in serious consideration. Even Finley seemed to be in agreement, although she remained her usual stoic self. The way Clemmins gestured excitedly in response to Rhome made me smile. Watching them all work together—for all the world like normal coworkers in the Bureau—warmed me, even as I itched to know what they were talking about.

When I got back to my bed, a brand-new breastplate, backplate, and set of knives sat on my blanket.

"Yes!" I said out loud.

Excitement surged through me as I tested the knife points on the tips of my fingers. They'd taken extra time to come because I preferred a specific type of curved blade that wasn't always available. I felt a wave of relief knowing that I'd have my armor strapped around me again for the next redbill mission, since my last plates had flown off just before I landed on top of Dorian in the desert.

I'd only been back at my bunk for about ten minutes when one of the girls called to me from the door.

"Lyra, the vampire wants you," Roxy said, sounding irritated. I wasn't sure if that was in response to Dorian's request or just her usual mood. I set down my gear and thanked Roxy while heading to the door, which she completely disregarded.

"We need your costuming skills again today for the vampires the captains have picked for the mission," Dorian said. That must've been what the vampires and captains had been discussing—each mission required a certain number of vampires to match the number of redbills, and apparently the captains had strategically picked who they wanted. Knowing how well Dorian and his close friends and family worked together, I had a hunch who we'd be putting makeup on. He stood at the door, smirking. "Apparently our trial disguise for Jim impressed the captains. They even want to recruit some other volunteers. If you could gather up some of your friends and their makeup and come to the vampire quarters, we'd appreciate it."

I felt my mouth quirk in amused disbelief. "Are you kidding? They were impressed by that makeup job?"

"Apparently they want us *all* to look like... what was it? Clowns in a bar fight?"

"It'll be like a mission to the circus," I joked.

He met my eyes as we laughed, and I noticed for the first time the crinkles that appeared around the edges of his blue eyes when he was amused. I still wasn't sure I liked this whole tingling limbs, nervous breathing thing that happened to me when he was near... but the warmth that suffused my body when Dorian smiled made the rest worth it.

"Well, I'm sure there's somebody here who can do better makeup on a vampire than me," I told him, then smirked at a sudden realization. "I bet Rhome and Kane are really stoked about getting human makeovers. Since they all liked yours so well."

Dorian's eyes glittered, and I could tell he would savor his miniature revenge. "They're going to be thrilled," he said dryly. "Come by our quarters in the next half hour or so. We also need two everyday outfits for women around Gina and Lily's size, if you could—"

"Of course," I said, and our smiles matched. This was definitely a step up from our previous costuming experience, and I clasped my hands in anticipation.

"Thank you," Dorian said, with a trace of irony. "I'll see you in a few minutes." Not "I'll see your group;" he'd said, "I'll see you." My heart swelled. I must have entered the stage of attraction where I read too much into offhanded remarks.

I beamed. My nerves about the first makeup session had mostly dissipated. This time, preparing human disguises might actually be fun. With that in mind, I set about getting help from my colleagues. Most were hesitant, but my excitement—not to mention my promise that it would be highly amusing—eventually persuaded Roxy, Louise, Lily, and Gina to gather up some makeup and clothes and follow me to the vampire quarters.

When we arrived at their cells, we found some of the male soldiers already there. Zach and Colin were laughing at the sight of Rhome, Dorian, and Kane dressed in their clothing: polo shirts and khaki slacks. *Holy crap.* It looked like a suburban vampire reality TV show unfolding before my eyes. I pushed down a laugh before it erupted from my throat. It was a little painful.

"Ready for a day on the links?" Roxy asked sarcastically, and I lost it.

Rhome halfheartedly played with the buttons on his polo, and Dorian struggled with a belt, undoing it, tightening it, and undoing it again, trying to cinch pants that were at least a size too big. Kane, meanwhile, simply attempted to murder the entire room with his eyes.

His just-too-tight shirt emphasized the muscles that rippled across his torso, making him look like a cover model.

Dorian looked up at the female soldiers who'd just entered. "Thank you for coming," he said. Even with his pants half-hanging off him, he managed to look casually collected. I tried not to let my gaze linger too long at the thin exposed line of skin at his hips. "As far as you know, there will only be humans on this mission today." He winked at us.

Gina covered her mouth to hide her amusement. I hoped she was having an aha moment regarding what *I'd* been doing with makeup the other day. Sike clung to the bars of his cell, laughing even harder than he had the night before, presumably at Kane. I eyed him sideways. He probably wouldn't be laughing so hard if his injured arm hadn't excused him from today's mission.

"All right, ladies. Let's get this show on the road," I said, trying hard to sound professional. No reason to make this part of the mission more absurd than it already was. We had a schedule to keep, even if it felt like we were in a bizarre species mashup.

At Dorian's instruction, I grabbed the jeans and T-shirts the girls had brought and handed them to Kreya and Bravi, who stood in a cell doorway, looking dubious. They cautiously accepted the clothing and went into their cells to change.

We each picked a vampire to make over. Roxy and Bravi paired up as usual, and Gina sat beside Rhome on his bed. Lily asked Kreya to be her partner. Quiet Louise squared her shoulders and approached Kane, who refused to speak to her but finally caved and sat still as she dabbed his face with concealer. The more Kane scowled, the more serious her face became.

Dorian walked up to me as if there was no other choice.

After practicing the night before, I thought my skills had improved. I'd always been a quick learner, a trait I was proud of. This time, though my stomach still did a weird somersault when he locked eyes with me, and my heartburn seemed to be acting up, I'd gotten control of my hands back. They didn't shake at all as I sat next to Dorian, quietly sponging his face. When I was done, Dorian still looked ridiculous, but less cakey this time.

We reconvened in the aisle, where the giggles continued. Harlowe stepped beside me and nodded in mild approval of Dorian's face, brushing her platinum hair out of her eyes. "That's actually not so bad," she said matter-of-factly.

"Practice makes perfect," I replied with a shrug. My mom said that constantly.

Thoth walked up to Rhome and pulled at the fabric of his polo. "That doesn't look comfortable," he said from under his silver beard in his aged, growly tone.

"It isn't that bad," Rhome replied quietly. His manners attempted to mask his displeasure with the costume requirements of the day.

Roxy had even given Bravi eye makeup, thick eyeliner in a startling shade of teal that complemented her bright green eyes. With her small, muscular frame, and her short dark hair styled a little bit, she looked like the kind of girl who was effortlessly intimidating. Her borrowed T-shirt read, "I'm not shy, I just don't like you." The shirt clearly belonged to Roxy, yet I had to admit that it worked for Bravi, too. They were quite similar, now that I thought about it.

Rayne studied Bravi's eye makeup, fascinated, leaning in close to Bravi's face. They were about the same petite height, so Rayne could examine the colors easily.

"Bravi, you look great!" I said, my excitement heightening my voice. She rolled her eyes but examined her face in the hand mirror with quiet satisfaction. I knew she wouldn't readily take any praise from me, but seeing her appreciate Roxy's work was refreshing. She didn't ignore all human kindness, apparently.

The disguises looked reasonably convincing, if you didn't know what they really were. I couldn't wait to see the captains' faces. Carwin and another little boy vampire crept into the aisle, pointing and laughing at Rhome, who grinned and shooed them back to the family quarters.

The soldiers gathered round the vampires to do last-minute fixes to outfits or add a bit more blush, everyone's excited chatter echoing through the cell block, and then we returned to our own quarters to gear up for the op.

By the time I reached the tarmac, most of the soldiers were already there. The captains discussed last-minute details off to the side. The aircraft, a Boeing V-22 Osprey, was new to the facility and a topic of much discussion among the soldiers already present. The plane/helicopter hybrid had hovering capabilities, allowing us to drop safely. The engine rumbled to life just as the facility door opened, and security guards began escorting the vampires out. Some wore human disguises, and the rest came along as backup, including Thoth, Rayne, Harlowe, and a couple of others I hadn't had much chance to talk to yet.

Upon seeing our costumed vampires, Bryce raised his eyebrows in amusement. Finley shook her head, while Clemmins allowed himself a chuckle. They'd agreed on this strategic approach, but it didn't seem to change the fact that it had a rather entertaining unveiling. The soldiers hooted and hollered. Though the vampires were visibly embarrassed, they quickly recovered their composure. A ripple of laughter rolled through the entire group—even some of the guards. Apparently humor crossed species lines. I felt a zip of happiness at how different this day on the tarmac was compared to the first.

Kane reached the tarmac last, moodily pulling his polo collar. Before we boarded, Clemmins handed the vampires more yellow tags for the redbills.

We humans boarded the aircraft first, the atmosphere distinctly more relaxed than usual, giggles still making the rounds. A group of Bureau guards sat all the way in the back of the craft. The vampires came next, scooting into seats between soldiers, the lighthearted conversations from the vampire quarters continuing. Captains Bryce and Clemmins boarded last.

Dorian and Kreya sat on either side of me. The redbills would stay near the facility that afternoon, as their presence at the site would probably draw unnecessary attention; the vampires had assured us that their calming effect was less necessary with the smaller number of birds that had been sighted.

Our aircraft slid into the air with a grinding roar. Kreya looked down at her T-shirt, which sported a retro paisley pattern.

"I don't much care for the colors," she said, bemused, taking the fabric between her fingers. "But I really like the flowers."

"You look great," I said. She truly looked beautiful—her auburn hair matched the shirt nicely. For as irritated as Kane was with his getup, Kreya seemed nonchalant.

"Thank you," she replied softly, a tiny smile pulling up her lips.

Dorian rubbed Kreya's shoulder affectionately, and she patted his knee, just like my mother did to me. The more I got to know this family of vampires, the more I wanted to spend time with them.

Our flight to Salt Lake City took an hour. Ten minutes before landing, Dorian asked Captain Bryce if he could give instructions to the group.

"Be my guest," Bryce said, and he didn't even sound sarcastic.

Dorian spoke loudly over the aircraft's engine. "We're going to split into teams," he said confidently. "The disguised vampires will be on foot on the golf course, our backup vampires will remain with the Bureau guards at the rear of the golf course in case of emergency, and the soldiers will secure the perimeter while we handle the flock. Lyra, can you organize your soldiers before we land?"

I met Bryce's eyes, and he inclined his head in permission. I smiled, pleased to add some muscle to my second-in-command training—especially alongside Dorian, who seemed to step into the leadership role so naturally. There wasn't a drop of discomfort in his voice, and I admired that. We'd worked together well in the field; hopefully we could organize our teams into a similarly seamless flow.

"Captain Bryce has arranged for the soldiers to use golf carts once we get there, so you'll be able to move quickly," Dorian said.

"Our aircraft will not stay on the course," Bryce added, his voice quick and loud. "It will land at a nearby hangar, to avoid drawing attention or antagonizing the targets. Clemmins and I will be on the perimeter with you, soldiers."

I got a closer look at the Bureau guards at the back. They had grenades strapped to their utility belts, and ARs sat beside them. They looked decidedly less comfortable than the rest of us in the presence of our vampire teammates. I noticed Dorian eyeing the guards' weaponry, too.

"The weapons are a precautionary measure, Mr. Clave," Bryce said curtly when he saw Dorian looking at the guards. "Every single one of you will be on your most discreet and professional behavior today," he added with a growl. "From the moment we land, there will be civilians among us."

For the first time, nerves traveled down my spine. How difficult would this be for the vampires compared to past missions? Would their hunger distract them? Or overwhelm them? The citizens here hadn't been vetted by the FBI and Bureau training; they could be a grab bag of darkness.

Bryce told us to prepare for the drop just as I finished discussing details with the other soldiers. Clemmins helped the disguised vampires adjust their comm earpieces. The backup vampires would receive necessary communication via the guards' comms.

Everyone lined up against the side doors as the aircraft descended, and I felt the familiar drop in my stomach as we lost altitude. Through the windows I saw jagged mountains ringing the neatly gridded city, and then the expansive green of the golf course grew in the view. We would aim to land near the clubhouse.

"Ten seconds to drop," Bryce said through our comms. And then —"Teams, drop!"

Security guards swung down to the pavement first. The backup vampires followed, and I raised my eyebrows at Thoth's agility as he slid down. I wouldn't let that gray beard fool me anymore.

I was the first human to zip down, and our captains descended last.

The aircraft immediately ascended again and buzzed away as we got into formation.

The disguised vampires broke away from the two other groups after an intense survey of the course, clearly avoiding looking at a group of tense-looking employees who gawked at us from a patio attached to the clubhouse. Captain Clemmins approached the employees and quietly spoke, gesturing for them to enter the club. They meekly disappeared inside. The Bureau guards surrounded the backup vampires, fully concealing them from the clubhouse's view. The guards then moved alongside their vampires and stationed themselves between the clubhouse and the field that rolled out in front of us.

My team made our way toward a group of golf carts parked at the first hole. We jogged to the boxy white vehicles, my mind settling into mission mode. It had been a while since I'd last taken command, but today I felt positive and in control, like the pieces slipped effortlessly into place.

I spoke calmly into my comm. "Soldiers, lieutenants, and captains, pair up and start your carts."

Bryce and Clemmins paired with Grayson and Sarah, the least experienced soldiers. I watched in amusement as Grayson's face turned the shade of the golf cart when Bryce plopped down beside him on the bench seat. Sarah gave a big, excited smile to Clemmins, who nodded to her. Their wheels started slowly rolling.

Zach ran up beside me and hopped into the passenger side as I started my vehicle. I would've been fine working with any of my teammates, but I would take Zach over any of them. Z and L.

"Remember when I taught you to drive?" my brother asked, grinning.

"Let's hope so," I said, with a feral grin of my own. It had been a while since I'd worked closely with Zach, and I felt the camaraderie we'd developed years before Bureau training slip easily into place.

I located the vampires walking down a slope toward a cluster of trees. Their pace quickened as I watched. The course was expansive, with many slopes. I couldn't see its full shape through patches of trees and the rolling hills.

"Soldiers, form a wide circle around the vampires and maintain distance until we have target confirmation," I said into the comm.

I hit the gas, and we started in the direction of the vampires over the rolling, flowing course. It could be risky for them to approach a wild flock of redbills without their own birds present, especially since they now resembled humans, but the makeup was necessary. I swallowed and increased speed.

"Yeehaw," Zach said into the wind, but his eyes narrowed with his typical focus.

My team spread out and established a drifting circumference around the vampires as they began sprinting. We tried to stay parallel with them, but they were too fast. Though, given what I'd seen of Dorian's speed in Las Vegas, they were probably holding back.

"We've sensed the targets. Soldiers, give us a wider berth," Dorian said into our earpieces.

We pulled off to the right, and I checked to ensure the other carts tapered off, too.

"Clave, what is the predicted location?" Bryce growled.

"Beyond those trees ahead," Dorian replied. A shiver ran up my spine at the sound of his dark voice focused on the hunt.

"Security, please follow and secure the rear with your vampires. Maintain a visual on all parties," Bryce ordered. Even though I'd been designated Dorian's second-in-command, Bryce still headed this operation.

"Yes, Captain." A gruff male guard's voice scratched over the comm.

The vampires pulled farther ahead than I was comfortable with, but I held steady. I had to trust them. By this point, I had very little reason not to. We rolled to the bottom of the slope, and the carts spread in formation around the trees.

"Targets spotted," Dorian said, his voice a bit quieter, as if to avoid startling the redbills in his eyesight.

I increased my speed to get a sightline past the trees, and our targets came into view. A flock of five redbills poked at the grass around a hole —until they spotted the approaching vampires. The bills stilled, in what I had come to recognize as a sign of caution.

"Soldiers, hold your positions until otherwise instructed," I ordered. I angled our cart's wheels toward the flock and hit the brakes. The other carts angled and stopped, mimicking me. Next to me, Zach sat silently, his hand resting lightly on his weapon, surveying the scene with focused eyes.

The vampires stopped and spoke in a huddle.

"That's one big bird," Zach whispered seriously, nodding toward the flock. I spotted it and nodded to my brother.

"I'm keeping my eye on that one," Zach said, his tone still hushed. "Got a weird feeling about it." His gaze fixed on his personal assignment.

Suddenly, that very bill let out a scream that carried far past us. The bird was easily twice the size of the others. At least this time it was less likely to snatch me, and there was no large body of water nearby to crash into. I tensed in discomfort, remembering the sight of talons wrapped around my body and the jolt of hitting the lake's surface.

The vampires spread into a line and loped cautiously toward the birds. The massive redbill shrieked again. I didn't speak redbill, but it sounded like a warning to me. I pushed fear out of my mind, focusing my eyes on the vampires. They didn't falter. Instead, they lengthened the space between themselves as they neared the birds. The vampires were attempting to encircle them, before moving in.

The lead bill screamed again and threw its beak from side to side. Then it tossed back its wings and began tearing up the grass in massive clumps with its talons. That was *definitely* a warning.

I looked back to locate security. They were in position to surveil the costumed vampires and wild flock. I debated calling security closer in my comm, but I stopped myself. The vampires had a plan, and I needed to manage my nerves to avoid disrupting their process.

The largest redbill carried on posturing, its screeches growing sharper. The other four bills swung their heads around, eyeing the calm vampires surrounding them. Kreya, Rhome, and Kane paused as Bravi and Dorian closed the circle around the birds. In graceful unison, the vampires held up their palms and tightened their circle around the flock. I waited; this was about the time that everything usually calmed down. Zach's previous comment about the largest bill circled in my mind, though, and I held my breath.

This time, daddy redbill wasn't having it. He jerked his wings and pointed his clacking beak at Rhome, then swung around to scream at Dorian. Unintimidated, looking perfectly calm, Dorian took another step closer, raising his open palms higher.

That did it for the bill. The massive animal lunged for Dorian, nearly cutting him in half with its beak. Dorian dove, rolling between the bird's ankles. It whipped around and stabbed at him again, howling between snaps.

"Holy crap," Zach said without surprise. "Should we be moving in?"

"Not unless the vampires request it," I said, gripping the steering wheel tightly. I prayed this was the right decision as I swallowed hard, committing. It reminded me again of watching Dorian in Las Vegas—it had always been harder for me to stand by and wait than to charge into battle myself. I reminded myself that it was necessary this time. I had to trust Dorian.

The other vampires held their positions but crouched, preparing to spring away or jump in to help Dorian. The giant redbill jerked around, stabbing and slashing and grabbing, but Dorian kept two paces ahead, dodging and weaving as it chased him through the flock. That same floating sense of pride I'd felt in Las Vegas swelled in my chest again.

I couldn't help my admiration. Even accounting for vampire speed and reflexes, he was undeniably one of the most skilled fighters I'd ever seen. But knowing that didn't stop me from holding my breath as Dorian suddenly stopped, and the bird closed in on him. It lashed out with a bony, clawed foot twice the size of a vampire. Dorian dipped, rolled three times, and popped up beneath the animal's tail feathers.

"What is he doing?" Zach exclaimed.

My fingers numbed around the wheel.

Before the bird could swivel, Dorian leapt, grabbed the bird's feathers, and yanked himself onto its back. The other vampires rose out of their crouches like they'd been waiting for him to do just that.

Zach and I turned to each other, mutually gaping. Dorian really wasn't predictable—at all. And I was extremely grateful for it in that very moment. Zach blinked hard, and then we wordlessly slapped a high five.

The huge bird howled and jumped into the air, its wings flailing. It bounced and bucked. I strained to see if Dorian would fall off, but he'd secured his legs around each side and had his hands on the back of its neck.

"This is one screwed-up rodeo," Zach said, pulling at a piece of his wavy hair. "I'm going to comm security."

"That'll make things worse," I said carefully, my thoughts rapidly filing through my memories of our trainings and previous missions. "Remember the redbill training in the facility yard? Every time we've brought weapons in, they've freaked out." And the redbills freaking out in this case meant they'd go straight for our vampire colleagues, some of whom I was beginning to think of as our friends.

My brother paused, squinted his eyes in thought, and then let out a tense breath. "You're right," he said firmly, as if still trying to convince himself, and gave a nod. "We don't want to blunder in and make things worse." His trigger finger twitched, though, and I knew he was imagining saving our friends with a well-placed bullet. Most people never caught on to it, but Zach's love and enthusiasm for weapons stemmed from the desire to keep people safe.

Just then, Bryce cut in over the comm. "Soldiers and security, be ready to jump in," he barked. He didn't sound anxious, but that didn't surprise me. That man never lost his cool.

The giant bill thrashed around the rest of the flustered flock, and their cries of fear carried across the course. The smaller birds grouped close together, beating their wings.

The other vampires stayed cemented in place, raising their palms to chin-level in a gentle pose that looked like surrender. The smaller birds quieted and stared, tilting their heads in curiosity. I was transfixed, impressed by the vampires' cool in this moment. They stood in the face of danger, but it looked like a calm, organized ritual.

Dorian's bronco bird stopped in one spot and pecked at Dorian's feet. I heard Dorian shout something, and the redbill gurgled. It swung around once more, then stopped moving. Dorian's hands remained locked around the base of its neck. At least he had something to hold on to in case the thing freaked out again—thank goodness.

After a few beats of stillness, Dorian leaned forward and moved his hands farther up the bird's spine.

I breathed out again in relief. "I think they're communicating," I whispered, more hopeful than sure. Zach just stared, his eyes intense, as through waiting for first blood to be drawn.

A chorus of gurgles from the flock of redbills turned to chitters. The vampires were almost close enough to touch them.

Dorian's mount lowered its wings and slowly tucked them back. And then it began to titter with the rest of the flock. The friendly, welcoming sound sent relief coursing through my body.

Zach audibly sighed with relief beside me, slapping his palms down on his thighs. "This is good. This is better," he muttered with excitement, mostly to himself.

The vampires on the ground placed their palms on the birds' foreheads. The chirping stopped. Dorian slid from his bird's back, and, without missing a beat, walked around to face it. It lowered its head to accept his touch.

Almost an entire minute passed. Every single creature stood completely still, until by some unspoken agreement, the vampires bent to fix the bands around the birds' ankles.

As every soldier, lieutenant, captain, and security guard stared, the flock clucked to each other and took flight in the direction of the desert.

"Targets not to be seen again," Dorian said over the comm. This time, I heard him smiling.

"All positions hold steady until targets are completely out of sight," Bryce ordered briskly, a hint of smugness in his voice.

The birds flapped into a V-shaped formation as they shrank away into the blue. Then they disappeared. I checked the time. It was startling how quickly peaceful missions passed, especially considering how insane it had been just a moment before. My heart rate didn't catch the memo immediately.

"All positions return to drop site," Clemmins said in my earpiece.

"Soldiers, retrieve our friends and get them safely back to the drop site," I added. I slammed my foot on the gas pedal, launching Zach back into his seat.

We cruised over the grass. The vampires watched the circle of carts close in around them, as they had done with the redbills. Their faces looked dispassionate. Even Dorian's. I wanted to shake him for being so casual about almost becoming a redbill's lunch, but not quite as much as I wanted to grin and cheer that they'd done it. As the leader of my team, I couldn't do either.

"That was impressive," Zach said, and I nodded my agreement.

"Great work out there, team," I told the vampires.

Dorian looked up at me, and his calm regard sent tingles through my chest. "Thanks for giving us space to work, soldiers," he said, but his gaze never left my face.

With a smooth motion, he jumped onto our cart, and the other vampires found rides as other carts pulled up.

The pack whizzed back up the slope. I hated having to keep my eyes on our path, because I could feel Dorian looking at me. But I knew if I looked, I would find something that I would obsess over later.

In short order, we returned the vehicles to the first hole and rejoined security, who had been mere onlookers on this mission. I wondered if the other soldiers felt the guilt I did, from having physically done so little on the course. Dorian's thanks for not interfering meant we'd made the right choice, but being backup for vampires might take some getting used to.

Bryce held a finger to his earpiece. "Pilots due back in three minutes," he announced to the group as we convened in yet another circle.

"Mr. Clave, that was bold," Clemmins said evenly to Dorian, his face a mixture of surprise and concern. It must have been pretty rattling to witness that, as one of the mission's captains. "Excellent execution, everyone." He clapped Dorian on the back.

Dorian looked startled, but a smile flashed across his face.

"Pretty good for a bro wearing khakis," Zach said, his voice revealing honest admiration, and held up a hand for Dorian to high five. Dorian stared at him blankly, so Zach used his other hand to bring Dorian's palm against his. Dorian blinked, nodding, and repeated the gesture without aid.

"What was up that bird's butt?" Roxy asked the vampires.

"They smelled humans—you were upwind, and apparently rather odorous—and they were confused by our appearance. They also didn't like the golf carts," Bravi said, tugging at her T-shirt again. "Well, and that giant one was a cranky old bastard."

The group's chatter soon drowned in the sound of the approaching aircraft. When we'd gotten underway, I made my way over to sit beside Dorian. Bravi sat on his left, and when she saw me sit down, she put more space between herself and Dorian. *What's that all about?*

I gestured for Gina to toss me a water bottle from the supply case under her feet. The burning ache in my chest had suddenly returned and felt like it was crawling up my throat.

I chugged the bottle in seconds. Dorian raised his brows.

"Thirsty?" he asked, as I wiped my mouth and set the empty bottle between my feet.

"Y-Yeah," I said, interrupted by a hiccup. My stomach hurt so badly my eyes watered, but I laughed through it.

He flashed a fanged grin in response. There was that spark of white in his irises again. The heat in my chest hurt, sure, but another warmth growing inside me felt a lot better.

Dorian's shoulder brushed mine. "Thank you for your help," he murmured.

I almost said, "You're welcome," but my words caught in my throat as our eyes locked for a few beats. I saw Bravi shake her head and lean away in my peripheral vision, but my own thoughts buzzed too busily in my head for me to pay much attention.

The humans spent the first few minutes of the flight back commending the vampires on their performance on the course, asking questions about redbills, and even cracking some jokes. After the chorus of chatter died down, though, most soldiers and vampires closed their eyes and dozed in the aircraft's lulling drone. I slipped into the quiet mood too, but I couldn't have slept even if I wanted to. Dorian leaned against me throughout the ride, the soft muscle of his shoulder gently pressing against mine whenever the plane rumbled a little, and the sensation kept me awake the entire ride back.

CHAPTER TWENTY-SIX

O ver the next few weeks, the days bled together as our redbill
missions became increasingly frequent. The facility's human-
vampire team developed a flawless track record. Soon we were being
sent to a different city every day. After the vampires had risen to the
occasion in Salt Lake City and handled being in a lightly populated
civilian environment without a hint of fangs, the board didn't shy away
from sending us into progressively closer quarters with civilians. I took
this as another great sign, and it fueled my burning anticipation of
hearing from Jim again.

Dorian and I moved into unspoken leadership roles in our respec-
tive groups, but because we were constantly in transit, reining in
redbills, or trying to eat and catch up on sleep, we mostly just spoke
strategy and logistics before each mission. It was difficult to focus on
business when he was near, his eyes pulling all of my thoughts right out
of my head... but I really didn't have time for much else.

Whatever sleep I did get was usually deep and dreamless. There was
still a hint of my heartburn from time to time, usually when preparing
for a mission, but I did experience some relief. Hopefully, the daily
supplement the medic had given me would resolve the problem.

"You're most likely experiencing digestive issues from the change in your diet; try to eat primarily raw fruits and vegetables," she'd said, looking unconcerned. "I can't say the food here is good for your insides. Not to mention the stress."

"Well, I can't do anything about the latter," I'd replied. Though lately, with the vampires handling the redbills so swimmingly, the stress had been less intense.

About four weeks in, we returned to the facility after an early-morning mission in Villanueva State Park, New Mexico. Everyone trudged down the main hallway, barely lifting their feet, which was to be expected after a 4:30 a.m. bugle call.

I ran numbers in my head as we walked—I'd been keeping a tally of the redbills we'd cleared out—when I noticed Kreya stop and lean against the wall. Rhome immediately materialized at her side, whispering to her. I slowed to see if I had cause for concern.

She shook her head. "Just tired," she mumbled. She'd never shown weakness before, but the weariness in her voice pointed to more than just a lack of sleep.

Shaking my own exhaustion off, I looked at the vampires with new eyes. They looked worn, the ripples under their skin sluggish and faded.

"You're hungry," Rhome said quietly, the concern in his voice taking the edge off his rebuke. "You let Detra feed too long last night."

"I'm fine," Kreya said irritably, pushing past him. "I'll ask Halla to feed her tonight instead." The couple made their way into their quarters.

I stood still for a second, considering what it would be like to not eat for days, weeks. And to have two children who needed to take sustenance directly from your body on a regular basis. Suddenly, the facility gruel didn't seem so bad. The vampires hadn't let their hunger show or affect their performance, and I mentally commended them for their poise. But if their behavior continued to impress the higher-ups, maybe they could earn a chance to feed somehow, under appropriate circumstances. Maybe I could figure out some way to get that for them. It wasn't like we could ask people to donate blood, though—we'd need to fund a blood drive at a prison or something.

I removed my armor plates and plopped onto my bunk, still musing about vampire feedings. We had another mission later, so Bryce had instructed us to get our shut-eye between shifts. Most of the women had already taken his advice.

I'd barely gotten horizontal and closed my eyes when footsteps came down the aisle toward my bunk, raising me from my torpor.

"Lieutenant Sloane," Captain Finley said. Her voice sounded like nails on a chalkboard to my tired brain. I wanted to like her, but sometimes it was so difficult.

I sat up. "Yes, Captain," I responded.

"Captain Bryce would like to see you in his office," she said, and turned on her heel to leave before finishing her sentence. Bryce must have asked her to summon me, since he couldn't come into the women's quarters himself.

I rubbed my eyes and grabbed the bar above my head to hoist myself up, trying to muster some energy for our project.

"Duty calls, princess," Roxy muttered into her pillow sarcastically.

I ignored her lackluster jab. I didn't have energy to spar with her.

I knocked on Bryce's office door and received the usual grunt to enter. Dorian sat in one of the chairs opposite Bryce. A smile spread across my face, and I felt excitement return, even through my exhaustion.

"Heard back from Jim," the captain said. "He's ready for another sit-down with us. This evening."

"And tonight's mission?" I asked, thinking that there weren't enough hours in the day. But one glance at Dorian, his face drawn, his eyes focused intently, and I could go without sleep for as long as I needed to.

The vampires were suffering for this too—and it meant even more to their species than it did to mine.

"There are two other captains and plenty of soldiers and vampires to handle the situation," Bryce replied. "The team can do without you two for an evening. We'll give them some excuse." He set his boots on the corner of his desk. "Sounds like Jim sorted through his files and found a nice little gold star for Mr. Clave to put on his resume, should he handle the task effectively."

"I will," Dorian said confidently. And, after his previous performance in Las Vegas, I didn't question his confidence. In fact, I enjoyed it.

Jim met us on the roof again. As we followed him to the stairwell door, Dorian's redbill grumbled in displeasure, possibly remembering how long he'd waited last time. Dorian shot the bird a sympathetic glance over his shoulder. Maybe Dorian felt bad for him because there were no shrubs to nibble at or desert rodents to catch on the roof. I was sure they got hungry, but did redbills get bored?

In Jim's office, on his desk, a thick brown file folder rested on his closed laptop, contained by multiple rubber bands.

"Dorian, thank you for your patience, and please excuse my silence since your last visit," Jim said, his usual charm a bit diluted. He sounded as exhausted as the rest of us. He snapped one rubber band off the file, then another. My eyes were glued to the file. I didn't even have an inkling of what Jim had for us, and it drove me nuts.

"I understand, sir," Dorian replied, cool as always when working with the brass.

"I have to be very careful with the task I offer," Jim continued. "These cases need to exhibit your value to the Bureau, and all humans, in the most convincing way possible. I settled on this one."

"We're listening," Captain Bryce said calmly, leaning back in the chair that he dwarfed.

"Let me preface this," Jim said, making a triangle with his hands, his eyes appraising despite the bags hanging under them. "What I'm proposing is far more complex than the test I gave you last time. This situation lacks thorough intel, so there is no way for me to properly gauge the true level of danger."

Dorian nodded for him to continue, and Jim gave the tiniest of smiles, as though he'd expected no less. Well, neither had I.

Jim removed the last two bands from the folder with a snap and pulled out several papers. He slid them across his desk toward Dorian, and all of us leaned forward to inspect them. They contained a long list of names accompanied by birthdates and addresses.

"What do all of these people have in common?" Jim asked. He paused for us to analyze the list but didn't wait for a response. "They're all Amish, and they're all missing."

Jim cleared his throat. "I told you last time, in general our missing persons cases have significantly decreased. However, that statistic is not reflected in several Amish communities. The primary communities affected are in Ohio."

Bryce, Dorian, and I sat in perplexed silence. I scrunched my nose. I wasn't educated on the Amish, but I knew they weren't common targets for crimes like this, and my stomach tightened angrily. They deserved to be left in peace, like everyone else. Bryce grumbled to himself, audibly putting together his thoughts. Dorian gazed steadily at the papers, studying the text. He was already at work.

"Somehow, their number of missing persons has quadrupled this year alone. We've been investigating and supplying extra police enforcement to the area, but we don't have a single lead." Jim sighed. He shook his head, frustrated, before continuing. "These vanishings haven't shown any sign of slowing. I do have one hunch, though. Based on the kidnappers' past patterns, I'm reasonably certain that their next target is probably this community in Elmore County."

Jim dug into the file folder and pulled out a map. He set it on top of the papers and placed his finger on it. "Right here."

Dorian studied the map, his chin resting on his fist. He remained so stoic, I had no idea what he might be thinking.

"I propose that you go, look for people with darkness, and report back to me," Jim said, watching the vampire with a steady gaze. "I understand that this is a rather involved operation, so if you need to sleep on it, that's fine. I do have some ideas to aid the process, should you accept. I think it might be best to take two vampires."

Bryce gave a very audible groan of irritation. Jim made a face at him. They could've been siblings.

"In fact, I'd suggest sending two skilled vampires *and* two soldiers to accompany them," he added tauntingly. "Depending on the situation, this could very well take several days. Pack a bag."

"Hold on," Captain Bryce said sternly, not letting Jim's game get to him. "We need to talk logistics, here. This is, yet again, explicitly against the trial period statutes."

"Come on." Jim grinned, wheedling. "Put that executive decision-making to good use, Bryce."

Bryce rubbed his temple, his breathing agitated. "The previous task didn't involve slumber parties," he grumbled. "And I certainly can't leave the facility for an extended period of time with the number of redbill missions we're drowning in. We'd have to bring more people into this experiment."

"Two able-bodied soldiers should be more than enough," Jim said enthusiastically. "Or you could just send Lieutenant Sloane, here. She's probably worth two." He nodded at me, and I smirked, just a little bit pleased with myself.

"All right," Bryce said. "If Clave accepts the assignment, I'll assign two soldiers. We've used tracking devices on the vampires before—we'll just tag them again. They take 'em off, trial period's over."

Dorian rolled his shoulders back and set his jaw. He opened his mouth to speak, but Bryce held up a hand, clearly spotting the vampire's displeasure. The vampire tracking devices had always been a bit demeaning, and I'd thought we'd gotten past that stage.

"It's not that I don't trust you," Bryce told Dorian. "It's about what the board will see as acceptable when we present them with the evidence. Our caution needs to be displayed so there's less blowback about doing a side mission without their approval. They don't know you. And I have to justify sending two vampires into a blood-filled candy store somehow."

Jim stifled a laugh. "Better you than me." Bryce rolled his eyes at his old friend.

"I understand, Captain," Dorian responded evenly. His confident air quelled some of my concerns, but I knew he was hungry, and this environment would challenge him. The vampires had proven their mettle—but that didn't erase their biology.

"Well, then," Jim said. "How does a vacation to the heartland sound to you?"

Bryce and I turned to the vampire.

"Thrilling," Dorian said, deadpan.

CHAPTER TWENTY-SEVEN

I fought off guilt as I slunk out of the women's quarters amongst my snoring friends at dawn the next morning. They hadn't returned from their mission the previous night until nearly three a.m. While most of the facility slept, Captain Bryce, Dorian, and I reconvened in Bryce's office to discuss Jim's proposal.

Bryce yawned and lazily indicated two cups of coffee sitting on the edge of his desk. He sipped from a third.

"Can't drink coffee anymore," I muttered.

"Why the hell not?" Bryce demanded, appalled.

"Stomach problems."

Dorian gave me a questioning look, but Bryce seemed to accept it. "Clave, the men drink alone," he said, chuckling.

"You're on your own, Captain. Vampires don't drink coffee," Dorian responded, though he gave a tiny halfhearted shrug as if to acknowledge that Bryce had tried his best. I tried to imagine the vampires acting this polite when we'd first brought them to the facility, and couldn't. Or, for that matter, Bryce making any of them coffee. Things had changed for the better, even if they were just little changes.

"Whatever." Our captain scoffed. "Last time I'm nice to you weirdos. Clave, any revelations reach you in your dreams about the Ohio gig?"

"I'm on board," Dorian said confidently, with an inclination of his head.

"Good. Picked a partner from your side of the hallway yet?" Bryce questioned.

"Not yet," Dorian said. "I haven't informed the others of the situation. I have a feeling I know who is most likely to volunteer and do the job properly, but it can't hurt to offer the spot to everyone at once and see who's interested. Although, that would mean revealing the experiment..." He gazed at Bryce with a furrowed brow.

Bryce considered this for a moment, then nodded, seeming to find this acceptable. "Whatever you think best. Just let me know who offers to smell cow poop for the next few days." Bryce chortled at his own joke, and that was funnier to me than his actual "zinger." Catching my smile, Bryce zeroed in on me next, and I hastily sobered up. "Lieutenant, I've decided on your partner. Seeing as you two are thick as thieves but also do your jobs properly and discreetly, I'm assigning your brother. I trust you not to lose your little heads should things get heated."

"Yes, Captain," I said, pleased with the praise. Zach and Dorian had been working together well lately, so the fact that I was excited to have him along was secondary. That just left the undetermined, fanged fourth wheel.

"All right then. Off to the vampire quarters with you. I need a decision ASAP." Bryce casually flapped his hand at us, shooing us out of his office in his normal grumpy fashion.

We walked down the empty hallway toward the vampire quarters, and once again, Dorian's steps synced with mine. This time, I didn't drop my gaze when his eyes locked with mine, letting the awareness spread through my limbs. If I could get a handle on the nerves and keep things professional while we were working—which was ninety percent of the time we spent together, anyway—I thought that maybe whatever feelings drew me to Dorian could be manageable, perhaps even enjoyable. I doubted those feelings would ever go anywhere, but if I could keep them contained, maybe they weren't so bad.

Seeing the warmth in his ice-blue eyes, I wondered what conclusion Dorian had drawn.

We entered the quiet vampire quarters, and Dorian glanced into cells to see who was awake. He made some gestures, indicating to a few vampires that he wanted them to follow him back toward the front of the hallway, where I waited.

While Dorian retrieved Kreya and Rhome from the family housing, the vampires he'd chosen emerged into the aisle, stretching their arms and faces in yawns. I nodded to the gathering, trying to meet each one's eyes; several of the vampires I didn't know very well had appeared as well. Thoth made a point to hold my eyes, and he slowly nodded to me in return, reminding me yet again of an ancient yogi with the way he always crossed his legs. Kreya's auburn hair was tousled, and her eyes were heavy but clear. Rhome rubbed her shoulder, and she accepted his affection. Kane came out and nodded to Rhome, a gesture of respect I'd never seen him perform in front of humans.

"It's time for me to explain," Dorian said, coming to stand next to me at the center of the group.

His voice was quiet, but all eyes focused on him. He lowered himself to the cement floor and crossed his legs, and we all followed his example. I wondered if everyone felt the magnetism that sometimes radiated from Dorian. He was a natural leader, and maybe they sensed that.

The vampires looked worn, relieved to be able to sit. I wondered what their hunger felt like, if their muscles ached like humans' did. Rayne rested her head on Harlowe's shoulder, dark gray circles under her eyes.

"As much as you all enjoyed my first makeover, it wasn't just for your amusement," Dorian said, raising his eyebrows as if to squash any giggles. "And it wasn't just a test for the golf course mission. The real reason I needed to look human that evening was because Bryce, Lyra, and I met with a leader at the human federal police force in Las Vegas. This man, Jim, wanted to use me to test what they call our 'specified feeding' theory."

Kane scoffed, and several other vampires rolled their eyes to the ceiling irritably. Dorian held up a hand. "Yes, it sounds ridiculous. But remember, they're not us, so they can't understand our physical experience. They're trying to, which is progress in and of itself. It might be the most efficient way to make them consider our request for asylum."

I nodded in confirmation, as the sole representative of my species. Dorian nodded slightly back to me, as though that proved it, and continued. "He believes we can build our case for asylum if we use our skills to fight and prevent human crime. Not only will we be able to do as we're naturally inclined, we'll help both of our species."

"How did you prove to this guy that you can sense darkness?" Bravi asked evenly. She didn't seem skeptical so much as cautiously curious.

Dorian explained what had transpired between him and the criminals in the alley. Listening to his account, I felt my own heartbeat speed up at the memory. I expected the vampires to be impressed, but they seemed unphased. A little reminder that I was the only one there without their skills.

"Jim has proposed a mission to showcase our skills," Dorian said, with an added spark of excitement. I admired him for mustering up the energy to encourage his clan, even when he was just as weary as they were. "I need one of you to go with us to a settlement where people have been going missing. He wants us to sniff around and uncover who's behind the disappearances."

The group contemplated the idea quietly for a moment. Kreya rested her chin on a fist, her brow furrowed. Bravi glanced at Rayne and Harlowe; Rayne shrugged lazily in response. Thoth stared at the floor stoically.

"It could be an extended stay. I don't know what the situation is going to look like once we get there," Dorian added, his tone unchanged by the less than enthusiastic response. "We'll basically conduct the investigation independently."

Another quiet moment passed. Sike looked around the circle with uncertainty, and when he met Dorian's eyes, he pursed his lips and gently shook his head. There wasn't much incentive for them to join us —extra work, travel, and risk probably didn't sound appealing on no sustenance. It would be particularly hard on Sike, with his injury, though he might have gone to support Dorian otherwise. Just as I started to worry about what we would tell Bryce if no one volunteered, someone finally spoke.

"I'll go."

I gawked at Kane before I could stop myself. *Really?*

"You want to?" Dorian asked. The surprise edging his voice was carefully controlled, but still audible.

"I'm bored out of my mind with these constant redbill heart-to-heart sessions," Kane grumbled, fixing Dorian with a stare that dared him to question that logic.

That couldn't be the real reason he was volunteering, could it? What if he wanted to sabotage things? I knew I should've been grateful for his offer, but wasn't there a single other person who wanted to go? Someone more… cooperative?

"Thank you for volunteering," Dorian said. He must have been concerned about how this would play out too, but to his credit, he didn't display an ounce of ingratitude. "I'll let you know when I have more details. And this conversation must be kept to present company only."

Kane shrugged indifferently. "We done?"

"For now," Dorian replied, still in that controlled tone. "We'll all be briefed before the mission." Without another word, Kane stood and stalked back to his cell, and some of the others exchanged looks that clearly said, "What the hell was that all about?" The vampires seemed as confused by his behavior as I was, and that wasn't particularly comforting.

Once Kane was out of earshot, Dorian turned to Bravi. "You don't want to go?" he asked her softly, his eyes fixed on her face. I realized he'd had her in mind earlier, and I didn't understand why she hadn't offered. Bravi had always been a go-getter; she and Dorian enjoyed each other's company to the point that the adventure should have been fun.

"I thought about it, but they need the most skilled vampires here at the facility to take care of the top priority," Bravi proclaimed, tossing her head with exaggerated pride.

Dorian chuckled and rolled his eyes at her joke. "Sure."

When he turned away from her to speak to Thoth, the humor fell from her face like a curtain dropping to the floor. I couldn't interpret what I saw before she caught me looking and glared until I dropped my gaze.

As the vampires dispersed, Dorian and I stood, too. He walked me back out into the main hallway, his footfalls resonating in time with my own.

"This should be interesting," I said, my voice tense. All I could think about was Kane's scowl, his nasty, undermining comments. I really didn't want to be trapped with that.

"Despite his sourness, it's not a bad idea to have him along," Dorian said thoughtfully. "He's discreet, and his skills are some of the best in the group."

"Fair enough," I replied, but my voice didn't carry the confidence I wanted it to. I couldn't hide my hesitation, when the thought of traveling with Kane felt like a nightmare.

"I understand your concern," Dorian added, with a hint of amusement. "I'll do my best to keep him in check." He offered a strong smile that reflected the amusement in his voice.

"We both will," I said with a bit more confidence, wanting to show him that I was on his team. Of course, I couldn't control Kane's mood swings, but I wanted Dorian to know that I was game for whatever came our way.

We split up to cement the plan's next steps, and as his footfalls faded away, the space next to me took on an empty feeling. I tried not to worry about missing his presence, throwing myself into my next task.

I knocked on the door to the men's quarters, mentally apologizing to my sleeping teammates. It took a few tries to rouse them.

Finally, Colin opened the door, his eyes mostly closed. "Holy hell," he groaned. "What do you want?"

"I need Zach," I said quietly. If the men had a problem with being up so early, they could complain to the bugle.

Colin disappeared, grumbling, and soon my brother filled the doorway, rubbing his eyes, his hair plastered against the left side of his head.

"Good morning," I said sweetly.

"What is it?" he asked, his voice sleepy but wary. "Is something wrong?"

"No, nothing's wrong. I need to discuss something private with you. Can we sit down somewhere?" I squeezed his shoulder in encouragement, keeping my voice calm. He nodded through a wide yawn.

We walked to the empty cafeteria. Leftover coffee sat in a carafe on the counter. Zach filled a cup, then sat next to me on a bench.

I took a deep breath, swallowed my jealousy about his cup of coffee, and dove in. "Bryce, Dorian, and I have been working on a side project under wraps. We've just received a new mission." I tried to be as succinct as possible, knowing how he could be in the morning. I watched the thought percolate in his tired brain.

Zach blinked. "Somehow that wasn't what I expected here," he said, and his eyes narrowed as he focused. "Side project?"

I explained Jim's desire to fight crime rates and how we intended to use vampires in the task. As the details came out, my brother nodded, his eyes serious, becoming more alert.

"Bryce assigned you to our next mission. We're going to Ohio, to an Amish community, to try and figure out why people have been going missing over the past year," I said.

"Hmm," Zach replied. He swallowed another sip of coffee, then swirled his drink in his hand absently. "Bryce is letting vampires take a mini vacation? That doesn't line up with the rules. Is this really a good idea?" His tone deepened and went quiet as he questioned Bryce, concern creating a line in his forehead.

"He made an executive decision for the sake of protecting human lives. And he's going to put tracking devices on them," I said, projecting confidence. He was already assigned, but I wanted my brother to be as excited as I was about the project.

"I see," Zach said. He blinked and scratched the side of his face. "Actually, sounds pretty interesting."

"I trust the vampires involved," I told him. "If this plan goes well, we could make history. And if something goes wrong, I'd rather have *you* there to help me sort it out." I gave him my best pretty-please-do-it-for-your-little-sister look.

"All right, all right," my brother said, and managed to dredge up an exasperated smile. "Don't lay it on so thick."

I threw my arms around his neck in excitement and gratitude. "Thanks for understanding."

"Get off," he said, laughter breaking through his façade of grumpiness. He removed my arm and stood. "Let me know when we're leaving. I'll be in bed."

CHAPTER TWENTY-EIGHT

The four of us arrived at the Elmore County settlement in a police vehicle driven by a local officer. Jim had issued us standard police garb to make our presence there less obvious, and the police in our vicinity knew that we were specialized officers from another state, called in to aid in the investigation. We expected full cooperation.

I grabbed my backpack out of the trunk and handed Zach his own. Green hills rolled around us under a bright, clear sky. Dorian and Kane stood beside the vehicle, nonchalant in their fresh coats of makeup. By now our vampire disguise skills had gotten more competent, and they hardly looked fake, even in full sun. We'd stopped at a store before heading into the farmland so I could stock up on ivory concealer and snacks for the next few days.

As I took in the landscape, I mentally mulled over the agenda that Bryce and Jim had briefed us on. This was a big step for my career—leading a private side mission to support the extremely important trial period. I was anxious, no doubt about it, but any time nagging worry sprouted in the back of my head, I just reminded myself of our set strategies and goals. It helped to have a plan.

"Thank you for the ride, Officer Shelton," I said to the cop who'd driven us.

"Yes, ma'am," he said. "We're grateful for your help here." He nodded to us and soon drove off down the gravel road.

We stood on that same road, which stretched through the village ahead. Brown wooden fences lined the roadside between hand-built cottages. Herd animals speckled the hills beside looming barns and silos. This was just one corner of the settlement. Five thousand people lived there, so it was important for us to quickly get the lay of the land.

I patted my vest pocket to ensure that the instructions Jim had written still lay folded inside. I also had a map to our sleeping quarters. A pair of young girls wearing black bonnets walked along the gravel road, stealing glances at us as they passed. I smiled at them, and they hurried away. I guessed that strangers were uncommon out here, but it stung a little. Usually kids liked me. Maybe my uniform had scared them? It dawned on me that they had good reason to fear strangers, given the current events affecting their village, and that took the edge off.

"Ready?" I asked, turning to my team.

"Locked and loaded," Zach said, his eyes alert. The vampires nodded. They had been extremely quiet since the beginning of the journey, their eyes constantly scanning. My curiosity about their immediate thoughts already ate at me. I wanted to know what Dorian thought about our tactics—and I wanted to know whether Kane already regretted coming with us. His posture and indifferent expression didn't look promising.

"Let's do our initial walkthrough and get a feel for the community," I directed. Our bags were light, so trekking with them would be no burden. We started down the road, circumventing a flock of bleating sheep.

The winding road took us past countless barns and fields. Most of the women wore long dresses and avoided looking at us, and the men hid under the wide brims of their hats. Young children stared before being shooed away by their siblings or parents. We hadn't seen police since being dropped off. An uneasiness floated in me, not threatening or scary, just... there.

The place was quiet, but for some reason, it didn't seem peaceful or idyllic. I got the sense that the people watching us didn't trust us; there was a tension in the air. We were outsiders in a community that had lost a lot of members with no explanation, and nothing to show for the police investigations. My heart got heavier at the thought. I might be upset with people in uniform too, if this were my home.

Finally, a teen boy walking a horse on a tether acknowledged us with a nod. We nodded back. At least not everyone here seemed hostile.

"Anything?" I asked Dorian quietly, more determined than ever to do this job right. I sounded more intense than the question deserved, but there was no way I would let this murderer slip through my fingers. If I annoyed my travel companions, so be it.

"Not yet," he replied earnestly.

"I haven't sensed anything, either, thanks for asking," Kane said. *This is a joy already.*

I hoped that the lack of dark energy at least helped suppress the two vampires' appetites. The exhausted circles under their eyes grew darker by the day, in contrast to their moving shadows.

After another mile of fields and swatting bugs, we ran into a police officer patrolling the same road.

"Good afternoon," he said. "You must be the visiting special officers."

"Hello, sir," I said evenly, and introduced myself and my teammates. Zach offered the man his hand, and they shook. Kane gave a curt nod. Dorian watched the way Zach shook the officer's hand and emulated it closely.

"Officer Wolf," he said. "Nice to meet you. I patrol here every few days." The officer's posture was relaxed, his attitude nonchalant, but there was care in his eyes. He reminded me of an old friend of my father's, who rarely visited but always brought my favorite candy bar when he did.

I exchanged some information about the case that the officer hadn't been briefed on; he'd been prepared for our arrival but had no new information for us. The vampires listened, and Dorian studied the officer without expression.

"We've never seen hide or hair of these kidnappers. It's a little depressing, after all this time." The officer's voice grew heavy and his gaze sad under his bushy brows. We moved on quickly; his admission made me impatient to get to the bottom of things.

"Ten four," Zach said behind his hand as we went on our way, and I fought the urge to smack his arm. I knew it was his way of dealing with tension, but now wasn't the time to be kidding around. Kane eyed him as though he'd spoken gibberish.

We walked until the sun became a blazing amber ball nearing the treetops.

I swiped a mosquito from the side of my face. "You guys haven't felt anything at all?" I pressed. My anxiety nagged in the back of my mind. I hated the idea of returning to the facility empty-handed, and I was projecting it onto the vampires. We'd walked the entire village, which comprised one road that looped in a giant circle, with no hints.

The vampires exchanged a thoughtful look, as if speaking to each other in their minds. I was *pretty* sure they couldn't do that. But not entirely sure.

"No one has raised any red flags yet," Dorian said.

Kane nodded, seeming not to mind the current lack of evidence. "Nothing interesting. There are always low levels of darkness in any community," he said, his tone neutral. It surprised me to hear him utter more than one sentence. "But those don't make us hungry. This place is bland. Nothing like some of the cesspool 'cities' we've been in."

Ah, there was the Kane we knew and loved.

I pulled out the map. "Okay, at this point, per Bryce's agenda, we should find our lodging. We can fine tune any last details for tomorrow there," I said with confidence, always more comfortable with an agenda. Nailing down the next day's details would be stress relieving.

"Aye-aye, Lieutenant," Kane replied, only a little sardonically. I was a little grateful for Kane's bitter humor, as it served as a distraction from my mental background of worry.

To my surprise, our lodging was not a house, but a barn.

"Rustic," Zach said, looking genuinely pleased, after he swung the door open.

They'd jazzed it up a bit with moveable plywood walls and some torn linen drapes, but the large space had clearly housed animals until a day ago—my nose was certain. Hay stuck out from the floorboards. The main room contained a rickety table and a few thin-legged chairs, and the plywood walls fit together to make two small "bedrooms." Each held two cots.

We entered and set down our bags on the cots. By silent agreement, we emulated the layout of our facility in the desert, the vampires taking one room and Zach and I setting our things in the other. I felt a twinge of disappointment, but professional Lyra nipped that right in the bud. This mission was about proving the vampires' ability and saving children, not about me indulging my desire to spend an evening with Dorian, talking late into the night.

"The evening shift patrol officers are going to drop off food for us," I told my brother, having been reminded of that detail by a gurgle in my stomach.

I heard Kane sigh heavily behind the plywood. I wondered if it was in response to my mention of food or if he was just being... Kane.

I took a seat at the tiny table and drafted a report of the afternoon's surveillance on a legal pad. Zach shuffled around, studying the barn's interior. He did this every time he settled into a new place—a trait he picked up from my dad. They had to know the nooks and crannies; maybe it made them more comfortable.

I clicked our walkie-talkie on. The officer who'd dropped us off carried the other. He was our primary point of contact should we need anything.

"Old school," Zach noted with a hint of wonder, wandering closer. "Way fancier than the ones we had as kids, though."

"Yeah," I said, smiling. "We could've gotten nicer ones, but Mom and Dad didn't want to spend money on something you were just going to strap firecrackers to again."

"Don't act all innocent, Miss Prissy Pants," Zach replied with his crooked grin, easing down into a chair next to me. "You were an accomplice to that crime." He hadn't called me "Miss Prissy Pants" in a good long while. I still lovingly hated it.

Dorian creaked open his plywood door and came out to join us. He took the chair beside me, leaning over to read what I'd written. I wondered if he'd heard the silly childhood story Zach had just related. My head buzzed when his forehead neared mine.

"Dorian, you ever tried a 3 Musketeers?" Zach asked, offering the candy bar. His eyes narrowed the slightest fraction.

Dorian waved a hand at it, giving Zach a tight smile. "I'm good. Thanks."

"Don't know what you're missing," Zach replied through his chewing. He sounded friendly, but a slight intensity tinged his studiously casual tone.

"I think I'll survive," Dorian said, with a flash of annoyance. *Maybe, but for how long?* Zach and I exchanged a look, and he gave me a tiny shrug. His experiment had failed.

Kane cautiously made his way from their room, too, feigning disinterest even when he joined us at the table. I looked around at our strange group. We were unusual, and perhaps some of us were crankier than others, but I was much more comfortable hanging out with these guys inside our little barn than walking around in that odd, pensive village.

"Let's talk about tomorrow," I said, preparing a fresh piece of paper on my legal pad. "We will run our planned interviews with police and civilians, and grab any extras we can, should they become available, focusing on relatives of missing persons. I think a lead could spring from that, and the vampires will get to be near potential suspects. Let's see if there are any supplemental interview questions we can add to Jim's list."

The group threw suggestions at me, and I organized them on the legal pad, my love of categorizing and making sense of things tingling happily. Even Kane offered a few questions, though I rephrased them when I wrote them out to be a bit more sensitive.

Someone knocked on the barn door. Officer Shelton stood there with a grocery bag.

"Evening, folks," Shelton said kindly, his mustache bristling. "It's nothing special, but this should get you through a day or so."

"Thank you, Officer," I said, setting the bag on a wooden stool beside the door. The snacks I'd grabbed from the store earlier had run out.

Shelton said he'd check in with us in the morning to see how everything was going, and then left.

Zach and I dug through the grocery bag. Granola bars, crackers, apples, packaged snacks. In this barn, we had no way to cook unless we built a campfire outside, so this would have to do. Remembering the medic's advice, I grabbed two apples and a bottle of water, which I sipped while swallowing my stomach medication. Zach inhaled three Twinkies.

The vampires watched us eat for a bit, but soon Kane began jiggling his foot, flexing his fingers. With an irritated sigh, he went back into his room. It had to be horribly frustrating for them to watch us enjoy food when they'd been starving for a month.

Dorian lasted longer, but he also retreated to his cot while Zach and I finished eating. A flicker of guilt flashed through me. I didn't like making him uncomfortable, but there was nothing I could do. Zach met my eyes and gave me a little frown, acknowledging the awkwardness of the situation.

Later, I explored the barn with a flashlight I'd found. Besides that one battery-operated piece of technology, lanterns provided the only other source of light in the barn. We'd set them around the main room, being careful to balance them on the dirt floor or hang them from the rafters. I was extremely grateful the Amish allowed certain battery-reliant devices.

The outdoor shower was as simple as it got: cloth curtain dangling from a metal frame, a rusty spout connected to a source of groundwater. The closest home stood two fields away.

The stars shone brilliantly. I'd never seen them like that back home. The heavy darkness might've seemed eerie to me if I hadn't been used to it, from the empty desert surrounding the facility. I stared up at the sky for a while, watching the twinkling Milky Way. The silence out here was almost deafening, with no ambient hum of generators and air conditioning, but I could kind of see the appeal.

I thought about all the Amish people from this settlement who likely would never see this sky again. I thought about Sike and Carwin in their bandages, and a hole in the sky that led to a world where flame-like lights drifted over desolate mountains. The silence around me began to seem more oppressive and less peaceful.

At least I was here, trying to make a difference for all of them.

I headed back into the barn and found the guys sitting around the table, a few lanterns flickering between them, casting their shadows against the wooden walls. It reminded me of childhood summer camps. I'd always loved the way fire flitted shadows across people's faces. Everyone looked so different in firelight.

"Kinda spooky atmosphere, huh?" Zach said as I shut the creaking door behind me.

I joined them at the table. The physical and emotional weight of the day's activities pulled at my eyelids, but the urge to hang out with the guys convinced me to stay up a bit longer.

A moment of quiet passed, and then Zach started rolling his fingers back and forth through the tips of the lantern flames, testing how much heat he could handle. Kane eyed him for a moment, then, without a word, stoically tested his fingers on the flame as well.

I hadn't lit a candle in years. I'd grown accustomed to the glaring fluorescents of the Bureau. There was something disquieting about that.

"Reminds me of our camping trips up in Wisconsin when we were kids," Zach said, transfixed by the flame. "Dorian, Kane, you guys ever take trips with your families?"

"Sometimes we'd spend nights high up in the mountains," Dorian said, a spark of memory lighting up his eyes.

Kane nodded. Without all the surly reticence, his face looked almost unfamiliar to me. "We'd build fires up there and tell stories when we were younger. Dorian's brother had the best stories."

Dorian closed his eyes briefly. Just watching that expression on his face, I felt shivers go through me. I wished I could take that pain away.

"We'd tell stories around the campfire, too," I added, wanting to stay in positive memories a bit longer. "Scary stories. My dad had great ones."

"We'd be up all night in our bunks," Zach said, laughing.

Later that night, as Zach and I tried to fall asleep, Dorian and Kane spoke on the other side of the plywood. I lay on my side, my eyes open, my ears picking out snippets of their conversation. Zach lay on his side, facing me, but I knew by his breathing that he was still awake and listening, too.

"We'll figure out what happened to them. We'll find them," Kane said, his voice low from exhaustion or subject matter—I couldn't quite tell yet. "I'm sure they're hiding out in the mountains. Not sure how they'd feel about coming to Earth and living like refugees, though."

Are they talking about Dorian's parents?

"It's better than the Immortal Plane," Dorian said.

"You keep saying that. But time will tell, I suppose," Kane replied, his tone sharpening.

"Even *you* have to admit things are going well." Dorian matched his tone.

"It's a crap situation, but I guess it's better than being dead," Kane said bitterly, any previous kindness vanished from his voice.

"Your positivity is awe-inspiring," Dorian snapped. Venom edged his voice in a way I hadn't heard before.

Zach shifted on his cot. "I think our friends are hangry," he whispered. Then his breathing shifted in the dark, and he sighed. "I can't imagine starving for weeks. Having to feed your children from yourself, losing even more energy."

"I know," I whispered back in agreement. "It can't be easy."

"It's bothered me for a while. It doesn't feel humane, especially with the little guys," Zach said. He shifted in his cot, his emotional discomfort evident in the movement of his body.

We fell into silence. Guilt weighed on my chest. The urge to discuss feeding options for the vampires with Bryce pushed into my head again. I promised myself I'd do it as soon as I got back.

"Just gotta hang on and do what we can for them," Zach mumbled, sleep sapping energy from his words.

This barn seemed to hold echoes of missing people. I looked over at Zach in the darkness, imagined only being able to reminisce about his memory over a table conversation.

I drifted off in the darkness, wondering what it would be like to have no idea where my parents were—or if they were even alive.

CHAPTER TWENTY-NINE

Dawn crept through the barn window. Zach's snore filled the space, contrasting with the silence emanating from the vampires' room.

For once, I was grateful to be up extra early. As the only woman, I didn't want to worry about a bunch of dudes milling around during my shower time.

I quietly dug through my bag and grabbed shampoo, soap, and a towel. My mosquito bites from the previous day itched, and I looked forward to soothing them with warm water.

I slowly opened the plywood door, peeking at the vampires' room. Their door remained closed. I was in the clear.

I scurried along the side of the barn in the pale light, my bare feet tickled by the dew-covered grass. Farmers and their horses tended fields off in the distance. The cool of the morning nipped my skin, but in a refreshing way. The land around this community was peaceful, despite the fear and grief of its inhabitants.

I turned the corner and jumped.

Dorian stepped from behind the shower curtain. Naked. Except for a towel hanging loosely around his waist.

A shock traveled up my body, embarrassment warring with other, less ashamed stirrings. I juggled toiletries, my shampoo threatening to jump out of my hands.

"Oh, I'm sorry," I said, trying for casual. "I thought you were slee—"

"It's fine," Dorian said, but I could hear barely concealed laughter in his voice. "Shower's all yours."

So much for my casual act. I couldn't help myself; I let my eyes wander down as the vampire stepped past me on the damp grass. His skin was pearlescent, and the ripples that usually traveled his cheeks wandered all over, down his angular chest, abdominals cleanly marked with muscle, and just the top of his hip bones... I tried not to imagine any further. Dorian was built lean, but the perfect amount of muscle covered his bones. Every single thing about his body seemed... taut.

"I'll be going now," Dorian said calmly, watching me watching him. I told myself it really wasn't that big of a deal. I mean, I'd been to a beach before. This felt much different than hanging out at the lake.

Someone had set my skin on fire.

"Right," I said, a moment too late.

I turned my head until he'd brushed past me and I heard the barn's front door squeak closed behind him. My entire face and chest tingled from flushing.

I stood in the grass for a moment trying to calm my racing imagination. Sometimes I felt like I was doing a great job maintaining my professionalism around Dorian, and then moments like this happened. Why did it seem like they came more and more frequently?

I remembered the time Kane had surprised me by coming out of the shower back in the facility and peered around, half expecting him to pop out of the woodwork as well. The response I'd had to him in a damp state had been much less embarrassing. The image I'd come away from this incident with would probably come back late at night when I couldn't sleep.

Well, this has been an interesting trip thus far.

"I wish I could put bells on those two," I muttered, and stepped behind the curtain to disrobe. I could still feel myself blushing, from my sternum to my shoulders.

The shower calmed me down. A little. I dried off and dressed before exiting the shelter of the curtain. I wouldn't be walking around half-naked, that was for sure.

Zach and I ate our leftover granola bars for breakfast. I chugged water and popped a double dose of my meds. No one talked much that morning. I put makeup on Kane while Zach tried his beauty skills on Dorian. Kane kept blinking and jerking his head as I dabbed at him with the sponge, which made me laugh.

"You have to hold still," I said. Who knew vampires could be ticklish?

"Fine," he snapped, steadying himself and closing his eyes tightly to brace himself.

Soon enough, we were out of the barn and making our way to the gravel road. I pulled the walkie-talkie out of my pocket. "Officer Shelton, do you read me?" I asked.

After a brief silence, the walkie buzzed in response. "Shelton here."

"This is Officer Sloane. Which officers will be on duty here at the settlement today? We'd like to ask everyone some questions." I waited.

Shelton sounded as unemotional as he had the night before. "You'll have Wolf and myself there shortly, and then around four we get a new shift. Not sure who. I'll let you know when we get there."

"Thank you, sir."

We made our way back to where Shelton had dropped us off the previous day. He and Officer Wolf leaned against their squad car as Dorian and I went down the line of questions on my legal pad. Zach and Kane studied the two men from a few feet away, and Zach scribbled in his own little memo notebook from time to time. The somberness I felt was reflected across the faces of my team.

The officers had very similar accounts of what they knew about the kidnappings. Usually at night. Usually when someone was outside doing a task before bed or walking home after dark. Almost every single missing person was under forty years old, but they seemed to have nothing else in common. They shared no resemblance or hobbies. Men and women carried equal risk.

"Officer Shelton, does your team patrol throughout the night here?" Zach asked, his arms crossed, his voice serious.

"As often as we can. We have our duties in town, too, so our time and staff are stretched thin," Shelton replied in his normal bland tone. "Unfortunately, we can't be here twenty-four seven, but we try to make it work." His voice was so monotone that I couldn't tell whether he was simply overwhelmed, or whether he meant "We do the bare minimum." If it hadn't been for his kind eyes by the road earlier, I wouldn't consider much of what he said. As it was, I questioned that initial impression.

"Do the officers bring the squad cars down this gravel road at all?" I asked, anxiously tapping my pencil on the legal pad.

"We try not to, out of respect for the village," Officer Wolf said. "It upsets the horses."

"I see. So, you don't patrol the settlement at night with spotlights or anything like that?" I thought I did a decent job keeping my skepticism out of my voice.

"Only if someone has recently gone missing and we think we might have a chance to catch the culprit," Shelton said.

"Have you taken any special measures to potentially prevent kidnappings?" After the question left my mouth, I feared my phrasing had implied judgment, despite controlling my tone. Regardless of what I thought of their system, I needed to keep them open to me.

"Like I said, we're doing the best with what we've got," Wolf said, shrugging. He looked lost, like he truly didn't know what else to tell me. I was relieved he wasn't visibly offended.

I looked levelly at him, focusing on not forming a judgment without knowing the whole situation. I understood respecting the villagers' wishes, but people—sometimes children—were being kidnapped.

Considering how many had vanished in the past year, these officers didn't seem very proactive about solving the problem.

I'd never dealt with anything quite like this, however, so I tried to temper my irritation. Maybe this lack of emotion was just their response to having to deal with the same unsolved problem, day after day, with no answers. Maybe all of this really was out of their control.

"Thank you for your time, gentlemen," Dorian said. Kane nodded to them, which I guessed was about as polite as he could get, but I still noted the gesture with approval.

We spent the rest of the morning and early afternoon walking through the community, knocking on doors. It felt rather intrusive, but we put on our most professional faces and tried to be polite and courteous.

Before we knocked on the first door, I turned and cleared my throat, stalling to collect my nerve for what I was about to say to my migraine-inducing teammate. *Be chill. Level-headed. Kane is logical. Mostly.*

"Kane," I started. "I love the curmudgeonly flare you bring to our team, but considering the cultural differences between you and these lovely people, I'm going to ask you to focus on observing and listening today. Not speaking." I offered him a sweet smile that I knew he would hate.

Kane pinned me with a glare. "What makes you think I plan to waste my breath?" he snapped. I took a moment to grieve for that moment of politeness earlier.

"Glad we're on the same page."

Dorian and Zach bit back laughter.

None of the families we interviewed welcomed us into their homes, so we asked questions on their front porches. Children gawked at us from behind curtains and legs. No one had ever seen the kidnapper, not even a trace. Worried families echoed the police. Always at night, always young. The victims seemed entirely random—they never knew who would be next.

Again and again, we heard similar stories, and saw the people who

told them in different moments of their grief. Our questions overwhelmed one mother. Her silent tears seemed endless. "My daughter is
always so careful, so smart," she said softly.

"And she was taken at night?" I asked, hating that she had to relive
her tragedy one more time, even for the sake of finding the culprit. I
already knew I couldn't bring her child back.

"Yes, she went to the outhouse as our family prepared for bed. She
never came back." The mother choked on her last sentence and wiped
her face on the sleeve of her long black dress.

I focused on my handwriting, blinking hard to disperse the tears
gathering at the corners of my own eyes. I couldn't cry in front of the
grieving mother of a girl I didn't know. I didn't envy investigators, who
did this every day.

Between houses, our team brainstormed.

"It's hard to believe that this is the only information they have," Zach
said, his voice hard and teeth gritted. "How can the police be this igno-
rant when this has been happening for so long?"

Dorian agreed with a terse nod, and our little group stood for a frustrated moment, simmering in discontentment. Even Kane seemed to
feel it, his lip curling into a silent sneer.

We continued down the road and passed some thickly wooded
areas. Crickets trilled in the tall grasses at the base of the trees. I caught
Dorian and Kane gazing into the woods before exchanging a glance, but
their eyes returned to the road. I made a mental note to ask Dorian
about that later, but I knew if he'd sensed something relevant to the
mission, he would've said so. Knowing that in my gut pulled back on
my "mission anxiety," too.

We hit a few more houses. The pain in peoples' eyes weighed on me.
It felt like the victims had been erased. The vampires remained quiet
and made sure to keep their distance from the villagers.

The afternoon waned, and we sat in the grass so Zach and I could
eat a few mouthfuls of crackers. I spoke directly to Dorian for the first
time since our interaction at the shower. I'd made a point to dive

deeper into our work that day and not think about the water droplets on his pecs. What I wanted to discuss with him was much more important.

"I've been thinking," I said.

He raised his brows, gently encouraging me to continue.

"I'm going to ask Captain Bryce if he'll allow the adult vampires to visit the Immortal Plane so you can feed. It doesn't make sense for you all to needlessly suffer, especially the children." I might've raised my idea with him in the morning, when it was just the two of us, if I hadn't been distracted by certain visual environmental factors.

"I hope he doesn't chew your head off for proposing it," Dorian said, but his low-key joke showed a hint of worry underneath.

"He might… but it's worth asking. For everyone's sake."

"It might help," Dorian said. "Though the Immortal Plane is still pretty dangerous."

From a few feet away, Kane turned his head, revealing that he'd been listening in. The topic of conversation made me focus even more on the dark circles under his eyes, heavy as bruises in the bright afternoon light. "Ah, so you'll consider going back to the Immortal Plane if *she* suggests it?"

I felt my mouth go dry. Dorian's, on the other hand, twitched irritably. "Kane, you know that Lyra's suggestion would be an entirely different situation."

Kane looked away again. If he were a cat, he would've lashed his tail in irritation. I knew he was sore about Dorian's plan to stay on Earth and request asylum, but I couldn't help lingering for a moment on what else he'd implied. It came with a sting, but I knew better than to take anything that came out of Kane's mouth personally.

"Guys," Zach said, bringing it back to the topic at hand. "Lyra's got a point. But I'm not sure others will see the logic. After all, it wasn't part of the deal."

I nodded my thanks to my brother. "If I can convince Bryce, I believe he could get everyone to fall in line."

"Doubtful," Kane said, as Dorian simultaneously remarked, "Worth a shot."

Dorian and I glanced at each other, sharing a smirk. If that moment didn't epitomize their relationship—and personality differences—I didn't know what would.

"We don't know if we don't try," Zach added cheerfully, tossing another point in the optimistic direction.

"I'll look for an angle," I said, remaining neutral. I didn't want Kane to feel ganged up on. "I'll emphasize to him how bad it would make him look if our six-week mission started strong and then flopped." I'd never actually say anything like that to Bryce. My gut told me that if I did bring this up with my captain, he'd hear me out. Gruffly and harshly, maybe, but at least he'd listen. If it meant the health and wellbeing of our new friends and our mission's bigger, universal picture, Bryce would consider it.

"And humans say that vampires are conniving," Dorian replied, smirking. He held my eyes for a moment and then sobered slightly. "Couldn't hurt to ask, anyway…" His voice trailed off.

My walkie buzzed, saving us from the need to disagree about further details of the plan.

"Two other officers are about to report for patrol at the village entrance," Shelton said through white noise.

My team looked at each other, and, without a word, booked it down the gravel path.

Approaching the entrance, we met the two new officers. Zach and I launched into the same questions we'd asked all day and received the same answers.

"It's an unbelievable tragedy that's gone on far too long," one said with a sigh, looking off over a farm field, clearly discouraged by the village's situation. "We're praying for it to end soon. Thank you for your help."

"Of course," Zach said, his face calm, giving nothing away, though I could still see his irritation in the speed of his notetaking, and hear it in the hardness of his voice.

As the sun began to set, our team returned to the barn to decompress and mull over the notes from the day.

"Okay, Kane, you can talk now," I joked, trying to get the vampires to smile again. They looked more worn than they had in the morning. I wracked my brain again, trying to think of anything I could do in the short term, but there was obviously only one, totally impossible option. Kane said nothing, but he cracked a slow, wry smile, which I took as a success.

We sat around the table, the silence of the barn weighing heavily on all of us.

"Now that we're in private," I said. "Dorian, Kane. Anything at all?"

Kane and Dorian glanced at each other, and I watched as some conflicted emotion passed between them. Zach caught it too, raising his eyebrows.

"An inkling," Dorian finally offered. He seemed thoughtful, pensive. "I can't describe it, but at one point today, I felt... a pull. It wasn't linked to anyone, but it felt like... a distant murmur, almost. I couldn't determine the direction, or I would have said something." That must have been the moment when the two of them seemed to tense up around the woods.

"I felt it too," Kane said, confirming my suspicions. "I agree, the source is questionable. I have an idea to help clear that up, though." Zach's brows quirked higher, mirroring my surprise that Kane actually planned to contribute something extra to the mission.

"Yes?" I asked.

"A night survey. The kidnappings happen at night, so maybe Dorian and I will be able to sense the source better if it's closer." His shoulders squared as he spoke, his voice even. It looked as if he was subtly bracing himself; his ideas did seem to get shot down frequently.

"*Great* idea." I placed my palms together, officially thanking fate for bringing this crotchety dude with us on this trip. I thought I saw a glimmer of pride in his stony eyes.

"We'll split into two teams and meet in the middle of the village. I'll find another flashlight," I said, getting up to dig around the barn.

Shelton called on the walkie that evening to let us know that some other officers had volunteered to do a "graveyard shift" squad car patrol that night so our team could rest after a long day of interviewing and investigating. I thanked him for their kindness, specifically leaving out the fact that we would be night-surveilling in secret. Shelton didn't need to know any specific details of our plans that didn't involve the cops. Besides, the last thing we needed was more officers in our way during our investigation. They had turned out to be of very little help up until that point, though they were kind enough.

We set out around ten o'clock. Darkness enveloped the village, save for a few windows glimmering with candlelight from inside.

"I'm with K-dog," Zach said as we headed toward the gravel road. He slapped Kane on the back, and I heard Kane suck an irritated breath between his teeth.

"Bros for life," I added, amused.

I paused to make sure that the infrared video camera I'd requisitioned for the mission hung securely over my shoulder. It was a fancy gadget, phenomenally lightweight yet jammed with features, including the most powerful zoom lens I'd ever used and a live backup-to-cloud mode. Jim set it up so he could receive notifications when footage was being relayed—and keep an eye on what we were doing.

Our pairs split and set out, each human with a flashlight, for emergencies only. We didn't want to be walking targets for whatever or whoever would potentially see us as such. Since the village's road was one big loop, Zach and Kane set out in one direction and Dorian and I in the opposite. The idea was to meet in the middle, sooner or later.

The moon helped us see the road. Crickets thrummed and chirped. Dorian and I walked quietly at first, moving evenly side by side, which was fine by me. If we spoke, he might bring up the shower event. The embarrassment was still too real.

We stepped lightly to avoid disturbing the gravel and drawing attention to ourselves.

I braved a whisper. "What were you and Kane talking about last night, before you fell asleep?" I asked.

I listened as Dorian's breathing turned choppier, hoping this didn't pain him too much to talk about.

"Sorry if we kept you awake," he replied softly.

"Oh no, it's fine. I just… wondered if you were talk—"

Dorian interrupted me. "Lyra," he uttered, his breathing completely stopped, his tone heavy.

A shiver crawled up my back at the change in his voice. "What is it?"

"Stop moving. Just wait," he said, gravel in his voice.

I froze, swiveling my head to listen. Only crickets. I couldn't even imagine how much keener his night vision and hearing were than mine.

We stood still for only a few moments before he spoke again.

"I feel something. Follow me."

He grabbed my hand, and we crept in the direction of a small cottage. The moonlight reflected from the dark windows. I physically shook my head to remind myself to focus on my steps, not his fingers wrapped around mine. Dorian slowed his pace, his shoulders tense but sinuous, like a hunting feline. Slowly, he led us around the house, maintaining a decent distance from the building. Until, without warning, he dropped into a crouch in the grass, pulling me down with him.

"Watch," he whispered.

I scanned the inky blur of darkness. I didn't hear anything. Then, a flashlight beam bobbed over by a barn about a hundred yards away. I sucked in a breath. Something was happening. That weird tension I sensed in the village felt much stronger now.

"Is that Kane and Zach?" I breathed.

"No," he said flatly. I knew he didn't mean to be rude. He didn't want to give away our position.

The beam bounced erratically, and then, for a moment, a young voice pierced the night, a gurgling cry of shock or surprise that sent anxiety coursing through my bone marrow.

The shout cut off abruptly.

A teenage boy—the one who'd nodded at us while leading his horse the day before—appeared in the flashlight's halo. Two men held his arms. One held a cloth to the boy's mouth.

"We have to do something," I breathed, concern straining my vocal cords as I raised the camera and hit record. We needed to capture evidence, but this was also our chance to make sure this boy didn't become another statistic.

"Hold," Dorian said.

My chest surged with irritation and a shot of adrenaline. I hated to sit still, sensing our window to help was tiny, but Dorian could sense things about the situation that I didn't. Begrudgingly, I kept still.

I trusted Dorian, but it felt fundamentally wrong to sit by and watch as the young man went limp in the pool of light shining on the grass. The two figures hoisted him up and carried him toward the moonlit tree line.

The flashlight beam disappeared into the edges of the forest that pressed up against the barn in a dark tangle. I tried to jump to my feet, but Dorian's iron grip kept me in the grass.

"Dorian," I pressed.

He waited a beat, just long enough for me to question. Then he bolted, dragging me behind him. I stumbled, unable to keep up as he darted over the uneven terrain.

Dorian stopped, turned toward me, and grabbed my other hand with his. I didn't even realize his intention before, without hesitation, he swung me onto his back. In silent understanding, I wrapped my arms tightly around his shoulders and gripped his sides with my thighs.

"Ready?" he muttered in the barest whisper, his voice tense and sharp.

"Just a minute." I pulled the video camera up by its strap and rested it on his shoulder.

I considered texting Zach but didn't want to waste another moment. More importantly, there was a chance his and Kane's arrival could inadvertently spook the criminals. The more of us there were, the more likely we were to draw attention to ourselves.

"Let's go," I breathed to Dorian. We could rejoin our teammates later.

Dorian flew silently over the damp grass. I knew his feet must be hitting the ground, but it felt like we floated over it. He ducked under branches as we entered the forest, the trees seeming to instantly spring up around us into thick woods. He slowed to scan the area for movement before taking us deeper.

I tucked my face behind Dorian's head as twigs slashed me. I felt gratitude for Dorian's eyesight, because I couldn't see anything outside scattered pools of moonlight. He slowed again and surveyed, breathing deeply through his nose, a predator checking the wind for scent. His back muscles were tense against my chest. He moved smoothly, as if I weighed no more than a feather.

"Found them," Dorian whispered triumphantly, his breathing remarkably steady. This guy was all business today.

I looked through the camera screen, but I heard them first. Cracking pinecones and voices about forty yards ahead.

I had to clamp down on my impatience as Dorian let them put distance between us, before quietly creeping after them again. We followed for what felt like ages. My memory flashed to the map of Elmore County Jim had given us—a forest preserve that stretched for miles. There was supposedly a river nearby, but I saw and heard no sign of it yet.

Light filtered through the tree trunks. More voices spoke ahead of us. Dorian slunk toward the light, using a shield of thick branches to guard us from sight. He carried me up an embankment and knelt there. Electric lights shone from a small cottage, perhaps a ranger or DNR station.

I was terrified. And I swallowed it, kept my eyes up, and thought about that boy and our mission. Dorian hadn't faltered and neither would I.

"You recording this?" Dorian asked softly.

"All of it," I said, switching the camera out of infrared mode. I gazed at the building through the screen, angling the device through one of the gaps in our cover.

The men cleared the brush and stepped into the floodlights, dropping the unconscious boy on the ground by the door.

I inhaled sharply.

The men were wearing police uniforms.

CHAPTER THIRTY

One of the officers opened the cabin door and dragged the boy inside. His companion looked back, scanning the forest.

As I watched, shock rattled my head and fury dried my mouth and throat. I was absolutely disgusted. These monsters had stolen the very citizens they were meant to protect. In my line of work, it didn't get much worse than that. The Amish mother's crying face flashed before my mind's eye, and a shudder traveled my entire body.

"Stay on my back." Dorian began to crawl toward the cabin, leaves and twigs crunching under his arms and knees. If they hurt him, he gave no sign.

I clung to his back and kept the camera pointed at the cabin as steadily as I could. Two of the building's windows faced us. Dorian made his way silently to the one farthest from the door, a spot where no floodlights exposed us.

We approached an open window, and men's voices drifted through the screen. Angling the camera up so it could see what I couldn't, I counted five police officers on the camera's side screen. Three other men in black shirts and trousers stood inside, their modern garb indicating that they, too, were not from the settlement. Their faces were hard and stern.

You getting all this, Jim? I glanced at the camera's side panel to double-check that backup mode was on. It was, and in spite of my radiating nerves, the sight filled me with a hard sense of satisfaction.

The boy lay incapacitated on a table in the middle of the room, while an officer argued with one of the men wearing black. Every muscle in my body longed to jump through the window and beat the crap out of every person in the room, but I fought it and emulated Dorian's quiet focus instead. I assured myself that karma was real and continued to stare at the camera screen.

"That's ridiculous," the cop snapped. "We never agreed to a price change."

"It's a fluctuating market," the other man said, completely devoid of emotion. "Nothing I can do about it."

"Don't be cheap," another officer interjected, visibly flexing his chest in the man's direction. "After all we've done for you, the least you can do is be consistent." He cracked his knuckles.

"It's out of my hands, gentlemen," the man replied, like he was ordering a pizza.

The officers scowled at each other, but one nodded. The other pulled the rag from his pocket and held it to the boy's face, like a cook might wipe down a counter. My stomach lurched from another wave of disgust.

"Good. Let's get on with it," the man said. He flicked a finger at one of his companions, who stepped up to a cop and began counting a lump of bills.

One of the officers left my sight and returned to the table with zip ties and a black cloth bag. He secured the bag over the boy's head, zip-tied his wrists behind his back, and tied his ankles together. *Hogtied*, I couldn't help thinking. My teeth clenched down hard. *Like an animal.*

"What are you using on that rag?" the man in black asked the officer.

"The last one woke up before we reached base. If that happens again, we'll be working with other people."

"This here's isoflurane. He won't be bothering you," the cop said through a dark smile.

"Good. Just don't kill him, for goodness' sake. We've got a long drive before we cut him open," the man said, typing into his phone.

My hands shook violently, but I held the camera as steady as I could. I had never felt so angry in my life. I could almost feel my blood steaming under my skin. Beneath me, Dorian remained perfectly still—almost too still.

I didn't recognize the officers in the room, but they knocked beer cans together like old chums and put the cash into a bank bag with "ECPD" written on it. Elmore County Police Department.

My stomach knotted, and I swallowed my rising bile.

"Move it. We've got a schedule," the leader in black barked. They wrapped a sheet around the boy's body and hoisted him off the table, toward the front door.

The cabin door opened, and footsteps plodded onto the grass. Dorian pressed us against the corner of the building, hidden deep in the shadows.

"Nice doing business with you, as always," the head officer said, his tone dripping sarcasm.

"Whatever you say," the leader of the men in black said dismissively.

The other officers continued their chatter, placing bets on an upcoming football game. A vehicle revved its engine from the other side of the cabin.

"Let's go around the back of the building so I can get the license plate," I breathed.

I had no doubt I could convince Dorian to follow them, once we got closer to the vehicle. We still had a chance to get our evidence *and* save the boy, but I was wary about exposing a starving Dorian to such evil people. In Vegas he'd controlled himself, but that had been a while ago.

We crawled, ducking low to keep out of the light flowing from the windows. At the end of the cabin's wall, I extended the camera just around the corner. A car sat running on a dirt road that disappeared into the woods. The car didn't have a license plate light, but I carefully zoomed in. I had to catch *something*.

"We'll be back in three weeks. Don't make us wait again," the leader growled. "And tell your Hanes County friends we'll see them in two days."

The two other men in black pulled the boy into the back of the car.

The officers stepped closer to the car, cracking jokes amongst themselves. The head cop stood watching, his hands on his hips. I wracked my brain, searching for a plan that would allow us to save the boy. If Dorian murdered a human, our cause would be lost. But we could—

The camera started shaking again, and I took a breath to steady my hands. But it wasn't my hands. Labored breaths shuddered out of the chest that my cramping legs were wrapped around.

Dorian's body was vibrating.

My chest went cold. "Dorian?" I whispered. "Are you okay?" I kept the camera on but shortened the strap, tucking the device under my arm.

He made a feral noise through clenched teeth, and I tightened my arms around his shoulders.

"Dorian," I pressed, alarmed.

I bent and peered down at the side of his face. In the dim light, the shadows under his cheek rushed down to his neck, eddying wildly.

The noise caught in his throat escaped his lips as the slightest hiss, and his hands tore at the grass beneath us.

Dorian tossed his head back, his lips curling in a wince. He clenched his eyes shut. This was exactly what had happened in the alleyway in Las Vegas—but worse. I couldn't tell if he was breathing or not. His fangs lengthened as I watched.

The men in black got into the vehicle.

"They'll be gone soon," I whispered into his ear, hoping I could talk him through this. The thought of these bastards potentially getting away with the boy tore me apart, but I steadied myself and put my mental priority list in order: calm Dorian, get the kid. We had a visual of the license plate to track them, and if Jim or any of his assistants were watching, which I was confident they would be, officials could already be on the way.

I silently thanked the stars I hadn't texted Zach. The last thing we needed was two vampires acting up.

I continued speaking gently to Dorian, my voice barely louder than a breath. "We don't have to let them out of our sight. We can follow from a safe distance. We can still do this, Dorian. Remember what happened in Las Vegas—"

Dorian released a low, deep vibration from his throat that I felt reverberating from his chest through my bones. Then his eyes snapped open to the sky. In the low light, I could see his pupils dilate to the size of quarters, the shadows rushing up his face and turning his irises into swirling inky pools.

His body went rigid, and fear stiffened my own spine—but not fear for myself. Fear for what was about to happen, for all the vampires who would lose their safe haven if we couldn't prove that they could overcome their urge to kill.

He was about to break, and bring our entire plan down with him.

"Dorian, no!"

Even as I abandoned our secrecy with my hoarse cry, Dorian moved.

With me clinging to his back, the vampire lunged at the police officers who lingered by the car, moving at insane speed. The officers barely had time to turn and stare in shock at us charging from the cottage. In the space of a breath, Dorian's hands reached for a throat.

Before he could grasp flesh and squeeze, I tightened my arms around his neck and threw my weight to the left, unbalancing him.

"Get out of here! Run!" I yelled at the men as Dorian tore at my arms. As much as I hated them, I couldn't let us fail when we'd come so far. Jim's team would have to deal with them from here.

A few of the scum bolted, but others pulled their handguns. Now two things could kill me: a bullet, or Dorian's seemingly uncontrollable fangs. *We have to get out of here.*

Dorian stumbled backward into the trees, digging his nails deep into my forearms. I winced in pain, shocked by how deep they sank into my skin, but I couldn't loosen my grip. He spun, trying to reach me, until I lost all sense of direction. I didn't let go, even when he slammed me into a tree so hard that I lost my breath. I gritted my teeth, clenching my legs tighter. A few more seconds and he'd pass out—I hoped. His knees buckled and he tumbled forward, me with him. But instead of hitting the ground, we fell and kept on falling.

We plunged down a steep slope, leaves and sticks flying about our faces. Fear of bullets dissolved into the terror of careening through the pitch black into trees or giant rocks. I lost my choke hold on Dorian in the fall, focusing only on keeping my grip around his chest. The video camera's strap jerked against my shoulder, and I lost it in the chaos. I tucked my head against Dorian's back, praying it wouldn't find a rock. *Hold on.*

We plummeted through sharp brush, a rushing sound like wind roaring in my ears, and suddenly I inhaled water.

A swift current propelled my body forward, the two of us thrashing, limbs everywhere. For a moment I had no idea which way was up or down, my lungs burning as I choked on water. Then Dorian's body jerked, and we broke the surface, spitting and coughing. We drifted down the river in the dark while I clung to Dorian's back, and his powerful kicks kept us afloat.

An awful sound emanated from his core. Fury, pain, and grief braided together into a long howl. If he got his hands on me right then, it could be ugly. I reestablished my grip on his shoulders in the shifting current, kicking beneath us, hoping we wouldn't snag. I couldn't try to knock him out—he'd drown.

In front of me, his mouth widened, his fangs glinting in the moonlight as he howled from his gut like an angry wolf. He turned his head toward a sky that was a tangle of black tree branches sliced with moonlight.

"Dorian." I coughed, fighting to keep my head above the water. "Stop!"

His nails sliced the tip of my chin, and I jerked my head to the side, barely registering the sting.

"*Dorian.*" I'd tried yelling and hadn't seen the slightest effect, but I couldn't float here and do nothing. I couldn't think about how he'd tried to attack me or the bleeding gouges in my arms. He wasn't himself. And he could've done so much worse.

I willed my voice to be calm, not to shake, even though this was the most fearful of him I'd ever been.

"You have to calm down," I murmured to him. "It's going to be okay."

His head swiveled, the howl deepening into a gurgling snarl. He tried to hit me again, swinging his arm around behind him, but missed my right eye. I grabbed his wrist to keep him from striking. He started sinking, unable to tread with just his legs, and I hastily let go, keeping my grip on his shoulder with my other hand.

Dorian's head went under for a moment, and I yanked frantically at his shoulder. He pushed up again, gasping. He still rumbled in his throat —I could feel it in his chest—but he didn't howl again.

As the water carried us downstream, Dorian grew stiller, and though he still halfheartedly tried to swim back in the direction of the officers, the distance between us and them grew.

I watched the side of his face to make sure he wouldn't lash out again, and loosened my grip on his shoulders. His pupils shrank in the few beams of moonlight that bled down to the water's surface. His skin, pale and pearly in the dimness, darkened, swirled, and lightened again as shadows spread over his body, predatory and unsatisfied. They seemed softer, after his exertion.

All the while, I murmured to him, resting my forehead against the back of his neck. I was barely aware of what I was saying, but I hoped it helped.

"It's going to be okay, Dorian. I won't let you hurt anyone. We're going to fix things. We…"

We continued floating. His breathing steadied, and he let out one last growl, his thrashing less desperate. I wondered if he was exhausting himself or feeling defeated that he hadn't caught his prey. I still wasn't entirely sure if I was currently in the prey category.

Deep inside, I trusted Dorian and couldn't imagine him seriously hurting me, but the truth was that I knew very little about the power of a vampire's hunger, especially considering what I'd just seen.

"Dorian?" I asked carefully over the burbling water.

He didn't speak, but he tilted his head slightly to acknowledge me.

Cold seeped into my bones, and I could feel my lip trying to tremble. "Shore," I bit out. "Let's get to shore."

I detached from him, and we pulled ourselves from the current toward a patch of shoreline touched by moonlight. Dorian's knees hit the embankment, and he started dragging himself out of the river. I crawled out of the water before collapsing beside him, our shoulders overlapping. The demon had left his body; he was finally fully calm, and my fear of getting gouged by his fangs disappeared in my turmoil over what we'd just seen.

I coughed on water. I stared at the sky as I panted, trying to wrap my head around what had happened. What *would* happen, if Jim's team didn't intervene in time. The boy would die; his organs cut out of him for money. More bile climbed my throat. Tears bit my eyes. I couldn't get the image of his limp, thin body on that table out of my head. The only one who greeted us. Jim couldn't let him down. He couldn't fail.

Dorian's chest heaved beside me.

"Are you okay?" I rasped.

"I have to go and kill them," he said darkly.

Maybe the demon hadn't fully left. I tensed, my exhausted muscles protesting.

"No," I said, dread rolling through me. "You can't… the regulations. Your people. This is for your people."

"What they did... unforgivable," Dorian managed through his breaths, his voice venomous but faraway, almost resigned.

"I know you're starving. I'm sorry," I whispered, closing my eyes.

I felt so powerless in that moment, the events of the past hour playing over in my mind like a nightmare. Dorian had cracked, we'd almost lost our mission, and the boy had been taken. It had been such a near miss—and still could be, in regard to the boy. The feeling shook me to my core, and I grappled for the strap on my waist, fumbling for my phone case. It had flown off during the tumble or the swim. I couldn't contact Jim to check that his team had caught the relay.

"It's not the hunger," Dorian said, his voice distracting me. It had leveled slightly, still resonating with a growl that came from deep inside. I thought I could sense his rational mind slowly coming back. "On the deepest, most fundamental level, what they did is unforgivable to vampires. Those who are supposed to protect others, selfishly abusing their power for their own gain... they're the worst beings in the universe."

I watched his face as he spoke. He looked worn out, angry and tired in equal measure, and perhaps a bit contemplative. Dirt streaked his cheek. His human makeup had completely washed off, leaving just his own swirling skin, heightened by the moonlight. It was oddly beautiful, and I couldn't help but become absorbed by it for a moment, despite the weight of everything else.

"That kind of darkness overwhelms us," he went on. "The craving is uncontrollable."

I exhaled, my own disgusted rage with those police officers souring my throat. That kind of darkness overwhelmed me, too. Black market organ trading, involving more than one police department. No wonder Jim had run into roadblocks gathering evidence. They'd manufactured, plotted, and schemed the whole damn thing. Part of my brain just couldn't process it yet.

"Jim will get them," I promised, trying to soothe Dorian, but also myself. Speaking the words aloud, they felt more real. "I recorded all of it, and the camera streamed the whole thing."

He turned toward me in the moonlight. His pupils had returned to their usual pinpoints, and the ice blue of his irises shimmered. He drew a breath, then paused as if sidetracked. I felt his hands on my forearms, testing for injury where he'd dug his nails into my arms. He winced when his fingers came up smeared with blood. Fortunately, the chilly river water had numbed it a little.

"I'm sorry," he murmured. That was the Dorian I knew, back firmly in control of his body. Relief calmed a bit of my internal anger.

"Sorry I choked you," I breathed, trying for a joke, but my voice came out mournful instead.

Dorian's words stayed low, disappointed. "You shouldn't have had to. I know I said this urge is uncontrollable. But hurting you... I should've tried harder."

"I've seen you fight, Dorian," I pointed out. "I know you could've done much worse. But you didn't. I never believed you'd hurt me too badly. I just worried about our project... all the work we've put into it..."

Even now, the thought of how close we'd come sent shivers up my spine.

Underneath the fear that had consumed my mind, my distress at the thought of him turning on me, there was a far stronger feeling. *I can trust Dorian with my life.*

I stared at him over the damp patch of riverbank between us. His eyes looked haunted and faraway.

"The project," he said, his voice going even darker. "If I'd killed those men, everything would've been ruined."

"Yeah, that's what I've been saying," I told him, expecting him to maybe crack a smile. But his response floored me.

"Thank you," he whispered, his eyes glinting with his glowing, ice-white honesty. "You saved everything."

Dorian brought his free hand up to my chin, as if to examine the scratch there. The brush of his finger stung, but it also sent spirals of feeling through my cold, exhausted body.

His pupils bounced between my eyes, studying them. He leaned up on his side, tilting his head forward, resting his forehead against mine. I brushed my nose against his and watched his eyes squint in a smile. A glorious happiness swelled in me, beautifully different than everything else lingering in my troubled mind.

I felt a sharp ache in my sternum. I sucked in a breath, unable to keep the wince off my face.

"Lyra?" Dorian asked, instantly drawing back.

Pain radiated through my chest, blossoming from my center without warning. A stabbing pain, like somebody'd knifed me in the ribs. I saw white for a moment, and came back disoriented, holding my body as if to keep it from falling apart.

"Lyra, what's wrong?" Dorian croaked, grabbing my shoulder. His fear tightened his grip on me to the point of pain.

The sharpness faded slowly, replaced by a dull ache in every muscle. I was so cold, and after that crazy rough-and-tumble, no wonder my body was acting up. It wasn't as tough as Dorian's.

I felt a flicker of disappointment as Dorian's eyes roved over me, concerned. I wanted to reset this scene back to whatever he'd been about to do or say with his finger grazing my chin. I wanted the moment we'd had back. But my body was spent. Even my disappointment was quickly sapped by exhaustion.

"I'll be okay," I said, running a hand along the side of my ribs. "I probably just pulled something in the fall."

His forehead creased in worry. "Let's get you out of here," he said softly.

Still reeling a little, I raised no resistance as Dorian scooped me into his arms and rose to his feet. He used his chin to pull my head into the crook of his neck. A few sharp jolts went through my chest, but they receded after I held my breath for a moment. I shivered. What exactly was going on with me? Was I getting sick? A torn muscle? More heartburn, exacerbated by the fight and fall? Frustration simmered in the back of my tired mind. I wasn't used to feeling sick.

As Dorian jogged along the shoreline and climbed the incline we'd fallen down, I tried to push thoughts of myself aside. He asked me to wrap my arms around his neck while he reached down to grab the video camera, his excellent night vision aiding us yet again. There was definitely no harm in retrieving it, just in case...

Once he'd ascended the slope, Dorian ran through the woods. The rhythm of his steps soothed my tired limbs, and I mustered groggy thoughts through my exhaustion.

At least we'd completed our mission. We had the evidence. We would stop those corrupt cops. Our government really did need the vampires' help; this would prove it without a doubt. And, hopefully, we'd save the boy.

"We'll be back soon," Dorian whispered, his gentle but firm voice enveloping me.

His grip around my shoulders tightened, and it coaxed me into unconsciousness.

CHAPTER THIRTY-ONE

The sound of beeping woke me. I slowly opened my eyes, a heavy fog stifling my brain. My arms, chest, and legs were dotted with Band-Aids, and I felt one on my chin, too. I noticed several new, blotchy bruises.

I blinked, searching through my clouded memory to remember where I was. We'd flown home. Zach had gripped my hand the whole time. I'd drifted in and out of sleep. Dorian had been watching me every time I'd opened my eyes. They'd admitted me to the medical wing the night before. Both had followed me until the medics told them they weren't allowed in the medical wing. They'd tried to speak to me, their expressions reassuring, but I'd been too out of it to register the words. They'd waved to me from the glass window, Dorian staying a heartbeat longer, as the staff ushered them away.

The rhythmic beeping continued as I sat up. My chest didn't hurt. Only a lingering dull ache remained in my muscles. I took solace in that, grateful for the relief. I wiggled my toes, warm under several blankets. My body remembered the feeling of Dorian's arms as he'd carried me back to the barn.

A zip of energy shot down my spine. I wanted to see him. The night had been hard on him, too.

I slid my legs over the bed. A bowl of fruit and toast sat on a table beside me. I snatched the bowl and inhaled the berries, then the toast, glad someone had realized I would be hungry. Surprisingly, my stomach felt fine—no trace of heartburn. It was odd, but I wasn't going to question it. There was work to be done.

I slipped my feet into shoes and made my way out the door. A medic stopped me as I walked out, his eyes going wide, probably at his patient's attempt to escape without a proper exam.

"Lieutenant Sloane," he said. "I'm not sure it's wise to be out of bed."

"Why?" I asked, feigning joviality. "I feel fine." I smiled to emphasize my point, though I wasn't much in the mood for smiling. I really did feel okay. Physically, anyway.

The medic gave me his most skeptical look and insisted on assessing my condition before I left.

He told me they suspected the root cause of my pain to be extreme heartburn, given that they couldn't detect a pulled muscle.

"I *am* surprised by how quickly it's tamped down, though," he remarked, eyeing me with a note of confusion—and perhaps suspicion. "Given your state last night, I expected it would be worse. Are you sure the symptoms have subsided?"

I nodded firmly. "I'm sure, Doc. Thank you." Recovering too soon was not high on my list of problems to worry about right now.

Nevertheless, his diagnosis put me at ease, at least a little. Heartburn was something I could deal with, and if I truly had recovered quicker than normal, maybe it wouldn't be too big of a problem in the future. I was just glad that I had escaped that tumble without a broken arm or leg.

His brow still furrowed, the medic released me with a clean bill of health, but demanded that if any pain returned, I come back to see him immediately.

I nearly ran face-first into Bryce as I walked out of the medical wing doorway.

"Just the person I wanted to see," he said, his grin especially warm.

"Good morning, Captain," I replied, a dozen questions jumping into my mind at once.

"Have some follow-up for you on your excellent mission," he continued before I could even ask anything, jumping straight to the subject I desperately needed to know about. "Jim caught the relay and wasted no time. We have already made several arrests, and a huge internal investigation began this morning. They're tracking down every single person involved. Their next step will be to review every police division's reports to look for inconsistencies and dig up any other corruption in the ranks."

"That's great," I said, taking in a breath before posing my most burning question. "What about the captured boy from the settlement?" I watched his face carefully, bracing myself.

"Jim was able to get someone trustworthy on the culprit's trail," he said matter-of-factly. "Paramedics revived the boy at the scene where the dirtbags were pulled over. He's in the hospital recovering."

"Oh, thank God," I said through a massive exhale. I looked to the ceiling, mentally thanking the inventor of that beautiful recording device. I felt I could sprout wings.

Bryce watched me, his smile warming me even more. "You did well," he said gently. He set a hand on my shoulder for a second, probably knowing I'd been torturing myself over that for hours. Sometimes he let his heart slip into view.

"Thank you, Captain," I replied. I had to find Dorian—I had to tell him immediately, in case he hadn't heard about the boy yet. "I'll catch you later."

I turned toward the vampire quarters, but Bryce stopped me.

"He's not here," he said, winking... I assumed to indicate that he was talking about Dorian. I ignored his implication without much effort; I

didn't have time to worry about who thought what about my relationship with the vampire.

But Bryce continued, "Neither is your brother, if you were planning
on looking for him, too."

"What?" I asked, in genuine surprise. That was news.

"Kane, Dorian, your brother, and another senior soldier flew to the
police station in Vegas right after dawn," he replied. "Jim wanted their
confirmations on the arrests."

My eyes widened. The sound of Dorian's howling the night before
echoed through me.

"Stop worrying. I can see it written all over your little face," Captain
Bryce reassured me gruffly. "Dorian let us know about the difficulty that
could arise due to their hunger, and he and Kane graciously agreed to be
restrained during the validation process. They won't return with regrets."

I exhaled. I was relieved, but a slow disappointment rose in my chest
at the realization that I'd have to wait to see Dorian. "They'll be back in
time for this evening's surprise," Bryce added, with an air of someone
bursting to tell you their secret.

Reluctantly, I took the bait, worried that Bryce's definition of a "surprise" wouldn't be much fun. "What surprise?"

Bryce grinned at me. "I can't tell you now, because then it wouldn't
be a surprise, eh? You'll see soon enough."

He left me standing in the hallway, nonplussed. I guessed I'd just
have to wait and see.

I returned to my bunk in the women's quarters, looking forward to
talking with someone about what had happened while I was away, but
found no one. Another redbill mission, most likely.

I plopped down onto my bunk, a little disoriented by the prospect of
an extended period of alone time and no to-do list. I wondered how
long the boy would be in the hospital, whether his family had gotten to
see him yet, how I could send a gift. Sighing as my feeling of triumph
warmed my belly, I hit the showers and enjoyed taking my time without

anyone telling me to hurry up. The hot water dissolved the tiny leftover aches in my muscles.

After the shower, instead of succumbing to boredom—which I tried not to ever do—I figured I should check in with my parents. It'd been ages since we'd spoken. A pang of homesickness hit me between the ribs, practically making the decision to video call them for me.

They answered the call, and the screen flashed to my mother sitting in the kitchen. She smiled ear-to-ear as we greeted each other. My mom swiveled the phone to show Dad's face, too. He gave me his usual casual wave, his eyes bright.

"Tell us everything," Mom said.

"Things are going really well. Better than expected. The species relations are calm, even friendly."

They looked cautious, exchanging a skeptical look.

"That's good," Mom said, drawing out the second word. "I'm glad they're not giving you any trouble. I never thought I'd see the day."

"So, tell us about these redbill missions," my dad said, taking over while Mom set the phone down on the table and continued eating her breakfast. "Everyone here is very impressed by them."

"They've gotten more organized since the beginning," I said, pleased that news of our work had reached home. "We have a set structure and protocol: two teams. The vampires handle the birds, and our soldiers provide backup and control the civilians. The missions are nonstop now. Last I heard, Captain Clemmins said our numbers were up to around three hundred."

"Three hundred birds gone?" my dad asked, shocked. "And no casualties?"

"No casualties," I said, and my dad gave a low whistle of appreciation.

Pride swelled in my chest. I appreciated praise from my captains and coworkers, but there was nothing quite like getting that glow of admiration from my parents—and my uncle. With everything they'd achieved and been through with the Bureau, their congrats meant the most to me.

"Well, that explains the unusually relaxed mood here recently," Mom said from across the table, shaking her head a little. "I can't quite believe it."

"Stop doing so well. You're going to put us out of our jobs," my dad joked. "By the way, we just hit the next milestone of development on the new satellite surveillance system. I hope to have it nearly completed by the time you guys get back."

"That's great," I replied, glad to hear about something other than my own work.

Dad described some of the hitches they'd overcome in the previous week. Business as usual.

"Everything else at home is good?" I asked.

"Totally fine. Almost boring, besides the surveillance," my dad said.

"We're a little envious of you kids and all the excitement you're getting," my mom added, chewing her toast. "And curious. You must be getting to know some of the vampires rather well. What are they like?"

I laughed at the impossibility of finding a description that included both Kane and Dorian.

"They're all very different from each other," I settled on. "Some are sweet and quiet"—I thought of Laini—"some are honest and gracious"—Rhome—"funny but whip smart"—Sike—"and... some are grumpy. But honorable, too." Kane, obviously. I shied away from describing Dorian. I'd never be able to hide my feelings from my parents, and having the entire facility already teasing me was more than enough. But I'd miscalculated.

My parents exchanged a worried look that I didn't understand. I retraced my words; I hadn't somehow given myself away, had I? That would take my parents' powers of observation straight to mind-reading.

"They sound," Dad paused before settling on a word, "charming." Somehow, he made it sound dangerous.

"Just be careful, Lyra," Mom said. "Remember, they're vampires. They're not like us, and they have a lot to gain from this experiment, if it goes well."

Oh, God. "So do we," I pointed out. "Imagine no more redbills, *and* no more vampire murders."

They nodded.

"That's true," Mom said, to my relief. "Just be careful, Lyra. Don't let them manipulate you."

"Yeah, yeah," I said, exhaling. "All right, guys, I love you. I'll talk to you later; I've gotta go run some drills."

We exchanged goodbyes.

I hung up and stared at my feet. That had only taken thirty minutes. How did normal people stand downtime? I wanted to be in Vegas with my team.

I searched the halls for any captains to discuss the recent redbill missions with, but they appeared to all be in a meeting in Finley's office. Stymied, I went to the cafeteria and sat on top of a table, chewing an apple. The empty facility felt sad when it was so vacant.

I plodded back down the main hall and remembered the vampire children. Maybe I could drop by to visit.

I shuffled past the empty cells, stopping momentarily to look at my quilt on Dorian's bed. It lay neatly folded on his pillow. I wondered if he had used it at all.

I closed my eyes, the sensation of his touch on the riverbank flowing through my body again. The warmth and openness and wonder that had suffused his voice when he'd thanked me for stopping him from killing the officers. In that moment, it felt like everything had mattered so much.

I wasn't sure I'd ever had a moment that left me feeling so connected to another person during a mission before. And my life had been mainly missions. I'd never had a boyfriend; I'd always had other things occupying my time.

I was beginning to think that what I felt for Dorian went deeper than physical attraction. And since that moment on the riverbank, I was almost certain that he felt something for me, too.

With all of that on my mind, a myriad of feelings crowding my thoughts, I entered the vampire family quarters. I approached Rhome and Kreya's chamber and tapped on the door, waiting for a quiet acknowledgment before looking in. Apparently, Laini was babysitting for the day.

"Hi, guys," I said, to Carwin and Detra sprawled on the floor. They'd acquired toys, some from the cells, others that I didn't recognize. Apparently, I wasn't the only one warming up to the vampires.

The children dropped their stuffed animals and hurried to their doorway, where they gazed up at me with their normal mixture of cheer and intense curiosity. I smiled down at them, pleased to see their little faces.

"Carwin, how's your arm?" I asked.

He held up his forearm, showing me that the bandages had lost most of their bulk since the first time I saw him in the desert cavern.

"Looks a lot better," I confirmed enthusiastically. The four weeks since we'd met had healed him well.

He nodded and nibbled a finger sheepishly.

Less shy than her brother, Detra spun in a circle to get my attention. "I've been good!" she said brightly. Laini grinned, shaking her head in denial.

"That's great to hear," I said, laughing.

I heard other children giggling down the hall. A boy and girl peeked out of another doorway, ogling me. I waved at them, and they scuttled behind the door. Maybe they'd be braver next time.

"May I come and stay with you guys? Everyone's out for the day, and I have no work to do," I said, turning back toward Carwin and Detra.

"Sure." Laini tapped the empty spot beside her on the bed. "We're playing a guessing game."

"I love games," I said to the kids. I sat beside Laini and crossed my legs, rubbing my hands together excitedly. The children shuffled over and stood in front of us, bobbing their heads with expectation.

"The adults think of something and the children ask us questions until they figure out what it is," Laini explained.

"Twenty Questions. Cool," I said. "Should I go first?"

"Yes," Detra said, tapping my knee impatiently as she awaited my readiness.

I thought over what a child would readily know… and then tried to think of what a vampire child would readily know. "Okay. I've thought of something."

"Is it blue?" Carwin inquired immediately, his voice very serious.

"Nope!" He was way off base, but that was the fun of this game.

"Can you put it in your pocket?" Detra asked.

"No," I replied, trying to keep a straight face as I imagined my word fitting in someone's pocket.

The children went silent, thinking of more questions.

Detra tugged at a lock of her hair. "I have a different kind of question," she said slowly.

"Okay," I said cautiously, glancing to Laini for approval. I didn't want to unintentionally say something vampire kids shouldn't hear. Laini leaned against the wall, smiling at me in encouragement.

"Go ahead, Detra," Laini said.

Detra looked me dead in the eyes. "Did you and Dorian go on a 'date'?"

My mouth opened, but nothing came out. I had no ready-made answer for that. I wasn't even sure if I knew the answer myself. *Technically, no, but maybe if he and I weren't in the middle of a dangerous, thankless job to save an entire species and improve the world for humanity, maybe I would want to do something like that?*

Laini shook her head, a little uncomfortable. "*Sike*," she muttered with gentle irritation. "He watched them yesterday. You don't have to explain anything, Lyra."

I held back a nervous laughter, still trying to find an answer.

"Of course they didn't," came a coarse voice from behind the curtain in the corner, causing me to jump. Halla pulled back the curtain and limped toward us.

"Vampires and humans don't do that, Detra," she grumbled. She lowered herself into a chair and settled her eyes on me, stewing.

"Why not?" Carwin asked.

"We don't need to talk about this anymore," Laini intercepted, her voice careful and firm. "Let's go back to the game. Halla, can you think of something for the kids to ask you about?" Distracted for now, the children hopped over to Halla and began asking her questions.

"Nice redirection," I whispered jokingly to Laini. My nerves had jolted with Halla's commentary, and I immediately wanted to ease the tension—and my own anxiety—with humor.

She gave me a gentle smile and folded her hands in her lap. Her face was delicate, diamond-shaped, and opalescent. Her large eyes contained hints of violet—and sadness.

"So, humans and vampires have never been friends before? Ever?" I asked under my breath as the children peppered Halla with questions. I hoped I wasn't making Laini uncomfortable, but she looked calm and comfortable. Honestly, my curiosity had plagued me for so long that it felt good to finally ask my questions.

"Not that I know of," Laini said softly, her tone genuine. "It never happened, back in the day. You know, predator and prey. Sorry."

"I get it," I said, and I did, though it reminded me of my uncle and the pain he experienced with his leg injury. I struggled to set that aside. "But I'm surprised that humans and vampires never just… talked. I mean, vampires don't feed on all people, so good-natured people could've met vampires and gotten along with them, right? Whether the person realized they were a vampire… or not?"

"Vampire and human relationships are not supposed to happen, let alone last, if that's what you're actually trying to ask," Halla said loudly, clearly having overheard our low conversation. The children went quiet. Halla's glare made my skin crawl.

I returned her angry gaze. I wanted to be respectful, but the woman's prejudice was toxic, and every part of me wanted to fight it.

"Our kinds can't and shouldn't mix," she continued bitterly, her furrowing brow adding more wrinkles to her forehead. The shadows moved under her face differently than they did on Dorian's, though I couldn't have said how. Slower, maybe. "We're not even supposed to be here now. It's all so abnormal. It's not the natural way of things. Wrong." Her glassy, steely gray eyes cut me on the last word. I hated admitting it to myself, but this woman unnerved me. I'd never experienced such unadulterated spite before I'd met her.

The children crawled onto the bed and huddled against Laini, like spooked ducklings. She wrapped a strong arm over each of them, scowling at Halla.

I stared at the old vampire, imagining her screaming at kids from her front porch. After the trial period's continued success, she still harbored so much hate? If Kane could come around to working with humans, why couldn't she?

I took a breath and kept my eyes steady on the old woman. "We have no idea what the future holds. And my hope is that the outcome of the trial period will help you feel differently," I said, keeping my words calm and earnest. She scoffed in return. I wasn't surprised.

I'd said my piece. My gut told me it was time to go.

I told the children I'd leave them to enjoy the rest of their game. Laini squeezed my hand before I left, her eyes apologetic, and I smiled at her and the children. Detra waved goodbye, but Carwin had frozen like a fawn. He watched me go with large, sad eyes. Halla said nothing, but I felt her eyes burning into me until I disappeared around the doorframe.

Flustered, I kicked at the floor, mumbling to myself as I puttered down the hallway.

What had I been thinking? Did I actually believe this thing I felt for Dorian would go somewhere? It felt so real now, a compelling part of my everyday life, but where could it ever go? Imagining myself and

Dorian on a date felt completely absurd. What would we even do together if we weren't hunting down criminals, sparring to prepare for some up-and-coming conflict, or planning a mission?

Maybe Halla was right. Maybe this collaboration between our two species was a weird once-in-the-universe thing doomed to fail from the start. The vampires would return to the Immortal Plane eventually—that was the whole point of Dorian's plan. And he'd said I couldn't go there. It wasn't like we could see each other after that.

What if these six weeks were the only time we would ever have together?

Trapped in my circling thoughts, I sat on a cafeteria bench, back where I'd started.

CHAPTER THIRTY-TWO

I sat alone, thoughts of Dorian and what my life would be like after this mission ended swirling in my mind, until the kitchen staff started cleaning. Then, to get out of their way, I headed to the side-door to walk aimlessly around the yard.

To my surprise, Captain Bryce was in the yard with a group of Bureau guards. I caught him climbing onto a stepladder, stringing up a line of lights.

"What's going on?" I asked his back.

He jerked in surprise. "Ah, blast." He turned to one of his assistants. "We've been found out."

I couldn't help but smirk at his reaction, putting the pieces together. "Is *this* your surprise, Captain?"

"Very smart, you are," he said. He climbed down the ladder.

"Something special we're celebrating?"

"Well," he said, brushing off his hands on his pants. "I figured I'm due to stop being a slave driver for a moment and let you all relax. Let your hair down, as they say. We have a lot of accomplishments to celebrate, and since everyone is getting along so well, I figured this called for... a mixer."

"Great idea," I told him. I wasn't particularly in the mood for a party, but maybe it would distract me from my swirling thoughts for a while. Besides, I knew a lot of other people in the facility were dying for some fun. My brother and Gina loved parties.

"That, and I'll get my butt chewed if morale dips too low. You're all so high maintenance." Bryce waved a hand as if to dismiss all of the prima donnas at the facility.

I laughed halfheartedly. "Need some help?" I hated being bored and also wanted to distract myself from Halla's nastiness, so this was the perfect scenario. Decorating always cheered me up—my favorite part about every holiday was spending hours with my family making our apartment look perfect.

"Sure, pick up where I left off," he said briskly, gesturing to the ladder. "I need to go and convince the kitchen to make party food."

Together, the guards and I strung up three more sets of multicolored lights. We dug through the facility to find speakers and a stereo, and set them up in the corner of the yard. Then, while some of the guards lined the perimeter of the yard with benches and chairs, the rest hauled a table out for a buffet line.

I surveyed the yard when we were done. To be honest, it still looked like a dry and desolate yard in the middle of the desert. Nothing could've changed it into a club. But the lights would look nice once the sun set, a good match for the desert's array of stars, and something about how makeshift it all was made it look heartfelt.

Once things settled into place, I went inside to wash my hands. As I left the bathroom, a crew of soldiers and vampires flooded the main hallway. The prospect of company sent a relieved wave through my body.

"How was the mission?" I asked the first person I saw.

Gina answered me. "Not a single hitch," she said, her eyes bright. "Twenty more bills on the 'bye-bye list.'" That was a relief.

Rhome and Kreya walked past and welcomed me back.

"How are you feeling?" Kreya asked, pulling down her loose auburn bun.

"I'm doing just fine," I replied, touched by her concern.

"We're glad you're all right. You weren't injured at all?" Rhome inquired, eyeing my Band-Aids.

"Just sore," I said, smiling. Their kindness was always appreciated.

Thoth gave me his usual gentlemanly, sincere nod, and I reciprocated. Bravi playfully bickered with Rayne about who'd performed better that day. Before the group could part ways into their separate quarters, I clapped my hands to get their attention.

"Everyone," I announced, "please get changed and relaxed and meet us in the yard. Captain Bryce has something special planned for us this evening."

A few people made "oohs" jokingly. I could tell they were tired, but their spirits were still high. This team felt so much different—warmer—than our human-only team had been only four weeks earlier.

Clemmins patted my shoulder as he walked by.

"Good job on your mission," he whispered, one of the few things he'd ever said to me individually. I took that as a good sign.

We gathered in the yard as Bryce set up the music. The sound of parade horns blared from the speakers; then an old-timey, scratchy recording of a trilling Scottish man played: "I love a lassie, a bonnie, bonnie lassie; she's as pure as a lily in the dell..." Bryce started bobbing his head to the music.

I'd always known my captain to be proud of his heritage, but this was a totally new level. Laughter pushed so hard at my throat, I thought I would choke on it. For the first time ever, I witnessed Bryce being a full-fledged dork.

Some of the soldiers groaned loudly. I thought that rather bold, considering who they were responding to.

"What?" he shouted at them, genuinely confused. "Have you no appreciation for good music?"

"Captain, we may want to get a little more contemporary," I said gently. It was so hard to keep a straight face.

He rolled his eyes and handed off the phone plugged into the stereo system.

"Suit yourselves," he muttered. "Hooligans."

I helped Clemmins and Finley carry platters of snacks from the cafeteria. Gina followed us with stacks of paper plates and plastic silverware. Human partygoers shook their shoulders to the music in the yard. Sarah made Grayson snort with her sad attempt at a moonwalk. Lily bravely opened a political discussion with Roxy, and Roxy's tone made her face fall in regret.

I scanned the crowd, the voices of my friends and acquaintances from the facility murmuring amongst the music in the calm desert evening. The sun touched the horizon, the sky filling with amber. Where were my guys?

For the most part, the ten or so vampires in attendance sat in a row of chairs to the side of the dance floor. Sike stared with amusement at the humans dancing—but tapped his foot to the music—and Bravi snorted. Some of the others looked genuinely transfixed by the soldiers' dance moves.

Little worries gnawed my brain, but a part of me hoped to steal a chance to talk to Dorian—the part that wasn't inundated with uncertainty after Halla's dressing-down. I wanted to see that he was okay with my own eyes, and I felt like I needed to say something to him, but I had no idea what.

After standing at the buffet line for a while, taking out my impatience with Dorian's absence on a carrot, I intercepted Captain Bryce as he strolled past me.

"Captain, any update on when my team is getting back?" I asked, trying not to sound obsessive.

"Relax, Lieutenant. Your beau will be here soon," he said, winking at me for the second time that day. "Speak of the devil."

I turned and saw my team members enter the yard. But the relief of knowing that they'd returned unharmed was drowned by another fluttering sensation flooding my chest. Unhurried but focused, Dorian moved through the crowd, never taking his eyes from mine. He made short work of the gap between us, weaving through other soldiers until he stood before me.

He left only six inches between us, searching my face for clues. I smiled, to give him one. My first impulse was to reach for him, but I didn't know what I'd do after that. What if, back in the facility with everyone watching, he responded poorly? My finger twitched as I held my hand back from touching his. This was the pull that I'd first felt in the yard with him, before Detra found us... the pull from a magnet inside my body that knew no other being but Dorian. Professional Lyra would've been irked by it, but I'd set her aside for that day.

"Sorry we're late!" Zach announced, like a cold bucket of water. He buzzed past me to the buffet table, knocking my shoulder with a brown paper grocery bag. "We brought drinks." I turned from Dorian to my brother, grateful for a distraction from trying to figure the situation out.

Zach and Kane set their bags on the table and emptied the contents. Zach's bag held glass bottles of colorful mocktails and two liters of soda. Soldiers rushed over, hooting and hollering. We weren't allowed to drink alcohol on the job, but we could get excited about drinks that were fancier than water and Gatorade. It was the little things when you were trapped in a drab old facility all the time.

It felt wonderful finally having my three guys back with me. The events of our trip to Ohio bonded us with an invisible warmth. I hugged Zach's side, and he asked how I was feeling. Kane greeted me with "Glad to see you're still alive," which I thought was pretty warm, coming from him.

"What are you drinking?" Zach asked me, reaching over the arms of Colin and Grayson.

"One of those," I replied, pointing to a bright red bottle. I had no idea what it was, but if we were having a party, I wanted the flashiest beverage allowed. Zach opened one for me and one for himself, and then we clicked the tips of our bottles together, both smiling goofily at the silly ritual.

I turned back to Dorian, who held a plastic cup I hadn't noticed before. In fact, I realized that all the nearby vampires now carried cups filled to the brim with red wine.

"Vampires are allowed to drink alcohol during the trial period?" I asked jokingly.

"No," Dorian said, smirking. "That's against regulations."

I glanced around again. The shadows on the vampires' faces rippled wildly as they chugged, the tips curling darker than they had in ages.

I looked down into Dorian's cup and confirmed that the liquid was too viscous, too opaque, for wine. My eyes widened in disbelief. *It can't be.*

Kane observed my expression and stepped in.

"Jim got us a little thank-you gift," he said quietly, eyes twinkling, which made his expression the merriest I'd seen him wear to date. "Compliments of some inmates' date with the executioner on Death Row."

"Cheers." Dorian tapped his cup against Kane's, then met my eyes over the rim as he took a long drink. I stared at him, partially because my heartbeat couldn't help but quicken at the look he fixed me with, and partially still in surprise. When I'd been thinking about feeding the vampires, I hadn't been thinking this way.

"Cheers, K-dog! To a successful mission." Zach bounced over and clapped Kane on the back. Kane scrunched his nose, but his eyes remained amused.

"It's about time we had a drink together." Zach didn't seem too bothered by what the vampires sipped from their cups.

I looked around, taking in this new information.

The sitting vampires mostly seemed focused on drinking, and

Harlowe winced after swallowing her beverage. Sike had long finished his cup and leaned back lazily in his chair. Thoth wiped a sprinkle of blood from his silver beard, his eyes also closed in a grimace. Rhome poured two smaller cups of blood and disappeared inside to give them to his children.

I eventually settled on feeling happily horrified about their little snack. If our vampire team had to drink blood, at least it was from convicted criminals who had been through the justice system. It dawned on me that regardless of my instinctual repulsion, this was completely in line with what we aimed to do with vampires and criminals in the future.

Dorian nudged me and pointed. The redbill flock had crept closer to the facility through the desert brush, their eyes curious, reflecting the shimmering strings of lights. They looked like they wanted to be part of the human-vampire flock—or they were confused by it. It was almost cute... and quite a change from them trying to bite us in half.

The music changed as Roxy and Bravi took possession of the stereo. An old techno beat pounded through the speakers, climbing in volume, and every soldier got up to dance. Dorian and I remained standing by the food table, holding our drinks, watching our friends jump up and down and shout the lyrics to each other. Soldiers worked hard, and when we cut loose, it was go big or go home—especially because we so rarely got to enjoy moments like this. The seated vampires seemed even more amused by this human display since they'd eaten, and even old man Thoth was giggling to himself now. I had a soft spot for older folks, and now I could add older vampire folks to that list.

A major oldie followed the techno, slow and crooning. I'd heard my parents listen to it, usually at their wedding anniversary parties.

Just as the song began, Rhome returned from family quarters. At the sound of the music, he perked up and took his partner by her hand. Kreya shook her head, embarrassed, but he whispered something in her ear that made her crack a smile. Sometimes those two deeply reminded me of my parents, and though I'd just spoken with them, I felt a touch of homesickness. Moving gracefully as always, the vampire couple found a quiet corner of the dance floor and swayed side to side, their eyes traveling each other's faces. I caught Bryce gazing at them, his eyes almost misty.

I felt Dorian watching me, and my chest fluttered. In the back of my mind, Halla's words still echoed, and as much as I hated to admit it, the worry had changed how I interacted with Dorian. I couldn't shake myself out of it.

It frustrated me that the cranky old woman had gotten under my skin, but the logical part of my brain had to consider whether there could be any validity to her words. I hadn't known how to sort out my feelings before; now, Halla had reminded me of another set of complications. Confusion clamped my mouth shut. Dorian's eyes were still on me, but I couldn't return his gaze.

Instead, I watched Louise. She had been standing at the buffet line for a strangely long time, twisting a cocktail napkin in her fingers—a motion I recognized as restless indecision from rather personal experience. Now, she crumpled the napkin in her hand, threw it away, and walked directly up to where Sike sat, her knees almost touching his. I assumed that she was just seeking Sike out for conversation, as I'd seen her do before, but her face looked... extremely determined. Too determined for mere talking. I held my breath. *Is she going to...?*

He leaned back in his chair, a cocky smile plastered across his face, and put his arms back behind his head like the most casual guy in the world. No shame, that one. He couldn't expect her to take that well.

I half expected Louise to shake her head and walk away. Instead, she put her hands on her hips, looking amused. I couldn't hear them over the music, but I could see her speak. Then, taking me totally by surprise, she thrust out her hand.

Caught up in their moment, I watched open-mouthed as Sike regarded her. Then, with his newly cast-less arm—he'd finally ditched his bandages a few days earlier—he reached out and took Louise's extended hand. When he stood, he twirled her by their linked fingers until she was caught up against his side. Louise flailed, looking torn between going along with his dance move and shifting into a fighting stance; they stumbled, then righted each other, and then the two of them burst into laughter. My heart nearly leapt out of my chest. Meeting the vampires had revealed amazing new sides to my comrades.

They moved onto the dance floor, keeping a slightly larger distance between them but swaying with the music all the same. I noticed Grayson glancing, somewhat sadly, in their direction from where he leaned against a post, talking with Colin under the glowing lights.

Her eyes on her dance partner, Louise beamed. Sike seemed very focused on dancing, maybe wanting to impress her. Or not trip over his lanky limbs.

My heart beat too fast. It looked like Sike and Louise were just part of our human-vampire team, dancing together, having fun. Was that so bad? Would Halla pop up out of the woodwork, pronouncing certain doom? But I doubted she'd come to the party... too many humans.

I could still feel Dorian's stare on my skin. This time I gave in and turned to him. It dawned on me that this was our first time socializing... not strategizing, not hurtling through the sky on a redbill, not chasing criminals.

"How did the assignment go?" I asked, instead of saying what I really meant. *I missed you.*

"As expected," he said, an edge of fatigue creeping into his tone. An experience like that would've wiped me out, too. "Appreciated the straps Jim's guys put on our chairs."

I considered that, furrowing my brow. What a weird thought. I imagined this was the only situation in which Dorian would appreciate doing his job basically wrapped in a straitjacket.

"I was drained when we landed, but I'm fine now," he added, indicating his cup.

I scrunched my nose but caught myself before I said something rude. "I'm glad Jim and Bryce could make this happen before it came down to a snack-time trip to the Immortal Plane," I said.

Dorian laughed. "Yeah, feeling much better. But..." His voice lowered, going dark and smooth as it slipped into something that I could only read as flirting. "Not just because of the blood."

I stared at him for a moment, feeling my cheeks heat, looking for a comeback. My head spun at the confidence in his icy eyes, and I had to look away. Dorian said stuff like this easily, as though it wasn't incredibly forward and embarrassing. How could I respond? Should I even allow myself to flirt with him, if humans and vampires really would just separate again?

Undecided and flustered, I focused on the dance floor again. But it didn't provide the reprieve I'd hoped for. Everywhere around us, I saw couples dancing together.

Sike and Louise twirled, more gracefully than I'd expected, then stood back from each other, Louise giggling as Sike made robot arms. I had no idea where he'd learned that. Kreya's head lay on Rhome's shoulder, and he held her close with a deep look of contentment. Some of the other soldiers had paired up too. I saw tall, burly Hank swaying a bit awkwardly with Lily. Their size difference was almost alarming. And off on their own stood Zach and Gina, forehead to forehead, barely moving with the music, having some quiet conversation meant only for each other. I'd always thought they would end up like our parents— insanely dedicated to their work, but also to one another.

Meanwhile, Bravi pretended not to aim side-glances at me and Dorian from her chair. Did seeing the human-vampire pairs bother her? I wondered if she secretly harbored some of Halla's less-than-friendly opinions, too. Bryce stood in the corner, having some merrily heated debate with Clemmins. At least *he* wasn't getting all romantic with somebody. At least—

Dorian interrupted my anxious surveillance by stepping directly in front of me, his crystalline blue eyes fixed on mine. "Lyra. Let's dance."

My heartbeat sped up wildly. I swallowed, then made my decision. Here was an opportunity for just a single dance, a chance to stand close to Dorian. A chance to see what might happen. And if I didn't take this chance, I knew I would regret it later.

"Okay," I said to Dorian.

His hand reached out; his fingers wrapped around mine. He pulled me forward through our mingling friends, to the dancefloor on the sand. I could feel my heart beating against his fingers.

"Something on your mind tonight?" Dorian asked as we threaded through the miniature crowd. He leaned in to speak with me over the music, and delicious shivers touched the back of my neck as he spoke near my ear. "You're being awfully quiet."

I debated trying to find a joke to brush it off with, and quickly gave up. "I'm not sure what to do," I admitted, my face flushing as I spoke into his ear in return.

"First Lieutenant Lyra Sloane, at a loss for what to do? Am I hearing this correctly?" His voice teased me, but his eyes were gentle.

"Hey, I've gone through a lot more training for team leadership than I have for... this," I muttered, more amused than annoyed, but still abashed. Dorian positioned himself in front of me on the sand, his hand still wrapping mine. And, once again, he surprised me.

"Well, to be honest, I have no idea how this 'dancing' thing works either. But let's give it a shot," he said, studying his feet, then looking up at me with a sly smile.

Just like every mission we went on, we were in this together.

The thought grounded me, and a burst of courage traveled up my spine. I took his other hand with my free one, noticing his long, elegant fingers, and how they looked next to my own.

"This goes here," I instructed, placing his hand on my hip. A tingle zipped up my spine as I remembered our afternoons of sparring on the sand beside the other vampires and soldiers.

He nodded, adjusting his grip until it felt solid against my skin, his face intent and focused.

A new song came over the speakers. A steady, chill walking bass line.

I could dance to that. And maybe Dorian could, too. A spark of excitement passed through me, transforming my nerves into something else.

"What next, First Lieutenant?" he asked teasingly, and I returned his smirk with one of my own.

"Next, I put this here," I said, placing my left hand on his right shoulder, covering the seven-ish inches of height difference between us, bringing the two of us closer together, only a few inches separating us. "And now we listen to the music and move with it." *No going back now.*

I caught the beat and curved my hips back and forth. Dorian gazed down at my waist, mirroring my movements. I caught his eyes traveling a little farther north, over my chest and up to my eyes, which he held confidently. A blossom of heat traveled up my neck.

We inched closer. Every so often, my thigh brushed his, reminding me of how firm his wiry muscles felt when he carried me on his back, and how safe I'd felt cradled in his arms.

"You're three steps ahead of the enemy, but you can't predict dance moves?" I commented sarcastically.

"At least I don't strangle and drown people," Dorian whispered, his lips brushing my ear.

A relieved laugh bubbled up in my throat. If he could joke about the previous night, then he couldn't be too traumatized or angry at me. Dorian drew closer, his hand sliding around from the side of my hip to the small of my back, pressing my face forward into his neck. He smelled like a breeze that had recently passed through the branches of a cedar tree.

"At least I don't waltz out of the shower half-naked in front of unsuspecting people," I retorted, continuing the joke.

I felt his smug smile against my cheek. On the downbeat to each measure of the song, our hips brushed briefly, then parted. I admitted to myself that I loved the feeling. I had really tossed aside Professional Lyra this evening.

Fire flared in my chest and moved lazily downward through my body. I ignored it as best I could, determined not to let it ruin my evening. I set my chin on Dorian's shoulder, no longer trying to suppress my smile.

Zach and Gina sidled onto the dance floor. Zach let out a whistle in our direction, and hoots echoed from the rest of our colleagues. Dorian and I grinned at each other but refused to acknowledge them. They did not need any encouragement. Especially Zach.

More drinks fell into cups; more songs played. Rhome, Kreya, and some of the other vampires slowly trickled back to their quarters, but most of the soldiers stayed a while longer before heading out. I had no idea how much time had passed, but eventually only a few couples remained. And there Dorian and I were, still dancing together.

As the dance floor emptied, Dorian squeezed my hand.

"Let's go for a walk," he whispered, and I nodded, feeling like I was in a dream.

I followed him into the desert, the music from the speakers drifting over the sand and through the brush. The redbills huddled close by under the explosion of stars above us. Some of the birds leaned their heads on each other, sleeping while standing. Others watched the remaining dancers with interested chirps—and the crickets chirped back at them.

After we'd walked out far enough to see the stars clearly, Dorian and I sat side by side on a large, smooth boulder, our shoulders leaning against one another. His fingers still twined with my own.

"Thank you for teaching me to dance," he said earnestly. The dim light from the stars shone on his cheekbones and eyes.

"You're a natural," I replied. I really meant it. A thought crossed my mind. "Do vampires not normally dance with one another?"

Dorian's eyes got somber for a moment. "Some of us do. I've never really had a chance or a reason to learn."

A moment of quiet passed in which we studied each other. The worries I'd pushed down all evening started to rustle inside me again, to my dismay. Halla's words circled through my mind. But how could something that felt so natural be unnatural?

"Dorian," I started, not entirely sure what to say. I exhaled and shook my head. Best to just acknowledge this head-on. "What are we doing?"

"We're sitting on a rock in the desert," he said, his voice completely deadpan, but I could still hear the teasing flickering there.

I gazed at him, brows furrowed. He was probably avoiding opening the conversation we both knew we needed to have, and as we sat there, I decided I was all right with just taking in the sight of him, at least for a little while longer.

Dorian's knees touched mine. He leaned forward, shifting on the rock until he could set his forehead gently against mine, the way we'd lain on the riverbank. I closed my eyes briefly and absorbed the feeling of his skin, all my thoughts fleeing as sensation overwhelmed everything else. This felt natural. It felt right.

I heard our breaths synchronize. After a few moments, I opened my eyes again, only to completely, utterly lose myself in his piercing pupils. This was a kind of happiness I'd never felt before. It was hot but didn't burn; it ached but didn't hurt. It was so big inside me, light but filling.

I couldn't look, turn, or move away. My body felt nothing but him drawing nearer, heard nothing but our breathing. I'd never wanted to be closer to someone in my entire life. My muscles leaned into him, that magnet inside of me acting up again.

Dorian's breath traveled down my neck. The breeze carried his scent over me. The bursts of white in his irises consumed my vision. His parted lips drifted slowly over mine. I closed my eyes, holding onto every slight skimming of his skin on mine.

His lower lip caressed mine.

Finally.

A jolt of electricity shot through my chest. Not the sweet warmth I'd felt a moment ago, but the hot poker of heartburn. Except now it had multiplied, a wheel of flame searing straight into my heart. Fire radiated between my ribs every time my heart pounded, growing stronger, harder, hotter. I couldn't breathe.

I cried out, clutching my chest, only vaguely sensing Dorian's hands on my shoulders, him calling out my name. I tried to power through by sheer force of will and pull myself back to awareness, but the pain in my body overwhelmed everything else.

"Lyra!"

My knees hit the sand. Everything went black.

CHAPTER THIRTY-THREE

I woke from a hazy dream to beeping and humming. My eyelids felt like lead, and it took me a moment to lift them. Medical machinery surrounded my bed. Their tubes extended from my arms; tape held another in my nose. I shifted in discomfort.

I didn't recognize the room at all. Unfamiliar voices carried in from the hallway.

A nurse shuffled in. "You're awake! Wonderful," he said, his friendly tone a little too abrasive for my fogged-up state.

"Where am I?" I croaked.

I knew something was up, because I wasn't immediately anxious about work—just confused, lost. A strange wave of déjà vu washed over me.

"You just relax. Everything is fine. I'll send in the doctor," he replied, heading back out the door. "Relax," "fine," and "doctor" did not belong in the same sentence, so his words had the opposite of their intended effect.

I lifted my hands to pull the tube from my nose, but the needles in my veins sent aches through my arms, so I gave up on that. The fog in my head made everything slow. What drugs was I on? Where was... Dorian? He was the last thing I remembered.

A doctor entered, a stethoscope swinging from her neck. "Hello, Lyra," she said calmly, approaching my bed. "I'm Dr. Weiss. Your family will be in shortly."

"Where am I? What happened?" I rasped, starting to feel some desperation through my mind's clouds. I didn't like this. I did not want to be here. I didn't want to feel slow.

"You're in the ICU in Phoenix. You've been in a coma for three days," she replied.

That... That wasn't possible.

"Lyra," my mother said as she hurried to my bedside. She pressed a palm to the side of my face, tears welling in her eyes. Zach, my father, and my uncle followed close behind. Their voices lilted in sighs and relief, their hands squeezing my shoulders. My uncle leaned over his cane and gripped my hand until it hurt. I attempted a smile for everyone, but my confusion and haze made that difficult.

"What happened?" I asked again.

My mind traced back to the party, sitting on the rocks by the redbills, Dorian easing toward me, his lip brushing mine... That happiness right before my blackout had consumed me. I wanted to just get back there, for just a minute.

"We're not entirely sure of the root cause yet," Dr. Weiss said. "But you showed signs of severe hypertension when admitted. We understand that you've been experiencing chest pains, and your recent loss of consciousness is another symptom. We want to run more tests, but what's important is that you rest now. We need to keep your blood pressure from rising unexpectedly again."

I rolled the doctor's words around in my head. This was more serious than heartburn. She patted my leg and left me with my family, promising to return shortly.

"You've been too stressed," my mother said, gripping my hand anxiously. "Being locked up in that facility with vampires has been too hard on your heart."

"Zach told us about this side project you're working on," my father interjected. "Far too dangerous and stressful, Lyra."

A tiny flash of irritation with Zach flickered through my mind, as secrecy had been important for our side project.

"I had to tell them," Zach said, his eyes pleading. "They needed all of the facts to make sure you got the right treatment."

Honestly, I would've done the same in Zach's shoes. His wellbeing would've meant more to me than anything else, had our roles been reversed. We'd made a lot of headway with the side project already, hopefully enough to get our point across to the board. My previous irritation dissipated into quiet gratitude for my brother, for always having my back.

I felt foolish for assuming that my chest and stomach pains had been heartburn. Maybe I had pushed myself beyond my limits. I hated to admit that, but today I'd woken up in a hospital bed after a three-day coma. This was beyond my diet.

"It's not just stress," I said, my voice weak, trying to explain to them that it wasn't simply the presence of vampires that had brought me to this state. "I fell recently. On an op. That was when I hurt myself, but it was necessary. I had to stop Dorian from..."

"Relax, honey," my father said, his voice gentle. "You don't have to strain yourself explaining."

Which was good, because as I said it, I realized I couldn't finish that sentence in front of them.

I mentally kicked myself for not getting a more thorough medical exam at the facility. My family continued worrying aloud, while I retreated into my still-blurry thoughts and exhaustion.

Dr. Weiss returned, having conferred with a colleague. She wanted to monitor me for another twenty-four hours before my release.

"Your routine needs to change entirely once you're out," Dr. Weiss added firmly, but her eyes remained caring. "You've suffered a severe medical emergency. No stressful assignments for at least three weeks. We're giving you a daily medication regimen to keep your hypertension under control."

I wanted to groan but hadn't the strength. After all our hard work, I would miss the end of the trial period? We still had so much to do.

I swallowed the doctor's orders and nodded. My usual stubbornness and workaholism needed to take a back seat—I could understand that.

My family read the disappointment on my face and returned to patting and comforting me. Gratitude for their presence pushed tears to my eyes.

"Lyra, it'll be fine," my uncle said gently, still holding my hand. "I've looked into your 'side project' with Captain Bryce. The evidence you've gathered is plenty for the board to consider. Between your recent assignment and your mission in Vegas, you uncovered multiple counts of police corruption. I've contacted Jim and will present this to my colleagues once I leave. This is bigger than you and Bryce now, so let the officials do their jobs for a bit."

I sighed, calmed by his voice and the assurance of his warm hand.

"No more worrying, honey. Rest. You've more than earned it," my uncle said, smiling. "I'm incredibly proud of you."

Tears stung my eyes. He was right.

"But it was supposed to be a surprise," I murmured, cracking a small smile.

My uncle brushed my cheek. "And it was. You've done a great thing, Lyra. Enjoy knowing that."

They left me to rest after my mother adjusted my pillows and blankets. My father dimmed the lights on his way out.

Calm washed over me. The side project had succeeded; all of our secrecy, the embarrassing makeup job, the extra shifts and lost sleep and the vampires holding themselves back from killing had been worth it. My eyelids required no encouragement to close again. I convinced myself that the more I relaxed, the sooner I could return to the facility,

the soldiers, next steps for our project after hearing from the board...
and Dorian.

The feeling of his lips brushing mine fluttered through my head
again.

I tried to block it out. That *definitely* wouldn't help my blood
pressure.

CHAPTER THIRTY-FOUR

The next day, I waited for the doctor on the edge of my hospital bed, already in my clothes and shoes. When she finally came in, surprise flitted across her face.

"Feeling better?" she asked.

"Great," I said. "I mean, I've been asleep for three days. Why wouldn't I be bright-eyed and bushy-tailed?"

The doctor laughed, startled. "That's not exactly how comas work," she said. "In fact, they often cause permanent brain damage. But your case has been a bit... different." Dr. Weiss raised her eyebrows slightly on the word "different," unnerving me slightly.

Brain damage? Holy crap. I felt ready to suit up for another redbill mission in less than twenty-four hours, but I didn't mention that. I felt fueled, energized.

The doctor went over my charts with me and explained my medication schedule. I tucked my prescription into the pocket of the hospital-issued sweatpants. She advised that I continue minding my diet, but above all else, keep my stress levels down.

"Yes, ma'am," I replied politely. It was not going to be easy for me, but I would do my darned best.

She smiled. "You really have bounced right back. Good to see it. Please take care."

Nervous energy tingled through my legs. It was time to get back to the facility.

My immediate family escorted me from my hospital room to the parking lot, where a Bureau vehicle waited for us. My parents insisted on driving back to the facility with me. They initially wanted me to come home with them, but they admitted that as long as I stayed on base and didn't exert myself with more missions, it wouldn't make much difference. After all, Zach would be there, and the facility had its own twenty-four-hour medical wing that could be instructed to keep a close eye on me. The latter was more than we had at home.

The car ride passed mostly in silence. I stared out the window, planning the days ahead. My parents still wore worry on their faces.

"I'll keep a close eye on her, guys," Zach said from the front passenger seat, responding to their wordless concern.

Even so, my parents struggled to release me from their hugs when they dropped us off.

"Don't miss your flight," I said, giving them a reassuring smile. "No stress. I know. I promise."

Zach took my arm, and we waved to our parents. He walked me inside, directly to the medical wing.

After talking through my new, stress-free daily game plan with the medics—which primarily involved writing reports and filling out paperwork, rudimentary daily facility chores—and giving them copies of my hospital paperwork, Zach and I went to the cafeteria. There, we found the rest of our team somewhat listlessly eating their dinners, until they spotted me.

Gina enveloped me, followed closely by Louise and even Roxy, a gesture I appreciated.

"My God, woman, what happened to you?" she asked, with her typical amount of tact.

The women drilled me, and even Grayson and Hank poked their heads into the circle.

"Were you seriously in a coma for three days?" "What happened right before you fainted?" "Can you go on missions anymore?" I raised my hands, overwhelmed. These guys were definitely not helping my stress levels.

It took some effort to convince them I was fine. "And I do need to rest again today, so I'll see you all later," I said, reluctantly peeling away from my team's huddle.

"She's going to see the vampires," Roxy muttered darkly to Louise. "Good luck with that."

I shot her a frown but brushed it off as her particularly harsh humor. After all, I'd never had problems with the vampires. Nor, to my knowledge, had Roxy.

My nervous energy returned to my legs, pushing me into a power walk as I neared the vampire quarters. I wanted to see Dorian smile again, and the crinkles that fanned around his eyes when he did. He would probably be relieved to see me up and about like nothing happened. I reminded myself to relax, for the sake of my blood pressure. It didn't help much.

I walked confidently down the cell aisle, took a breath, and walked into Dorian's cell.

Kane lay on the bed, reading, his bag on the floor. None of Dorian's things were in sight. I knew I was in the right place, but I couldn't help looking around in confusion, as though I'd accidentally walked into the wrong cell.

"Where's Dorian?"

No response. I thought he and I had moved beyond the silent treatment days. *What gives?*

I tried again. "Hey, Kane. Where's Dorian?"

Nothing.

What the hell is going on?

"Kane," I said, irritation lining my voice. I snatched the book from his hand, staring at him.

His gaze rose slowly to mine, icily indifferent. He shrugged his shoulders and ripped his book back out of my hand without a single word.

"What the…" I muttered to myself. I knew Kane could be cold, but this felt different. Before, he'd at least answered my questions, even if he did so bitterly. He'd even told me he was glad I was alive last time I got out of the hospital. Had I done something to offend him? But I'd been unconscious the whole time. A tiny spark of dread entered my mind, but I pushed it away.

I walked down to Kane's old cell. He and Dorian had probably switched rooms. The vampires sitting in their own cells didn't greet me, but that wasn't unusual. Pretending that a wall separated them from the hall gave them a sense of privacy.

Besides Kane being a worse jerk than normal, all of this could be explained. But I fought my growing sense that something was terribly wrong.

Bravi and Sike sat on Kane's old bed. I waved, halting their conversation.

"Hi, guys," I said, smiling, though the nerves I'd felt in my legs had turned to a totally different kind of jitter. "I'm back from the hospital. Where's Dorian?"

Their eyes dropped to the floor. Sike looked at my face, seeming conflicted, about to speak. Then, abruptly, he looked away from me, staring pointedly at the wall. Bravi crossed her arms, her lips turned down in a grimace.

"Hello?" I asked. My stomach knotted, and I swiveled, searching the aisle for anyone who looked friendly, then looked back to the two vampires I'd begun to think of as allies, if not friends. "Guys, did something happen to him? Why won't anyone speak to me?"

Sike sighed and closed his eyes, tuning me out. Bravi's face just got colder.

I approached Thoth's cell and peered in. "Hi, Thoth. How are you?" I pushed cheer into my voice, though it was increasingly difficult to start fresh with each vampire. He was reading, as always, but this time, he did not meet my eyes and give me a stately nod, as he usually did. I waited, hoping, but he simply turned a page after a minute.

Refusing to give up, I stepped ahead to another cell and waved at Rayne and Harlowe, who chatted quietly. At least, until they saw me. Their faces fell, and they went silent. My heart sank. This was bigger than I'd let myself believe. The two young women swiftly exited their cell, brushing right past me as if I wasn't even there.

I stood there, staring at their backs for a moment, legitimate shock creeping over me. They disappeared into another cell. Was everyone making a practical joke? This was the strangest vampire behavior I'd seen since we'd arrived at the facility. Dread prodded me.

I walked past another set of guards, moving quickly into the family quarters. Surely Rhome and Kreya would explain what was going on. They'd always been understanding. Surely...

I knocked on their chamber door, and Detra slowly opened it, sucking her thumb. Rhome, Kreya, Carwin, and Laini sat around the room. They'd been talking, laughing, but at my appearance, silence fell among the adults in the room. Their faces turned to stone, shadows swirling hypnotically across them. It took Carwin longer to catch on, and he looked from face to face, his giggles trailing off.

Detra pulled her thumb from her mouth, reached out toward me—then changed her mind and scurried to join Carwin behind their father's legs.

"I'm back," I said, pushing a smile through my worry.

"Glad you're back," Laini said softly.

Kreya shot her a hard look, which she returned, but closed her mouth.

"How... How are you guys?" I asked.

Another long, awful silence. Like Bravi and Sike, the family refused to look at me. The children didn't move from behind Rhome's legs, though Detra's wide little eyes stared at me unerringly from her hiding place.

Kreya milled about, folding the children's clothes in the corner.

"Rhome?" I asked.

He turned his back on me, focusing on stitching a little frock that I'd seen Detra wear before.

I searched the women's faces but received only a small, strained smile from Laini.

"Lyra, can we play the question game?" Carwin asked suddenly, his young voice so bright in the heavy silence. His eyes met mine, worried but hopeful. It broke my heart watching him try to fix something broken and knowing he would fail.

"Not right now, Carwin." Kreya immediately shushed him, her eyes narrow and severe. He frowned and set his head on his father's leg.

A new pain stabbed between my ribs, unlike the others I'd felt recently. This had nothing to do with my blood pressure. This was the pain of rejection.

I stepped away from their chamber door, my palms growing sweaty. It felt like I'd entered an alternate dimension. Had the past few weeks even happened?

Where were my friends?

My desperation led me to open conversation with the guards.

"Did something happen recently?" I asked them.

They glanced at each other and shrugged.

"Moody bastards, I guess," one said. "It's been like this for days now. Tight-lipped, little to no engagement. Soldiers say they've been the same on missions."

"I think it's communal PMS," the other guard said, grinning. "Or maybe there's a full moon comin'." They chuckled to each other.

I ignored the misogyny in favor of a more pressing issue. "Dorian. Where did Dorian move to?"

"Down at the end," a guard answered. The other elaborated with a gesture. I tipped my head in thanks and took off in that direction.

My breath wavered as I neared the door, the last in the hall. This was when Dorian said, "Gotcha!", right? Or at least explained the issue —did the vampires and humans have a tiff while I was in the hospital? There was no way Dorian was part of this. Still, that dread sat inside me like a stone, growing by the second as I got closer to Dorian's door. I picked at a fingernail, worry rushing through my muscles, listening for movement behind the closed door. I heard nothing. I knocked softly anyway.

More of that unbearable quiet. My emotions toyed with me. Dorian would have opened the door for me instantly. What if he really wasn't there? Or had he just not heard me knock?

I knocked again, harder. "Dorian?"

Nothing. But I had to be sure. "Dorian? I'm not going away."

My pulse picked up as the silence stretched. The doctor would be pissed, but I had to figure out what had gone wrong. This would stress me no matter what, so I might as well get to the bottom of it.

The door creaked open. Finally. Dorian's dark hair gathered away from his eyes, the curling ripples flowing calmly over his cheeks.

He looked like a statue of himself. Not the Dorian I knew. His eyes held the same dead-eyed gaze as the others', like a robot had taken his place. Any hope I'd felt that he would be different fizzled out with a little dying spark of hurt.

"What is it?" he asked.

I squinted at him in disbelief, my anxiety slowly hardening into something else. Even *Dorian* was going to be this way? After everything we'd gone through?

"What's going on?" I asked. My dread had burst and splattered disappointment all over my insides, leaving only determination behind. I would find out what had happened if it killed me. And in this case, that was a possibility. I took a deep breath and ordered my muscles to relax.

"Nothing. Do you need something?" His voice was devoid of emotion.

"Excuse me?" I didn't try to hide the hurt in my voice.

"What do you want?" He stood in the doorway, his lean, toned body stiff and formal. His eyes stared blankly over my head.

"Dorian, I... just got back from the hospital in Phoenix." The words had to grind up my throat to get out. There was so much hurt inside me that I felt pressure on the back of my ribcage.

He nodded, not saying a word, but his lips twitched, as though struggling to contain an expression. What, I couldn't say, but at this point, any reaction was encouraging. Maybe I could talk him out of this.

I tamped down the heat in my belly and started again. "How are you doing? I haven't seen you since—"

"I'm fine," he snapped, cutting me off before I could mention the party. For a moment, his eyes squeezed shut, as though in pain. The tightness of his voice said anything but *fine*.

"Okay," I said, his irritation infecting my own tone. I was so done with this runaround. "Why is everyone so weird today?"

"I don't know what you're talking about." He'd returned to his flat, dead-eyed demeanor.

I put a hand on my hip. "Are you serious? You sound like a child right now."

He didn't respond, didn't move a muscle. I couldn't even see his breathing. I'd been annoyed by Dorian before—terrified and really angry, even, at the beginning—but what rose inside me now felt like what a redbill scream sounded like.

"Dorian," I said, through an exhale. I tried to steady my breathing so my heart would stop pounding so quickly. *Keep away from stressful situations...* "Please, tell me what's going on. Talk to me."

"Nothing is going on," he replied tersely. "We're just here, doing what we were asked to do."

His stare continued to floor me. It was like looking at a corpse. A *mean* one.

I couldn't help the shiver that shook my spine. Twilight zone. Dorian's eyes seemed to stare at my face, and yet he refused to meet my eyes.

"Look at me!" I exclaimed, my voice bursting out of me before I could tamp it down. "Tell me why you're doing this. Did you have your memory erased?"

"No, Lyra," he growled, finally meeting my eyes. *Be careful what you wish for.* It was like a burst of Arctic air. "We're doing what needs to be done: protecting ourselves. Now we've seen what happens when our species mingle, and it's not safe for us—or you, apparently."

I stared at him. "What are you talking about?"

I saw a spark of something in his icy gaze, but it vanished before I could interpret it. Annoyance? Frustration?

He spoke sharply. "Lyra, what happened to you wasn't heartburn. It was a sign—a confirmation, rather, from the universe—that our proximity isn't natural. We knew all along..." He trailed off, his face returning to corpse status.

I tried to keep my teeth from clenching. All that crap inside of me, dread turned anxiety turned hurt, swelling up and festering, soured my mouth.

"Dorian... All I'm asking you to do is explain to me, so I can understand." Preferably without words like "natural" and "sign from the universe," but right now I would take what I could get. At least someone was talking to me.

He continued. "We both know that vampires are here under emergency circumstances. That's it. This arrangement was a requirement. Could you just accept that?"

I continued to stare. I'd prefer the vampire I met on the cliff to this strange and cryptic one.

"I'm sure your kind are coming to realize that you need us as much as we need you," he went on coolly. "That's all this arrangement needs to be about. We should have known from the start that this place was not a clubhouse, but we let ourselves forget. We made a mistake. It's not happening again. There are no friends here. This is a business transaction."

"What the hell?" was all I could manage.

Even if he were right about this "sign," it seemed like he'd forgotten everything that came before. If some mystical message from the universe had happened, couldn't they at least have let us know and gotten our take on it? Even as a courtesy? We'd been working together as a team for weeks now, building goodwill to benefit both our species. And they'd tossed it aside, for no understandable reason.

"So you're planning to pretend we're complete strangers now? Because you think my health issues are some kind of omen?"

His gaze remained stony. He was serious.

"Dorian, that's crazy," I said. Frustration coiled in my stomach, expanding and heating up my core. This discussion felt like it belonged in the Middle Ages. I'd never experienced something so irrational.

He crossed his arms and shifted his feet, his eyes back to staring at my forehead, or wherever they were going to not meet me in the middle.

"It doesn't make sense," I continued, unable to stop the words pouring out as I tried to apply reason to this scenario. "Other humans and vampires have gotten close to each other and nothing's happened. Even Sike and Louise danced the other night. And Kane and Zach have... I mean, they *had* that stupid handshake that we couldn't get them to stop doing. Our teams have grown tight, and that's important for the goal. For *our* goal. How are we supposed to work together long-term like this? How are we supposed to trust each other? That is what you want, isn't it? A long-term alliance with humans? Otherwise, what the hell have we been wasting our time on these past weeks?" I couldn't stop the barrage of questions as they tumbled out.

His silence chewed a hole in me. It gnawed at my frustration, trying to suck the life out of it. But I couldn't give up yet. Somewhere inside this creature staring at me was the vampire I knew. The vampire I thought I'd... I looked directly into his eyes, willing him to understand.

"My health problems could be—and very possibly are—totally unrelated to this. The doctor says it's stress. Blood pressure. Are you seriously going to shut down and erase *everything* we've built based on one human's illness? When no other humans have shown symptoms? Dorian, this isn't like you. You're smarter than this."

He shook his head but remained silent, his lips pressed together, his face severe. Through the blankness of his eyes, I thought I could see the tightness of pain. But maybe that was wishful thinking.

"Please help me understand," I said, drowning my exasperation to try another tack. "If there's some other issue, let's talk about it. This isn't logical. If there's a problem between humans and vampires, we can fix it. Just tell me the real reason you're doing this. Has anything else happened? Did I... Did I do something wrong?"

Dorian's voice growled. "I did explain."

"Is it because..." I steadied my breathing and organized my thoughts. I'd never spoken with anyone like this before, and having it out in the open would tear me apart one way or another. "Do you... Do you think I collapsed because we got *too* close? Because... you almost kissed me?" My voice cracked.

"Oh, please," he snapped suddenly. He jerked his eyes from me, his posture leaning away, his voice becoming bitingly clear. "Why would I *kiss* you? You daydream a lot for a soldier."

I blinked. Tears bit my eyes. That hole that had opened up inside of me swept more of my frustration away, leaving me feeling drained.

I didn't know the man standing in front of me. And maybe I never had. Maybe I'd made it all up. He clearly thought so.

Maybe vampires were exactly what I'd been taught. Manipulative, calculated, temperamental animals who'd turn on you in an instant. Maybe I was seeing the final act of a master deceiver. But...

"Why?" I asked hoarsely. "Why go through... all of this, and pretend to get close to me, just to... What does that even get you? What game are you playing?" I closed my mouth, my face hot, my eyes pricking. Why embarrass myself?

"I only wanted to help," I said, not even sure what I was going for anymore. There was nothing left to say; his dragging silence made that clear. The ache inside me wasn't from my stomach or hypertension. My hands clenched into shaky fists. My vision tunneled, all the feelings I'd experienced up until now pinpointing into a burning bitterness.

"Really? This is it?" I finally snapped.

Dorian offered me one more dead, lifeless stare. It looked like a mask of Dorian, worse than any makeup or clown paint, frozen into a hideous Greek statue, a parody of the vampire I'd spent an entire evening dancing with.

"Obviously," I spat, "I'll be more careful about who I help in the future."

And with that I stormed out of vampire quarters—before he could see me wipe my cheeks.

CHAPTER THIRTY-FIVE

The following days passed in a slow, dragging blur. My chest and stomach pains disappeared, replaced by a new dull ache. An ache that was not quite physical but seemed to hold my body in its sway just the same.

With the side project over, our remaining redbill missions absorbed my energy, though not as much as I might have liked, since Bryce benched me on the aircraft per doctor's orders. That seemed stupid to me now, though, because I hadn't had a glimmer of pain or stomach issues since I'd stormed out of the vampire quarters.

I was so bitter that I hardly cared if Dorian was right about him being the source of my medical issues or not, but I mentioned it to Bryce after a mission. He wasn't fully convinced, but he did agree to assign more kinds of tasks around the facility to alleviate my torturous boredom and lack of distraction. I was grateful, but that feeling usually got lost somewhere between my intense swings from anger to heavy melancholy.

Every day, the vampires only spoke when absolutely necessary, and our groups sat apart in meetings. A malaise enveloped me, a fog that never drifted or lifted. Worse, it shrouded everyone else, too. Everybody at the facility looked like zombies, shuffling from one task to the next, day after day. Even the security guards had lost their humor. The air thickened with disappointment.

The vampires' silence spread through the facility like a plague.

On the rare occasion that Dorian was near me, my despondency broke into burning bitterness. He never said anything more to me than the mission required, but every time I heard his voice, sharpness and indifference flooded me again. Eventually, the initial shock wore off and grew into anger, holding firm. I regularly woke with a sore jaw from relentlessly clenching it, even in my sleep.

A week after I'd returned from the hospital, we passed each other in the main hallway. This time, Dorian fixed his eyes on me and held them for a moment as he passed, his gaze less icy than before. I couldn't help it—a flicker of hope that everything would turn back to normal soon flashed through me.

But I had to crush that hope. I couldn't bear the thought of getting pulled in again. Not after he'd thrown my friendship away so easily for only a suspicion, a temperamental assumption. That minimal amount of acknowledgement in the hallway physically hurt. And after we floated past each other, my anger dissipated back into the massive hole inside me.

He wanted to keep everything between our species a "business transaction." It could be done, I supposed. But it sucked the life out of everything.

I began to despise it all: every minute, daily detail about the facility. So much so that I seriously considered returning home in disgust. It wasn't like my current work couldn't be performed by someone else, and given my recent health issues, Bryce would release me. But we were so close to the end now that I decided to hold out. I wasn't one to leave a task unfinished, no matter how unpleasant it became.

I resorted to reminding myself that this was probably inevitable; apparently our incompatible species were not meant for interaction or friendship. Vampires came from another realm, another world, and

CHAPTER 35 | 353

they would return to it eventually. We were too different. What I'd thought was growing between me and Dorian was just an unnatural, random occurrence that could never have lasted. Just like Halla had said.

In fact, Halla seemed to be the one person in the facility positively affected by the change. From what I saw, she suddenly enjoyed her daily doings. In fact, some days her voice lilted in a way that was almost chipper, like something lost had returned, which made me want to slap her. My tingling resentment over the situation reignited every time she shot me a smug smirk around the facility. Kane hadn't spoken to me since I saw him in Dorian's old room. I never returned to the vampire quarters.

Captain Bryce made a point to start morning briefings with energy and jokes, but the effort he put in always dissolved after the first few minutes of everyone's deadpan, indifferent stares. His confusion and disappointment lined his forehead.

Sometimes I felt worse for him than anyone else. He was powerless to fix something he'd been so invested in.

Our missions wound down as the trial period neared its end. No one seemed to care how many redbills we'd relocated anymore, but the captains continued to sing praises to our deaf ears.

On our second-to-last day at the facility, I found myself scrubbing the bathroom tiles just to avoid being alone in my bunk. My phone vibrated in my back pocket.

"Hi, Uncle Alan," I said.

"I have news for you," my uncle told me, sounding somewhat distracted. Hopefully he was too busy to notice how dead my voice sounded. "I presented your case to the board at our last meeting, and they've finally given me their verdict, after a predictably prolonged debate. Excuse me." He covered the microphone and spoke with someone else in the room before returning. "Sorry, juggling a lot right now. We will extend our support for the vampires beyond the trial period. Despite some reservations, most board members were impressed with what you pulled off."

"That's good," I replied, feigning cheer. His words meant so much, but so little.

"The next step in discussion is accommodation, where to house them in the longer term, because we expect they'll need something a bit more spacious. And perhaps less prison-like"

"Oh," I said softly, my warmth slightly more genuine this time. "I'm glad to hear that."

"Your superiors have been informed, and they're making necessary preparations. I just wanted to tell you personally, as you've gone above and beyond on this mission."

"Thank you, Uncle Alan," I said.

Despite the board taking steps forward, the success rang hollow. At least I'd helped a group of people who needed it, and I still believed that had been the right thing to do, though they no longer seemed to want me as anything more than a means to an end.

I hung up and went back to scrubbing at the grout.

It was strange, feeling so much but so little. I wiped a tear from my cheek.

This had not been how I envisioned celebrating our success.

Late the next morning, I roamed the halls searching for a captain to give me a task. By now, they'd grown adept at avoiding me. Finally, though, I found another job: helping Bryce set up another party in the yard.

"Time to celebrate!" he encouraged, handing me the cords to set up the speakers.

"I suppose it is," I replied, forcing a smile. My thoughts flooded with memories of the laughter and dancing—and Dorian's eyes on my hips—from the previous party. I didn't have high hopes for this upcoming one.

"Lunch is in the works. I've asked the kitchen staff to join us, too," he chattered.

We moved tables and chairs. Bryce unfurled a banner with "GOOD-BYE, 700 REDBILLS!" scrawled across it in multicolored marker. We hung it between two posts on either side of the food table.

After Bryce scurried inside to alert the soldiers and vampires of our final gathering, I stood staring at the banner. I read the number over and over in my head. We'd cleared more redbills in six weeks than I'd imagined I would in my entire career, and the number felt so abstract. Frustration sparked that I couldn't feel the joy this accomplishment deserved. But even that fizzled out.

It was a rare cloudy afternoon. It felt like the facility's demeanor even affected the weather.

After a shower, I headed back to my bunk to change. Soldiers milled around, most of them already packing their bags.

"You guys coming to the party?" I asked in Roxy and Louise's direction. Roxy simply walked away as if she hadn't heard, but Louise offered a small smile and nod.

I made my way back to the yard, finding only a few soldiers milling about the food and drinks. Zach and Gina sat in the corner with their elbows on their knees. I joined them.

We sat in silence, listening to Hank and Lily discuss plans for relocating to the vampires' next facility. Apparently, some of the soldiers would stay with the project, but most of my team would return to Chicago. Just a week ago, it would've stung to be excluded from the new project. Now I just felt relief to put all this behind me.

"Well, it's been fun," Zach said bitterly, staring at the bottom of his plastic cup. Gina rested her head on his shoulder.

Bryce burst through the door with papers in his hand.

"I have an announcement." He glanced around at the small group, then mumbled, "Er, I'll wait a few minutes for everyone to arrive." He hooked up a microphone to the speakers, looking around anxiously every now and then.

An entire hour passed before Bryce finally admitted defeat and stepped onto a chair, rustling his papers to get the attention of the five soldiers in the audience. He cleared his voice in the mic.

The door creaked open, and everyone's eyes darted to it. Two kitchen employees came out. They feebly waved and took seats.

"All right," Bryce grumbled into the microphone. "I have a few words about how I, uh… feel things went."

Zach rolled his eyes and muttered to me, "Looks like the old man's finally lost it." I smacked his shoulder.

"We relocated seven hundred redbills, which *well* exceeds our expectations for the trial period. Congratulations!" He forced excitement, clapping his hand against his papers, his voice getting marginally stronger. The seven of us clapped in support.

"I want to take this moment to commend all of you on your hard work, and especially your professionalism and… teamwork." I could see him struggling with the last word, but he got through it and continued. "Your efforts have been and will continue to be felt across the country. You've saved lives." He paused, staring at his paper in the dead silence.

My heart ached for him. It all felt so unfair. So stupid. I hoped the vampires were happy with themselves. This moment would have really felt like an accomplishment if we had all been celebrating together.

"I guess that's it. Good job," Bryce concluded, before stepping down from his chair and turning off the microphone. He pressed play on the music, and some obscure rap beat pumped out of the speakers. Even the music felt halfhearted.

I approached Bryce at the food table.

"Thanks for the speech, Captain," I said quietly. My chest tightened as I looked at him. I wanted so badly to magically transform all my bitterness into a better day for my captain. "We really do appreciate it. And the party." I felt a certain solidarity with his futile attempts to make things feel normal again.

"Aye," he said, cracking a carrot stick between his teeth. He looked lost. "Just thought I'd get us all together one last time."

"Yeah," I said. I patted his shoulder lightly with a sigh. The kitchen staff crept away, and I couldn't blame them. The crowd of ghosts at this party left little room for the rest of us.

CHAPTER THIRTY-SIX

I stood on the tarmac as evening fell, the cooling wind sweeping my hair around my face. The facility looked the same as it had the day we landed. The inside had changed a lot, though. So had I.

As the other soldiers boarded the aircraft, I patted my pockets for my phone and keys. I felt a lump in my breast pocket and sighed. Dorian's stone. I'd put it there intending to return it on my way out, but I'd turned back after I reached the vampire quarters. I'd had enough rejection for a lifetime. If Dorian wanted it back, he'd have to ask for it.

Zach walked up, backpack slung over his shoulder. "All set?"

"Yeah," I said quickly, ready to be done with this place. I followed him to the aircraft.

Zach hopped in and turned to offer a hand. But before I took it, I heard my name through the wind.

Laini ran up, waving. I cautiously set down my bag.

"I wanted to say goodbye," she called over the thrumming engine. "I'm sorry that things… didn't end on the best note, but I want to thank you. For everything you've done for us." Her violet eyes shimmered. "It won't be forgotten."

"Thank you, Laini," I replied, my words catching.

Laini had been kind to me, in her own quiet way, even when the others acted like I didn't exist. I was grateful for her to my core in that moment. Smiling sadly, she squeezed my hand and backed away.

I grabbed my bag and boarded, plopping down beside Zach. Through the window, I watched Laini stand at the facility entrance as the plane pulled away. The camaraderie we'd built, and then lost so suddenly, hadn't been entirely in my head. Knowing that made my chest ache, but it also helped.

We lifted from the pavement. Zach put his arm around my shoulders. Grayson stared out the window, his eyes lazily gazing at the scenery. Louise had borrowed Sarah's pillow and dedicated herself to a nap the moment she'd put her butt on the aircraft bench. A heavy sleepiness floated about all of us, even before we'd reached higher elevation.

We landed in Phoenix shortly, to drop off a few soldiers who had business there before the transport moved on to Chicago. As the plane touched down, something stirred in my mind. Uncle Alan had mentioned the board would gather in Phoenix today, expressing his regrets that we would miss each other.

I turned to Zach, the spark of an idea in my head.

"I'm going to hop off," I said. "Uncle Alan is here, so I can fly back to Chicago with him to discuss details about the vampires' long-term feeding plans. The team doesn't need me on the plane with them." I stood and picked up my bag.

Zach and Gina exchanged a worried look.

"What they do with the vampires isn't your responsibility anymore, Lyra," my brother said, his tone protective.

He gestured for me to sit down, but I hesitated. Zach might be right, but I wasn't ready to slide back into my normal life again. Not yet.

"I know. But I can still offer some help. So I'm going to," I replied.

I headed for the aircraft's door. Rejected or not, I wasn't a quitter. I still cared about the vampires' wellbeing, and my uncle might be willing to listen and take more of my ideas to the board.

Casting a glance back as I reached the exit, I saw irritation and then guilt flash across my brother's face. He knew I wouldn't budge. After a brief exchange, Zach and Gina grabbed their things and followed. I didn't try to stop them. After all, Zach had promised our parents that he'd keep an eye on me, and it would be nice to have company.

We passed Bryce and a pilot on the tarmac discussing the wings on a new aircraft model parked there. I nodded professionally to him, and he squinted back, seeming confused that I was off the plane, but continued his conversation.

Zach and Gina followed me for a few more steps, having a quiet conversation, then Gina called out behind me, "You go ahead and talk to your uncle, Lyra! We'll stick around to fly back with you, but we're going to see what Bryce is learning about these new wings."

I waved my assent and continued on my way. I knew that I needed to go home and exercise off the previous six weeks, but getting closure felt necessary. I wanted to make sure the vampires would be all right. And right now, the thought of sitting at home with nothing to do made me want to crawl out of my skin.

I entered the Phoenix headquarters and made my way to the front desk.

"Alan Sloane will be in a meeting for another two hours," the receptionist informed me when I inquired.

I hadn't planned for that, but of course my uncle would be busy. I could wait. I checked the wall clock, tapping my foot restlessly; the plane with the rest of the soldiers had likely already taken off for its next stop.

I decided to take a walk.

After studying the building map, I went to the stairwell and ascended a few floors. Truly, it didn't matter where I went or what I saw. My legs just needed to move.

Once my muscles started to protest the continuous stair climb, I exited a stairwell door at random. On the other side, a guard sat behind a desk. Before I could apologize and back away, he held up a hand.

"Name?"

"First Lieutenant Lyra Sloane," I replied.

"Here with Director Sloane?" he asked blandly. Someone didn't want to be at work that day.

"Yes," I replied. It'd be true once my uncle left his meeting, and I didn't see the harm in wandering about before then. I wasn't going to be poking through people's desk drawers, just walking the hallways. It wasn't like I didn't work for the Bureau.

The guard nodded and let me pass.

Motion sensor lights lit the dim hallways as I quietly walked the marble floor. Inscriptions on the doors designated different conference rooms. Silence thickened the air, interrupted by a few drifting murmurs from some of the meeting rooms. The quiet made my restlessness deafening.

I avoided the rooms that seemed occupied. The voices that carried were mostly muffled by the walls, so I figured I was far enough away to forego any accusations of eavesdropping.

I walked each hallway on the floor twice before I decided to find somewhere to sit and write my questions for my uncle. I approached a dark room with a cracked door and peeked inside to see if anyone occupied it. Lights flickered to life at my presence, revealing a long mahogany table covered in organized papers. Plenty of empty chairs clustered around it. It reminded me a little of the room I'd given testimony in, back when this all began. It would do.

Pulling out a chair, I dug through my bag for my notebook and pen. I set the spiral pad on the table, moving a few papers to the side to make room. My eye caught the word "vampire" on the top page. Without really thinking, I looked closer.

The Bureau had purchased a half-developed gated community in a remote area, with plans to finish the homes and retrofit them for vampires. Each organized row of papers displayed structural blueprints for the new vampire lodgings, their rooms a variety of shapes and sizes. The plans included outdoor spaces, common areas. One building even had a playroom for children. A full smile flashed across my face for the first time in ages. Carwin and Detra wouldn't have to play question games to amuse themselves anymore. At least they'd be more comfortable, despite being stuck on Earth.

I slowly scanned each building on the blueprints, visualizing what they would look like, a warm feeling growing in my belly at the thought of the vampires having a permanent home. Each building had its own name and completion date at the top of its blueprint. I nodded, impressed by the Bureau's organization and preparedness.

Then I reread the nearest scribbled mention. "Completion date: 6-11." I blinked and looked closer. That had been two weeks ago. Obviously a mistake.

I moved along the table and saw another date. "Completion date: 5-15." We'd just arrived at the trial facility that week. Why would the Bureau have put money into these lodgings if the trial period had only just started? They'd only made their decision about giving the vampires asylum in the last few days—at least, that was when I'd heard about it. Beside the "completed" layouts were detailed construction outlines and billings for expedited services and overtime. They had multiple crews working through the night. The Bureau spared no expense, apparently.

I grabbed one completed residence blueprint and compared it to several others, my eyes picking out more incongruous details. Each one included what I'd thought to be an outdoor storage space, with illustrations of detailed pipe systems in each shed, leading into the apartments. Sheds didn't usually contain AC or heat. Why would they need to connect to the housing?

I picked up a different paper from the tabletop, this one looking like a written report. My breath stopped. My heartbeat heightened in my ears. The report was titled "Efficacy of Hydrogen Cyanide Compared to Carbon Dioxide and Carbon Monoxide."

I flipped through the other completed lodgings and found them all to contain that same shack in the yard connected to the lodging via pipes.

I stepped back from the table, still unable to breathe. My hands felt like they'd touched something poisonous. Did this prove the horrible thing my thoughts had immediately leapt to? Fear gripped my chest—or was it panic? In the rush of disbelief, I couldn't tell.

No, there had to be an explanation. I shook my head, placing my tingling fingers against my lips.

Heightened murmurs caught my attention, drifting in from the room's air vent. They came from another meeting room. Creeping closer to the vent, I held my breath and listened.

"That requires some discussion," a low masculine voice said, muffled enough to be vague... yet familiar.

"A realistic timeline is necessary, Director Sloane," a male voice replied tersely.

My heart beat faster. I was next to Uncle Alan's meeting.

I pulled a chair over to the wall and climbed it, pressing my ear against the air vent. The voices rewarded my effort, becoming more distinct. If I got caught like this there would definitely be questions, but right now I didn't care.

"That's why it's imperative to make them comfortable as quickly as possible," Uncle Alan replied, his voice sounding the way it always did: official, confident, and smoothly persuasive. "The sooner they feel secure, the sooner they'll call the others to join them in the other residences."

"Would either of you like to propose a final date?" a woman's voice asked with a trace of impatience.

"I say two months. No longer. We don't want to risk the population changing its mind over time and bleeding thin," the other man remarked.

"Ah, but that might be hasty. If we give it longer, say four months, we're more likely to get the entire population into the lodgings, or at least closer to it. We could take care of it all at once," my uncle said. I detected something unusual in his voice this time. It was completely cold. Devoid of even the slightest hint of emotion. So much so that if I hadn't known it was him speaking, I'd have barely recognized it.

"Vote?" someone asked. "All in favor of four months say aye."

A choir of "ayes" rang through the vent.

"All opposed?"

Only one man said, almost too faintly for me to catch through the vent, "nay."

"Four months. Final day marked in the meeting notes as October 22nd," a woman said banally.

"I just received an update," my uncle's voice said. "The transportation team will move the trial group to the new lodging in a little over an hour. I'll phone security and make sure they lock the utility rooms where the extermination gas is kept before the vampires arrive. No need to raise unnecessary suspicions."

My vision went white.

No. This didn't make sense.

My uncle wouldn't be part of this. He couldn't. Maybe it hadn't actually been Uncle Alan's voice. It could be someone else.

But whoever it was, he'd said the word himself. *Extermination.* There was no mistake there. That panic started rising in my chest again. I suddenly felt so unsafe, like the world was actually a completely different place than I'd ever imagined. A nightmare.

My knees shook as I quietly lowered myself from the chair and slid it back under the table. My mind focused on action, tuning everything else out. The shock and panic I'd felt earlier numbed down into a list of things to do. If I told anyone on my team about this plan, they'd look at me like I was crazy. I'd need proof.

I put the blueprints I'd been scanning back exactly as I'd found them —except for one, which I folded and shoved into my pocket along with the report as I packed up my notebook and slipped out the door. I was never one to steal, ever, but this was beyond necessary. Many lives could be saved by that one paper, even though its original purpose was the exact opposite. My boots moved silently over the marble, but my thoughts raced ahead. I had to warn the vampires.

I rounded the corner that led to the stairwell. A new guard sat at the desk, looking more alert than the last. When he saw me, he stood.

"I don't recognize you. What are you doing on this floor?" He stepped up to me. His eyes narrowed, and a bolt of fear struck me, even though he probably didn't know I'd taken the paper—or know that the paper existed at all.

"I'm here with Director Sloane," I answered, holding my tone as even as possible. "He's my uncle." I reminded myself on a loop to breathe, be calm. The thought of being calm felt insane, but I had to get out of this building as efficiently as possible.

"I see. Please wait here a moment, miss, while I call to verify," he said, having pumped some politeness into his tone. The guard pulled out his walkie-talkie and took a few steps away from me down the corridor, pacing back and forth as he called whoever he needed to call.

As he spoke into the radio, received an answer, and spoke again, I felt time trickling away. I had maybe an hour to somehow reach the vampires and warn them before they were taken to the new facility. If this guard actually managed to get ahold of Uncle Alan, then I could still pretend I knew nothing... but my window of opportunity would be gone. Sweat tickled my spine as I hesitated—but only for a moment. There was no time for me to listen to the fear in my chest.

The next moment, when the guard's back turned as he paced, I tore past him, opened the stairwell door and pounded down toward the ground floor.

"Hey!" the guard yelled at me. Then I heard him reporting a breach and giving my description over his walkie. I channeled that lingering fear into fuel for my flexing muscles.

Reaching the ground floor, I rushed through the lobby, carefully zigzagging between two small groups of high-ranking soldiers who had probably just recessed a meeting. One uniformed man's sentence trailed off as I rushed past him, his wide, confused eyes following me. I prayed no one immediately recognized me, and I made a point to avoid direct eye contact. I had to get out of there.

I finally got back to the tarmac. Bryce, Gina, and Zach stood beside the new plane, still jawing with the pilot.

"Captain!"

Bryce turned and glowered at me. "Why are you yelling at a superi—"

"We have to go." I rushed up, trying to speak through my panting. "Now. The vampires aren't safe at the facility. We have to go back and warn them, immediately!"

"Lieutenant," Bryce started to chide, but he trailed off, studying my face, his eyes narrowing at what he saw. Gina and Zach stared openly.

"What the hell are you talking about?" my brother asked.

"Please, Captain. We have less than an hour," I said. "I swear on my career. They plan to murder the vampires. All of them."

Bryce shook his head, as though waiting for the punchline of the practical joke I was playing. "Sloane, that's crazy talk. I'm sure it's not all that bad. Where is all of this coming from?"

Without a word, I pulled the blueprint and report out of my pocket and shoved it toward Bryce's face. He squinted at the paper, his eyes bouncing back and forth. And then I saw his eyebrows climb his forehead, utter disbelief washing over his face, horror in his eyes.

A moment of icy silence passed. Then he looked over his shoulder at the jet he'd just been admiring, and back to the three of us. A wild look sparked in his eyes. "Get on the plane," he growled.

Gina and Zach still looked bewildered, but I yanked them after me as Bryce and I leapt into the little jet. Bryce sat in the pilot's chair, and the rest of us took the back. When I'd woken up earlier that day, I never would've imagined this turn of events—or seeing Bryce casually fly a military jet, for that matter.

"Please hurry!" I urged, nerves shaking my voice.

I gripped the armrests. We pulled away from headquarters, and the tiny craft sped down the airstrip. It still didn't hold a candle to a redbill flight, but I could tell this model was much faster than our typical transport. Our heads rattled against the backs of our seats.

I craned my neck to look back at the headquarters. Guards had flooded the empty tarmac behind us. The entire Bureau would know what had happened in no time.

Sitting next to me on the small plane, Gina whistled softly. "That's... a lot of guards," she said, her voice concerned. "Lyra, what did you do in there?"

The plane took off with a gut-dropping lurch, and Zach leaned forward from Gina's other side so he could see me, clearly on the edge between confusion and anger.

"No kidding," my brother said. "Lyra, you better have a really good reason for all of this, because from what I'm seeing, we're all about to lose our jobs."

I didn't bother to preface it. "I saw these blueprints in an empty meeting room." I handed the paper I still gripped in my fist to Gina, and Zach peered at it over her hands. "Plans for the new vampire lodgings. Each building is essentially a gas chamber. The shacks in the yards house gas, and these connecting pipes will pump gas into the lodgings while the vampires are in them. Here's the report on the kind of gas they intend to use for the executions." I gave it to Zach.

"I overheard the board's meeting in the other room when I saw the blueprints. They set an extermination date. They're going to kill every single vampire they can."

Bryce cursed from the cockpit, and I felt more force as the plane accelerated faster.

Gina's hand covered her mouth.

Zach looked at the paper, then me, then the paper again. For once, my brother was completely dumbfounded to silence. He swallowed hard and slowly extended the blueprint back to me. I refolded it and shoved it deep into my pants pocket, so it wouldn't slip out.

Even though panic still riled my brain, logic resounded. I realized what could happen to Zach, Gina, and Bryce in this situation. And what would happen to me.

"You guys don't have to warn the vampires with me, or even get off the plane when we get back to the facility." My voice carried a pain that emanated from deep in my core. The Bureau was my life, and I'd just thrown it away. I didn't have time to think about that now. "But I have to tell them. I have to try and save them. I don't want any of you to suffer for my decisions."

Zach looked at me so deeply I thought, in the panic and terror gripping me, I might even sprout tears, too. He drew in a breath and set his hand on top of mine.

"You're stuck with me," he said, earnest, but almost resigned, like he knew what he had to do and it sucked. My heart leapt. *Thank God.*

"I won't stand for something like this," Gina said angrily, pointing at the blueprint in my pocket. "This isn't my Bureau. Those vampires are people. Good people. It's my duty to protect them, not fall in line with something like this." Her eyes glistened, her voice sad like Zach's—but she sounded determined. I used my free hand to grip hers. That was my girl.

Even though I was absolutely horrified and knew my life was about to splinter into a million pieces, I was grateful for my brother and closest friend. I was lucky to have them.

"How long is this flight?" I yelled to Bryce.

"Thirty minutes or so, I'm thinking," he called back. "Longer if you distract the pilot."

I squeezed my eyes shut and pushed my head back against the seat. *We're going to make it. We'll make it in time.*

As our jet descended on the facility, I craned my neck to look out the window. Two large Bureau aircraft sat on the tarmac. Were we too late?

"They're already here," I yelled.

The plane touched down and braked to a stop. I tossed off my seat-belt and leapt to the pavement a moment later.

Zach, Gina, and Bryce disembarked behind me, their faces strained, and we gathered on the concrete in the hot night air.

"They're bringing them out," Zach said gravely, looking at the main entrance.

I followed his gaze. Guards and soldiers that I didn't recognize walked in front of the vampires, escorting them from the facility toward the large aircraft. The vampires stared at their feet as they walked, as if they somehow knew they were actually prisoners.

Bryce shot us a look. "Time for another executive order," he said under his breath.

He marched over to the thirteen approaching guards, his hands raised in the air to command their attention. We followed, the three of us instinctively gathering in formation behind him as though we were on a mission. And, I realized, the stakes were so high, we might as well have been.

"Captain Bryce, facility captain, here," Bryce blustered in his most official voice. "We need you to escort this group inside for an assessment before they're relocated."

That man was good on his toes.

"We have orders from the director and a schedule to keep, Captain," an unfamiliar soldier replied, looking confused as he stepped up to Bryce. He knew we were not supposed to be here.

"There's been a change in the schedule, for confidential reasons. Please escort them inside, and I'll explain in my office," Bryce told him cheerfully, and I watched the two of them face off, sizing each other up.

I glanced down at the waists of my bare-bones team. Everyone had their handguns. *Thank God.*

The other soldiers closed their fingers on the triggers of automatic rifles. One spoke over his comm. About ten more unknown soldiers filed out of the facility doorway, making their number twenty-three. They had more of a force here than I'd expected. That didn't bode well at all.

I glanced at the vampires. At the edge of the crowd, Thoth and

Rhome breathed heavily, clenching their jaws, eyeing the soldiers surrounding them with irritation. The children seemed restless, their parents hard-pressed to keep them under control. Kane's glare reminded me of the one he'd worn when I first met him in the cavern. His dislike of humans was more justified in this moment than ever before, whether he realized it or not.

"I won't ask again," Bryce growled at the other captain, squaring his broad shoulders. He was pulling out his scare tactics. I was grateful; if they scared this team as much as they did mine, maybe they'd work now. "Will you please—"

"Your orders are not sanctioned by the board. Step aside and leave this facility," the first soldier ordered. "Or we *will* treat you as hostiles."

Dorian's eyes caught mine. His expression was darkly rigid—just like in the alleyway in Vegas before his fangs sprang out. I inclined my head toward him, trying to communicate everything I could in one plaintive look: my fear for them, that we were here to help, that all his instincts were correct.

Please trust me. Even if it's just one more time.

Bryce clicked his tongue against his teeth. "Well, I was worried about that," he mumbled to himself, then turned to the vampires. "Friends, accompany us inside, would you?" He jerked his head toward our jet.

The vampires on the tarmac no longer moved toward the Bureau transports. Instead, they stood completely still, their eyes flickering between my group and the soldiers who directed them forward, the tension in their decision unmistakable.

"Final warning, sir!" the lead soldier yelled.

The unfamiliar soldiers cocked their weapons, and I got to experience the new, uncomfortable sensation of Bureau gun barrels pointing at me. This was really happening.

Bryce turned toward the lead soldier, his voice hard. "It's *Captain*."

And then Kane's jaw snapped open and he sank his fangs into the neck of the soldier standing beside him.

Screams reverberated over the tarmac, and Gina, Zach, and I drew our weapons as the vampires exploded into action. One moment they were still, and the next a flurry of teeth and horror scattered about the pavement.

Gunshots rang out, but the soldiers couldn't move faster than the vampires. Vampires washed over them like a tsunami—fangs flashed and soldiers toppled, their guns flying from their hands. Bryce leapt into the fray, cracking a soldier's cheek with the butt of his gun. Zach fired a shot into a foreign soldier's leg as he ran to accost Bryce.

My brother had just shot a soldier. A vice of dread closed around my chest, but I couldn't stop moving.

A soldier stormed me, fumbling to get his weapon aimed. I put a bullet in his foot, and he toppled to the ground with an angry cry, dropping his weapon to clutch his boot. *And now I've shot one.*

More screams bounced off the facility walls. Rhome and Kreya left two soldiers drained on the ground and leapt onto others, their growls mixing with the gunshots, their faces suffused with rage. Carwin and Detra sat on an unfamiliar soldier, their teeth deep in either side of his neck.

More soldiers swarmed, and Gina deflected a fist that nearly caught the side of my head. She twisted the arm, breaking the elbow, and kicked its owner to the ground. There were still more soldiers than we could handle—because the vampires were slowing down to suck them dry. I lashed out again and again, my pent-up anger flowing through me like fire.

"Keep fighting!" I yelled to the vampires, pounding a soldier with my fist. "We have to escape!"

I spotted Dorian crouched over a limp body, drinking deeply as blood flooded from the soldier's neck. Couldn't he move faster? But from the desperate way he gulped, threw his head back, and went back to drinking with blood streaming down his chin, I could see that he'd gone to another, darker place, controlled by his instincts. Shadows writhed in his eyes. I'd seen this demon in him before.

Dorian was so engulfed in his feeding that he took no notice of a soldier rushing up behind him with a gun pointed at his back. A yelp caught in my throat, and before I could think, I shot the soldier in both thighs. The man toppled back, his face contorting in painful screams, his gun clattering on the pavement as he fell.

The fight had taken over me. There were no feelings, just thoughts. Prioritized, logical, step-by-step thoughts. Getting Dorian on his feet was next on my list.

I ran over and pulled his arm. He jerked away from the man's neck, snapped his fangs at me, and yanked his arm free of my grasp. I'd dealt with this side of Dorian before, and I wasn't afraid of him.

Our eyes bored into each other. Weeks of frustration boiled in my guts and pushed at my throat. I'd put my neck on the line for him repeatedly, thrown away my career, stolen a *plane* to be at his side. I'd had enough.

"Don't push me away!" I roared. "I'm trying to help you!"

Dorian startled, then his face softened in recognition, almost like he was waking up, the muscles going so lax his jaw lowered.

Then his eyes flickered, and a snarl raged from him, spit flying from his mouth.

He lunged at me, and I instinctively jerked to the side, furious that he'd decided I was also an enemy. But Dorian flew past me and sank his teeth into a soldier preparing to unload a bullet into me from behind.

I stood in shock, watching the man's blood spill over his uniform and the concrete. Dorian rose to his feet, wiped his face, and met my eyes. We took one moment to hold each other's gaze. *Thank you.*

He nodded as if he'd heard me.

There was no more time for communication. Three soldiers rushed us, and we dodged the crosshairs of their guns. I clocked one in the jaw with the butt of my weapon, and then Dorian rushed in, grabbed his head, and snapped his neck. I heard the sickening crack.

Another soldier lunged at me from the side, and I put my boot in his groin before Dorian tore his neck open. Screams continued ringing out all around us, and as I scanned, I realized there were still more soldiers than we could handle if the vampires kept slowing down to feed. Another dozen had spilled out of the facility. A kind of fear I'd never felt before built in me.

"Vampires, keep *fighting*!" I cried again, before putting a bullet in the back of a soldier's leg.

I caught sight of soldiers restraining Sike. They signaled to one of their cohorts to aim at the writhing vampire.

Without a thought, I wheeled toward them, a spike of fear turning into protective rage. They couldn't do this to him. But I didn't know if I would make it in time to stop them. He was thrashing so much, I feared I'd hit him if I fired at this distance.

As I raced toward Sike, I felt wind and heard the pounding of wings above me.

The redbills screamed, clacking their beaks and diving to the tarmac to defend their vampires. They continued the war call as they grabbed soldiers with their talons, slamming them against the concrete. More redbills landed, lashing out and closing their serrated beaks around the unfamiliar soldiers. With horrifying, gurgling growls, they shook them violently, one taking off a soldier's arm with a single snap.

I busted the chin of an attacking soldier and looked around. The vampires leapt onto the last of the enemy soldiers. Bryce pivoted, searching for any still-conscious enemies. Zach clutched his thigh, Gina pulling his other arm over her shoulder. My heart stopped in my chest. I hadn't seen him get hurt.

The soldiers would have backup in no time. We had to get out.

Dorian's eyes scanned the perimeter, his thoughts clearly parallel to my own.

"Fly!" he roared.

The vampires rushed to their birds, picking up my team without a second thought. Rhome lifted Zach onto a bill. Harlowe grabbed the three children whose names I didn't know and thrust them up onto her redbill. I rushed to Dorian's animal and, without missing a beat, he took my hand and pulled me up behind him. Fear still pounded through my veins, but feeling his hand in mine sent those old tingles up my spine. I threw my arms around his middle and held on, relieved to be flying on one of these animals—for the first time ever.

Kreya wrapped her arms around her children atop their redbill and cried out to her bird. Around us, the vampires' birds worked their wings, jumping into the air.

We rose into the dark sky, forming a V-shaped flock. The lights of the facility shrank to tiny blinking dots. They suddenly reminded me of the glowing amber specks on the mountainsides of the Immortal Plane. My chest clenched. The vampires were fleeing for their lives from our facility, which had turned on them just as their old home had.

Dorian growled, and his bird flew even faster, the speed shaking my insides, the wind buffeting my face. Through my blurring vision, I saw Rhome holding Zach steady on his bird. Nearby, Bryce clung to the back of Laini. Gina held Bravi for dear life, trying to shield her face behind the vampire's small but muscular frame.

My team was accounted for, as were all the vampires. No bird lacked a passenger. We cut into clouds, and I closed my eyes, enveloped by the chill, swirling fog.

CHAPTER THIRTY-SEVEN

Our birds carried us for miles through the dark. I had no way of telling our location after we entered the clouds. The birds chirped to each other through the wind.

I listened to my heart racing in my ears until we slowed and descended. If the birds were riled from the attack, I couldn't tell. They gracefully fluttered to the ground, landing within seconds of each other. Desert crickets thrummed around us in the cool night air.

I still felt shell-shocked from the fight on the tarmac. Numbness layered on top of anger, fear, and worry in my mind. And now a sense of uneasiness settled in, as I had no idea what our next steps would be.

I had no idea where we were. The night gave scant light. I could pick out some pale rocks in the dark. Sand shifted beneath us.

Dorian dismounted. I took his hand and slid down, holding it just a bit longer than necessary—which he didn't protest. Part of me wanted to drop it and shout at him for ignoring me for so long; a bigger part wanted to ask if this meant he would speak to me again. But we had more pressing concerns. For now, just the pressure of his fingers for a moment longer than necessary, a tiny sign of solidarity, helped me keep myself together.

The others dropped from their birds, their labored breathing audible in the dark. Gina approached Rhome, and together they eased Zach off the bird. He sat shakily in the sand. I rushed to his side, my heart clenching at the sight of his limping. I'd rather be injured myself than watch his pain.

Bryce came up, after thanking Laini for his ride, and tore some fabric from his undershirt to bandage Zach's leg. I crouched next to my brother, silently assuring myself that he would be okay. He winced in pain as I set my hand gently on his back but shot me a watery smile to show he would be fine. My training told me that because the bullet had scored the fatty tissue of his outer thigh, he'd be okay. We just had to keep it wrapped and clean. Walking wouldn't be fun for a while, though.

The moon crept from behind the clouds, painting the sand white.

For a few moments, all of us sat in shaken quiet, the vampires in a circle and we humans in our tiny cluster nearby. I guessed that everybody else was also trying to wrap their heads around what had just happened. I kept shooting anxious glances at the vampires standing in the moonlight, unable to formulate an apology that would make up for what my species had done. Or tried to do.

"We have everyone," Dorian said on a hoarse exhale, his eyes scanning the dark. The vampires all clustered together, their birds huddled nearby in protection.

"And we're lucky to!" Kane said harshly, his anger passing through the group as a wave of mutters followed. "So, Dorian," he continued, his voice dark and mocking, "I'm assuming that you sensed what I did in those soldiers back on the tarmac. I guess I should be grateful that those four showed up," he tossed a hand in my direction, "to confirm what I suspected. Was this how you envisioned your grand, harmonious plan? We all join hands, work together to make humans happy, and then get murdered as the finale?"

Dorian looked at Kane. His sleeves dripped from our trip through the clouds; his face was worn and fallen, sadness hanging under his eyes.

"I had no way of knowing what the Bureau was planning," he said. The defeat in his voice was palpable enough to make me wince. "How could I? They outsmarted me, Kane. I'm not proud."

"You should've known not to trust humans from the beginning!" Halla hissed. "We may as well have handed ourselves to the firing squad the moment we got to the facility."

Thoth nodded beside Halla. "She's right. We went against our better judgment," he said lowly, shaking his head.

Dorian raised a weary hand to his hair, looking from group member to group member as though trying to figure out how to proceed.

"I can't believe I took my children there. I feel so *stupid*," Kreya said, a sob caught in her throat. "We starved ourselves for weeks, suffered, lived in cells. We should've trusted our guts. We knew better." In her arms, Detra whimpered.

"Should've left the minute that girl fell ill," Halla snapped, then corrected herself. "Never should've been there in the first place."

Her words fired up the anger still lingering in my gut. I'd swallowed it out of fear for the vampires' safety, but it hadn't been extinguished. So Dorian had been telling the truth, or the vampires' version of it, when he'd told me that they'd iced us out because of my coma. Did they all believe this "sign" crap? Halla seemed to. Around the group, I saw Rayne and Harlowe nodding, but Sike and Bravi had their arms folded, and Sike particularly looked as though he wanted to disagree.

Was the pain I'd been going through really because of the feelings Dorian had for me? The thought shot sparks of anger through my mind, but other kinds of sparks kindled too. I pushed them down, irritated at myself. This argument wasn't about that. It was bigger.

Trying to stay out of the vampires' argument, even if it pained me, I gazed around at the rock formations as the vampires argued. By now, my eyes had adjusted, and I could make out a familiar stone wall with a jagged crack down the middle in the moonlight. Canyonlands.

"We have to leave," Kane said. "There's surveillance everywhere. These bastards have probably already ratted out our location to them."

Kane threw a hand in our direction. As irritated as I was with Dorian, Kane was getting dangerously close to nabbing first place.

"Leave them out of this," Sike interjected, his voice less angry but no less firm. "You're not even making sense, Kane. Why on earth would they have risked their lives for us back there just to turn on us now?"

"Lyra has never done anything but help us," Dorian added sincerely, heaviness in his voice. "Same goes for the others."

His defense of us pained me even as it warmed me. Was he going to support me now as if he'd never tried to cut me out of his life? I reminded myself, again, that this wasn't about that.

I had to speak up. "We truly didn't know what the Bureau had planned, Kane," I said, rising to my feet and moving forward so they could hear me better. "They were planning to harm you after relocating you. I found out about an hour before the soldiers came to take you away. We got there to warn you as quickly—"

"Don't listen to her!" Kreya said, her voice cracking apart from her fury. "This whole thing happened because of her."

Kreya's words cut me like a knife. A flood of guilt and anger battled in my chest, and I placed a balled fist against my lips, unable to respond.

"She was only trying to help, Kreya." Rhome grabbed her shoulder, anxiety straining his voice. "Why would she have attacked other soldiers to help us escape if she were lying?"

"You're still believing humans?" At that moment, Kreya lost it. Her previous anger was nothing compared to her snarl now. "Rhome, listen to yourself. Have you lost your mind? Our children were nearly killed. You sensed what those soldiers knew. They planned to murder us."

"Yes, and I've never sensed any deception in Lyra or her friends. Neither have you, Kreya," Rhome replied evenly. "We're safe here for now. We need to work together to figure out a plan."

"Just because these four aren't trying to kill us right now doesn't mean we should risk staying around humans. Not after this. They're backstabbing murderers. I will not stand around and let us get that close to death ever again!" Kreya shouted, whirling on her partner, her face warped by anger into a feral grimace. Her children clung to her legs. Detra started sobbing. "I can't do that to our boy and girl."

Kane growled in his throat. "The plan is, we're going back to the other plane. Now."

"No," Dorian said, but without strength. Hope had dwindled from his posture. "It's more dangerous. A few humans trying to kill us is nothing compared to what we'd face there."

"That excuse won't work anymore, Dorian," Kane snapped. "We tried your way. It's time to stop playing games and do what we should've before. We were never supposed to come here." He clicked his tongue and helped his mother onto their bird.

I opened my mouth to speak, but stopped, reminding myself that nothing I could say anymore would convince them my species was trustworthy. Because we weren't.

I couldn't blame them for being angry with humans. But I hadn't forgiven Dorian for what they'd all done to me, to Bryce, to our loyal human team, either. The guilt, hurt, and anger swirled through me, warring, as I tried to separate everything.

"Kane," Dorian started, his voice still broken but resolute. "I know I let you down. I let you all down." He paused, gazing around at the other vampires, trying to meet their eyes. "I won't try to stop you from leaving. But I still think it's safer here. I'm not going back, but I understand if you all do. It's your choice." His statement was met with combinations of pained, confused, and furious stares.

Kane scoffed at Dorian and turned his back on him. "Everyone who wants a chance to live, get on your birds. We're not dying in this wasteland," he announced harshly. "May as well die at home."

Kreya took her children's hands and led them to their bird. They looked around at the surrounding adults frantically, confusion warping their mouths. Detra pointed back at her father, and a whimper rose in her throat.

"Kreya, wait," Rhome called, following her. "We have to think this through!"

She snarled at him and lifted her children onto the redbill. "Come or stay. It's up to you. But *I'm* protecting our children." Carwin froze on the redbill's back, white-faced, but Detra howled and struggled in her mother's arms.

Rhome winced, sucking in a breath, struggling to find words. He glanced at Dorian, then back to Kreya.

"We can't go back there, Kreya. Not after what happened. Some humans may be evil, but there's far more evil in the Immortal Plane," Rhome said firmly, over Detra's sobs. His hands trembled as he raised his palm pleadingly to his partner. "It's not safe for our children there. We've started something here. Let's finish it, make a safe place here for our children with the humans that we *can* trust. That's better than walking into certain death back home."

Kreya acted like she hadn't heard him. She gripped the redbill's feathers, preparing to leap onto it. Detra leaned toward her father, tears flowing, arms outstretched. Carwin grabbed her to prevent her from falling forward. He'd started crying too, silently.

"Kreya, please," Laini cried out, her voice cracking. She rushed to Kreya's side, gripping her arm. "Please stay, just for tonight. We can talk about it in the morning. Don't separate your family."

"I'm *saving* my family," Kreya hissed, yanking her arm from Laini's hold. She mounted the bird behind her children. Laini choked on a sob. Rhome tried to mount as well, but at a growl from Kreya, the bill hopped backward.

"You know what?" she said viciously, eyes on Rhome. "If you love humans more than your own family, you can stay here. Don't follow me. You'll just try to convince me to come back."

"No," Rhome said, devastated. He reached for Kreya, but she hissed at him. Her redbill leapt into the sky, Detra's howl trailing away as it faded into the darkness.

Dorian stood silently in the dark, watching the group splinter. Thoth passed Kane and Halla, nodding to them sullenly, and then mounted his redbill. Harlowe briefly set a hand on Dorian's shoulder on her way to her bird. Rayne had remounted in the middle of the argument, her mind already set.

Rhome remained statuesque, the life drained from his form, staring helplessly at the stars. With vampire hearing, it was possible that he could still hear his daughter, even if I couldn't. Bravi and Sike approached Dorian, setting their hands on his shoulders. The three gazed at each other, their faces fallen.

Tears bit at my eyes. Everything was ruined. We'd all been betrayed. Everything we'd hoped for was a lie. I held my head in my hands, unable to handle putting all of these pieces together. The bitterness from the past weeks, my frustration with the vampires... the fear I'd flown through to get here on time, the horror at what the Bureau had done. It was too much. My ears rang. The guilt weighed so heavy on my chest I felt faint.

Bryce watched with pained eyes. The silence thickened the air, broken only by small gurgles from the redbills.

"Let's go," Kane shouted. The birds carried the vampires into the air. I watched them rise, sand whipping my face in the wind.

The only vampires that remained—Dorian, Bravi, Sike, Laini, and Rhome—watched their families and friends disappear into the night. Rhome's shoulders jerked, as though he'd been shot, and he fell to his knees, gasping for air. Laini dropped down beside him, wrapping him in her arms.

I collapsed back to the sand beside Zach.

Dorian groaned softly, tugging at his hair. His expression flowed from fallen to distraught to livid and then back again. His hopes, his clan, had dissolved before his eyes in a matter of hours. I watched him pace the sand.

"What do we do?" Sike asked. "They're going away, and we're just going to sit around waiting for the humans to find us?"

"I don't know yet," Dorian murmured. His grief and frustration gripped his voice, and as he talked to Sike, he was clearly trying to convince himself. "But we're going to find a way. We still have to tell the group we left in hiding. Some of them will support us. Somehow, we *have* to fix this."

Dorian, always a decisive leader, looked as lost as I'd ever seen him, and my heart ached for him.

But he was right. It *couldn't* be over yet. Without the vampires to hunt it, darkness thickened and roiled in the Mortal and Immortal Planes, growing powerful. The words Dorian had spoken to me in his cave, the day he kidnapped me, came rushing back.

"Without us, evil will continue to grow."

It had apparently already seeped into the Bureau, into the hearts of its leaders... *My uncle.* I could still hardly process what I'd witnessed. That it was *his* voice I'd heard talking in that meeting room.

And it made me wonder, my heart gripped in a vise of fear, how many other people in our world with positions of power and influence had been corrupted. How many other cops, captains, senators, people whom we trusted to lead and keep us safe.

And how much farther would the darkness spread, without the vampires to beat it back?

"In the end, it will consume everything. Everyone."

A shiver ran through me as I clenched my fists, my chest rising in short, ragged breaths. *No.* We might have lost this battle, but we couldn't lose this war.

"Let us know if there's anything we can do to help," I managed, my eyes fixed on Dorian. This problem was so much bigger than what had gone on between us. I could accept that.

Or I thought I could, until Dorian looked sharply over at me, startled from his grief. A flood of emotions warped his face too quickly for me to figure them out, before he schooled it to an all-too-familiar blankness. His face wasn't quite the mask it had been for our last weeks at the facility, but it was close enough.

"This isn't your fight, Lyra," he replied, staring at me with dead eyes. "You've helped us, but do you really think you have some kind of say in this?"

I couldn't let him speak another sentence. At that look, the horrible collection of emotions I'd been feeling combusted into flames. Adrenaline flooded my limbs.

I was so over his arrogance. Like he could just use me and set me aside at whim. *My* life was ruined now, too, as he'd apparently forgotten. He thought he could defend me in front of his group and reject me to my face. And now I was supposed to feel bad for him because people he trusted had turned their backs on him? That felt a little too familiar to me.

"Yes, I do!" I said, bolting to my feet. "I've been with you on this from the beginning! Do you have any idea what I've done for you? If we're going to stand even the smallest chance of 'fixing this,' we need to work together. If you had kept your head instead of believing in 'omens' or whatever the hell—"

"I already explained—"

"You explained nothing. We don't even have proof that it's true! What you did was very effectively alienate our teams. We could've worked together once we figured out the Bureau's plan. You keep saying you can read our intentions, so you *know* my team would've supported you. But no. This divide wasn't the real one. The split happened ages ago."

It came as a relief for my words to fly from my mouth like this, my internal truth finally resounding outside my own mind. The relief did not temper my rage, though.

Dorian growled, swiftly crossing the sand to get in my face. "We did what we had to do to protect both of our species," he hissed at me. "But clearly you're too selfish to see that."

"I'm selfish?" That was *it*. "At least I didn't throw the entire mission away because I was afraid to admit I tried to kiss someone!"

Silence fell over the sand. Every pair of eyes fixed on us.

Dorian's breath shook and wavered over my face. I stared into his eyes; tiny rivulets of white flickered through his irises. A rush of adrenaline surged through my limbs, and I couldn't even care anymore who was watching. After all the crap he'd put me through, I was not letting him get away with this. I was going to find out once and for all if it was true. No more second-guessing.

I threw myself up against him, wrapping my arms around his neck, and pressed my lips to his.

My mind exploded.

Searing, beautiful, glorious pain careened through my veins as I breathed him in, the scent of cedar and wind flowing over me. Red-hot pokers slid between my ribs as I grabbed Dorian's face, pulling him deeper into me. He stumbled forward, eyes wide, filling with bursts of white.

Then he grabbed my waist, swinging me up against a rock and returning my kiss. The impact knocked the wind from my lungs, stealing my breath and spilling it out over his face. That joy—that unprecedented joy consumed me again, the sheer elation of his presence so close, everything he was on the inside pressing into me, wanting to be closer to everything I was on the inside. I had never been so happy to be in pain.

Dorian's fingers wrapped my cheeks, and he shoved his lips harder into mine, pressing me against the stone. Another jolt of fire burst from my sternum, filling my empty lungs with delicious, hellacious pain.

I gripped his wrists and twisted away, breaking our lips apart. As my vision darkened, I sucked in a breath, teetering on the edge of consciousness, and my back slid down the rock.

"Vindicated," I whispered.

Dorian's shoulders heaved as he panted. He stared down at me, the white flares still billowing in his eyes. A fierce smile split the side of his mouth, and I grinned at him, my vision slowly growing less snowy.

"Dammit, Lyra," Dorian said.

Yes, our physical—or rather, emotional—closeness appeared to harm my body. Yes, Dorian's fear of hurting me through his attraction for me was valid. But now I knew, we both knew, that what we felt was real, and there was good to it, not just pain.

But whether his touch hurt me or not, whether anything would come of these feelings, as we stared at each other in the moonlight, it was clear we would have to come to terms with it. Now we were both alienated, pariahs in our worlds, hunted. But we were in this together, more than ever before.

"Um... guys?" Sike murmured from behind Dorian. "Hate to butt in, but we've got, ah... things to sort out..."

I pressed a hand against the rock wall behind me and pulled myself up. Zach gaped at me, then groaned at some jostle to his leg. Bryce didn't bother to hide his smug smile.

Bravi cleared her throat, sounding uncomfortable, eager to change the subject. "Let's get moving. We can't sit out here, waiting to get shot." She led us through the rock crevice pathway to the vampires' cavern. Laini helped Rhome, when he proved too dazed to follow.

In the pitch-dark passage, I felt Dorian put the corner of his cloak in my palm and tug it. His fingers brushed mine only briefly, then pulled away.

Once we reached the torchlit cavern, our five vampire friends greeted the other fifteen or so surprised vampires who had remained behind at the start of the trial period. We humans stepped away from the group out of respect and helped Zach lean against the stone wall.

"There really is more," Bryce said in awe, staring at all the new vampires.

Zach groaned, but I wasn't sure if it was from the pain or to express his feelings on the matter.

The vampires huddled, murmuring, communicating the worst imaginable outcome of the last six weeks. Gasps rang out against the stone walls. Fear gripped faces.

As Dorian whispered to the group, taking in their reactions, I saw a tear roll down his cheek. I had to look away. The guilt returned too strongly for me to bear, wrapped up in the desire to help, if only he'd let me. My victory had drained all the anger and fear from me, but I was left with all the oppressive, helpless feelings of our untenable situation.

Still, there was work to be done, and too few of us to do it. Bryce, Gina, and I helped Zach get comfortable in Dorian's room, before Bryce and I left Gina with him. I would have stayed, but it looked like they wanted privacy to talk.

I spent the rest of the night leaning against the cool rock wall, speaking quietly with Bryce about why the Bureau would've done this. He had no answers. Just as my brother had been silenced by confusion earlier that night, the most opinionated person in my life had a lost, numb face and nothing to say. His pale blue eyes had heavy circles under them in the torchlight. My career had just begun and ended. His, on the other hand, had consumed a majority of his life before going up in flames.

Between our few words and numerous long silences, I checked on Zach, who finally found sleep through his pain.

I woke along the cavern wall the next morning, lying on Dorian's cloak. I sat up, rubbed my eyes, and cringed from the aches lingering between my ribs. I walked around, whispering good mornings to the conscious members of our small group. I noticed there were fewer vampires in the cavern than there were the previous night, but our friends were all accounted for—except Dorian.

"He's down there," Bravi murmured, pointing to the hallway entrance.

I peeked into Dorian's room as I walked down the hall. Gina and Zach snored in a pile on Dorian's bed, so I kept going.

The hall ended with a set of crude steps carved into the stone, ascending toward a flood of sunlight and fresh air. I climbed the stairs and walked out onto the flat top of a tall rock formation looming over the expanding desert.

Dorian sat before me, staring out over the red sand dotted with sage bushes. Part of me didn't want to sit beside him. Part of me did. I still had no idea where we were with each other, besides in the middle of a desert. And both hunted.

I sat beside him with an exhale, ignoring my little bite of resentment. I didn't know exactly what was going on between us, and I still wanted deeper explanations, but just being able to sit next to him without being pushed away was bracing. With my mind pulled in so many directions, the silence we sat in felt comforting.

Everything I'd believed about the Bureau, my life's work, was a lie. Uncle Alan's cold, indifferent voice filtering through the air vent filled my mind for the umpteenth time. I felt hollowed out, my internal truth evaporated. I knew nothing about the Bureau at all, and maybe I never had. I felt used.

And we were all enemies to the Bureau now. I'd gone from rising star to target in a matter of moments. What lies would the Bureau—my own uncle—tell my parents? How would I reach them ever again without the board finding out?

A sense of loneliness engulfed me. I had a lot more in common with the vampires now than I wanted to admit.

I just wished I understood why the board had done this. Their exact, specific reasons. I wanted to believe that it wasn't simply because "darkness" was spreading. I wanted to believe they'd thought this through rationally. The vampires had proven, over and over, to be sincere, and to be useful to the human race. What could the Bureau possibly have to gain from their planned massacre? They'd be acting against their own self-interest. It made no sense.

What was the bigger picture? I was missing something. At least one massive piece of this strange, dangerous puzzle. And it both chilled and frustrated me not knowing what it was.

I pulled my knees up to my chest, attempting some form of self-comfort, and felt a hard poke against my leg. Reaching into my breast pocket, I pulled out Dorian's stone. I had no use for it anymore. It was time he had it back.

Lowering my legs again, I slowly reached over and offered it to him.

But instead of taking it, his cool hand closed my fingers around it, pushing it back against my chest.

His lips were tense, much like the air between us.

"Please don't lose that," he said quietly, his eyes searching for danger in the expanding, echoing desert surrounding us. "You might need it."

READY FOR THE NEXT PART OF LYRA'S STORY?

Dear Reader,

Thank you for taking a chance on this book. I hope you enjoyed it!

Book 2 of the series, **Darkthirst**, releases **October 28th, 2019!** (Or possibly sooner).

Visit: **www.bellaforrest.net** for details.

I'm thrilled to continue Lyra's journey with you. See you there...

Love,

Bella x

P.S. Sign up to my VIP email list and I'll send you a heads up as soon as my next book releases:

www.morebellaforrest.com

(Your email will be kept private and you can unsubscribe at any time.)

P.P.S. Feel free to come say hi on **Twitter** @ashadeofvampire; **Facebook** facebook.com/BellaForrestAuthor; or **Instagram** @ashadeofvampire

The Gender End (Book 7)

THE GIRL WHO DARED TO THINK

(Action-adventure/romance. Completed series.)

The Girl Who Dared to Think (Book 1)

The Girl Who Dared to Stand (Book 2)

The Girl Who Dared to Descend (Book 3)

The Girl Who Dared to Rise (Book 4)

The Girl Who Dared to Lead (Book 5)

The Girl Who Dared to Endure (Book 6)

The Girl Who Dared to Fight (Book 7)

THE CHILD THIEF

(Action-adventure/romance. Completed series.)

The Child Thief (Book 1)

Deep Shadows (Book 2)

Thin Lines (Book 3)

Little Lies (Book 4)

Ghost Towns (Book 5)

Zero Hour (Book 6)

HOTBLOODS

(Supernatural romance/adventure. Completed series.)

Hotbloods (Book 1)

Coldbloods (Book 2)

Renegades (Book 3)

Venturers (Book 4)

Traitors (Book 5)

Allies (Book 6)

Invaders (Book 7)

Stargazers (Book 8)

A SHADE OF VAMPIRE SERIES

(Supernatural romance/adventure)

Series 1: Derek & Sofia's story

A Shade of Vampire (Book 1)

A Shade of Blood (Book 2)

A Castle of Sand (Book 3)

A Shadow of Light (Book 4)

A Blaze of Sun (Book 5)

A Gate of Night (Book 6)

A Break of Day (Book 7)

Series 2: Rose & Caleb's story

A Shade of Novak (Book 8)

A Bond of Blood (Book 9)

A Spell of Time (Book 10)

A Chase of Prey (Book 11)

A Shade of Doubt (Book 12)

A Turn of Tides (Book 13)

A Dawn of Strength (Book 14)

A Fall of Secrets (Book 15)

An End of Night (Book 16)

Series 3: The Shade continues with a new hero...

A Wind of Change (Book 17)

A Trail of Echoes (Book 18)

A Soldier of Shadows (Book 19)

A Hero of Realms (Book 20)

THE SECRET OF SPELLSHADOW MANOR

(Supernatural/Magic YA. Completed series)

The Secret of Spellshadow Manor (Book 1)

The Breaker (Book 2)

The Chain (Book 3)

The Keep (Book 4)

The Test (Book 5)

The Spell (Book 6)

BEAUTIFUL MONSTER DUOLOGY

(Supernatural romance)

Beautiful Monster 1

Beautiful Monster 2

DETECTIVE ERIN BOND

(Adult thriller/mystery)

Lights, Camera, GONE

Write, Edit, KILL

For an updated list of Bella's books, please visit her website: www. bellaforrest.net

Join Bella's VIP email list and you'll be the first to know when new books release. Visit to sign up: www.morebellaforrest.com